W9-BFR-400

FRACTURE GRADIENT

A NOVEL

JIM McCULLOCH

Mossy Mountain Publishing
Banks, Oregon

Fracture Gradient is a work of fiction. The characters in this novel are entirely fictional, with the exception of certain public persons that appear in the novel and are used fictitiously. All events and conversations depicted in the book, including those involving public persons, are entirely the product of the author's imagination. Names, characters that are not public persons, places, businesses, and incidences are either the product of the author's imagination or are used fictitiously, and any resemblance to actual persons, living or dead, business establishments, events, or locales is entirely coincidental.

Copyright © 2012 by Jim McCulloch

Published in the United States of America by
Mossy Mountain Publishing, Banks, Oregon

ISBN: 978-0-9857745-0-9

Edited by Arlene Prunkl at PenUltimate Editorial Services
Book Design by Karrie Ross   www.KarrieRoss.com

Printed in the United States of America

This book is dedicated to the
memory of my friend,
Colin Kennedy

Fracture gradient *n* 1: an oil and gas industry term used to define the brute-force hydraulic pressure required to induce fractures in solid rock at a given depth for the purpose of enhancing the flow of hydrocarbons to the well bore. 2: the quantity and quality of product development pressure required to fracture or destroy an established industry through the introduction of new technology that effectively renders the former obsolete and worthless. 3: the point at which extraordinary technological development decisively fractures the international balance of power paradigm.

FRACTURE GRADIENT

Best wishes

Jim McCulloh

—|||— One —|||—

February, 1981

FLETCHER BOYD GRIMACED WHEN THE right rear wheels of the transport he was backing toward a trailer-mounted acid pump dropped into the soft ground on the edge of the dirt pad where the gas well sat. He could feel it. Some locations were more difficult than others to position all the equipment, and this was one of them. He was dead tired, having already worked nearly ninety hours this week…and was now without any sleep for close to twenty-nine hours. Still, there was no excuse for poor driving and he knew his supervisor would appear shortly to offer up his very personal opinion. He quickly jammed the gear selector into second and popped the clutch, back into reverse, and back to second in an effort to rock the truck with its five thousand gallons of twenty percent hydrochloric acid out of the eroding sinkhole he was creating. The big transport trailer settled deeper into the soft Oklahoma earth. The sun wasn't even up yet. He mumbled to himself in disgust as he climbed down from the tractor to eyeball the problem.

Hollis Cade was already shining a flashlight on the rear wheels.

"That's the sorriest damned excuse for spotting a truck I've ever seen," he boomed. The large-boned, six foot six inch, 240 pound supervisor seldom minced words. He towered over Fletcher's sinewy six foot, 175 pound frame. Well, six feet with boots on and 175 pounds soaking wet, though his muscles were in the best shape since his Army days. "I told you to stay off that soft ground but you just had to back right into it didn't you."

"Yeah, I screwed up, Hollis," Fletcher said as he pushed his cap up and rubbed his forehead with the back of his hand. "I'll move it."

Fletcher fought the frustration knowing it wouldn't help to bitch about not getting any help from the other drivers as he tried to spot his truck in the dark. He had put the truck there, and it was what it was. He looked the other way, sighed, and waited for Hollis to finish.

"You're driving like a damn worm. Look, there's only one way to get good at backing up these big rigs and that's by doing it…a lot. If you need help, just say so and I'll have one of the trainers work with you. Or you could just find some open space on the yard and practice on your own. I'll do it for you this once but I can't be spending my day driving everyone's truck. Now get in the passenger seat and pay attention."

Hollis pushed past Fletcher as he climbed up into the tractor while Fletcher scrambled around the front of the rig and up into the cab. Fletcher watched him flip the "Quad" switch on the dash, drop into low range granny, and ease the heavy truck back to firm ground. Just as quickly he pulled forward fifty feet, slipped into reverse, and deftly backed the big transport around the hole and up to the acid pump. He had asked to be assigned to the toughest and most competent service supervisor, and was reminded one more time that he had been granted his wish.

"Hook two hoses up to that pump and don't do anything else until I tell you," Hollis yelled over his shoulder as he moved to his next problem of this very early morning.

Fletcher did as he was told and then eased himself up onto the wet truck bumper. The cool dew wicked into his pants and soon made his backside itch as he replayed how Hollis had backed the transport so effortlessly into position. He'd have to step up his efforts to learn and better understand how the oilfield worked on the ground. That was his goal and he had no problem with doing the hard, dirty work in the meantime. He fully understood he couldn't expect to successfully lead men in this business if he couldn't do the job himself.

— || —

When the president of Westcona had come up with the idea of fast-tracking some promising corporate employees into district manager positions, Fletcher had jumped at the chance. To actually operate a stand-alone business instead of evaluating the performance of others who were already doing it was an energizing thought. He wanted the prize job and didn't care that getting it required him to work in the field as a "super trainee" for a year or so. He could stand on his head for a year if it meant moving into this high-profile and respected position. It would open career doors that he could only dream of as an auditor.

In the end, he had been one of only ten men selected from a pool of thirty-seven corporate office volunteers. Each of the lucky ten had been assigned to one of Westcona's district locations in the Mid-Continent Region. The Region Manager was Jake Taylor, and Fletcher knew that Taylor was an accomplished iron-ass with a big reputation that rumor held to be well deserved.

Accustomed to being a star performer in the corporate world, Fletcher was finding that driving tractor-trailers, swinging a hammer, and operating heavy oilfield pressure-pumping equipment was tougher than his former desk job in many ways. He had been a suit and tie guy in the corporate office but was now wearing the green work-uniform of an oilfield equipment operator. He was learning as best he could and feeling more comfortable in this new labor-intensive role, but knew he wasn't as competent as many of the men he was working with. They were good, really good. And like most oilfield workers, they were a rough bunch. He smiled when he considered how harsh his new work environment was from that of Westcona's elite internal audit department where he had spent a year as one of their top operational auditors. Now his former workmates would hardly recognize him.

What had sounded so promising in the Dallas corporate office wasn't working out quite the way it had been presented, and Fletcher was less than pleased with his progress. He seemed to be learning less than he should be, sleeping less than he needed, and being openly encouraged to quit despite knowing that he was performing at a better than acceptable level. The pace of his training was unnecessarily slow and disjointed...at least in his mind. The service supervisors consistently harassed him, and the equipment operators mimicked their behavior. He had endured much worse in Army officer's training where more than half the cadet's had washed out. In that environment, he knew the cadre wanted the capable to succeed. But this new corporate training program was tinged with a maliciousness that gave him the impression it was designed to wash everyone out. Was it his imagination? Were the other "super trainees" experiencing the same treatment at their districts? No, this was just too obvious to ignore and he had no idea where it was coming from or why. What troubled him was the uncomfortable feeling that he was a target and that someone wouldn't be satisfied until he failed or quit. The very thought of failure, or being considered unworthy, was just not in Fletcher Boyd. He didn't complain, he didn't fail, and he sure as hell didn't quit.

— ‖ —

Hollis Cade walked away from Fletcher's truck wondering why Fletcher was out in the oilfield doing this kind of work when he could be back in the Dallas corporate office in clean clothes doing whatever it was he had done before coming to Lindsay. He had heard that Fletcher was being groomed to be a district manager but didn't understand why he'd been told to be particularly hard on the guy. He reflected on his ten years in the Navy and how many times, as a Chief Petty Officer, he'd been required to help train newly commissioned Ensigns in how the blue-water Navy really worked. He hadn't liked that part of his job then and didn't like the idea of doing much the same again now. There were enough problems just getting his job done without having to deal with the politics of who should or shouldn't make it into district manager jobs. He leaned on Fletcher just as he leaned on everyone on his crew because he wanted to get the job done safely and correctly for the customer. As far as he had seen or heard from other service supervisors, Fletcher didn't complain, make excuses, or cause any problems. The same couldn't be said about many of the regular equipment operators assigned to him. He wasn't sure Fletcher was as tough as the career oilfield workers but then again maybe he was. The guy was taking a lot of uncalled for abuse and sucking it up, something Hollis tended to respect...at least to a point. He made a mental note to talk to some of the other supervisors about Boyd when he got back to the yard that afternoon.

— ‖ —

Jake Taylor, known widely in the Oklahoma and Texas oilfields as JT, slipped into his winter robe, opened the French doors to the deck, and looked at the empty swimming pool in his large back yard. He had come a long way since joining Westcona as an equipment operator nearly thirty-two years ago. JT had joined Westcona with little more than the clothes on his back, and now had a beautiful home, a cabin in rural northern Minnesota, a jet airplane he was licensed to fly, a retirement plan worth north of seven figures, and money in the bank. Not bad for a guy who started out swinging a hammer.

Lighting his first cigarette of the day, he strode over to the love seat and sat down to look at the sky. It wouldn't be light for another couple of hours, but the pre-dawn humidity and cold reminded him of his many years working in the field as he literally fought his way up the food chain to a district manager position and finally to his current position of region manager. Ten districts located in Oklahoma and north Texas now report-ed to his Mid-Continent Region, and he had every reason to be proud of his accomplishments. He thought of the dozens of Westcona crews already hard at work at customer's oil and gas wells across his region, and felt a tinge of nostalgia. Those had been some of his best years, and he sometimes wished he could still be part of the rough and tumble rather than a "suit" in his Oklahoma City office. He was extremely thankful to Westcona for giving him the opportunity to demonstrate his ability and progress in the company despite his lack of a college education. The company had always been loyal to him and he felt very protective of it as a result. It was a matter of pride, something most of the new "college boys" at the Dallas corporate office seemed to lack. He knew he was already considered a dinosaur in some circles…though he was only fifty-three years old.

That was still young by most standards, but not necessarily true in the oilfields where youthful vigor, strength, and stamina were highly prized and a necessary part of many jobs. He was strikingly handsome, fit, and energetic. Some folks thought no one his age could stand up to the rigors of working in the oilfields, but JT had no doubt he was the exception. He always had been. He was lucky and he was special. He lit another smoke and wondered if the coffee was ready.

The damp cold finally drove him back into the kitchen. He doubted that his wife would be up before he left for work, but had made a full pot just in case. He decided to call each of his district managers yet again and make sure they were keeping the pressure on these "super trainees" to quit and go back where they belonged. The thought of getting rid of all ten had become his obsession over the past few months. He hadn't met any of them but strongly disliked them on principal. Engineer trainees were necessary in his districts because they had critical knowledge that could only be learned in college. Management trainees were another story. Those guys seemed to think they should jump ahead of everyone else just because they had a sheepskin that didn't mean a whole lot in his oilfield. JT was convinced that a district manager needed at least ten years of field work, training, and experience under his belt to be successful and respected. A college degree and a year of equipment familiarization just didn't cut it. His oilfield didn't need more candy-assed college boys pretending to be real men. The young college-educated staff people at corporate headquarters, region offices, and now even in his districts just plain chapped his ass like few things had in years. He marveled that he had been sent these prima donnas to turn into district managers. Him of all people. Corporate had to know he was going to run them all off. Some of the other region managers might think this training program was a good idea but it had to be pretty damned generally known that he'd never agree. He would not pass over the people he'd been grooming for years to give these college boys the coveted district manager jobs. They hadn't earned the chance and didn't deserve the honor and privilege.

— ⫴ — Two — ⫴ —

August, 1981

EIGHT MONTHS INTO HIS TRAINING program and Fletcher's progress was still artificially slow although he was occasionally working on more sophisticated and complex equipment. Instead of always driving a stake bed or transport and then being used as general labor on jobs, he was now being trained on the pumping equipment that was the bread and butter of Westcona's revenue generation model. They were paid for pressure pumping expertise and that's what he was learning, especially when he was dispatched on one of Hollis Cade's jobs. Hollis had taken to changing Fletcher's assigned equipment when they all got to the yard in the middle of the night to prepare for the job. He would simply tell one of the pump operators to get on the stake bed or transport while he directed Fletcher to the pump. It pissed off the crew and certainly made Fletcher more unpopular with the men, especially with the displaced pump operators. Fletcher briefly wondered what kind of hassle Hollis got into when his boss, the operations supervisor, heard about it. He was beyond caring what most of them thought of him but was starting to feel appreciative and loyal to Hollis because Hollis seemed to be trying to do the right thing and was probably risking something in the process. Fletcher had decided months ago to just keep his mouth shut, his head down, and learn what he could while working exceptionally hard. He knew the other nine "super trainees" had already quit and that there were bets down as to how long he would last.

The day was cloudless and sweltering, well over one hundred degrees according to the thermometer in Hollis's van. They had just pumped a hydraulic fracturing job consisting of nearly three quarters of a million pounds of sand blended into one hundred twenty thousand gallons of gelled diesel fuel, a particularly dangerous and unpleasant product in Westcona's arsenal of services. The gelled diesel was akin to what the military called napalm, with the addition of a few proprietary chemicals to achieve the desired result in the specific downhole treatment they were performing. Fletcher's head was pounding from the heat, chemical smells, hunger, and constant roar of large engines over the blistering four hours of pumping time.

"Take a break and get some fluid in you," Hollis yelled to the crew. "Then let's get this equipment broken down and back to the yard."

The men sat scattered around the trucks trying to cool off in the scant shade provided from the nearly overhead sun. Most were drinking water or Gatorade and dipping bandanas into the ice water left in their coolers. Fletcher had a dripping bandana spread over his head and another draped around his neck as he sat on the ground near a group of equipment operators, hoping the three aspirins he had just swallowed would kick in soon. One big stocky man, tagged with the nickname "Motormouth" for obvious reasons, was loudly complaining about everything that came to his feeble mind. He seemed mostly angry that Fletcher had bumped him from his assigned pump that day, but was also sharing some of his self-proclaimed expert opinions on a variety of subjects. A number of the men aggressively encouraged Motormouth to quiet down and let them sit in peace for a few minutes, but the guy just wouldn't shut up. Fletcher's pent up frustration finally erupted. He scooped his yellow hardhat from the ground and threw it at Motormouth to quiet him down and let them rest for a few minutes in the stifling heat. The rocketing hard hat glanced off the big man's shoulder, cutting his cheek before bouncing noisily off a truck behind him. Rage filled the man's face as he charged at Fletcher, kicking dirt and lacing the searing air with obscenities and threats. Fletcher was still sitting on the ground when the fight began but didn't stay there long. One of his steel-toed boots shot out like a piston and caught Motormouth in the mid-section. He bounced to his feet and delivered a flurry of quick blows…and then it was over.

Hollis arrived moments later.

"All right, who started it?" he demanded. The crew just got up and went back to work without answering or looking at Hollis.

"I asked you damn bastards a question. Who started it?" Hollis bellowed at the departing men. Not one looked back or said a word.

Fletcher was about to admit he had started it by throwing his hardhat when Motormouth got up, dabbing at his swelling lip and eye with a now muddy bandana.

"I tripped and fell, Hollis. That's the whole of it."

The burly equipment operator with fifteen years experience among this tough bunch of oilfield workers picked up Fletcher's hard hat and handed it back to him before walking away.

— ‖ —

Hollis corralled the other supervisors as they arrived back at the yard from their jobs.

"Fletcher Boyd punched out Motormouth on my job today," he told the small assembly.   "I don't know what happened but by the time I got over there, Motormouth was down and Fletcher was the guy standing over him."

"Damn, I didn't know the boy had it in him. I'm surprised nobody's gone after Motormouth before now, but I'm impressed it was Boyd. Still, here's our chance to fire him for starting a fight," one of them said.

"You know he's the last of the super trainees and the boss will be happy to get out from under JT on this," another spouted.

Hollis just stared at the group and then asked them, "Doesn't this whole thing bother you? Boyd hasn't done anything but put up with everyone's bullshit since he's been here. He's done everything we asked and hasn't complained to anyone. He must have friends in the corporate office but, as far as I know, he hasn't been in contact with anyone down there."

"What did your crew do after the fight?" another supervisor asked Hollis.

"I'm not sure there was much of a fight. Looked to me like Fletcher must have just kicked his ass. The crew didn't do a damned thing," Hollis responded. "They just walked away. Motormouth said he had fallen down. I do believe Fletcher earned some respect out there today."

Hollis suggested that the supervisors get out on the yard and talk to their crews about what happened as they made sure the trucks and equipment were post-tripped, washed, and re-fueled. He had no doubt that the story was the hot topic all over the yard by now.

When they returned, all had the same impression. The men were clearly supporting Fletcher and were going to make him one of their own. The supervisors agreed that Fletcher's training would accelerate and they would make sure it was done properly...and on time. Hollis was selected spokesman and directed to the district manager's office to give him the news. This was now a matter of principal, and the supervisors and men were in agreement. Hollis had a wry smile on his face as he ambled down the hallway to the corner office. Sometimes justice is slow in arriving, but it usually makes it just the same.

— || —

"What do you mean they're protecting Boyd and training him?" JT roared into the telephone. "I told you to get rid of him. No candy-assed college boy from the corporate office is going to complete this bullshit program while I'm running this region. You run his ass off," he demanded.

"No, JT. You're wrong about Boyd," the district manager countered. "You know how these guys are in Lindsay. They won't back down and nothing good can come of forcing the issue. They rallied around Boyd even knowing you want him gone...maybe because of it. Boyd could have dropped a dime on us anytime over the past eight months and hasn't," he continued.

JT was livid. "He wouldn't dare whine to his old boss or those Human Resource weenies in Dallas. None of the others did and Boyd won't either. You run his ass off today," he angrily demanded.

"You're not listening, JT. I've got over a hundred of the roughest sons of bitches working in your oilfield who say you're wrong...and I agree with them. Boyd could take a small district right now and do better than most people already in the job. You come down here with my replacement and fire both of us if you want it done."

JT was stunned by the temerity of his district manager and with the news that the Lindsay employees were helping Boyd.

He'd never heard of such a thing, or considered for a moment that this could happen. He knew from experience that Lindsay was one of his toughest districts and just couldn't quite get his head around them wanting to help Boyd. He lit a cigarette and sat quietly thinking for a moment.

"Tell you what. I'll put him on the company-wide promotion list. You pull him into your operations supervisor's office and get him up to speed on that job. We'll pass him off to some dummy who likes college boys with just enough knowledge to be dangerous. I want that bastard out of my region."

The district manager shook his head in disbelief before answering. "Yeah, JT. Good thinking. Let your competition take the talent. He'll be happier in another region anyway."

JT didn't even hear the insolent comment. He was too busy feeling smug about getting rid of the final "super trainee" — one way or another.

—‖— Three —‖—

ALICE, TEXAS

October, 1982

FLETCHER'S SURPRISE PROMOTION TO WESTCONA'S Alice district had been one he welcomed and was disappointed in at the same time. Still, getting away from Jake Taylor was like suddenly recovering from a nearly fatal illness.

The Alice district was the largest in the South Texas Region but his employment offer had been for the operations supervisor position…second in command at the district. That had been eight months ago and he now knew just how fortunate he had been. The domestic oilfields were continuing their decline in lockstep with the price of oil on the international markets. Many experienced district managers were being offered early retirement and some were being let go as Westcona's senior leadership continued the process of retrenchment and consolidation. It was an industry pandemic of historic breadth and depth.

When Fletcher interviewed for the Alice job, he felt an immediate connection with the South Texas Region Manager, Roland Dupree, and the feeling had apparently been mutual. Dupree was young, aggressive, and educated. His region consisted of eleven operating districts scattered around south Texas, and his executive office provided the same engineering, sales, and operational support as Jake Taylor's did in Oklahoma. Fletcher and Dupree shared the common bond of both being former Army officers and the sincere desire to be the best at what they did. Neither was bound by tradition when it came to excelling at their jobs. Fletcher was promised a district of his own in the near future and was in regular contact with Dupree, something his current district manager in Alice found inappropriate and threatening.

— ‖ —

An unexpected call from Dupree ramped up Fletcher's level of anticipation. There had been a managers meeting in Corpus Christi that morning and the Alice district manager, Fletcher's boss, hadn't yet returned. The guy didn't seem to fit Dupree's idea of what a district manager should be, and Fletcher had wondered how long he would last without making some major changes in his leadership style.

"Fletcher, I'll be over there in an hour. Get the department heads together in the conference room for a short meeting. Then I'll buy you lunch," he said before abruptly hanging up. Fletcher wondered if he was buying lunch for all the department heads or just for him. He had a curious feeling in his stomach as he picked up the phone to make the calls.

— ‖ —

"Gentlemen, I met with your district manager in my office two hours ago and relieved him of his responsibilities," Dupree calmly explained to the surprised department heads. "I want each of you to tell your employees what happened and that a replacement will be named in a few weeks."

"Who's in charge until then?" the sales manager asked.

"Fletcher Boyd," Dupree answered without hesitation. "Any other questions?"

No one said a word.

"If that's the only question, get out there and take care of your people. Fletcher, let's get some lunch."

Fletcher drove Dupree out to Highway 281 and then south over Highway 44 to a little Mexican restaurant he favored. They ordered lunch and made small talk until the food arrived.

"I'll be up-front with you, Fletcher. Another corporate reorganization and downsizing is happening in a couple of weeks and I doubt you'll be the permanent manager here. I assume that I'll still have a job because they told me about it in advance. All I know for sure is that there will be some experienced people available and I'll be expected to find a home for some of them within our region. If they offer me a good fit for Alice, I'll have to take him to save his career and make the region stronger."

Fletcher was disappointed. He'd thought this was likely his big moment but understood the position Dupree was in and appreciated the personal attention.

"What do you want me to do until then?" he quietly asked.

"I want you to clean this place up. You know how I like things to work, and the kind of people I want in supervisory positions. I want people with good attitudes, leadership skills, and drive to be in key slots. There are no sacred cows. Make any changes you need to. Just stick with me on this, Fletcher, and I'll take care of you when the dust settles."

— ‖ —

Fletcher followed Dupree's instructions and made the appropriate changes at the district. It was no surprise that he enjoyed sitting in the district manager's office, even if it was for only part of each day. Deep in his heart, an ember of hope glowed softly and told him there was a slim chance the district would be his. That perhaps nobody would want to move to south Texas and it would just fall in his lap. The ember extinguished itself when the phone rang again.

"Fletcher, bring the district manager car over to my office at nine tomorrow morning. I'll have some news about the reorganization and someone for you to meet. Schedule a district meeting around eleven so you can introduce the new manager."

The line went dead leaving Fletcher humbled but ready to get on with the change. He had been told the job would not be his so he had no right to be disappointed. Still, he was. He called the facilities supervisor and asked him to clean and paint the curb in front of the district manager parking place by the front door of the office.

"Have your stencils ready in the morning and I'll call you with a name around ten o'clock," Fletcher said. "I want his name on it when we get back from Corpus around eleven."

— ‖ —

Fletcher drove the freshly washed and polished white Oldsmobile Delta 88 to Corpus Christi, arriving at Westcona's region office at eight forty-five. That car was a coveted and highly visible symbol of achievement at Westcona. Only district managers drove one while the salesmen, engineers, and operations supervisors all drove identical yellow Ford LTD's. He had not touched the Olds while he temporarily functioned as the "acting" district manager, although the temptation had nagged him. It would have given the wrong signal to the Alice employees...and he hadn't yet earned it.

The drive from Alice was normally one he enjoyed as the flat, lush delta turned to coastal landscape, but today he'd hardly noticed the beauty.

He entered the modern office tower on the downtown hillside overlooking Corpus Christi Bay and T-head. Strolling through the lobby to the coffee cart, he caught the glint of water-reflected sunshine through the spotless windows. It reminded him of the quirky coffee houses and stands around Seattle and Portland, and he always bought a large cup when he came to Dupree's office. Today it was a vanilla-flavored Caribbean roast with three chocolate-covered espresso beans on top of the plastic lid. The little bastards provided a potent buzz as he chewed and washed them down with the strong coffee in the elevator.

The doors opened on the seventh floor and he made his way down the hallway into the Westcona office suite. A couple of staff people waved or said hello as he weaved his way through to Dupree's rear corner office. The door was closed so he sat down with Dupree's secretary. He always worked to stay on her good side with his unique brand of humor and playful flattery...and it certainly helped that he genuinely liked her.

"Hello, pretty lady. It's kind of quiet back here. Am I the only one coming to this meeting?" he asked.

"You wish. Hello Fletcher. Your new boss is here but there's some good news, too, even if it's not what you want to hear." She knew Fletcher was disappointed in not being named the permanent district manager in Alice. "I see you're into the caffeine from downstairs again. It's having the usual effects on you — talking too fast and those weird, jerky eye-movements."

"Naw, that's the effect you have on me."

"Fletcher, you pig," she said with a laugh. "Roland got a promotion. He's pretty excited and can't wait to tell you about all that's happening. Now put on your big boy face and try to talk slower," she admonished him with a smile.

Fletcher was heartened by the news and hoped for the best as the intercom buzzed.

"Send Fletcher in when he gets here."

He knocked smartly and opened the door. Dupree stood and directed Fletcher to a man standing with his back to them, gazing at the magnificent view of bright blue water under a crisp azure sky.

The man turned slowly with a tight sterile smile, hard eyes, and an extended hand. "Hello, Boyd," Jake Taylor said quietly.

—‖— Four —‖—

ALICE, TEXAS

May, 1983

JT's ARRIVAL IN ALICE HAD BEEN the result of a corporate reorganization and downsizing that eliminated his region manager level position and consolidated the former seven regions into two divisions under newly named division vice presidents. Dupree was one of them, and now his new boss. He wasn't overly surprised that he had not been selected for one of the new vice president positions because he'd been watching the insidious infiltration of flashy corporate executives into the old regions for the past couple of years. Some of them didn't even have oilfield experience but rather came from big name companies outside the industry. Some had Ivy League degrees and impressive Wall Street connections. They were administrative types, not oilmen, and they were all college boys.

JT's information pipeline told him some of the corporate leadership had recommended his dismissal but that Westcona's Chairman of the Board had prevented it. There had been a time in the early 1950's when the company had been so cash poor that it couldn't always make payroll. JT had accepted company IOU's in lieu of paychecks during those lean times, and that same private company owner was now the public company Chairman. Although he no longer worked full time, it was well known to the small cadre of long-term employees that the old man had insisted on chairing the Human Resources committee for the express purpose of making sure none of his loyal employees from the old days were hosed by the new corporate executives brought in after the company had gone public.

Still, JT's options had been limited. He knew he wouldn't fit in at the Dallas corporate office although he had been offered a job in executive sales and another in the credit department. He wanted no part of them. The clincher came when his wife of thirty years announced that she was leaving him. He was completely blindsided...again. In the end, he decided to return to the work he enjoyed and held in the highest esteem. He had asked for a district to run and was told to take his pick. Alice, Texas, was a Westcona crown jewel...and the farthest from the people he had worked with in Oklahoma. He could lick his wounds in private. It was also less than a two hour drive from his home town of Hargill. When told that his number two man was Fletcher Boyd, he sighed with resignation and thought, *but of course he is.* JT was just plain exhausted and drained of his usual fighting spirit.

Now, after a few months in Alice, JT was actually enjoying his job and getting to know his south Texas customers. Many were his age and just as beat up by the industry — and life. His personal situation was still a mess and he was compensating for it by drinking more than he ever had in the past, usually with his new customers under the guise of salesmanship. Still, he was up early and back at work the next morning seemingly none the worse for wear. The loneliness wasn't quite as hard to live with when he immersed himself in work...and J&B scotch.

JT learned from Dupree that his supervisory staff had been picked by Boyd before his arrival, and was impressed with the selections. He was also more impressed than he wanted to admit with the job Boyd was doing. The employees seemed to respect Boyd, his costs were in line, his sales skills were good, and he was extremely low maintenance from a supervisory perspective. In fact, JT rather begrudgingly admired the fact that Boyd basically ignored him unless he needed something specific. Dupree was something else altogether. He really had a difficult time taking the man very seriously or paying him much mind. It also bothered him that Boyd was so close with Dupree, and he wondered if they were discussing him or his performance as a district manager. Hell, he had twice as much experience in the oilfields as those two put together.

— II —

After stopping at a downtown store, Fletcher was on his way home as he passed the Holiday Inn. It was raining hard and unusually dark. He noticed the cars of a few of his best customers in the lot and decided to stop for a quick drink. One of the men had mentioned a squeeze job he might need on one of his wells, and Fletcher hoped to set that up for the next morning if the man hadn't already made other arrangements. It wouldn't be much revenue but every bit of cement he could pump helped the bottom line.

The bar was quiet, a casualty of the weather and setbacks being experienced by those who made their living in the oilfields. OPEC was flooding the market with inexpensive high-grade crude which made domestic exploration and production unattractive to the major oil companies. They could buy OPEC oil, transport it to the United States, and refine it at a lower cost than taking it out of the ground right here.

Fletcher flashed a casual index-finger salute off his silver-belly Stetson brim to the bartender and took a seat with the customer he was targeting. He closed the sale of the squeeze job in the customary fashion…a price on a cocktail napkin and a handshake. He then moved to another table with another customer. As they chatted, he noticed JT's reflection in the mirror…alone at his rear corner table. The customers called it an early night and when Fletcher looked around the bar he saw that most of the other patrons had followed suit. JT, however, was still sitting quietly in his protective corner cocoon. Feeling a little annoyed at his boss's lack of sales participation, Fletcher went to the bar, ordered a drink for JT, got quarters from the bartender and plugged them into the jukebox before sitting down on a barstool to listen to his first selection, *"You're the Reason God Made Oklahoma"*. He could have a little fun provoking JT with a song about Oklahoma before he went home. He intended to duck out as soon as the song ended, but JT must have sensed what was happening.

"Boyd, that's a hell of a fine song. You gonna join me or did she make a mistake with this drink?"

"No mistake, JT," Fletcher said, more than a little surprised at the civil response.

"Come on over then. I was beginning to think you didn't like me."

Two hours later they left the bar, and in the months that followed became frequent companions in JT's quiet corner after working the room for sales opportunities. Soon they were having lunch together on a fairly regular basis. Their work relationship didn't really change but, while neither man would admit it, both looked forward to the time they spent together. They talked about a variety of subjects; politics, history, science, country music, books, firearms, the military, and sometimes their personal lives. Fletcher began to understand what his boss had been through while JT saw some of himself in Fletcher Boyd. After a few drinks he even felt an occasional and vague regret at his instructions to have Boyd fired just a couple of short years before.

Fletcher was pleased that JT still left him alone at work and didn't second-guess or try to micro-manage him. In fact, JT had quickly acclimated himself to being back in a district and had smoothly assumed control of the business. The old man was a natural, performing his job with an easy calm that belied effort. JT obviously expected people to work hard and excel at their jobs. Fletcher noticed that the old warhorse didn't talk behind anyone's back, was unquestionably loyal to the company, and was completely focused on doing a good job. He also noticed that JT ignored Dupree much of the time but never brought it into their conversations. When he expressed an interest in joining Fletcher on a dove hunt, Fletcher hesitated until JT explained that he hadn't hunted in years but thought it would be a good idea to organize some hunts for their best customers, and needed some practice before he embarrassed himself in public. Fletcher wasn't sure how much he wanted to share his hobby time with JT but couldn't very well say no when it was being portrayed as a company sales opportunity. It was also obvious that his new boss was aware of his frequent sojourns to his dove lease just outside of town. JT was a continuing cycle of surprises.

— || —

Fletcher grimaced as he sat up on the edge of the bed and answered the telephone. As he tried to calm the agitated Westcona dispatcher, he noticed it was 2:35 a.m. on a Sunday. Mother's Day, in fact. Well it would be once the sun came up.

"Slow down and tell me again what happened," Fletcher said as his head cleared from a deep sleep.

"The Highway Patrol called and said JT's been in a bad car wreck. I think they said he rolled his car. Happened at the junction of 281 and 624 north of town, and they're bringing him to the hospital in an ambulance. What do I do?" the upset dispatcher implored.

"Are they bringing him to Alice?" Fletcher asked.

"I think so. They just said they were transporting him. Alice is the closest."

"I'll meet them at the hospital. Call the maintenance supervisor and have him get up to the accident scene. I want JT's car towed back to the yard, not to the Police Department or some impound lot in Alice. Don't call anyone else until you hear from me. Got it?"

— ‖ —

Fletcher ran into the emergency room reception area and was stopped by a State Trooper.

"Whoa," the Trooper said as he grabbed Fletcher's arm.

"What happened to Jake Taylor?" Fletcher asked as he tried to catch his breath.

"You related to him?" the Trooper asked.

"No, but he's my boss and I'm about the closest thing to family he's got around here," Fletcher explained quickly. The Trooper looked vaguely familiar but he was too concerned over JT to give it much thought.

Before the Trooper could answer, a tall, tired-looking doctor came out of one of the treatment bays.

"Do you know the injured man?" he asked Fletcher.

"Yes. How is he?"

"He's a mess and we could use some help in here from somebody he knows."

Fletcher's stomach churned when he saw JT sprawled out nearly naked on the examination table. Two orderlies were trying to hold him down and keep him still while the medical team was trying to flush and examine his eyes for glass, and pick shards out of his face, neck, and upper body. Another was trying to get the bleeding under control. JT was very drunk, in shock, and combative.

"Get over on this side and take his hand. Squeeze it and try to calm him down. Be as loud as you need to be with him and ignore us," the doctor commanded.

Fletcher did as he was told but couldn't help but pay attention to what they were doing. It was purely bad as far as he could tell. The sights, sounds, smells, and intensely bright lighting gave Fletcher a headache and queasy stomach. JT finally settled down somewhat but was in no condition to think rationally. After a long quarter-hour, Fletcher was told to step outside the treatment area. The doctor followed a few minutes later.

"We're going to x-ray him and move him to intensive care. He's badly hurt and in shock, as you could see. Go home and come back in a few hours. He'll either be in a room where you can see him, or in the morgue."

— ‖ —

Fletcher walked out to the parking lot behind the ER where he found the Trooper standing by the door smoking a cigarette.

"How is he?"

"I don't know," Fletcher admitted. "The doc said to come back later this morning. He may not make it but they should know by then. Can you come in and vouch for me so I can get his wallet and personal property? They won't release anything to me without your approval. Oh, and I sent our maintenance supervisor out there to arrange for the car to be towed to our yard. Is that okay with you?" Fletcher asked the Trooper. He wanted to sanitize the car before anyone from the corporate or region office decided to poke their nose into what may have happened.

"Yeah. I talked to our people on the scene while you were in the ER. Your guy can have the car as soon as our accident team finishes up."

"Thanks. Wrecking a company car isn't exactly a career builder at Westcona. He'll be in a world of hurt if he lives to face it," Fletcher told the Trooper.

They went back into the ER and got JT's personal effects taken care of before walking back toward their cars in the parking lot.

"Has your boss been with Westona for a long time?" the Trooper asked.

"He has. I think the earth was still flat when they hired him."

The Trooper smiled weakly and paused as he looked at Fletcher. He seemed to be conflicted over something.

"Say, I picked up some of his stuff out at the crash site and here at the hospital that I haven't had a chance to look over yet. It's in my trunk but if you happened to see anything that looks like it doesn't belong there, I probably wouldn't even remember that I picked it up. I'll be right back. I need to call in and report myself back in service."

Fletcher wasn't sure what he meant but the squad car's trunk popped up as the Trooper picked up his microphone in the front seat of his Ford LTD cruiser. Fletcher peered into the trunk, illuminated only by the parking lot lights above him. He had forgotten that, for nighttime security purposes, police cars were set up to not automatically turn on any interior lights. He squinted as his eyes slowly focused on the trunk contents. There was a Playmate cooler with empty beer cans in it, a bent and mutilated black cowboy hat, a small handgun, and three vials of red liquid in a small holder. Fletcher gathered it all up and put it in his car before returning to the cruiser. The Trooper climbed out of his car when he saw Fletcher in his side mirror.

"I just hope your boss makes it. At least nobody else got hurt by his stupidity out there. See you at the range," he said as he got back into the car.

Of course, Fletcher thought as he recalled seeing the Trooper out at the county fairgrounds public firing range in civilian clothes. He hadn't recognized him in his uniform. In fact, Fletcher remembered helping him adjust the sights on a new handgun a couple of months ago. Just a couple of guys practicing at the range. One of them with a new gun that had adjustable sights and another with the proper screwdriver to fit them. He hadn't known the guy was a cop at the time...and it wouldn't have mattered if he had. The guy was going way out on a limb for JT for some reason and, like many issues surrounding JT, it was an enigma.

Fletcher got back into his car and headed to the Westcona yard to see if JT's car was there yet. No sense going home. He wouldn't be able to sleep anyway. He briefly considered calling Dupree to inform him of JT's wreck but thought better of it. If JT died, none of it would matter anyway.

— ‖ — Five — ‖ —

THE POP OF AN OPENING BEER can made Fletcher sit up and look around to see who had silently approached him. He was on the edge of an orange grove that had not been replanted after the 1982 freeze.

With the birds not flying, Fletcher had unloaded his Browning A-5 shotgun, stretched out in the dry grass, and pulled his camo baseball cap over his eyes to daydream. He and Katie had purchased a beautiful home in nearby McAllen, and he was still ecstatic that his career dream had finally been fulfilled, even though Katie was frustrated by yet another move. Still, the considerable raise and inexpensive real estate market bought them a spectacular home in McAllen, and she had no difficulty finding a teaching job in the local school system.

After JT's 1983 auto accident, Fletcher had again assumed temporary responsibility for the Alice district. JT had nearly died twice in the days following his wreck but Westcona had quickly arranged for HALO-Flight to transport him to Ben Taub General Hospital's trauma center in Houston, and ultimately on to a Baptist Health System rehabilitation facility in San Antonio where he could be closer to relatives. Before JT was out of the hospital, Fletcher had finally been promoted to district manager and transferred one hundred miles south to Westcona's small district in Edinburg, although he had run both for nearly eight months while JT made a slow and painful recovery.

"You can't shoot birds with your eyes closed," chided Hollis Cade.

"I suppose walking around with a shiny beer can is a new way of decoying them in."

"If it was, we'd probably be doing better. I left my shotgun in the trunk when I took the cooler out and started looking for you. No birds today so we might as well enjoy the weather."

"Yeah, let's just watch the sun go down," Fletcher agreed.

"We gonna have to cut more employees?" Hollis asked.

"Depends on revenue. What are your customers saying about their plans?"

"Oh, we'll keep working over in the Willimar Field, but if you weren't an investor they'd give it to somebody else. The deep stuff along the river and up towards Laredo is slowing down. The McAllen Field is still pretty busy but I'm having trouble getting jobs off those operators."

"Pick up a few cases of twelve-gauge shells in the morning and I'll ride out there with you to do some PR. They all dove hunt, and we need their work," Fletcher offered.

Fletcher had taken the first opportunity to offer Hollis a promotion and transfer from Lindsay, Oklahoma, to Edinburg as a field salesman, a job at which he excelled. No surprise there. Hollis excelled at most things he put his mind to. Ten years Fletcher's senior, Hollis sported a strong, rugged face that matched his no-nonsense demeanor. After traveling the world for ten years with the United States Navy, Hollis couldn't help but keep an avid interest in world events. Each Sunday, he bought every different newspaper he could find on the McAllen newsstands, still concerned with what was happening around mother Earth. He also had a portable shortwave receiver for listening to international broadcast stations from around the world. His interest in world events was insatiable.

Fletcher and Hollis agreed on almost everything, although sometimes for divergent reasons. Fletcher followed world affairs for financial and investing purposes while Hollis was a serious news hound and observer of the human condition. Different as they were, Fletcher's respect for Hollis had grown strong. Hollis was as steady and dependable a man as Fletcher had ever met and had the privilege to call a friend.

Hollis jumped as three doves closed on them from the west. "Hey, I kicked over a perfectly good beer and you didn't even shoot," he complained despite having already noticed Fletcher's unloaded Browning.

"Kind of clumsy of you," Fletcher said as he poured the bottom inch of warm beer onto the dirt where Hollis had spilled his, and opened the cooler for two cold ones. "Grab one of those little oranges and see if there's any juice in it," he told Hollis, who was relieving himself beside a nearly dead orange tree.

"They put lime in beer around here, not orange juice. This isn't Oregon, Fletcher."

"These frozen-up old trees will never grow anything again except these little dwarfs. Funny they didn't bulldoze this grove and replant it like the others. Throw me a couple and I'll see if I can get some juice out of them."

Hollis threw Fletcher a half dozen of the golf ball size oranges. Fletcher cut one open and tried to squeeze some juice out of it. Six oranges later he had succeeded in getting no more than a half-teaspoon of the tart juice into his beer and the rest on the ground.

"I did a fine job at that, didn't I?"

"Yeah, for somebody with ten thumbs you did okay."

The sun was setting in a blaze of tropical colors over the dark rich farmland while they enjoyed the end of another beautiful south Texas day. After a couple more beers, Hollis got up and reached into the cooler for another.

"We're empty. Let's call it a night." He spit his cigarette among the spilled beer and squeezed oranges as he stood up in the near darkness. The flash was loud and blinding. Hollis recoiled and nearly fell as he stumbled awkwardly away from the explosion while bringing his hands to his face to protect his eyes.

Fletcher instinctively dove for cover and rolled as he reached for the rifle he wasn't carrying. Embarrassed, he was thankful for the darkness so Hollis hadn't seen his involuntary reaction forged deeply into his psyche by his combat experiences. He mentally inventoried his limbs, rubbed his face, and sniffed for blood. He couldn't see anything but knew he was in one piece and not bleeding much, if at all.

"Hollis, are you alright?"

"I don't know and I don't think I can see. Where the hell are you?" he asked as he turned toward the sound of Fletcher's voice. "How'd you get over there?"

"Are you alright?" Fletcher asked again.

"I think so, but the flash damn near blinded me—I'm just seeing stars."

"What exploded?"

"I don't have any idea," Hollis said.

— ‖ —

Steve Addison had worked late in Westcona's Edinburg district lab and now wished he hadn't promised to meet a customer at the Cattle Baron. It was nearly seven when he pulled into the parking lot. He had overheard Fletcher and Hollis talking on their company radios and hoped they would stop by so he could leave without offending the customer. He was a district engineer, not a salesman although Westcona demanded both skills from their engineers.

His pregnant wife, Shelley, was getting more nervous by the day about the baby. However, the oilfield never slept and he had an important job in it. His drive to succeed, combined with his view of Fletcher and Hollis as role models, was taking a toll on his family life. Shelley wanted him home with her in the evenings rather than gallivanting all over the Valley. She had twice miscarried and was understandably worried about being left alone. Katie Boyd and Sara Cade had tried to befriend her but they were older women and had very little in common with her. That and the fact she really didn't like their husbands made for mildly uncomfortable times when they were together. She appreciated their intent but couldn't understand how they could be married to guys who were always at work or off having fun with people from work. According to Steve, his father had been much the same in his younger days, and Steve had promised to be different.

Steve Addison was a twenty-six-year-old Texas A&M graduate with a double major in petroleum engineering and chemistry. All that study and little play produced a man who fit the classic engineer stereotype. He was highly intelligent but shy and generally lacking in confidence when in the presence of other accomplished adults. Nonetheless, his highly impressive educational credentials, winning smile, and underlying potential impressed nearly everyone.

Fletcher had worked with Steve in Alice when Steve was a newly hired field engineer, and he was extremely impressed with the younger man's command of the petroleum sciences and his ability to charm customers on the telephone. Steve's flattering telephone manner was among several traits that convinced Fletcher his protégé would, with a little more experience and coaching, soon break out of his social shell and grow into a very successful oilfield engineer. He thrived on compliments and acknowledgment of his obvious talents. Fletcher and Hollis provided the necessary support for him, anticipating that their efforts would be paid back tenfold in the near future. The three already had a good working relationship.

— ‖ —

Hollis was less than a mile ahead of Fletcher when he approached the Cattle Baron on his way home to McAllen. Slowing to scan the parking lot and not seeing Fletcher's lights in his mirror, he keyed his microphone.

"You wanna stop for a nightcap?"

"Cattle Baron?"

"Yeah, I see Addison's car. Maybe he can explain what happened."

"I'm right behind you."

Steve appeared relieved and happy to see them come through the door, and Fletcher knew Steve probably wanted to go home to Shelley and leave the customer entertaining to them. Still, he wanted to impress on the young man that a good social relationship with decision-makers and customers was important to his career.

"Hello Steve," said a mostly recovered Hollis.

"Hi Hollis. What happened to you?"

In the light of the bar, Fletcher could see why Steve asked the question. Hollis had soot all over his face.

"I'm sure nothing happened to me that you couldn't explain."

"Hollis was in a small explosion," Fletcher interjected. "We have no idea what caused it."

As they explained the sequence of events that led up to the explosion, Steve grew visibly more annoyed as the nonsensical story unfolded. "Beer and orange juice don't burn," Steve responded as if to a couple of grade school boys. "How much beer did you have out there?"

"Look, I'll show you," Hollis said as he poured a little beer into an ashtray, went to the bar for a slice of orange, and triumphantly returned to his experiment. After squeezing the orange slice into the ashtray, he adjusted the flame on his lighter. "Pull back your face—she's gonna flare." Firing the liquid produced nothing but smelly black smoke.

"Maybe it only works in the dark," Steve chided as he headed for the door. "See you in the morning if your orange juice doesn't explode and kill you at breakfast."

— ‖ —

Fletcher and Hollis delivered shotgun shells to the McAllen Field operators the next morning. They received a few promises for upcoming work, but their minds were elsewhere. After quietly driving around for another half hour, Hollis couldn't take the silence any longer.

"Did we have too much to drink last night?"

"A little, but you didn't sweat that soot on your face. Somebody must have dumped a gas can or something flammable where you threw your cigarette."

"I didn't smell gas. Damn, Fletcher. We spilled and dumped almost a full can of beer on top of whatever it was. It wouldn't have exploded like that even if there was gas on the ground."

"I don't know, Hollis. We do know that beer and orange juice don't burn, don't we? Let's go back out there after work and see what we can figure out."

Hollis dropped Fletcher at the office and said he had an errand to run. He didn't like being made fun of and wasn't about to wait all day to solve this problem. After stopping to buy a six-pack, he headed for the orange grove. He sniffed the ground for gas. Nothing that smelled like a hydrocarbon. Kicking dirt into a small pile, he poured a little beer on it and fired his lighter. Nothing. Bewildered, he went to his car to light a cigarette and think about last night while he drank a beer to prevent it from getting warm. *The oranges!* he thought as he carried the beer to the explosion site. Moving over five yards, he again got down on all fours and sniffed the ground. No gasoline or other hydrocarbon that he could smell. He scooped more dirt into a pile, poured all except one last swig of a newly opened beer on it, and walked over to the orange trees. After squeezing six of the dwarf oranges onto the pile, he lit another cigarette and sat back to enjoy the smoke while tension built in his gut. When the cigarette was almost finished, he took a deep breath and tossed it on top of the wet dirt and was rewarded with a boom!

"Is Addison in the lab?" he asked the dispatcher.

"Yes, sir. He just walked in."

"Tell him to stay put until I get there. And ask Mr. Boyd if he'll meet us in the lab in about twenty minutes."

A sooty, euphoric man without eyebrows walked into the Westcona lab in Edinburg. Any six-foot-six-inch man without eyebrows would be an amusing sight, but neither Steve nor Fletcher moved until Hollis grinned. "I did it again," he said as he threw a bag of dirt and six small oranges on the counter before pulling a lukewarm can of beer from a paper sack.

"I should have thought of the dirt last night," Steve said, laughing. "That'll make a huge difference in its combustibility."

"College boy, your daddy sure didn't get much for that Aggie education he bought you. Try citric acid, alcohol, and whatever else is in that dirt. They use chemicals on orchards, don't they? Do some of that chemical engineer shit you're suppose to know and figure out what's in it," Hollis challenged the young and suddenly serious engineer.

— ‖ —

Steve went to work on the dirt after he thought through what Hollis had said. He took his results down to the county agriculture agent for confirmation. By six that evening he had a weak, flickering blue-yellow flame burning in the lab. He stopped by the Cattle Baron to tell Hollis and Fletcher the astonishing news.

"The dirt has a pesticide in it that was outlawed by the EPA years ago. The alcohol and citric acid acted as a catalyst with two chemicals in the pesticide. That resulted in a change in the citric acid's ionic bond."

"What you're saying is that it burns, right?" Hollis asked impatiently.

"Sure. There's a synthesis of compounds containing rhodium, platinum, and tungsten. It's heavy."

"I don't follow you, Steve. Metals don't burn either," said an increasingly irritated Hollis.

"No, they don't, but the result is an effective production of hydrogen through a chemical reaction, and hydrogen is flammable. A simple distillation process turns it into a flammable liquid."

"So what's this all mean?" Hollis asked in complete befuddlement.

"Well, we get a product that has the same characteristics as natural gas. The acid and alcohol make it happen but aren't part of the end product. We can then turn it into a liquid without much work."

"Hold on a minute. You're not saying we have a gasoline substitute?" Fletcher asked incredulously.

"I think so. Natural gas, gasoline, diesel, kerosene all those kinds of fuels. There's more, though. Once I found the molecular structure of the pesticide chemicals, I got into the Westcona applied chemistry library on the computer. We don't need the alcohol and citric acid for a catalyst. I think I found a more efficient way to create the molecular structure by using two of the pesticide's raw materials; pet food protein supplements and a thermal catalyst."

Reaching for his three-dollar calculator, Fletcher asked, "How would the cost compare to gasoline or natural gas?"

"That's what I'm trying to tell you, Fletcher. It's cheap, real cheap. The base substance I'm working with is seawater!"

"Seawater? As in ocean water?"

"Yeah. I think I can make a natural gas, gasoline, or any other liquid fuel substitute out of ocean water, a handful of inexpensive chemicals, and heat. The seawater already has trace amounts of the metals needed for the conversion process. It would be almost free! The product presents itself in a gaseous form, which can be substituted for natural gas. Liquefied, it's a substitute for gasoline or any other liquid hydrocarbon-based fuel."

The stunned men looked at each other, unable to speak. Finally, Fletcher quietly broke the silence.

"Sonofa…bitch!"

— ‖ — Six — ‖ —

"Anyone having problems yet?" Fletcher asked.

Steve and Hollis were seated behind closed doors on the sofa in Fletcher's corner office.

"I'm not," Hollis said. He stood and flexed his muscled arms in excitement. "I've run two tanks through my car and used some in my lawnmower at home. It works just like gasoline."

"How are the other vehicles doing?" Fletcher asked.

"I had four of the service supervisors fill their pickups early in the week. We're using it in the lawnmower here on the yard, and I'm testing it in the road engines of the tractors that are on a job over by Raymondville right now. Everybody thinks its gasoline or diesel."

"You having any problems?" Fletcher asked Steve.

"No, I'm seeing it about the same as Hollis. I made it to Corpus Christi and back on one tank without any trouble. It's in my lawnmower at home, too."

Over the past ten days, Steve had worked nearly nonstop while he refined, adjusted, and tweaked the formula. While it seemed incredible, the basic science was sound and repeatable.

The gasoline and diesel engines they tried it in seemed to run without problems or adjustments. Steve and Hollis had created a still of sorts in the bulk-chemical warehouse to distill their new discovery which was then piped into drums sitting outside on the edge of the raised loading dock. The newly created fuel was pumped out of the drums with a hand-operated drum pump. Workers on the yard wondered about all the activity surrounding the contraption and drums, but just shook their heads when they learned that it was some kind of a lab experiment Steve Addison was running with the help of Hollis Cade.

Fletcher was adamant that absolute secrecy be maintained and that none of the information was shared with anyone, even their wives. He was comfortable knowing Hollis didn't put up with many questions about his personal business or activities on the yard. When told to fuel their pickups from the drums that week, the service supervisors were informed that Steve was testing a new fuel additive, and it was left at that. Hollis had personally supervised the addition of the new product to the fuel tanks of the road tractors used to pull the heavy oilfield equipment to a job one of their crews was now pumping. They continued to use diesel fuel in the deck engines used to power the pumps and other job-related equipment to avoid the risk of damaging a customer's well with engine failures brought on by their new fuel.

Fletcher leaned back in his chair and lit a cigarette. He wanted a preliminary action plan before the meeting ended but was nervous about what his colleagues would want to do.

"I assume you have all your data in the computer?" he asked Steve.

"Yeah, but nobody can get to it without my password."

"The corporate computer jocks in Dallas could—easily."

"They don't have any reason to be looking at my stuff."

"Today they don't. But this company, along with a huge piece of the oil industry, will cease to exist if our discovery becomes public knowledge. I think that's reason enough."

"What about the agreement we all signed when we were hired? It said that Westcona gets anything we discover while working for the company," the ever-practical engineer recalled.

"I know. That's why we need to decide what we're going to do with it," Fletcher said.

Hollis had a disturbed look on his face.

"What do you think?" Fletcher asked the big man.

Hollis was even more agitated, pacing the room now. "There's no doubt that this'll ruin OPEC and all the world's oil and gas producers. They'll be mighty pissed if they find out about it. Westcona probably does have rights to it, but the U.S. government needs it more than anyone. Think what our country could do with something like this. I think we should talk to the feds."

"Every oil company and government in the world will want it. Do we just give it to Westcona and let them deal with the government?" Fletcher countered.

"I don't know, Fletcher. They'd probably just sell it to the government or the highest bidder anyway."

"Yeah, that's my concern. And we'll be out of work when the oilfields disappear in the very near future. Think of all the other careers that would be destroyed if this suddenly bursts onto the scene."

"Well, I think we should get something out of it besides unemployment checks," Hollis concluded.

"Me too, but there are a lot of good people who could be hurt by this if it was handled poorly. I guess we can't much control what others will do with it though," Fletcher said.

Steve was quiet. His mind was whirling and digesting the possibilities. He'd been thinking about the fame this would bring, not the money. His dad would be impressed with his participation in the discovery but could also be financially devastated by it. Logan Addison had made his own success in the oilfields and was now a vice president of one of the world's largest oil companies, and Steve had always wanted to succeed on the same scale. It wasn't easy living up to your father's reputation, especially when you were in the same industry. He saw this as a way to show everyone that he was Logan Addison's son. Some walking-around money certainly sounded reasonable, too. And Shelley, once she became aware of what was happening, would surely agree that he should be compensated in a significant way. Maybe now she would stop worrying about all the hours he put into his career and the people he worked with. Maybe now she would understand the pressures he endured to make a life for her and the family they hoped to have.

"I could talk to my dad and see what he thinks," Steve offered.

"Hell, no!" Fletcher and Hollis shouted in unison. "He's the last person we should let in on this until we decide what to do. We don't even have any outside verification that it's commercially viable," Fletcher said.

"I've got an old shipmate friend who's an attorney in California," Hollis added. "I'll call him tonight and ask about the employment agreement."

"No. It really doesn't matter what Westcona or the law thinks about ownership. They're going to claim rights to it no matter what we do, but we aren't going to give it to them without some serious compensation...if at all," Fletcher said as he stood and paced nervously.

Hollis had confided in Sara, although he had not admitted it to his friends. She possessed rock-solid judgment and often helped Hollis work through complex issues that would impact their life together. He was not a demonstrative or overly-talkative man, but the years he had spent with Sara had been the best of his life. He relied on her strength and especially her judgment. Sara Cade was a six-foot-tall redhead with a big-boned, low-fat, full-figured architecture that matched her vibrant personality. Fantasize a Nordic warrior woman, and Sara was close to what most men would dream. When Hollis was working in Lindsay, she attended college in Chickasha where she earned a bachelor's degree in business administration. Hollis was attracted to her free spirit and boundless energy, something he wished he had more of. She enjoyed having Fletcher in their lives and trusted that Hollis could steer through the storms Fletcher seemed to attract. More importantly, she knew that Hollis had a true friend in Fletcher, something he needed in his life.

Her response to the discovery was one of skepticism until she heard the lawnmower and saw his car idling in their driveway powered by the new fuel. She also expressed a certain foreboding that Hollis felt but couldn't verbalize. This could prove to be a very dangerous adventure depending on how they decided to handle it. Hollis was drawn to the concept of what nearly free energy would mean to humankind. This discovery could eviscerate the Middle East's oil stranglehold on the rest of the world and ignite a jihad like the planet had never seen. He had observed much of so-called civilized man's unseemly behavior, and here was an opportunity to contribute something very positive to the world or start another world war. Fortunately, they both trusted Fletcher and felt the intoxicating attraction of significant wealth, something they had never really considered before knowing him.

"Okay then," Fletcher said. "We're in agreement that we deserve a lot of money for our discovery and that we're not going to let anyone take it away from us. I think we have to offer it to Westcona first just because we owe them some loyalty. Do either of you see it differently? JT's coming down for the weekend and I'll get his take on how to approach Westcona, okay? In the meantime, you dismantle the still and get the chemicals out of here. Dump whatever liquid product you have so there's nothing here except a small amount we can use for a demonstration or two."

As Steve and Hollis prepared to leave, Hollis added, "I'll make sure the road engines have real diesel in them when the crew comes back today and see to it that all the service supervisors add gasoline to their tanks. That just leaves our three cars and our home lawnmowers. We need to get rid of that product, too."

"Yeah, good idea," Fletcher agreed. "Make sure there's none in the lawnmower here on the yard either.

"I'll print out all my data and notes, and erase the computer records," Steve said as he opened the door. "I'll also copy it to a floppy. There's hardly any ingredients left in the lab, just a couple of sacks. I'll make sure those are gone, too. That should make it impossible to duplicate without my notes."

"Give me your notes and floppy disc, Steve. I want everything in the safe and off the computer before we leave here today. I can't stress this enough; don't trust anybody on the outside," Fletcher warned as his colleagues left his office.

He smiled to himself. His friends now agreed that they deserved something significant for the discovery. They were beginning to recognize the value of what they'd found and, most importantly, felt as if they were contributing to the solution Fletcher already had in his mind. He wasn't manipulating them so much as just opening their minds to the enormity of their discovery. Each man had his unique value perspective that Fletcher acknowledged and respected. He just had to make sure the dollars were maximized as part of the overall decision. Fletcher also knew he needed their judgment and help in getting his mind around the complexity of the actions they needed to take, as well as the reactions they needed to anticipate from the outside world—the government, the press, oil producing companies and countries, industrial energy users, and others he hadn't yet recognized.

— ‖ —

Fletcher heard JT's voice as he hung up the phone. He was putting his investment files into his briefcase when JT walked into his office on a late Friday afternoon.

"I'm early, Boyd. Couldn't sit in Alice thinking about doves all afternoon. How are things around here?"

"Fine, JT. Just tying up some loose ends. Let's change and get out to the groves. The doves should be flying low today and, hopefully for you, they'll be flying slow, too."

JT had been known to fill the sky with lead when he saw doves, but the quick little birds normally just kept on flying. Fletcher seldom missed a chance to needle the older man about his shooting skills. Fletcher's secretary interrupted them before JT could respond.

"You'd better answer line two, Fletcher. It's Mr. Jacobs, and he sounds upset."

She couldn't have cared less that JT was in her boss's office. Doris had been the district secretary in Edinburg for more years than she would admit. At sixty-three, she had helped many a new district manager cut their teeth in a relatively easy-to-manage location. Doris was tough and exceptionally good at her job. She always made sure the district operated efficiently and that her temporary charges looked good to the region office. If she liked the manager, she took a motherly interest in his career. Doris took to Fletcher Boyd right away and hoped he wouldn't be leaving Edinburg any to soon.

A long time smoker, Doris had recently quit and was using snuff while trying to wean herself from the cigarettes. No one dared mention the spit cup beside her telephone. In fact, most employees gave her a wide berth on general principle.

Fletcher picked up the phone to speak to his broker. "Hello Ed," he said before a long pause ensued. "That's right, I want out. I know they're good programs but I need the money for something else. I know, I know. No, I won't change my mind. I want the money soon. Yeah…yeah, bye."

"You're not getting out of those drilling programs, are you?" JT asked after Fletcher hung up.

"I am. Energy is not the place to be right now."

"Never thought I'd hear you say that. What about your other investments?"

"I'm shifting everything into transportation-related issues and maybe Westcona stock. Then again, maybe I'll get into some heavy industrial stocks of companies that use huge amounts of energy to produce their product."

JT's facial expression changed from confusion to agitation. "Are you out of your mind? Westcona stock's dropped from seventy-five to less than two dollars over the past four years, and you're getting in? I've been almost suicidal over my million-dollar ESOP account changing into a twenty-five-thousand-dollar pile of steamy horseshit. High-energy-use manufacturing companies?"

"I think energy prices are going lower…much lower," Fletcher responded calmly. "I also think Westcona stock will skyrocket in response. Let me explain."

JT looked thunderstruck as Fletcher poured out the story from the beginning in the orange grove. He immediately forgot about an afternoon dove hunt. Initially, he didn't believe the tale but knew that Fletcher was serious after hearing about the trucks, cars, and lawnmowers. "Westcona stock will go up at least a thousand times, maybe more. I'll be rich again!"

"*If* we give it to Westcona," Fletcher said flatly. "I'm not entirely sure we're going to do that."

His ex-boss exploded. "What do you mean? It's Westcona's property and you know it."

"JT, think about it for a second. They'll take it from us and the company will be rich beyond words. What about us? They won't need us. The company won't even be an oilfield service company."

"Your stock will make you rich," JT countered. "What do you care?"

"A thousand times a little is still a little, JT. This is worth billions, or trillions, or whatever comes higher than that. It'll change the whole world forever. Steve, Hollis, and I are going to be very, very wealthy. If Westcona wants to do that for us, fine. In fact, that's what we'd prefer."

"I'll talk to Dupree…aw, shit, no. I'll take it to the top in Dallas on Monday morning. Don't tell anyone else about this until I talk to Cole. Don't worry; he'll take care of all of you… I know he will," JT assured him.

"That's fine, JT but make sure he understands that the three of us own it and that the company is going to buy it from us. He can save his strength and not even bother with the legal stuff because we're simply not playing that game."

When JT left to use the restroom, Fletcher went to his safe and removed the documentation Steve had given him. He had an uneasy feeling as he hurriedly threw it into his briefcase. *This is going to get complicated*, he thought as he walked out the door to join his disquieted ex-boss for a drink. *I hope to hell we can trust him.*

— III — Seven — III —

BY EARLY MONDAY AFTERNOON, AN OBVIOUSLY confused Roland Dupree was in Dallas after being summoned from his Corpus Christi office for a meeting with Westcona President Branton Cole. JT had called Cole's office earlier that morning and left a disturbing and confusing message with an assistant when Cole was unavailable. Cole wanted immediate clarification and, following the proper chain of command, called Dupree looking for answers. Dupree didn't know anything about JT's call or the message, and admitted as much. When he finally understood that JT had gone over Dupree's head, Cole demanded Dupree's presence in Dallas and then quickly tracked JT down by phone to find out what this was all about.

Cole was not a career oilman or petroleum engineer, but rather an MBA senior executive who happened to run an oilfield service company. This discovery gibberish made no sense to him. Anyone with half a brain would know that the R&D Department needed to verify something like this before wasting his time.

His indignation became palpable as JT did his best to explain the situation. Cole had never heard such an outrageous proposal and, if this discovery was viable, just who the hell did these people think they were dealing with.

Though Cole had met JT, he didn't really know him. Just the same, he was very aware of JT's reputation as a hard-charging maverick with a distinguished record. And because JT had not followed the proper chain of command, he also understood that JT had little or no confidence in Dupree...and that concerned him. He wondered if the young Division VP would be up to the task he was about to be assigned.

Cole's meeting with Dupree was short, sweet, and blunt. He explained the information and ultimatum from Fletcher Boyd as relayed by JT. He was irate over being communicated with in such a manner by two lowly district managers, and finally offered some harsh and pointed career counseling to Dupree. He then offered Dupree the opportunity to redeem himself and his career when he instructed him to ascertain the basic veracity of this wild claim. Then and only then, and subject to substantiation by real scientists, was he to respond to Boyd's ultimatum with an offer of compensation. While it was unthinkable that the alleged discovery was for real, Cole instinctively covered his ass. The offer would be made only to shut down any notion Boyd might have of putting out feelers to prospective buyers. Cole had no intention of actually paying or honoring the offer he sent with Dupree. Boyd would certainly fall for his little ruse if there was anything to this discovery. While he was confident that the company would legally own anything Boyd might have discovered while in its employ, he also knew that possession was nine-tenths of the law. Whatever this cowboy thought he had must be controlled until brighter minds could sort it out.

— ‖ —

The corporate propjet bearing Roland Dupree was waiting for clearance before landing at McAllen Miller International Airport. As they entered the pattern, Dupree looked for JT's company car in the parking lot. From the air, McAllen looked like a tropical oasis sitting in a sea of parched landscape. Only the replanted orchards, groves, and trees bordering the Rio Grande River provided any color to the flat brown desert that stretched beyond both sides of the international border this late in the year. JT was supposed to pick him up for a meeting with Fletcher. He didn't see the car but was confident JT had made the 110-mile drive from Alice in time. Dupree's plan was to see what this new discovery was all about before arranging a demonstration at Westcona's research and development lab the following day if he was convinced it was viable. As the plane touched down, he wondered once again about the reality of this bizarre situation. He was already on high alert because JT had warned that the men were considering other options, even though they were leaning strongly toward Westcona at the present time. Their confidence level was obviously off the charts, and he knew Fletcher well enough to know he wouldn't be acting this way without ample cause. Dupree also had a bone to pick with JT for going over his head.

"Over here, Dupree," JT yelled as he walked out of the FBO. JT was sitting in his car, cowboy hat pulled low, sucking the bottom out of a beer can. Dupree thought it ironic that two people as different as Jake Taylor and Fletcher Boyd had become such close friends, even to the point of JT buying a black cowboy hat after Fletcher began sporting his silver-belly.

"I really appreciate you calling Cole this morning," he said sarcastically and without effect.

"Fiddle-fuckin around with you just wasn't in the cards, Dupree. This needs to be handled right damn now...and Cole should be the one getting off the plane, not you."

Dupree's face and neck colored in anger and embarrassment. Their former boss-subordinate roles no longer existed...if they really ever had.

"You shouldn't be drinking in a company vehicle."

"I shouldn't be sneaking around McAllen holding your hand either," JT responded without apparent interest. Dupree was depending on JT to control Fletcher if the need really existed. There shouldn't be a problem, but he could still feel the situation getting away from him. It annoyed him that JT was calling him by his last name and openly drinking beer in a company vehicle, but under the circumstances he couldn't do much about it. He knew that JT seldom called anyone by anything other than their last name, but it was disrespectful and he didn't like it. While it wouldn't have been the case just a few short years ago, he also knew that JT had a lot more influence with Fletcher than he did, so he let it slide. As to the beer, well these were the south Texas oilfields, a place where cold beer flowed like water twenty-four hours a day. They were both big boys and he suspected JT had never really fully adjusted to the diminished role he was being forced to play within Westcona since his region-level job had been eliminated a few years ago.

"You tell Fletcher what this is about?" he asked JT.

"You really amaze me, Dupree. What the hell do you think he thinks you're coming down here for? To go whoring in Mexico?"

"No, I just meant have you told him that I went to Dallas and got my ass reamed over this already today — and that I want answers."

"Pass me that last beer before it gets warm. I think you underestimate Fletcher Boyd."

— ‖ —

Hollis Cade watched JT's car disappear before he dialed Fletcher from the payphone in the public terminal.

"JT just picked him up and they're headed your way."

"Was anyone else with him?"

"Nope, just Dupree."

"Good. Stay off the radio in case JT has his on. I'll have Steve meet you at the Cattle Baron and I'll be over as soon as I get rid of Dupree."

— ‖ —

Roland Dupree was strutting around playing his vice president act to the hilt as he demanded a demonstration of the new discovery. Fletcher handed him a small jar of their liquefied product.

"Here, Roland. Sniff and decide for yourself if its hydrocarbon based. Rub some between your fingers and you'll see that it's not slick either."

"I'm not sure that means anything, but you're right. It doesn't smell or feel like gas or diesel. Does it really burn?" he asked as he reached for a lighter.

"Put that away or you'll blow us up!" Fletcher yelled. "I'm not kidding! Here, let's put some in the lawnmower and I'll show you."

Dupree theatrically verified that the gas tank on the mower was empty, and then tried to start the machine anyway. He carefully traced the gas line from the carburetor back to the fuel tank with his finger to make sure gas wasn't being supplied from anywhere else. Satisfied, he poured a small amount of the product into the tank and primed the engine. Two pulls later the engine was running like it would on high quality gasoline. Dupree looked stunned, then excited.

"We've been using it in our cars and the tractor road-engines, too," Fletcher said.

"Can you make some from scratch tomorrow in Dallas for the R&D guys?"

Fletcher shifted and glanced at JT. "We can, but we need to talk money first. We're not just giving this to Westcona...or anyone else for that matter."

"In your office, now," Dupree ordered as he walked away leaving them standing with the lawnmower. Fletcher and JT looked at each other and shook their heads in unison before following their boss inside.

Fletcher was not impressed with the offer. JT sat in an over-stuffed chair in the far corner of his protégé's office, quietly listening and watching. Dupree carefully framed the offer subject to verification by the Westcona chemists in Dallas. Fletcher's scowl told the story.

"That's not enough," Fletcher said.

"What do you mean, that's not enough?" Dupree exploded defensively. "Three hundred thousand bucks is a hell of a lot of money when you know company policy says you get fifteen hundred for a patentable discovery."

"Get your head out of your ass, Roland. A hundred grand each is hardly going to turn us into Rockefellers."

"Westcona doesn't have to give you a dime for it. We're just trying to do the right thing, not make you rich. You signed your rights away when you were hired."

"You think so? For one thing, that agreement says the company has rights to anything that can be used in the business which our discovery can't be. It'll destroy this whole industry. We'll be out of work and a few hundred grand won't change that. No, Roland, this isn't some invention like ball sealers or a new gel breaker. This is going to make us enough money so we don't ever have to work again."

Dupree turned to JT for support. JT just smiled. Perspiration formed over Dupree's upper lip as he collected his thoughts.

"I'm not supposed to offer this yet because the board hasn't approved it, but Westcona will guarantee lifetime employment for the three of you and at a pretty damn good salary."

"And how much is that?"

"One hundred thousand dollars a year each."

"Would we have to work or would we just get a check in the mail?"

"Get off it, Fletcher. For that kind of money, you'd damn well have to work."

"You must be visiting California soon, Roland, because that's where Disneyland is. You'll feel right at home in Fantasyland. Now listen up. With our discovery, Westcona would become some kind of a holding company that wouldn't need people like us. Secondly, that's less than twice my current salary and hardly enough to consider. Now that I have this opportunity, working for the rest of my life has kind of lost its appeal. I'm sure Hollis and Steve agree."

"Are you speaking for them? Don't you think we should get them in here and ask?"

"They're indisposed right now, but yes, I'll ask them. When do you need an answer?"

"When do I need an answer? I need it right now. Today. I have to call Mr. Cole before I leave here."

"Well, that isn't going to happen. Tell you what, Roland. You get back on your plane and toodle on back to Corpus. I'll call you at home by seven tonight with our answer."

"No later, Fletcher. I can't put off calling Mr. Cole for long. He'll start hunting me and I'll be embarrassed for the second time today thanks to you."

"You don't seem to grasp this, Roland. I don't care about Cole. I'm setting the schedule and I don't need any ultimatums or direction from any of you. I'll call you tonight."

— || —

Dupree was livid as JT drove him back to the airport. "He can't talk to me like that. I'll run his skinny ass off and get the formula from Addison."

"He did talk to you like that, and Addison won't talk to you without Boyd's approval. He's loyal. Look Dupree, you're taking yourself way too seriously. If Westcona gets their discovery, you and I will be just as unemployed. Besides, they discovered it on their own—outside of Westcona. The patent may not be Westcona's to claim. And even if some court says it is, they aren't going to give it up. Get a grip on yourself, boy. Think this through before you have a stroke. Like I told you on the way out here, you underestimate Fletcher Boyd. I'll go back and talk to the three of them after I drop you off. Any chance I can expand the offer?"

"*No*, but you can get a counter offer. Cole's going to hang me by my nuts if I can't get this taken care of fast. He's still convinced they're blowing smoke, but wants to know for sure to cover his own ass with the board."

"You've seen it with your own eyes...and now you have an advantage on Cole, at least until you tell him. Rather than fret about what he might do to you, why don't you think about how much Westcona stock you can buy before Fletcher agrees with us? Call your broker when you get back to Corpus. Then you'll at least have some walking-around money while you look for another job."

After dropping Dupree at the McAllen airport, JT shook his head in wonder as he switched on his company radio to call the Edinburg dispatcher.

"Is Boyd still around there?"

"No sir, he's meeting with Mr. Cade and Steve Addison."

"Cattle Baron?"

"Ahhh err yes sir."

— ‖ —

Logan Addison looked through his telephone messages as the sun was trying to burn through the smog and mist that enveloped downtown Houston. It was already hot and the stifling humidity had soaked through his shirt before he even reached the building. Like most men in the city, he kept a fresh shirt hanging on the back of his office door to change into after lunch. That was just self-defense in this swampy steam bath of a city. The lush green sub-tropical landscape was beautiful and made for a terrific place to live if you had gills and webbed feet. It took some getting used to, but he had sure lived in less hospitable places.

Logan had spent the previous week in Midland, Texas, and Los Angeles trying to calm his employees. Rumors were again circulating that Global Oil was planning more layoffs and early retirements. As vice president of domestic production, Logan Addison was responsible for all U.S. oil and gas production for the fifth-largest oil company in the world. Global's drilling and completion activity was decreasing due to the continuing slump in OPEC-driven oil prices, and people were being retired and forced out of some segments of the company. Logan's thirty-six thousand production employees were concerned that they would also face layoffs if the market didn't

turn around soon. He shared their concerns and did his best to
allay their fears. In no rush to return to gloomy Houston, he
had spent the weekend in sunny California and returned this
Monday morning on a red-eye.

He stopped sorting through his messages when he noticed
one from his son, Steve. It was dated Friday afternoon and
simply said, *Houston, we have a problem.* Even on a Monday
morning, that made him smile. He and Steve did not have as
close a relationship as either of them really wanted but
both were trying to improve the situation. Logan's career
had been all consuming, especially when Steve was a boy.
They had been transferred almost a dozen times and lived all
over the world. Their life had been vigorous and dynamic in
those days, and he still missed the excitement.

Logan had sent Steve back to the States to live with his
sister and her family after his wife died in Malaysia. A year
later, he was transferred back to Houston in his present capac-
ity. By that time, Steve was enrolled at Texas A&M. Despite his
urging, Steve refused Global's employment offer and accepted
one from Westcona when he graduated. They had very
different personalities, something Logan found difficult to
understand. Still, he was a good kid and now had a terrific
wife. Perhaps the time was finally right for them to enjoy
closer family ties.

He immediately dialed Westcona's district office in
Edinburg hoping Shelley wasn't having problems with her
pregnancy.

"Hi, Steve. What's going on in the Valley?"

"Where have you been all weekend? I've been trying to
find you."

"I was in L.A. and decided to stay the weekend. Got back
to Houston this morning. What's up? Shell's all right, isn't she?"

"She's fine but you won't be. I've discovered something that will put Global out of business. Well, really I helped discover it."

"Sure you did. Look, I'm kinda busy. What do you need?"

"I just told you. I'm serious. You are about to be out of work."

"Yeah, right...and just what is this great discovery?"

When Logan hung up the phone, he loosened his tie and shut his office door. He sat down on his sofa, his head spinning at the gravity of Steve's words. He thought he had seen and experienced everything in the business world that could possibly stun him but...damn, this just couldn't be true! Steve was well trained and certainly a competent chemist, but this was way beyond his pay-grade. Still, if there was anything to it he'd better notify his boss that something was about to break within the industry. Then again, he couldn't very well go to his boss with something as farfetched as this without incontrovertible proof...and this was just too far out in left field to even seriously consider. Still, it was not like Steve to just dream up something like this.

He sat in his office, still unable to grasp what he thought his son had told him. Neurons snapped frenetically through his brain as his imagination ran wild. Finally, he took a deep breath and tried to reason through what he must do. Although he had promised not to tell anyone at Global right now, he would have to bring it to the top quickly if what Steve said was even partially true. This thing would be worth trillions, if real. But then the likelihood of it being even partly real was pretty damn small, and he already had enough on his plate to overwhelm most people without adding a cockamamie story to the mix. He looked out the window for a few moments, sighed deeply, and hit the re-dial button on his telephone.

"I'm coming to McAllen."

"Driving or flying?"

"Flying. I'll have to make arrangements to get a company plane but I should be there later this afternoon. In the meantime, you get a demonstration set up for me. I'm not saying I don't believe you, but you'll have to admit this is pretty damn hard to swallow. You're absolutely sure of your science?"

"I've never been so sure of anything!"

"Sit on it until I get there," Logan instructed.

— ‖ —

The Westcona pilot listened intently on the McAllen tower frequency of 118.5 MHz as he swung the propjet around to the northeast and set a heading for Corpus Christi. He heard another pilot say, "McAllen tower, this is three six Gulf Oscar. Request clearance for landing on runway one three. We're eight miles out with Bravo." He reached behind him and banged loudly on a cabinet to get Roland Dupree's attention, motioning him to plug in his headset. Dupree was rooting around in the refrigerator looking for a diet Coke when he saw the pilot's gestures. He grabbed the headset and plugged it into the jack in time to hear, "…six Gulf Oscar, McAllen tower. Altimeter two niner eight one; wind is light variable; you're cleared to land runway one three. You have a corporate propjet climbing out at your ten o'clock. No other traffic in the pattern."

"Roger McAllen, runway one three. Three six Gulf Oscar."

The pilot switched on the intercom and spoke into Dupree's headset.

"Mr. Dupree, that's one of Global Oil's planes out of Houston Hobby. I bump into them all over the country."

Dupree knew that Global Oil had wells in south Texas and may have a valid reason for landing in McAllen today.

However, he also had encouraged Steve Addison to solicit Global Oil work for Westcona through his father, and it was likely no coincidence that Global's plane was here now. Steve must have told his father about the discovery...and now Global was after it! Dupree's stomach tightened as his bowels loosened. It was up to JT now.

— || —

Logan Addison was in the right front seat of the small Global jet as they made their approach into McAllen Miller International Airport. He couldn't help but notice the distinctive yellow and red markings on the Westcona propjet as she climbed out in front of them. A sharp pain throbbed in his left temple at the thought of Westcona beating him to his son's discovery. Logan deplaned and walked over to the public terminal for his rental car. McAllen was only slightly cooler than Houston. Perspiring, he removed his coat and tie while pondering how in the hell this place got so brown with all the humidity. He dug in his pocket for change to make a phone call.

"Shelley, is Steve home yet?" he asked his daughter-in-law without preamble.

"Not yet, but he should be soon. Where are you, Logan? Steve was trying to find you all weekend."

"I'm at the McAllen airport. Do you think he's still at the yard?"

"Probably. They can reach him on the radio or telephone if he's not."

"Thanks. Don't start cooking, hon. I'll take you out for dinner. I trust you're doing well?"

"I guess we are, Logan. Steve's been acting rather strangely the last few days, and now you show up in McAllen. Something's going on, isn't it?"

"I meant you, dear. Are you well?"

"I am. Just a few more months and this will be over," she said, laughing. "Not going to answer my question, huh?"

"See you in a little while, Shell."

Logan thought the world of Shelley. After the death of his wife, he and Steve had lost the warmth of an understanding and loving woman in their lives. Shelley filled the void so perfectly that Logan had known almost immediately she was going to be part of their family. Shelley had been completing her elementary education degree when Steve met her. Kind and considerate, she also recognized the underdeveloped potential in Steve. She had endured two miscarriages within a year's time but had not let it get the best of her. Now she was in her sixth month and doing well. Steve, Shelley, and Logan were exuberant as they planned for the baby's arrival. To say Shelley was sweet was an understatement, and he loved her like a daughter. She was bringing his son back into his life after a long drought. Logan dialed the Westcona yard in nearby Edinburg and asked for Steve.

"I'm sorry, sir, Steve's in a meeting right now. Can I take a message and have him call you back?"

"This is his father. I'm in town and he's expecting me."

"Yes, sir. Hang on and I'll patch you through to where he's at."

— || —

The air-conditioner compressor was again frozen up like a block of ice so the bartender propped the front door open and plugged in the fans. They did little to cool, just barely moved the hot, smoke-filled air around the Cattle Baron bar. Fletcher stood in the doorway for a moment to let his eyes adjust to the relative darkness. Seeing him, the bartender poured a stiff J&B scotch with a splash of water and carried it to the corner table where Hollis and Steve were having a spirited discussion and their fourth round of drinks.

"Come on over, Fletcher," boomed a half-pixilated Hollis Cade. "They got the Yankee air-conditioner on again. You should feel right at home."

Fletcher tipped his silver Stetson up on his moist forehead wishing he'd not switched from his straw hat so early this year.

"We agreed on a name, at least if you like it," Hollis announced proudly. "We're gonna call it Neptune, after the Greek god of the sea. Steve wanted to call it a bunch of numbers but I talked him out of it."

That didn't sound right to Fletcher. Hadn't he just seen a documentary about the Roman Empire and their efforts to adopt all the Greek pagan gods to keep control of the people without admitting they were the same set of gods? The Greek name for their god of water was Poseidon. *Yeah...and the Romans named him Neptune.* He was also the god of earthquakes, if Fletcher remembered correctly. Hollis didn't often mess up a history fact, especially if it had to do with the sea.

"Had a couple already, Hollis? I'm not sure I agree with your memory on the Neptune thing. Poseidon was the Greek god and I think the Romans re-named him Neptune."

Hollis' face twisted in thought, quickly followed by the spreading pink of embarrassment across his well-tanned features.

"Damn, I've been landlocked for too long. I knew that," the former blue-water sailor said quietly. "Poseidon doesn't do it for me though. Neptune has a better ring to it."

Steve didn't seem to care and just shrugged his shoulders in good-natured disinterest.

"Neptune's fine," Fletcher finally conceded.

"What did Mr. Dupree say?" Steve asked.

"He said Neptune belongs to Westcona, but they'd reward us handsomely for the outstanding work if we could prove it was for real." Fletcher squeezed into the rear corner chair against the wall and took a long drink. "They want a demonstration tomorrow but Dupree and I had a disagreement over money. We'll have to go up to the Dallas lab and put on a show for them sooner or later, but it's off the table for now."

"We can sure as hell prove that it works. How much money did you argue about?" Hollis asked.

"They offered us a three-hundred-thousand-dollar cash bonus to split between us, plus a life-time employment contract worth another hundred grand a year each." Fletcher looked quickly at their faces, hoping to see disappointment. He had spent hours trying to keep them focused on being multi-millionaires. Steve reached for his calculator as Hollis ordered another round and lit a cigarette. Neither displayed any emotion as they mulled over the information.

Steve stopped poking at his calculator. "If we all work until we're sixty-five, that's about four million for me and about…two and a half million plus change for each of you due to your advanced ages."

"How much do you think we'd earn normally if we worked until we were sixty-five?" Fletcher pushed the young engineer without taking the bait about his age.

"I don't know how much you two make, but for me it would be about two million, assuming raises every once in a while."

"And for Hollis and me it would be about the same because we make more than you do, although we're of advanced age, as you point out. That means they're really giving Hollis and me about an additional half million dollars each, maybe a little more spread out over the next twenty or twenty-five years. We'd have to work all those years to get it and hope the company stays in business to boot. For you, it would be about two million more spread over forty years."

Fletcher could see his strategy was working. While the arithmetic wasn't precise, it adequately demonstrated the point he wanted to make. Both men were thinking hard about what he had just said and neither was looking particularly happy.

"Write those numbers down on this napkin would you, Steve?" Hollis asked. "You said we'd get more than this, Fletcher."

"I did, and we will if we stick together and play our cards right. What do you two think?"

"I think they're trying to take advantage of us," Steve said.

"Me, too," Hollis added. His tone was somewhat menacing. "I think we oughta look at other options. They must think we're as dumb as a sack of rocks."

"Steve?"

"I agree with Hollis. Let's ask for more. I know I wasn't supposed to but I talked to my dad this morning. He's coming down today to see what we've got. I bet Global will make us a better offer once he's convinced it's for real."

Fletcher and Hollis flashed angry looks at Steve and then caught each other's attention. Hollis nodded nearly imperceptibly and spoke in his most ominous Chief Petty Officer voice. "If you ever fucking go behind our backs again or do something Fletcher or I tell you not to do, you're going to need surgery to get my boot out of your ass."

Steve turned pale and then blushed red when he realized Hollis was serious. He glanced nervously at Fletcher and saw only hard, unblinking eyes.

"Now, what about the feds?" Hollis asked as if no words had been exchanged. "I want Uncle Sam to have a chance at this, too."

"I agree, and even though Steve jumped the gun, it may be time to talk to Global anyway. Let's put it up for bid and see what happens." Fletcher grinned and raised his eyebrows. "We *will* become multi-millionaires if you stick with me on this."

The three men sat in silence. Fletcher figured his cohorts were trying to imagine life with so much money. Steve was likely thinking about a new home with a baby nursery and swimming pool. Hollis would be envisioning a prosperous United States, finally free of OPEC, in which he could buy a few hundred acres of land and build a rustic log home that nobody could find without a map. Fletcher himself was pondering the counter-offer he had already prepared and wondering if he should ask for even more. He shared Hollis's ideas of retirement heaven; a remote spread where he could choose when he wanted to be around people. A satellite dish, phone lines, and a computer would allow him access to the financial markets and the world. The silence was not awkward, just comfortable as it can be between friends.

JT walked into the Cattle Baron as the bartender yelled at Steve to come to the phone. Swaggering over to the bar, JT ordered a Lone Star longneck and threaded his way across the room.

"Move your ass over, Boyd. You know I can't sit anywhere except in the corner."

"What a surprise," Fletcher said without smiling as he slid around the table. "You should trust people more so you could sit with your back to a crowd once in a while."

"That's a bad habit I don't intend to get into."

— ‖ —

JT had thought about his approach to the trio on his drive from the airport. It was indefensible that they would not sell their discovery to Westcona, but he did think the offer was pretty chicken-shit. He was confident the company would sweeten the pot enough to make everybody happy once the science people verified their discovery. The boys deserved a lot for their formula, and Westcona would become the wealthiest company in the world. It was only right. He also knew that talking tough to Boyd wouldn't help.

"Boyd, you were kind of hard on ol' Dupree this afternoon."

"I was, but he needed it."

"Don't blame Dupree. The offer came from Cole and the big boys in Dallas. Money's tight right now. I'm sure they were just feeling you out a little."

Fletcher snorted. "I think there are better words to describe what they're doing."

"We figured out the financial end of it," Hollis blurted as he searched the cluttered table for his napkin. "It adds up to only about an extra half million for Fletcher and me. More for Steve, but still not that much once you consider what we already get paid."

"So, what are you saying?" JT asked Hollis.

"We're putting it out to the highest bidder," he said before Fletcher could get his boot onto Hollis's foot. He needed to get control of the situation from his loose-lipped friend who already had too much to drink.

Fletcher grimaced. JT's eyes widened, his neck bulged, and his fists clenched…but he held his fiery temper.

"Cade, that's a shit load of money. I'm sure we can work out the finances to suit everyone. Let's put a counter-offer together. They'll be reasonable if you are."

"Yeah, and if a buzzard had a jukebox up his ass there'd be music in the sky," Hollis said with a penetrating glare.

Fletcher smiled as he pulled a piece of paper out of his pocket.

"This is what I came up with, JT. It's right off the most recent Westcona annual report. Once this is out, the company won't be a well service company anymore, right?"

"Right."

"So, if Westcona sold its facilities and equipment, it would generate about seven hundred and fifty million dollars after paying off all its loans. Its operating expenses would drop off because they'd lay off all the field people and most of the division and corporate people. Bankers would be standing in line trying to lend them money to develop and distribute their new product. I propose that the three of us split six hundred million dollars in cash and part ways with Westcona. We'd have fair compensation and Westcona would still have some operating capital, bank financing, and the most valuable product on the face of the earth."

Hollis nearly choked on his drink. JT looked as if he might be having a stroke. He became even more disquieted when Steve returned from the phone.

"That was my dad. He's in town and driving over from the airport right now."

— ‖ — Eight — ‖ —

HOLLIS, STEVE, AND FLETCHER HAD breakfast at the Rincon Gaucho restaurant in Edinburg the next morning. Fletcher's head hurt and it looked like Steve and Hollis weren't in any better shape.

"Where's JT?" Hollis asked.

"He was dead to the world when I left home" Fletcher said. "I rattled the guest room door but didn't hear him stir. His head has to be pounding this morning."

Fletcher knew that JT would promise the good Lord to quit drinking in exchange for making it through this day. He also knew his former boss would be back in Alice by noon and still get in a full day's work before stopping by the Holiday Inn for three drinks to take away the nagging headache he will have endured all day. Only then would he fall into his own bed feeling vaguely guilty about his earlier discussion with the Almighty.

"What did your dad say last night?" Fletcher asked Steve who was pouring large quantities of hot sauce on his Spanish omelet.

"He was pretty excited. He called some people before he flew back home, and he's in a Global board meeting this morning in Houston. He said he'd call me as soon as he could."

"I imagine Westcona's having a meeting today, too. Dupree could hardly talk when I called and told him what we wanted," Fletcher said. The men laughed at the thought of Dupree's reaction.

Hollis had also liberally doused his eggs and hash browns with hot sauce, and now had a line of sweat over his upper lip and still visibly seared eyebrows. Fletcher marveled at the amount of hot sauce these guys used, and already felt better just being around them.

"You didn't tell your dad how we make the stuff, did you?" Hollis asked as he mopped his big face with the third napkin of the meal.

"No, but he sure tried to get it out of me. He just kept telling me that Global would pay much more than Westcona could. He also wanted to see the lawnmower run, and fortunately I had what was left of the Neptune we saved for demonstrations. That's the end of it. He's convinced, although he warned me that Global would have their lab rats verify our science before they pay us."

"I guess he wanted to be able to tell his boss about it from his own personal observation. Can't blame him for that. We need to get the wives together and bring them up to speed, too," Fletcher said. "I had to tell Katie most of it last night because JT couldn't keep his mouth shut."

"Shelley knows, too, after my dad got so excited," Steve admitted. "She's apt to side with my dad on what to do, but she's really tickled."

"Sara knows, too," Hollis said with a trace of guilt in his eyes. "She's pretending to have a hard time buying our bullshit, but she's happier than I've seen her in a long, long time, Fletcher."

"I'm not sure Katie believes what we told her either but they all need to know exactly what we're up to," Fletcher insisted.

"Let's get them together at my house tonight so they'll have the same information and understand how serious this thing is."

— || —

Global's emergency board meeting was not going well for Logan Addison. The executives became reluctant and skeptical believers after Logan explained what he had witnessed the previous evening. While the idea stretched credibility, they agreed that doing nothing was unacceptable in the off chance Neptune was real. They were not responding to his proposal to offer a billion dollars to the Westcona employees, particularly when one of the recipients was Logan's own son. The discussion covered many areas, including attempting to steal the technology before Westcona gained control. The board also thought Logan should be able to talk his son into betraying his friends for much less money. After all, what could they do if young Addison defected to Global? The meeting adjourned without a planned offer, at least not a firm one. Logan felt ashamed and embarrassed when he was instructed to persuade his son to bring the formula to Global and abandon his friends. Without Logan's knowledge, the board ordered a six-man security force to Edinburg. The team was to await instructions, pending Logan's success with Steve.

— || —

Westcona's board met in Dallas and was incensed at the terms of Boyd's counter-offer. The members ordered Branton Cole to summon Boyd into their presence to threaten court action if he refused the original offer, deemed extremely benevolent for something that was legally theirs. After all, each of the men had signed a boilerplate agreement that said any process, device, or well treatment they invented while in the company employ belonged to the company. They softened somewhat when Cole explained that the offer was nothing more than a trick. He had no intention of paying the men anything once Westcona had the formula. Still, they directed a security team, posing as auditors, to Edinburg. The same corporate jet would bring Boyd back to Dallas where they would explain the facts of life to the upstart district manager.

— ‖ —

"I'm so proud of you I could burst," Logan told Steve, who was smiling broadly on the other end of the phone. "I underestimated you son, although I shouldn't have. You'll soon be one of the richest and most famous men in the world!"

"What happened at your meeting?"

"They loved it! You bring the formula to Global and you'll never have to work another day in your life."

"How much, Dad?" he asked with sudden uneasiness.

"Don't worry about that now, son. I'll take care of the money for you."

Steve's reaction was as immediate as it was emotional. Trembling in anger, he tried to light a cigarette but failed and finally just threw the matches and cigarette on the desk. He didn't smoke and didn't even know why he had grabbed a pack from Fletcher's desk that morning. Old feelings welled up in him as he looked at his window without seeing past the dirty glass.

"I *am* worried about it, dammit. You come up with an offer and I'll give it to Fletcher. He's making the deals for all of us."

"Forget him, Steve. You discovered it. You don't owe him anything. Just bring it to Global."

"Bullshit!" Steve exploded, swearing at his dad for only the second time in his life. "I owe Fletcher Boyd. He promoted me into Edinburg and has helped my career more than you or anybody else. He and Hollis really made the discovery. I just refined and documented it. I can't believe you're doing this."

"Steve, listen to me. This is the big leagues. It's every man for himself, and you don't owe them anything. Global will make you rich and famous. We're not dealing with those other guys."

"Forget it, Dad. It's going to the highest bidder. If Global wants it, make us an offer. We're a package deal."

Steve had been taking unsolicited advice from his father his whole life and was sick of it. While he had never said anything, he still had strong and unresolved feelings about how his father had shuffled him back to the States when his mother died. He had wanted to stay with Logan during that difficult time but his dad was too busy with work to keep him. All those old feelings unexpectedly surfaced. He was shocked that his father was siding with Global and expecting him to be disloyal to his friends. That just wasn't how he had been raised.

"Don't make a hasty decision, son. I've been around a long time and you're making a mistake. You sleep on it and I'll call you in the morning."

"Apparently you haven't been around long enough to understand me. I'm embarrassed for you. Call with an offer," Steve ordered flatly as he hung up. Then he felt sick.

— ‖ —

Fletcher walked into Westcona's boardroom late in the afternoon wearing what he had gone to work in that morning: starched jeans, a long-sleeved dress shirt, and cowboy boots.

Branton Cole was seated near the head of the long, highly polished mahogany table surrounded by hard-bitten old men he had never met but had heard stories about. They didn't look very friendly.

The tenth-floor boardroom offered a spectacular view of the Dallas skyline. Crystal water pitchers sat every three feet up and down both sides of the table, and each man had a matching goblet and ashtray in front of him. The air was redolent with expensive cigar smoke. Branton Cole shook his hand and introduced him around the table. Each man curtly nodded without speaking or rising from the dark maroon high-back leather chairs. *Nope, not friendly at all.* A year ago, he would have been very nervous in a meeting like this but now he felt a strange calm, almost as though they were working for him instead of the other way around.

After motioning Fletcher to a seat, Cole cleared his throat and spoke for the group. Fletcher brazenly lit a cigarette and sat back confidently in his chair. They were being assholes and trying to intimidate him. He could show them a thing or two about being an asshole.

"Thank you for meeting with us, Fletcher. We want to make sure you understand our very generous offer, and are concerned that it was somehow mis-communicated to you in Edinburg."

The darkly tanned, sixty-year-old Cole trained his glacial, steel-gray eyes on Fletcher. His silky-smooth demeanor, accentuated by a finely tailored midnight blue suit and shock of pure white hair, was impressive. After presenting the offer again, Cole asked if he understood it.

"I understood it when Dupree made it yesterday. He speaks English reasonably well, you know," Fletcher answered without flinching. "You need to consider our counter-offer. I'll go over it again if it was too complicated for you."

"I'm afraid your offer is out of the question, Mr. Boyd," responded one of the board members. "Our offer is quite generous, especially when you consider that you won't get a penny or have a job if we take you to court."

"Court? Really?" Fletcher smiled easily. He was still amazed at his own confidence.

"That's it, then?"

"I'm afraid so. Just remember we hold all the cards, Fletcher," Cole said icily.

Fletcher got to his feet and walked toward the door while shaking his head, his body language expressing nothing but contempt for the group. He paused, leisurely lit another cigarette, and turned to Cole.

"Do you really think you hold all the cards, Branton? I'm going back to Edinburg. Fire me if you think that's a smart move. It would be your second mistake in as many days."

"Mistake or not, you're on very dangerous ground, son." said Cole. "We'll get you a room for the night and talk about your offer. We'll meet again in the morning after we've all had a little time to calm down and reflect on our positions. How's that, son?"

"I'm not your fucking son," Fletcher stated calmly as he continued toward the door. "But I'll stay overnight. This is your one and only chance to get it right before Neptune goes on the open market." He felt sure they were lying but couldn't think of anything to do except stay and give them some time to work on the offer or tip their hand.

"No offense intended, Fletcher. For the sake of discussion, is your six-hundred-million figure negotiable?"

"It was but I'm not sure anymore. You really don't seem to be taking this seriously, and now I'm thinking the price needs to be higher. I'm looking for a warm, fuzzy feeling that I'm not getting here and I don't like it." He strode from the room leaving the door open behind him.

Cole pressed an intercom button and asked his assistant to arrange transportation and lodging for Fletcher at the Greenbrier Inn just west of the office. As soon as Fletcher was out of earshot, Cole dialed his security team leader waiting patiently in Edinburg.

"Dutch, I'm keeping Boyd in Dallas for the night. He's most uncooperative and unpleasant. You arrive on the yard at four-thirty when the office staff is getting ready to leave for the day. Tell them you're internal auditors conducting a surprise audit. Get Cade and Addison in and pressure them for the information. Tear the office apart if that's what it takes. I want that formula and any documentation you can find. Don't mollycoddle the bastards," he ordered vehemently.

— ‖ —

Logan Addison received a call from Mark Streeter, Global Oil's president, at 4:55 p.m.

"Addison, what's your kid going to do?" he demanded.

"Well, Steve's thinking about it and will have an answer in the morning," Logan sidestepped.

"Don't beat around the bush with me, Addison. Is he coming over or not?"

"I'm still hopeful," Logan lied. "A firm offer that included all of them would help it along."

"Bullshit," was all he heard as Streeter slammed down his phone.

A surge of anger flowed through Logan. Everyone was telling him *bullshit* today and it wasn't something he gracefully tolerated. His feelings of contempt and resentment toward

Streeter were immense even under normal circumstances. Who the hell did this guy think he was? He was nothing but a daddy's boy with very little real industry experience. Logan had spent more than twenty-five years working the Middle East, Far East, and Africa for Global. He had friends, business relationships, and experience all over the world. Yet Streeter had foolishly put him in charge of domestic production where he couldn't begin to leverage his real strengths. Streeter was going to get a lesson in how the world really worked if he screwed with Steve. Indeed, Mark Streeter was a daddy's boy. Born into a family of wealth and influence, Streeter's father had been a high achiever within Global Oil. By the time Mark was in high school, his father was chairman. Mark was a pale imitation of his father, not especially bright, yet smart enough to complete a bachelor's degree in business administration from a state university. His personality was that of a salesman; vibrant, confident, and outwardly positive. He was an accomplished public speaker who had grown up with the catch-phrases and vernacular of the international oil industry. However, he never actually worked in the field, nor did he really understand the details of petroleum engineering, drilling and completion, or refinery operations. In a nutshell, he didn't fundamentally understand the business world at this level, and was an obnoxious, ill-tempered bully. His arrogance, which knew no bounds, created little but hostility, paranoia, and hard feelings among the people he worked with. Logan detested him and now felt tainted by the association. He felt dirty. Steve's embarrassment for him was no match for what he was feeling about himself.

— ‖ —

At 4:35 p.m., Westcona's security team walked into the Edinburg district office.

"Hello ma'am. I'm Dutch Peltier with my crew of auditors from Dallas. Is Mr. Boyd in?"

"No, he's not," replied Fletcher's wary secretary. "Mr. Cade's in charge. Would you like to speak with him?"

Doris didn't like the look of this group. There were too many of them. None had briefcases. All had a physical bulk that indicated just a slightly better level of fitness than one normally associates with men who make their living with their heads from behind a desk. No, she didn't think they looked like any auditors she had ever seen, and she was glad Hollis was in the office. She thought about making a quick call to Fletcher but didn't know how to contact him in Dallas; something else that was out of sync with the way he normally operated. Her well-tuned BS meter was telling her something wasn't right.

Hollis didn't like auditors, and he especially didn't like people from Dallas snooping around when Fletcher was away. Fletcher's guidance about not trusting outsiders had not fallen on deaf ears, nor had Hollis just fallen off the turnip truck. He studied the group with the skilled eye of a man familiar with physical confrontation. Doris had already given them the thumbs down and he usually trusted the old girl's judgment.

"So, whadda ya'll want?" he asked, reverting to his good old boy persona. He could smell trouble and didn't like the way these guys spread out around the room.

"The name's Peltier, but my friends call me Dutch. This is just a routine audit," the man said to Hollis. "It's a little late to get much done today so we thought we'd stop by and let you know we're here. We just found out Mr. Boyd's in Dallas. Must have passed each other going in opposite directions."

"Yeah, he left this morning. Don't you people at least find out if the manager's going to be in town before you come to a district?"

"Usually we do, but we didn't know he was going to be in Dallas today. And like I said, this is just a routine audit. His going out of town sure doesn't have anything to do with the internal audit department. I wonder if we could get your engineer in here so both of you know what we're doing—you know, in case one of you has to leave for some reason. We'll lay out what we're going to need and how the audit will go in the morning."

Hollis's hackles rose along with the hair on the back of his neck. *Who in the hell are these hombres?* he wondered. He wished Fletcher was back.

Mr. Rodney Peltier was, in fact, a tough guy who made his living through deception and intimidation. Calling him Rodney was one of the quickest ways to send him into a rage. His résumé portrayed him as a former Navy SEAL, part of SEAL Team One based in Coronado, California, with two deployments to Southeast Asia during the Vietnam War. In fact, he'd had two deployments to Vietnam, but as an Underwater Demolition Team frogman, not as a SEAL. He'd been hired by Westcona and was expected to progress quickly through the ranks within the security department because of his alleged experience and unique skills.

During a company training class, two other former Navy UDT guys working for Westcona's Houston-based offshore drilling subsidiary learned that a former SEAL was working in Dallas. When they heard Peltier's name, they immediately recognized him as one of their former teammates in UDT-12 in Coronado. While the two groups shared some extremely difficult training, the jobs were completely different. No one ever identified himself as a SEAL without having earned the significant distinction…an honor Dutch Peltier had not attained.

When the office staff left for the day, Peltier proudly made known the real reason for the visit, who he worked for, and what his mission entailed. Belligerent questions turned to threats. Hollis responded poorly to such impropriety, causing tempers and testosterone levels to swiftly intensify. Steve sat in an oversized chair with a big man on each side of him, not daring to get up.

"We know you've got the formula and you're going to give it to us, now," Peltier demanded.

"Not likely, sonny boy," Hollis said, trying to stay calm as the five men alerted for action. "Now get your ass out of here or I'll rip you a new one," he said with more feeling.

Peltier walked up to Hollis, his face close enough to smell his breathe. Hollis met his stare, not willing to show weakness or the anxiety creeping into his gut.

"Look tough guy," Peltier barked, "you cough it up or we'll tear this office apart and find it ourselves. You people aren't smart enough to have hidden it very well and we're not afraid to hurt you to get it. Now speak."

That was all Hollis needed to hear. He pulled Peltier toward him with his left hand while his huge right slammed into the man's stomach with a sickening thud. Before Peltier hit the floor, another of the men expertly kicked Hollis's feet out from under him and struck him with a forearm to the jaw as he collapsed, glancing off the desk and crashing to the floor. After shaking his head, he looked up into the barrels of four Heckler & Koch P-7 semi-automatic pistols.

Hollis saw the men turn to Steve with menace in their eyes. He hoped Steve knew better than to try anything after watching how easily they had dropped him. Steve remained seated, apparently trying to look calmer than he felt.

"Do you need some of that...or are you ready to hand over the formula?" Peltier asked in a low, quiet voice. Hollis shot Steve a look meant to scare him more than the men posing as auditors already had. Steve looked at them and then back at Hollis, knowing it was time to make a choice.

"Not in this lifetime," he said.

The heel of an open hand promptly landed on his chin and lips, bloodying his nose in response. Surprised at the speed and effectiveness of the assault, Hollis realized just how well trained these men were.

They were escorted to the dispatch office where a guard was posted to monitor telephone conversations and keep them from causing any further disturbance. Steve was pale, visibly pissed, but determined to withstand the assault for information. He held his shirtsleeve to his nose, trying to stop the flow of blood. Hollis was furious but knew he was hopelessly outnumbered. The dispatcher looked confused and scared out of his wits.

By six o'clock, the security team had turned the offices upside down without finding anything related to Neptune. Hollis heard them on Steve's computer and hoped Steve really had deleted his files. Finally, they brought him into Fletcher's office and demanded he open the safe. When he refused, one of them cracked it and found nothing. They were clearly unhappy and becoming more troubled as time passed. The threat of other employees coming into the dispatch office increased with every minute.

"This is your last chance before things get serious," the frustrated team leader blustered.

"You better do this real well, Peltier, because if I ever get my hands on you without your friends around to protect you, I'm gonna put you out of your misery," Hollis promised the former Navy frogman.

"Dutch, I told you my friends call me Dutch."

"Yeah, Peltier. Someday I'm going to show you how friendly I can be."

Dutch sighed and dialed a number from Fletcher's office phone. "Mr. Cole, Dutch Peltier. We came up dry. There's nothing here and these men won't talk. Yeah, we checked the safe and computer. Okay, Mr. Cole. I'll tell them."

He hung up and turned to Hollis. "Mr. Cole apologizes for any inconvenience we may have caused. I suggest you forget about tonight or you really will get hurt," he said as he motioned his men to the door.

— ‖ —

After leaving the corporate office and settling into his room at the Greenbrier Inn, Fletcher called Spencer Wainwright, Westcona's Director of Internal Audit. Fletcher seldom made a trip to Dallas without getting together with Wainwright for dinner, although tonight he also needed some pleasant and trusted company. Wainwright was his former boss and mentor, but he wasn't sure he wanted him involved in the events surrounding this trip so he also extended the invitation to Wainwright's staff to deflect any personal talk until he got a better read on Wainwright's attitude.

Wainwright was fifty-six years old and had recently taken up jogging, which accounted for his suit looking just a little baggy on his small frame. He had initially hired Fletcher and helped him get into the field-training program after spending a year working with the audit staff.

They became personal friends and business confidants, with Fletcher serving as a sounding board when Wainwright's auditors received questionable explanations to audit findings. Fletcher had always been impressed by Spencer's willingness to admit he didn't know everything and his obvious comfort level with asking for help in understanding new problems. Fletcher very quickly learned that Spencer Wainwright was extremely bright and seldom missed a trick when dealing with people.

Joining them were four of the six auditors on Spencer's current staff. The auditors held Fletcher in high regard, even with a certain sense of unwarranted awe after seeing what he had accomplished from the same position they now held. Wainwright enjoyed seeing his former employees succeed, and used their success as a training and motivational tool within the department. No one except Fletcher had ever made the transition from any corporate office position to field operations, so they jumped at the chance to spend some time with him. A district manager, while not considered a senior executive, held a prestigious position within Westcona; much like a company commander in the Army. He had accomplished what they perceived as impossible, or nearly so.

Tonight Fletcher had a lot on his mind. He wanted some advice from Wainwright but didn't want to cause his mentor any trouble. He assumed Wainwright's unofficial, in-house intelligence-gathering network may have told him there had been an emergency board meeting today, and he may even suspect his former employee was somehow involved in whatever was happening. During dinner, Fletcher entertained and answered questions with good-natured humor, but when the staff auditors departed Spencer and Fletcher moved their meeting to Fletcher's suite for a nightcap and some privacy. Spencer had questions and he was characteristically plain-spoken.

"So what's going on and how are you involved?"

"You're the head of the Internal Audit Department, Spencer. I'm just a simple country boy from south Texas."

"I'm not humored, Fletcher. You're not a country boy and neither are you from south Texas. Remember, I hired you and saw your résumé. I knew you before you became a living legend around here. The tenth floor has been extremely busy and secretive recently. When the corporate officers come to work on a Sunday night and are still in panic mode on Monday morning, I hear about it. It makes me wonder what's happening and whether it involves something I should have found and told them about in advance. That makes my nerves grate on each other. Then you show up on Tuesday while the swirl is still like a category five hurricane. Cole's secretary mentioned seeing you when I pumped her for information. You were in the emergency board meeting today, weren't you?"

"I was, and then I was pretty much ordered to stay the night and meet with them again in the morning. You have my word that it doesn't reflect on your department."

Fletcher noticed the blinking red light on his telephone and suggested that Spencer mix drinks while he checked his messages from the bedroom phone. Fletcher watched through the door as Wainwright poured drinks at the wet bar. He knew his former boss was eavesdropping.

"The auditors are not in Edinburg, Hollis. Because I've been with them since five-thirty. No, they don't carry guns. They called Branton Cole in front of you? That bastard conned me into staying here tonight with a promise of reconsidering our counter-offer in the morning. I'll check commercial flights right now and call you back in a little while. I'm coming home tonight if I can get a flight out of here."

Fletcher dialed Southwest Airlines before calling out to Wainwright. "Can you get me to Love Field within the hour?"

"Sure, if you tell me what's going on. We're not going anywhere until you let me in on what's happening around this nuthouse."

"Dump those out and I'll tell you on the way."

Fletcher told Wainwright what Hollis had said. He also

provided a thumbnail description of the reason he was in Dallas as they drove to the airport.

"It had to be some kind of a security operation, Spencer. They just used the audit cover to get into the building and wait out the office staff. Apparently things got a little rough when my guys didn't cooperate."

He was confident that Wainwright knew he was hearing only part of the story, and was also smart enough to understand that something significant was going on. Still, he knew that Spencer's curiosity was running wild as self-defense mechanisms long buried in his DNA were kicking into action. He remembered when Wainwright had coordinated with Westcona's security department after the audit department uncovered cases of employee or vendor fraud, and had expressed that he was always thankful the security people were on his side. They could be an intimidating bunch, and Wainwright was likely experiencing some anxiety as he considered what might be happening.

Security departments in this industry were filled with former federal agents from all the alphabet-soup agencies and sometimes the military. Westcona's was no different. These people were well trained and played by their own rules. Fletcher had befriended a few of them and learned that many had failed in or voluntarily cut short their federal service. He had often speculated that it was due to their seemingly unstable personalities or expansive and unrestrained sense of self-importance. In any regard, he hoped Wainwright wouldn't worry unnecessarily or do anything that might cause himself trouble down the line. He really liked the guy and felt a little guilty for even telling him what he had.

"Fletcher, be careful. You call me if you need help…any kind of help," Wainwright yelled as Fletcher dashed out of the car and into the old terminal.

— ‖ —

"Hollis, my flight leaves in twenty minutes. Find Steve and pick me up at the airport at twelve-thirty."

Fletcher had run into the terminal, paid for his ticket, cleared security, and found a telephone kiosk near his departure gate. He was angry, flustered, and disheveled from the long and intense day. Despite the emotion, he deftly dislodged a cigarette from the pack and lit it with one hand while talking to Hollis.

"I've been trying to get Steve on the phone but there's no answer," Hollis said. "He was really shaken up, Fletcher. He must have taken Shelley out for dinner or something. You'da been real proud of him when those guys pressured up on him. I was worried that he might fall apart, but he sure as hell didn't."

"I'm impressed," Fletcher said genuinely. "But with Shelley being pregnant, you wouldn't think they'd keep very late hours. They'll probably be home before eleven. See if he'll come with you or let us come over to his house to talk. We need a strategy meeting tonight," he insisted.

— ‖ —

Hollis was alone when he picked Fletcher up at the McAllen airport.

"Where's Steve?"

"Still no answer. He's not at the yard and he doesn't answer the radio. We can drive past his house on the way home. It's not like him to be out of pocket."

Fletcher and Hollis exchanged notes on what had happened in Dallas and Edinburg as they drove north on Tenth

Street toward Steve's house. Hollis pulled over on North Depot Road to let an ambulance pass before turning onto Thunderbird and into the Addison's new subdivision. The flashing blue, white, and red lights from the squad cars and ambulance nearly blinded them as they rounded the corner onto Swallow Avenue. The police were stretching yellow crime-scene tape around the small trees in front of the house.

"Ah, Mr. Boyd, this does not look good," Hollis said with a heavy resonance in his voice. "Maybe we should get the hell out of here."

"No. Steve works for me and we're just trying to find him. The cops won't question that, especially since we're in a Westcona car."

"Who's in charge here, Officer?" Fletcher politely asked a young policeman as he and Hollis exited the car.

"Lieutenant Hernandez," answered the cop. "He's the one with the flashlight by that yellow Ford."

Fletcher glanced quickly at Hollis before ducking under the tape. They walked purposefully toward the familiar car that was the apparent focus of the detective's attention.

"Lieutenant, my name's Boyd and this is Hollis Cade from Westcona. What's going on?"

"Who the hell are you?" Hernandez barked suspiciously, obviously unhappy with the uniformed officers for letting them into a crime scene.

"This is one of my employee's house and we're trying to find him. I just got in from Dallas and couldn't get him on the phone or radio. We drove by to see if he was home yet."

"His name Addison?"

"Yeah, Steve Addison. He's our District Engineer."

"Is this his car?

"His company car, yes," Fletcher answered as he walked to the front end and felt the hood for heat. "We were hoping to find him yet tonight," he added.

"Believe me; we want to find him more than you do. His wife's inside on the kitchen floor with her brains splattered all over the wall."

— ||| — Nine — ||| —

THE SILENCE WAS DEAFENING. FLETCHER glanced at Hollis whose face was contorted with the same confusion and horror mirrored on Fletcher's. *Shelley dead? She wasn't even involved in this. And the police think Steve murdered her?*

"My God, Fletcher. She was pregnant," Hollis said softly."

Fletcher fought the overwhelming disconnect as he realized just how high the stakes had been raised, and that he wasn't remotely prepared for the abrupt change in direction this was taking. There was no wind blowing on this warm Texas night but a cold chill ran down his spine. Fear of the unknown, like he hadn't felt in years, crept into his heart as he looked around half expecting to see the people who had done this lurking around the houses. His focus had to be on leaving as quickly as possible without arousing any more suspicion than was already apparent in the detective's eyes.

"We thought we might be able to save the baby, but too much time had passed," the detective said as he studied the men's reaction.

"Who called you?" Fletcher asked. He was trying to think about Steve and what might have generated the call to the police.

"We got a call from the neighbor lady across the street after she tried to deliver some cookies and couldn't get anyone to come to the door. She said she knew the lady was home and got nervous enough to call us. Now, you mentioned you just got off an airplane. You got a boarding pass or your ticket with you?

Fletcher went to the car for his briefcase and boarding pass.

"How 'bout you big fella?" he asked Hollis after handing the boarding pass back to Fletcher. "Where have you been tonight?"

"I've been over at our yard in Edinburg until it was time to go pick him up at the airport."

"Witnesses?

"Yeah, the dispatcher and a handful of employees who were in and out of there over the past few hours."

After spending another thirty miserable minutes with the McAllen police detective, they were told they could leave but warned to remain available for more questioning. They made it unsteadily back to the car where they sat quietly for several minutes trying to make some sense of this nightmare. Both were military veterans but this was so far out of context that neither could quite get their head around it. Fletcher finally broke the silence.

"We need to get to our wives," he said. "Let's swing past your house to pick up Sara and then go to my house and try to figure what to do."

— || —

After the four settled in at the Boyd's home, Fletcher explained the day's events to Katie and Sara. Both were horrified and shaken by what Fletcher told them. In short, this Neptune thing was turning into something very ugly. Now their lives could be in danger, too. He could see that they all felt like they were being sucked into a vortex of hideous proportions.

"You're saying Westcona's responsible for Shelley's death?" Sara asked incredulously.

"I'm saying that the people who came to the yard today must be who killed her. Unfortunately, the cops could easily suspect us after we showed up at the crime scene. Steve's gone so they have him figured as the prime suspect, at least for now. But I think Westcona must have kidnapped him because they think he has the formula in his head," Fletcher said. "And some could still be around, seeing there were five of them when they visited Hollis at the yard this afternoon."

"Did you tell the cops about Neptune and what happened at the yard?" Sara asked.

"We didn't tell them anything," Hollis said.

"Well, don't you think that would be a good idea?" she asked.

Katie was obviously in shock. She was trembling and crying softly. Taryn and Felecia were in bed and had been for hours. Once asleep, they seldom stirred until morning. She made her way to their bedrooms to check on them, and returned looking somewhat relieved but only slightly more in control of her emotions.

"It'll be alright, Katie," Fletcher reassured as he put his arm around her. "Hollis and I will have to leave to straighten this out, but we won't leave you alone here. We'll get you all to a safe place first thing in the morning."

"My mother still lives up north on her ranch between Blossom and Paris. They could hide there," Hollis offered as Sara nodded in agreement.

Fletcher agreed. "Good. That's close to Dallas, and they wouldn't think any of us would be in the area. You stay here tonight," he motioned to Hollis and Sara. "We'll leave in the morning. I don't see any other option if we're going to protect ourselves and get this straightened out."

"What about the cops?" Hollis asked. "They told us to stick around town."

"The cops can hang around trying to figure out what happened, but we're leaving. Nobody's trying to kill them," Fletcher said.

Katie and Sara began packing clothes while Hollis and Fletcher planned a hasty defense of the house. Lady, the Boyd's black German Shepherd, was not a trained guard dog but she could be fearsome when her protective instincts kicked in. They'd keep her in the fenced back yard as an early warning alarm.

"I'll stay up until 0400 hours and cover the front. You relieve me then," Fletcher directed as both men fell back on their military training and protocols.

"Have you got a gun in the car?" Fletcher asked.

"Yeah, my forty-five."

"Good. I'll grab mine and all the forty-five ammunition I have. I think there are five or six boxes around here someplace. I've got a case and a half of 5.56 millimeter ammo for my Mini-14 rifle. We'll pick up another Mini or two before we're out of Texas. Let's stick to those two calibers and weapons so we're both using the same magazines and ammunition. The Mini-14 is like a scaled-down M-14 you fired in the Navy so it should come right back to you. Pull your car into the garage and grab your Colt before you crash. I'll load all the spare .45 and Mini-14 magazines during my watch."

Both men had been to war and immediately fell back into the combat theater mode of quiet and alert emotional numbness. Emotions were turned off until danger was past. Fletcher knew that Hollis felt the horror of Shelly's death just as strongly as he did, but couldn't and wouldn't let it interfere with their own survival. Such behavior appears cold and uncaring to most people, but it's the only way to fight a war without losing your soul in the process. And this was now a very real war.

— || —

Hollis inched Fletcher's bedroom door open at 0700 hours, hoping Katie was covered and asleep. He was rather old-fashioned about such things and felt awkward being in their bedroom despite the circumstances.

The ceiling fan whirred silently over Fletcher's bed. Katie had the sheet pulled over her waist, her colored t-shirt visible in the waning darkness. He gently shook Fletcher.

Fletcher was in a near coma-like state. Startled, he lunged for the .45 lying on the floor next to the bed. His mind reeled as he tried to remember why his friend would be in his bedroom. Reality rushed in and he laid his head back down.

"I was hoping this was just a bad dream," he mumbled groggily. "Then I remembered the phone ringing. I finally unplugged it in here. Did you answer it?"

"Hell no. I was afraid of who it might be," Hollis admitted.

A quick shower and shave made Fletcher feel a little more human as he joined Hollis in the kitchen. Hollis was adjusting the fan and light, the blinds still closed.

"That was a short night," Fletcher said as he sat down at the table.

"Yeah, the garbage man came through the alley an hour ago and I almost sent him to that big dump in the sky. We need to get out of here before I do something really stupid. Any new thoughts about what we should do?" he asked as they sipped the Navy-strong coffee Hollis was so fond of.

"Let's stick to what we talked about last night. We'll take the women and kids to your mother's and then put some distance between them and us. If the bad guys find the women, which I highly doubt, they'll leave them alone once they realize we're long gone. I'm thinking Shelley was a mistake, and that they'll be more careful going forward."

"It damn well better have been a mistake. The last thing I want is to leave the women and girls alone, but we can't very well drag them around with us when we don't even have a solid plan for ourselves yet. The ranch will be safe and my mother will take good care of them."

"That's what I'm hoping, too," Fletcher said.

"You still think the .45s and Mini-14s will be enough for us?" Hollis asked.

"I think so. I've got quite a few thirty-round magazines for the Mini and a dozen or so magazines for the .45s.

"I'd rather have a pump-action shotgun."

"Then we'd have to carry shotgun shells, too. Let's just stick to the two weapons so we have interchangeability of ammo and magazines."

"I don't have a holster that's very concealable."

"I've got a couple of inside-the-waistband holsters and magazine carriers we can take, but today I'm going to wear a shoulder rig. It's more comfortable to drive in. I think I've got another shoulder holster we can adjust for you if you want to try it. I'll throw in a couple of regular belt holsters, too. We'll be fine with untucked shirts or light jackets. We'll have everything we need after we pick up another Mini-14 or two on our way north. Shotguns for the women are a good idea though."

"Yeah, Sara's pretty good with a shotgun. I'll pick one up when we stop at our house."

"We'll take another from here for Katie. Say…how much money do you have in the bank?"

"About fifteen thousand, I think," he said. He and Sara were rather private about their finances and he felt a little uncomfortable talking about it.

"Take ten grand in cash. I'll get more at our bank and meet you out on Highway 281 at 0930 hours. That should give you time to pack, shower, and change clothes. Grab your passport, too. Hard telling what we're going to need by this time next week. Keep your radio on but maintain radio silence until we get up near San Antonio. That's where Westcona's net frequencies change. We'll take I-35 to Dallas, and you can lead us to the ranch from there."

Once the smell of coffee wafted through the house, everyone was up and about. Katie and Sara fixed breakfast. They were still visibly shaken and became even more so as they watched Fletcher and Hollis adjust holsters and slip into light windbreakers to cover the weapons. They explained the situation to the Boyd twins as delicately and briefly as possible, omitting the part about Shelley's murder. Both Taryn and Felecia were happy about missing school and staying on a ranch in north Texas, although neither grasped the gravity of what was happening. At thirteen, they questioned most things their parents told them but didn't mind the idea of an adventure. As soon as they had eaten, Hollis and Sara left while Fletcher loaded the car with all the things three women and a dog would need for an extended vacation while Katie went through the house one more time making sure they hadn't forgotten anything.

After stopping at the bank, the Boyd family made their way to Highway 281 where they pulled in behind Hollis and Sara parked on the side of the road. Taryn, already complaining about the close quarters in the backseat of the Delta 88, asked if she could ride with Hollis. They sent her to the other car, and Felecia and Lady settled in for the long ride north.

As they approached Premont, Fletcher heard JT begin calling on the radio from Alice. They were obviously already considered missing. He resisted answering. JT and anyone else listening would know their approximate whereabouts if they did. They couldn't risk that, especially when they didn't really know for sure who had killed Shelley and might be after them now. Fletcher thought about it for a moment and decided to avoid driving through Alice. Highway 281 passed within a couple of blocks of the Westcona yard and he didn't want to risk being seen by any employees. They skirted around Alice on farm-to-market roads and caught Highway 281 north of town. JT was still calling them on the Westcona radio system.

Fletcher took a mental inventory of the firearms he had in the car for the women. A Mossberg 500 shotgun, an old .380 Walther PP he had traded another army officer for in Saigon to use as a non-regulation hide-out gun, and a Colt Government Model 380 he had bought just this year as a gift for Katie. She had fired both handguns at the range and seemed comfortable with them. She was also more than competent with the Mossberg.

— ‖ —

Logan Addison walked into his Houston office at a few minutes past 7 a.m. with the intention of calling Steve to make one more desperate attempt at getting him to sell out his friends. His phone rang before he had even set down his coffee. It was Branton Cole, President of Westcona.

"Mr. Addison, I'm sorry our first contact is under these unfortunate circumstances but I feel I owe you an explanation even though we may be competing for your son's discovery. I'll be very frank. I had a security team in Edinburg yesterday afternoon to pressure up on your son and Hollis Cade. I also had your son's boss, Fletcher Boyd, here in Dallas for the same reason. Boyd disappeared from his hotel last night about the time of the murder and we haven't been able to find him since. Hollis Cade is also missing. My team had nothing to do with it."

"Murder? What the hell are you talking about?"

Cole was mortified when he realized Logan had not yet been notified of the tragedy in McAllen.

"I'm sorry, Mr. Addison," Cole said gently. "We thought you knew. Damn, I can't believe I'm the one telling you this." He paused, gathering his thoughts and taking a deep breath before continuing.

"Your daughter-in-law was murdered last night and your son is missing. We assumed you'd think it was our doing, so I called to assure you we had nothing to do with it..."

Logan collapsed into his desk chair and sat staring out the window in shocked disbelief.

"What? Dead...missing? You had security people at the district and now you're telling me Shelley's dead and Steve's missing?"

Logan instinctively stood, then sat back down again in confusion. His brain had not yet processed the horror. He was perspiring and blood was pounding in his head making it difficult to think.

"My people were only at the district office, not your son's house. We were looking for the formula but it wasn't there and they couldn't get Steve or, ah...the other guy to talk. My team left for Dallas at six-thirty last night. The police came to the district at two this morning to find out when Steve had last checked in with the dispatcher. His last radio contact was at 8:49 p.m. with no indication that anything was wrong. In fact, Steve joked with the dispatcher about having to go to the store to get something for his pregnant wife. We've since found out that Boyd and Cade showed up at the house and talked to the investigating officers at about one this morning. The woman was dead and Steve was missing."

"That woman is my daughter-in-law and she has a name," Logan shouted angrily, his voice trembling. "I think...I think you bastards *are* involved in her death and I'm going to tell the police that when I get there." He had never felt so utterly helpless.

"If we were involved, I wouldn't be talking to you," Cole said in a controlled tone. "If it was just a break-in or robbery, Steve would be dead, too. The way we see it, Global put a team in to get the formula. Something went wrong. They killed your daughter-in-law and kidnapped Steve. I'm very sorry you had to find out this way."

"That's preposterous," Logan exploded. "Global would never do that. And I had until this morning to sway Steve over to us, so it couldn't have been our people. I'm leaving for McAllen right now."

"I'm telling you, Mr. Addison, it was Global. You may not want to hear it, but it's the only scenario that fits. I personally controlled our team, and they left town before Steve left his office to go home. It had to be a Global operation. There's just no other explanation. The police think Steve may have committed the murder—"

"You asshole!" Logan screamed into the phone. "How dare you insinuate my son killed Shelley."

"but they might tie it to Global if they find out that one of your planes left McAllen about the time of the murder. You stay in Houston for now. We'll work with you to find him. But Mr. Addison, forget the formula. It belongs to Westcona," Cole said.

Neptune was the farthest thing from Logan's mind. He dropped the phone and violently vomited toward his waste basket, splashing his partially digested breakfast on his desk in the process. He blindly stumbled to his private bathroom, washed his face and swished some water around in his mouth before awkwardly maneuvering back to his sofa with spittle dribbling to his chin. He couldn't swallow it fast enough. His office already reeked but he didn't notice. He just sat numbly for several minutes before snapping out of his stupor and vowing to himself that he would find and kill the men responsible for bringing this pain to his family. And find them he would, if he had to track them into the bowels of hell.

His telephone rang but rather than answer it he ripped the cord from the wall and hurled the phone at the window. When the glass didn't break, he muscled a heavy wooden chair up into his arms and violently swung it at the window with a wail heard throughout the office. Broken glass and chair parts rained down toward the sidewalk eight stories below.

— ‖— Ten —‖—

JAKE TAYLOR'S STOMACH TIGHTENED WHEN the phone woke him long before the sun was up. He knew it could only be bad news when he heard Roland Dupree's voice.

"JT, we've got big trouble in Edinburg," blurted the Westcona Division Vice President.

JT lit a cigarette as he swung his legs out of bed. The news struck him hard as Dupree laid out the story. His military experience was over thirty-five years in the past and he had softened considerably when it came to hearing about violent death. A feeling of dread washed over him as he thought through what he should being doing while Dupree droned on in his ear. He didn't really know Shelley but considered the family of any Westcona field employee to be his family. Then there was the issue of the top three salaried Edinburg employees gone missing. Dupree hung up and JT immediately dialed Boyd's home number. It rang, unanswered. He lit another cigarette as he nervously considered the possibilities. All were foreboding. He called the Edinburg dispatcher, who told him what little he knew; Fletcher, Hollis, and Steve were not answering their phones or radios. JT assured the troubled man that he would take care of the district until Boyd showed up. He took a quick shower before driving over to the Alice yard without remembering to shave.

JT repeatedly called Boyd's home number from his office. He began calling on the radio and continued sporadically throughout the morning. Just before noon, he received a call from Westcona's Director of Internal Audit, Spencer Wainwright.

"Jake, I've been trying to reach Fletcher at his office all morning. Finally they told me that you're running Edinburg. What the hell is going on?"

"Boyd disappeared along with two others last night. I'm just helping until they show up for work," he half lied.

Wainwright filled him in on what Fletcher had told him the previous evening in Dallas and of Fletcher's surprise and anger when he realized that Westcona's president had lied to him and had sent people to Edinburg.

"Wainwright, I know you and Boyd are friends, but things are happening faster than I can keep up with and I don't know who I can trust. I'm trying to help him. You find out what you can around the corporate office and let me know what you hear. I'll either be here or in Edinburg."

— ‖ —

The two-car convoy was into San Antonio traffic by mid-afternoon. Katie had decided that running was foolish, and tried to persuade Fletcher to go to the federal authorities with Neptune. Surely the feds would protect them from whoever had killed Shelley. Fletcher fought his irritation at Katie's suggestion. While he knew Katie should have a say in what happened to them, he couldn't get past the feeling that she was not willing to deal with what was at stake. This was war and he had reverted to the mode that had kept him in one piece while in Vietnam. She just wouldn't be talking like this if she really understood. Well, perhaps that was a somewhat unfair statement. She didn't seem to feel the ardent conviction to take Neptune to its rational conclusion; one in which they gained significant financial reward. He was conflicted but unmoved.

"Look, Fletcher. I don't care about the money or legalities. We need help and you know it," she appealed. "Let them have the damn formula."

Felecia was becoming upset as she listened. Lady rested her head on Fletcher's shoulder and occasionally licked his ear as he drove.

— ‖ —

The conversation was mirrored in the Cade vehicle. Sara strongly urged Hollis to stop at the Federal Building in San Antonio.

"Dead people can't enjoy money," she said.

The more Sara talked, the quieter Hollis became. Taryn Boyd obviously didn't like that they were arguing and didn't like it when Sara yelled at Hollis. Hollis saw no alternative to their current action, hellish as it was. This was a once-in-a-lifetime opportunity and one of the most important discoveries in the history of modern man. Sara didn't seem to understand. Nothing would bring Shelley and her baby back, and the fact that they were gone didn't alter the importance of Neptune. He had seen others die over much less and was hardened to violence like many with wartime experience. He wished they were already at the ranch. Sara tried one more desperate tactic.

"You haven't been the same since you came home from Vietnam," she railed.

"Nobody that came home has ever been the same," he replied gently.

"You think this is exciting, an extension of the war. We could all get killed and you're enjoying it."

"I didn't enjoy the war, Sara. Believe me; I was scared as hell more than once even on the carrier. You're right about one thing though; dead people can't spend money. But we're not going to die. Our plan is solid and this'll be over soon," he calmly assured his flustered wife.

"Fletcher has never had a plan," she said. "You think he's so great, but he's not. He's just using us, even threatening our lives over some stupid get-rich-quick scheme. He doesn't care about us. Let's just give it up," she pleaded.

Taryn wasn't having any more of that kind of talk.

"Don't talk about my dad that way," she admonished Sara. "He's way smarter than you are!"

"We're already committed, Sara…and I'm one hundred percent for it. It's all right, Taryn. Sara didn't mean what she said about your daddy. She's just kinda mad at me."

Hollis tuned Sara out as he followed Fletcher's Oldsmobile into downtown San Antonio. Maybe Sara was partly right. He didn't have any doubts about Fletcher or what they were doing, but maybe he did like the excitement. In the Navy, he had been one person among thousands on two different aircraft carriers. He never saw the ground war close up but had seen shot-up airplanes and pilots. He had felt the agony and anger when planes didn't return. The conduct of carrier-based air operations was dangerous, exhausting work in the best of times. It was absolutely brutal during wartime. Hollis had seen men die in explosions and fires, and pilots and flight deck personnel die in crash landings. He had watched pilots throw their shit-filled flight suits off the stern after returning from missions, and heard strong men whimper in their sleep. He hardened himself by pushing the fear and emotion so deep into the recesses of his mind that he felt nothing, at least when he was awake…and he seldom talked about his experience to anyone. He also knew that the soldiers and Marines who fought in the jungles had it far worse. That's why he never pushed Fletcher about his Army experience.

They were finally out of Westcona's south Texas radio system area of operation. Hollis picked up his microphone and keyed it. "There's some good restaurants on the River Walk," he said to Fletcher. "We need a break. How about something to eat?"

They found parking places and walked to the Alamo. Hollis was very self-conscious with a handgun under his windbreaker, and steered clear of the Texas Ranger guarding the entrance to the shrine. His spirits improved somewhat after a meal and a cold beer. Sara appeared resigned to what they planned to do, if he was reading her body-language correctly. Katie's body language was indicating something else altogether, but he'd leave that for Fletcher to figure out and deal with.

— ‖ —

Fletcher wanted to find a gun shop, but for the obvious reasons also wanted to divert the women's thoughts away from the horrors they had just left behind. The lighter mood and festive atmosphere that always prevailed along the river wouldn't make them forget but might provide a distraction while he and Hollis went shopping. They could get an early start in the morning and be at the ranch by mid-afternoon.

After renting a couple of rooms and sneaking Lady in through a side door, Fletcher looked up gun shops in the Yellow Pages. Ten minutes later, Hollis met him in the hotel garage.

"We need to get the company markings off these cars," he told Fletcher. "They might have reported them stolen by now."

"The decals are attached with some kind of adhesive. We can take them off at the ranch," he said as they pulled out in the Oldsmobile.

The first gun shop had a lot of traditional hunting rifles but no Mini-14s. Its clientele must have been mostly the once-a-year hunter who lived in the city and leaned toward traditional bolt or lever-action rifles. Ranchers found the little Mini-14 rifles more useful and sturdy for knocking around in their pickups, and for predator control.

"I really can't help you boys," the owner said. "I just don't have what you're looking for."

"Who might?" Fletcher asked.

"Well, there's a place on the south side of town that probably carries Mini-14s in stock. It's a little run down over there…and they don't have the best reputation."

Fletcher realized the warning had been understated when they pulled up to the store. The decrepit warehouse building had a small sign that simply said, *Surplus Warehouse*. There were bars over the front windows and door.

"Kind of a shitty looking place," Hollis observed.

The inside of the store did little to buoy their confidence. Staffed by three pugnacious-looking men wearing military fatigues, the shelves were full of paramilitary weapons and gear. Nothing illegal, but inauspicious just the same. Fletcher immediately approached the mangiest clerk and told him what they wanted. He also asked for slings, flash hiders, and a dozen thirty-round magazines, preferably PMI brand.

"You want folding stocks or full wood?" the clerk asked.

"Let me have one of each," Fletcher said. He had never seen or fired one of the folding stock versions but thought the shorter overall length might come in handy. His order was placed on the counter within minutes. While Fletcher filled out the federal paperwork, Hollis carried ten boxes of 230 grain

.45 ACP hollow point ammunition over to the counter and plunked it down next to the rest of their booty. The clerk grinned.

"That'll be thirteen hundred and thirty bucks," he said after happily punching on the cash register keys.

"You sure that's right?" Fletcher asked. "We can buy this stuff anywhere for less than a grand."

"Then maybe ya'll oughta do that," the man snapped back as he picked up the two rifles from the counter.

"We'll take them," Hollis intervened as he peeled C-notes from his wallet.

They picked up the boxes, carried them out to the car, and put it all in the trunk.

"You think they might have any military type stuff we could use?' Hollis asked before they got into the car. He offered Fletcher a cigarette as he lit one himself.

"I was wondering the same thing. They're a damned surly bunch for being a legitimate store. Let's go back in…and be surly right back at them when we ask."

"You jug-heads got anything more potent that we might be interested in?" Hollis asked gruffly when they stepped back inside.

The man hesitated for a moment and then motioned Hollis to a room behind the counter. "Hands on the wall, big guy," the cashier ordered as another clerk pushed Hollis from behind.

Hollis complied while Fletcher backed up and stopped just out of the men's reach. Finding the handgun caused momentary excitement but the clerk calmed down and smiled when he found no badge as he continued frisking Hollis. Fletcher held his hands out and let them frisk him to confirm his lack of a badge. Cops were obviously not welcome in this shop.

"We have some stuff you might like if you got the cash," he said.

In a back room down a dark hallway, the men looked through the boxes and bins. Fletcher smiled at what he saw. He rummaged around and quickly picked up an M79 grenade launcher, an ammo can of forty-millimeter high-explosive ammunition, and two cases of hand grenades. It cost them dearly at the cash register, and then again as they strained under the weight of carrying it all to the car.

"I don't know how to handle that stuff," Hollis said when they were back in the car. "Do you?"

"Yeah…I do."

— ‖ —

Steve Addison was handcuffed to the bed frame in a dark, musty-smelling room. The strong odor implied that it had been unused for quite some time. Though his captors had removed his blindfold, he could barely see his hand in front of his face let alone find a clue as to where he was. After dozing fitfully in a drug-induced haze, he had finally come out of it and was now trying to solve the puzzle as to where he was and how he had come to be imprisoned. The why part of the equation was quite evident. They were still after Neptune.

He recalled driving to the store at a little before 9:00 p.m. to buy Shelley some Alka-Seltzer and ice cream. An unfamiliar car was parked in his driveway when he returned. He heard Shelley scream, followed by an explosion of some kind as he raced up the rear sidewalk. The next thing he remembered was coming to, blindfolded, with a throbbing headache in a car full of men. They had driven to an airport and left on a small jet, judging from the short steps and engine sounds. He recalled being injected, and then only an odd and disorienting floating sensation. Based on his watch, they had traveled for hours. *What was the explosion in the house? Where was he? Where was Shelley?*

—‖— Eleven —‖—

THE LANDSCAPE CHANGED DRAMATICALLY AFTER leaving McAllen. Rough brush and parched brown field grasses replaced the lush semi-tropical foliage and trees. Driving toward Austin, the hills were rolling and the grass less brown. Not green, just not as burned-looking. Resplendent with vibrant wildflowers each spring, the hills were anything but colorful this time of the year. It was a cool, cloudless fall morning. Everyone was visibly tired. Shelley's death would hound them until exhaustion provided some much needed relief.

The extent to which they were being forced to go to protect themselves and their right to Neptune was daunting — and confusing. Fletcher knew Neptune was real but Westcona didn't know for sure. Why would they resort to killing and kidnapping when they could just buy it? He wondered how much the pressure would increase once the United States government became involved, as Hollis kept insisting was necessary and appropriate. Would they also try to take Neptune by force and be willing to kill for it? Paranoid? Perhaps.

Fletcher had always tried to abide by the rule of law, but that law was created for normal times and circumstances. This was anything but normal. The right to self-defense trumps everything, and he had been operating under that principal since Shelley's death. Someone had elevated what should have been a highly publicized discovery and business opportunity into obscene violence...and he would push back. He had no intention of harming any innocent people, but they sure as hell would defend themselves and their lawful interests.

"We brought a couple of shotguns to leave with you and Sara at the ranch," he told Katie.

"Why would we need shotguns if they can't find us? We aren't even sure they're after us."

"They are or soon might be, and you need to be prepared for anything no matter how much we wish it wasn't so. You and the girls can't come with us so it'll be up to you to defend yourselves and them if need be."

"I think you've gone over the edge," she chided him. "They'd know we don't have the information."

"Shelley didn't have anything useful either but look at what happened to her. I still think her death was a mistake but we don't know that for sure. They might hold you for ransom if they find you."

"And then you'd give them the formula, right?"

"If you're prepared to protect yourself properly, it should-n't come to that."

Fletcher knew Katie was hoping for a different response, but he also knew she agreed that people should be willing and able to protect themselves and their families, even in her liberal-tilting world. He knew she didn't share his enthusiasm for firearms but did understand that they sometimes were all that stood between evil and her family. She was quite accomplished with firearms and knowing that gave Fletcher a measure of comfort about not being there to protect them himself.

Though the drive north into the Dallas/Fort Worth Metroplex was uneventful, Fletcher grew increasingly nervous as they entered the area Westcona called home. His concern was largely unnecessary because the Metroplex covers such a huge geographic area that anonymity was almost assured. Yet he would have felt a little better if the Westcona decals weren't on the cars. The farm country just south of the big cities was comforting and a welcome distraction after the barren plains they had driven through north of Temple. They had taken I-35 East after passing Hillsboro and hit traffic and suburban housing developments soon after crossing into Dallas County.

They caught I-20 on the south side of Dallas and followed the loop east around to I-30. After a lunch stop in Mesquite, Hollis took the lead to his mother's ranch. They crossed the Lake Ray Hubbard Bridge, bisecting the large body of water glistening in the fall sunshine.

— ‖ —

Hollis hoped his mother would be able to handle the stress of having two women, two kids, and another dog around. She was spry for a seventy-one-year-old and actually might welcome the company. A widow for nearly a decade, Ellie Cade reveled in her independence as she continued living and work-ing on the farm without much help from anyone. She had always lived that way and trained her nine children to do the same. One son and his family lived over to the west in Sherman, and one daughter was within reasonable driving distance in Texarkana where her husband and sons operated a lumberyard and hardware store. Sherman and Texarkana were close enough in the old lady's mind. Like Hollis, the others had left the area many years ago and were scattered all over the country.

They arrived shortly after two o'clock, greeted by a surprised but happy Ellie Cade. After hearing an abbreviated version of the story, she stated in no uncertain terms that she would watch over her guests and keep them from harm. Hollis always felt emotional when he returned to the farm and this time was no different. It was relatively isolated and, like most farms, well stocked with dogs. She had sold off some of her land over the years but still retained a quarter-section that she leased to a neighbor. She loved to see cultivated fields, and the lease provided a reasonable income to augment her Social Security checks.

While Fletcher was uneasy at the thought of leaving Katie and the girls without his protection, he felt better after seeing the calm confidence Mrs. Cade exhibited. He took to her immediately. Hollis assured Fletcher that his brother, brother-in-law, and nephews would ride to the rescue if trouble brewed. While still uncomfortable, he trusted his friend's judgment and didn't really have a whole lot of other options if they were to go forward with their plan to sell Neptune. Giving it up was not an option. Their wives were strong and would be able to handle themselves on their own.

Hollis helped the women move into their new quarters while Fletcher watched Taryn, Felecia, and Lady explore their new playground. He wanted to evaluate the basic security of the place and get a feel for how it could be attacked. While Mrs. Cade no longer kept many animals, she still had some chickens, a couple of goats, and her dogs. The barn still put off the smell of cows that had once called it home. Lady romped ecstatically in the riot of exotic odors and uncharted territory she could explore with Taryn and Felecia. They had a great time in the barn trying to scare each other with imaginary villains. As long as they had Lady to watch over them, they seemed unafraid and happy.

Fletcher was pleased with the isolation and noted that no one could get within a few hundred yards of the buildings in daylight without being seen. The road was also far enough away from the house that nobody could drive by and casually observe any activity. Even better, there were farm dogs roaming all over the property to sound the alarm at anything out of the ordinary.

Fletcher began pulling Westcona decals off the cars, and Hollis joined him when the women were situated and he had spent a little time with his mother. It was difficult work, the baked-on tape adhering securely to the metal until Mrs. Cade brought them a hairdryer and extension cord.

"One of you brain surgeons oughta run this cord out from the house and use the hairdryer on that tape while the other pulls on it."

Thirty minutes later they had both cars stripped of all company identification.

"Funny how mother's get so much smarter with age," Hollis grinned.

The shade from a huge oak tree sheltered the men as they spent the rest of the afternoon preparing the new Mini-14s and planning their next steps. Fletcher disassembled and cleaned the rifles before re-assembling and lubricating them while they talked. He attached the flash hiders and slings before they sighted the little rifles for one hundred fifty yards. He liked the folding stock Mini-14 and decided it would be perfect for the backseat of the car where it would provide additional firepower without them having to get to the trunk in an emergency. Hollis paid close attention and learned from the precautions Fletcher was taking on their behalf. This concept of close combat was new to him, and he was relying on Fletcher to give him some pointers.

— ‖ —

Global Oil's board of directors was again convened in emergency session at their Houston headquarters. Details of the McAllen debacle were reviewed and spirited discussion followed. Mark Streeter explained the details as best he knew them from the report called in by his security team leader.

Shelley Addison had put up a fight in the kitchen, throwing everything she could reach at the men who had charged in and surprised her. One had drawn his handgun as she moved towards a set of carving knifes. When she picked up a knife and lunged at him, he instinctively fired, killing her instantly. After verifying she was beyond help, the men left her lying on the kitchen floor. Steve Addison arrived home while this drama was unfolding. He was thumped on the head and put in their car while they searched the house and his car for the discovery documents. None were found. The team drove to the airport where Addison was loaded aboard the waiting Global jet and drugged. He was not aware of his wife's fate.

Global's security chief explained that generally accepted use-of-force doctrine within law enforcement circles treats a knife attack within twenty-one feet as a deadly threat, and the former federal law enforcement officer had acted in a fashion consistent with his training. The board members were obviously more concerned with the location of the new discovery than the murder. The dead pregnant woman was just unfortunate collateral damage that would have no effect on Global Oil. Steve Addison was to be kept in isolation for now. After considerable argument, they decided to promise him a swift reunion with his wife in exchange for the formula they only now understood to be code-named Neptune. Steve would be told that his wife was being held at another location and would be freed only upon his acquiescence to their demands.

Boardroom decorum prevented them from discussing his ultimate fate but it was understood that he would indeed join his wife as promised.

Logan Addison was a potential problem. The board decided to keep him under loose observation for a few days in case the McAllen police department contacted him as part of the investigation or somehow made the Global Oil connection. As soon as was practical thereafter, he was to be transported to the corporate retreat where his son was being held. He, too, was expendable once they had Neptune.

— ‖ —

Despite being instructed to remain in Houston for the next few days, Logan Addison was already on the way to McAllen to help Shelley's parents with arrangements to transport her body home, secure the house, and talk to the local police. He was angry and beyond caring what Global Oil thought about Neptune or his whereabouts. He needed thinking time, something the seven-hour drive would provide. His mind replayed the events described by Branton Cole while comparing them to the lack of detail or suggestions from his own boss, Mark Streeter. Streeter wanted him to believe that Westcona was responsible, which was not out of the realm of possibility. He recalled that Steve's original boss when he had been first hired by Westcona in Alice was an experienced manager who had been around the block a few times. Both Logan and JT were in their mid-fifties, alone, and energy industry lifers. He had been impressed by the man when they first met and recalled that Steve thought very highly of him. Logan considered contacting JT but wasn't sure if he should.

After stopping for gas and a hamburger in Robstown, Logan made a fateful decision when he turned off Highway 77 to follow Highway 44 into Alice. He would talk to JT and get his take on the situation before proceeding to McAllen. It really wasn't out of his way and he needed the seasoned perspective only someone like JT could provide. If JT seemed more concerned with Neptune and Westcona than he did about his young colleagues, then Logan would know he had misjudged the man. He wasn't quite sure what to expect, but he needed an ally right now.

— ‖ —

In Dallas, Westcona's senior management was in a frenzy. A murder, a suspected kidnapping, the disappearance of Boyd and Cade, and confirmation of Global's active involvement in the Neptune search stripped the veneer of sophistication and propriety from their behavior. Branton Cole sent his security team, headed by Dutch Peltier, back to the Rio Grande Valley to once again search the Edinburg district office for clues, and nose around the men's homes in McAllen.

Peltier brought two former FBI agents with specialized information technology forensics training to Edinburg for their second search of the Westcona district office and Addison's computer. With no concern of employee challenges or law enforcement intervention, they were free to do so openly. Their search was again fruitless. Steve had apparently repeatedly overwritten his hard drive after deleting the Neptune files from his computer.

He reported their lack of findings, and suggested telephone surveillance of the Alice district office in case Boyd contacted Jake Taylor. Branton Cole quickly instructed the security department to make it happen. The company did not have the means of tapping Taylor's home telephone without breaking into the building, which Cole rejected as too risky at this point.

It was going to be a cat-and-mouse game for now. So far only one crime involved law enforcement. He hoped the fragmented jurisdictional boundaries would prevent anyone from tying the murder to the inevitable leak or outright disclosure of Neptune. Global Oil's involvement raised the likelihood that rumors would become more widely spread, and that could be disastrous to Westcona.

The rest of Peltier's team drove to the Addison residence in McAllen where they found crime-scene tape stretched around the front yard and across the door. They moved on to the Cade and Boyd houses which appeared deserted and had mail accumulating in the street-side mailboxes. They considered breaking in but rejected the idea. Getting caught would certainly alert the police to the fact that far more was going on with Westcona employees than a suspected domestic violence case that ended in a death. They also instinctively knew that the homes would yield no clues. These men wouldn't have left anything behind. Nosing around a Westcona-owned facility was vastly different than private homes, and they knew it.

— || —

Steve Addison was roughly escorted to a large dinner table. As his eyes adjusted to the light, he could see he was in a well-furnished lodge with heavy forest visible through the large bay windows. He was famished and ate lustily under the watchful supervision of two guards.

"We have a fire going in the great room. There's booze behind the wet bar. Help yourself but don't consider going outside. You couldn't walk out of these woods even if you knew where you were. You'd be lost in ten minutes, and bear shit by tomorrow morning. There's a bathroom off the hallway."

Steve was caught completely off guard by the sudden hospitality. He was disoriented, afraid, and worried sick about Shelley and the baby. He knew he needed to stay alert and try to pick up on clues as to his location but didn't know how to begin. He walked into the next room and looked outside at fog shrouded, late autumn mountains. It appeared wet and chilly. He mixed himself a drink and nervously settled into a soft leather chair beside the fireplace. As he reached to put his glass on a side table, his eyes fell on a coaster bearing an official and familiar logo. Leaning over the table and squinting, he recognized the Global Oil corporate seal. Only the numbing shock kept him from snapping when he realized that his father was involved in his kidnapping. He was momentarily mortified — and then felt a rage beyond any he had thought possible.

—‖— Twelve —‖—

JT GAVE UP TRYING TO CONTACT Boyd on the radio and phone. He was feeling old and tired. *What the hell was going on?* He called Branton Cole for updated information and Cole still maintained that Westcona had nothing to do with the murder or the disappearances. JT wanted badly to believe him but it didn't feel right. Then again, maybe it really was the work of Global Oil. Cole's logic was hard to dispute but JT still had that niggling feeling that something was seriously fucked up.

JT knew Boyd well enough to know that he would accept Westcona protection if he felt the company could be trusted. Obviously that was not the case. He sent two of his more senior employees to help in Edinburg, with orders to call immediately if they came upon any new information. He also instructed his dispatchers in Alice to listen closely for any radio transmissions between Boyd, Cade, or Addison, especially at night when their radio network was quieter and it was easier to hear weak signals. With the help of an air traffic controller acquaintance in Corpus Christi, he had even taken the Falcon 20 up hoping to spot the company cars traveling together.

He was lost in thought when a knock on his open office door stirred him from his reverie, and was surprised to see Logan Addison standing in the doorway.

"Addison, I don't know what to say," JT said quietly as the two acquaintances warmly shook hands.

"Taylor, I think it's time for a couple of old hands to figure out what's going on."

They left the office and drove to the Holiday Inn where the bar was almost empty this early in the day. Logan explained all he knew about the recent events, and JT responded in kind. Though they differed in perspective, they quickly developed significant common ground and contradictions in the events as they understood them. Two points were undisputed. Their employers were both involved, but how and to what extent was uncertain. And, they were going to find out who was behind the deception and violence.

"Where are you staying tonight, Addison?"

"Here, I guess. I had planned to be in McAllen, but I'm not in any shape to drive down there and face that mess right now."

"Why don't you stay at my house? We can keep working through this over some good scotch."

"Thanks, JT," Logan said with heartfelt sincerity and relief that he had not misjudged the long-time Westcona employee.

— ‖ —

Ellie Cade was up before sunrise to prepare a hearty breakfast for Hollis and Fletcher. By six-thirty they had eaten and were scavenging the yellow Ford LTD for anything they might want to take with them. They had already decided to leave the Ford at the farm.

Sara, Katie, and the girls had slept fitfully. Now they were all bustling about the kitchen filling thermos bottles with strong coffee and packing snacks for the hopefully short but successful trip. Both men could go for a day or so without much food, but coffee was a survival necessity.

Fletcher's white Oldsmobile Delta 88, with Westcona decals removed, was not readily identifiable as a company car. It had tinted windows, power seats, door locks, windows, and trunk release. It also had an AM/FM radio with custom sound system. The yellow LTD, even stripped of company logos, was still the Westcona primary color that would certainly make it more difficult to hide from potential pursuers. It also had none of the Oldsmobile's creature comforts the men would appreciate.

Hollis removed his toolbox, a small duffle bag of work clothes, and an old pair of Redwing steel-toed boots from the car. A first-aid kit was already on the ground, and he was holding a pair of FM handheld radios set up on the Petroleum Radio Service VHF frequencies that matched their mobile and district base-radios. Hollis carried the small, low-power units so he could hear what was happening when he inspected jobs without having to stay in his car.

"You think we might want these?" he asked Fletcher.

"I've only used them on jobs. What kind of range do they really have?"

"Handheld to handheld they're only good for a half-mile or so, but I've heard crews close to a mile away on my car radio when I was in open country. The car's outside antenna makes a big difference."

"Sure, why not? They might come in handy," Fletcher agreed.

Both men were dressed in starched blue jeans, dress shirts, and sport coats to cover the .45 Colt Combat Commanders on their hips. The shoulder holsters they had worn since leaving

McAllen had turned out to be less comfortable than either had expected after wearing them for a couple of days. In cowboy hats and dress boots, no one would give them a second glance in cowboy or oil country. The goodbyes were more difficult than either wanted to admit. In just a few days, their lives had been turned completely upside down. Leaving the women behind, though the only action that made any sense, was not at all what Fletcher or Hollis wanted to do. Promises were made to be careful and to keep in contact as best they could. Neither was sure he would see his wife again.

Feeling the burden of separation, both were quiet on the drive to Paris for gas. After fueling, they turned north on Highway 271 and crossed the Red River into Oklahoma thirty minutes later. Their intention was to drive to Kansas City where they could contact Westcona, Global Oil, and the Department of Energy in an effort to find Steve Addison and complete negotiations on Neptune's sale without the constant threat from the two companies. Neither company had operating locations in Kansas or Missouri.

"You think Steve will give Neptune to Westcona?" Hollis asked as he poured them each a cup of coffee.

"Not if he knows they killed Shelley. If he thinks she's alive and in danger he might, although it would take him a little time to reinvent it. Have you seen how complicated his notes are?"

"Naw, I never saw them. It's just orange juice, dirt, and beer as far as I'm concerned. We've got that stuff with us, don't we?"

"In my briefcase in the trunk. I had a bad feeling and took it all out of the safe when we told JT about it last Friday."

"Steve's safety has to be a condition of the sale. And we need to get that done before they crack him and he gives it up for free."

"Yeah, but where do we start if not with Westcona?"

"Fletcher, we could take him back by force if we could find him. His dad's got a lot of pull at Global Oil. Maybe he could swing some help from their security people."

"Maybe. We'll call him when we get to a phone."

When they pulled into McAlester an hour and twenty minutes later, the hilly countryside was greener than they had seen since leaving south Texas. High cumulus clouds scuttled across the autumn sky and the sun was warming the morning air. Westcona had a small district in McAlester where they offered little more than acidizing services. Fletcher had never been there but Hollis had. The men looked at each other when they saw the yard.

"You think we dare go in and use the phone?" Fletcher asked. "I don't know anyone here and the manager's Oldsmobile isn't out front," he added.

"They know me from my Lindsay days but you could go in posing as a Global company man. Just tell them you need to call your office in Houston. You might get by with it."

Fletcher walked into the building like he owned it and politely asked to see the manager. Fortunately, the district manager was out so he asked to use the phone after identifying himself as a Global Oil manager. The secretary showed him to a bullpen area where Westcona salesmen made telephone calls to customers when they were in the office. Looking at the wall near the desk where he sat down, he noticed a chart listing the telephone numbers of many area customers, including Global Oil. He dialed the number on the chart only to find that Logan Addison was out of the office due to a personal family emergency and could not be reached. *It couldn't get more personal, could it?* He then dialed Westcona's Alice district number and asked for JT.

"Boyd, where the hell are you?" JT exploded excitedly. Fletcher could hear that JT had punched the speaker button on his phone.

"We're in your old neck of the woods, JT. Things went kinda haywire in the Valley. We need some help."

"Addison isn't with you, is he?"

"No, that's the first thing we need help with. Hollis and I think our security people have him. We're trying to find his dad but he's not in his office. I suppose he's in McAllen but we don't know where."

"This is Logan Addison here, Fletcher. Why do you think Westcona has Steve?"

Fletcher was startled to hear Logan's voice, especially from JT's office. *What the hell's going on?* He paused for a long moment, thinking furiously before responding.

"Because Westcona security people held Steve and Hollis at gunpoint in Edinburg, ransacked the office, and threatened them just a couple of hours before the murder."

"Fletcher, I'm working outside normal channels with JT. We think Global is also involved although neither company is admitting any real knowledge of what happened. Lots of finger pointing but nobody with the balls to own up to anything."

Fletcher was taken aback at the thought of Global Oil involvement. They hadn't even considered it, and that certainly shot the hell out of their idea of asking for Global's help.

"If Global kidnapped Steve, where would they have taken him?"

"No idea, Fletcher. They could have him anywhere in the world by now. Your division guy in Corpus Christi thinks he saw a Global jet in McAllen on Monday."

"Have you checked to see if they filed a flight plan? JT knows an air traffic controller in Corpus who could get that information."

Logan explained that the Global plane Dupree had seen at McAllen Miller Airport on Monday afternoon was likely his own, and that he had met with Steve to hear about Neptune before taking Steve and Shelley to dinner that evening. Also, that he had returned to Houston soon after dinner. However, Global could have sent another plane with a security team on Tuesday just as Westcona had done while Fletcher was in Dallas. They should be able to track which company landed airplanes in McAllen, when they departed, and where they planned to go when they left. Before they hung up, JT agreed to call his air traffic controller friend and ask about flight plans.

Hollis was behind the wheel and ready for a hasty getaway when Fletcher walked calmly out of the office. Neither man said anything until Hollis had turned north on the Indian Nation Turnpike toward Tulsa.

"You're not gonna believe this shit," he told Hollis as he lit a cigarette and prepared to repeat what he had just learned.

— ‖ —

Within ten minutes of the telephone conversation, Branton Cole was listening to the recording. The tap on the Westcona telephone switch in Alice had paid off. They would know where JT stood if he failed to report the contact with Boyd. Logan Addison working outside normal channels with JT? Now that was interesting and something Westcona could certainly use against him if the need arose.

"Go pull Boyd and Cade's HR files," he ordered his chief of security. "Taylor used to run our Mid-Continent Region in Oklahoma City. They've gone a long way north if that's where they are, and there must be a reason. See if there's a clue in the files. Also, have our aviation people check out the flight plan before Taylor does. You should've thought of that yourself."

"Should I send a team to Oklahoma City?"

"Not yet. It won't help if they keep moving, and we don't know if that's where they really are. Can you put a bug on Taylor's home phone?"

"Yes sir, but not without breaking in. We could put a pretty sophisticated listening post on the street in front of his house though. I can have a van in Alice yet tonight."

"Do it," ordered Cole.

— ‖ —

JT and Logan had just finished a late dinner at JT's home when the telephone rang. It was his elderly next-door neighbor, Mrs. Walters, who he had befriended and quietly kept an eye on without appearing obvious. She was proud and seldom asked for any help but he could tell she enjoyed their conversations and was frequently more than a little lonely.

"Jake, there's a van been parked out by my driveway all evening with the motor running. I think there's people in it. Do you know who it is?"

"No, Mrs. Walters, I sure don't," he patiently informed the overly cautious eighty-six-year-old who spent most of her time watching cable television and peeking out her windows. She was a one-person neighborhood watch program. "It's probably just a repairman."

"Well, the van isn't marked and it just sits out there like someone's watching my house," she persisted. "Will you please go out and see what they're doing? What with women getting attacked and raped all the time, I can't go myself." A light came on in JT's head.

"I will if you call the police and tell them what you just told me."

Within minutes, a City of Alice patrol car came down the street shining a spotlight on parked vehicles. The blue strobes came on as the squad car accelerated up to the van. Mrs. Walters, Logan, and JT were already standing on his lawn when the policemen removed the two men from the van.

"See, they look just like rapists," she whispered.

One of the cops asked the security men for identification while the other radioed the license plate number to the dispatcher. Within seconds, his radio crackled the news that the van was registered to Westcona. When asked if they possessed any weapons, the men replied that they did. They were instructed to keep their hands away from their weapons while the cops opened the rear van doors exposing the bank of rack-mounted electronics. They were frisked and relieved of their H&K P-7 handguns and ordered to put their hands behind their backs.

"You boys have some explaining to do," one of the cops told the silent duo as he guided them into the squad car's back seat.

"I'll send a tow for the van," the other cop told JT, Logan, and Mrs. Walters. "We'll probably be back to talk to you after we hear their story and get this sorted out," he said to JT while tipping his head toward the van. "Oh, and thanks again, Mrs. Walters. You're always a big help to us."

The police left with their detainees, and Mrs. Walters scurried toward her front door to avoid being out alone.

"I would imagine that your phone at work is tapped," Logan said with a heavy sigh.

"They'll try to get the flight plan information if they heard us this afternoon."

"Addison, your people may not have filed a flight plan and those plans are not public information anyway. Westcona must not have a bug in my house or those sons of bitches wouldn't have been sitting outside with this equipment, right?"

"Right. They sure didn't want to explain themselves to the police so they must be worried about repercussions for getting caught."

"Or just plain embarrassed," JT said. "They'll get cut loose in a hurry and be on their way back to Dallas once their story is verified."

JT's ringing telephone interrupted them and he hurried to pick it up.

"You get the information, JT?" Fletcher asked without preamble.

"Boyd, where are you now?"

"In a phone booth. What did you find out?"

"My friend in Corpus is off work for the weekend. I tried him at home but he didn't answer. He's not supposed to give out flight plan information, but I think he will when we catch up with him."

"We need to find Steve, JT. Is Logan staying with you or has he gone to McAllen?"

"He's here with me. Westcona had some guys outside my house with listening equipment like you see in the movies. Alice's finest just arrested them but they won't stay in jail after a phone call to Dallas. Your call to the office this morning was probably monitored."

"Then they might guess which state we were in. Has Logan been able to find out anything or even guess where Steve might be?"

"No, but he's staying here and we'll work on it together. Hey, how much do you trust Spencer Wainwright?" JT asked.

"I trust him like I trust you. Why?"

"He called and wants to help. Now that Cole knows I'm not cooperating, Wainwright might do us some good in Dallas."

"Go ahead and talk to him," Fletcher agreed.

They agreed to leave messages for each other at the Holiday Inn front desk, and were just finishing their conversation when JT had the idea of offering the men the use of his Minnesota cabin as a hide-out.

"Thanks, JT. We might take you up on it. Is there a telephone up there?"

"Hell no. This is a real wilderness setup that I use to get away from telephones and people I don't want to talk to. The nearest phone is eighteen miles away in Gatzke. Ah, there might be one in Skime, which is a little closer."

"I thought you had some of your ham radio equipment up there. Could we use it?"

"Not without a license you can't."

"Not even in an emergency?"

"Only in life-threatening emergencies."

"And this doesn't qualify?"

"I doubt the FCC would buy it and I'm not willing to lose my license and gear unless this thing really turns south. You let me know if you decide to go up there and we'll deal with radios another time."

— ‖ —

"Where's my wife?" Steve Addison demanded.

"She's safe, and she'll stay that way if you give us the formula," the Global guard said without warmth.

"I want to see her before I give you anything."

"Sure, kid. You write it down and we'll bring her here while we test the formula. You can both leave as soon as it all checks out."

"Bullshit," Steve responded. "Not until I know she and the baby are safe." His anger with his father and Global Oil was now competing with the fear he felt at being kidnapped and separated from Shelley.

— ⅲ — Thirteen — ⅲ —

THE MOTEL WAS LOCATED AT THE junction of Highway 169 and I-35, just southwest of Kansas City in the town of Olathe, Kansas. The trip had been easy and uneventful. Huge farms dominated the brown rolling plains, with wheat fields stretching to the horizon in all directions. These fields were so broad they created an almost surreal image. Large pieces of farm equipment were mere dots in the distance, their perspective skewed by the vastness of the land upon which they toiled. Hollis had mentioned that it reminded him of being at sea, and idly contemplated how Neptune would ultimately impact food production.

Fletcher leafed through the Kansas City telephone book to find the U.S. Department of Energy office. He found federal agencies but was disappointed and surprised that the DOE was not among them. He had just assumed it would be there. The public library would have the information they needed, but it would have to wait until Saturday morning. They called their wives and JT from a phone booth and ate a late dinner before retiring for the evening. Fletcher was tired, despondent, and already lonesome for his family although he didn't mention it to Hollis.

— ‖ —

Hollis was awakened very early by the rumble of passing trucks. He showered, dressed, and left his room for some fresh air, deep in thought and troubled by what was happening. A discovery of Neptune's magnitude should be welcomed by the world, not put innocent lives at risk. Shelley Addison was dead, Steve was likely kidnapped, and he and Fletcher had run away from their own homes and families. He detested Global and Westcona's actions but was not surprised when he really thought about it. Countless millions had died over much less throughout history. Was greed the underlying motivation for what he and Fletcher were doing? The thought struck hard.

They had discussed the economic benefits and many of the possible catastrophic possibilities Neptune could cause if it weren't phased into use while careers and industries adjusted. Who, if not the government, could enforce such a phase-in period...and would they do it? Neptune was a "genie let out of the bottle" but it was their genie, at least for now and they deserved some credit.

He knew Fletcher viewed their current activities as those of men at war, with normal civilian laws and rules of conduct temporarily suspended. While he agreed that the situation called for unusual actions, he was nagged by what a jury would think about it once Neptune was no longer theirs. He had never gotten away with anything in his life, and this event would be no exception if history served as an example.

Drawing on his cigarette, he noticed bright lights come on in the motel office and recalled a coffee service in the lobby from when they checked in. Hollis strode into the office and volunteered to make coffee for the desk clerk. No sense in just hoping it was Navy strong. He drank one cup as a test, then refilled his cup and poured another for Fletcher.

He heard Fletcher moving about after kicking lightly on the door with the toe of his boot. Probably woke him up but that was fine. Sure enough, Fletcher cracked the door, pistol in hand, and smiled sleepily before reaching for the cup. Sunrise was still thirty minutes away.

"Bout time you got up," Hollis grunted as he pushed through and closed the door. "You know if those assholes had found us last night we'd have been sitting ducks."

"Yeah, I thought about it but was just too tired to deal with it. We need to be more careful but it's hard to find motel rooms with back doors. Where have you been?"

"I was walking around until the desk clerk was ready to make coffee. Just thinking a little, I guess. Get cleaned up so we can find some breakfast. I'm starving."

Dressed in casual clothes and windbreakers, they drove up to 119th Street where they hoped to find a hearty breakfast. The cool October temperatures allowed them to blend in well with the locals, even with cowboy hats. This was still cow country and they felt right at home. They happened upon a buffet restaurant and spent the next hour enjoying a large hot breakfast with copious quantities of strong, black coffee before heading for the library.

The Olathe Public Library wasn't yet open when they pulled into the parking lot. They killed time sitting in the car smoking cigarettes and listening to the radio. The sun was up but wasn't warming the air much. An Olathe squad car passed through the lot, slowing while the lone cop looked them over before continuing on his patrol. Both sighed in relief and checked their watches. Not knowing precisely who was after them made them nervous and suspicious of everyone, especially the police. Technically, they had stolen the company cars and could be considered witnesses in a murder investigation. They could also be accused of stealing company secrets.

Then there was the instruction from the McAllen police that they not leave town without letting the cops know. Had they been missed? Were there warrants out for their arrest? Fletcher dismissed the thought as unlikely because their alibis on the night of the murder could be easily verified. They cautiously assumed Westcona and Global were both actively searching for them, and their pursuit would be relentless and without conscience or concern for anyone who got in their way.

When the library finally opened, they began the search in the reference section.

"Here's a book with all the federal agencies listed in it," Hollis said happily. "The Department of Energy starts on page sixty-seven."

The book showed no DOE offices or facilities in either Kansas or Missouri. In fact, they were surprised to see that, except for northern Illinois and eastern Tennessee, all DOE facilities and offices were on either coast with one exception. Ames Laboratory was listed as a federal government-owned DOE research facility with "a focus on solutions to energy-related problems through the exploration of chemical, engineering, materials, mathematical, and physical sciences". According to the book, it was operated under contract by Iowa State University.

"Where do you suppose Ames is?" Hollis asked.

"I'm not sure, but there couldn't be a more perfect place to take Neptune."

An hour later, they were checked out of the motel and driving north on I-35 toward Ames, which they estimated to be about two hundred and fifty miles ahead. Endless flat cornfields stretched to the horizon. They hadn't planned to go this far and Hollis truly hoped it was the right thing to be doing. He knew that Fletcher was only playing along because he trusted his judgment. Hollis knew in his heart that it was the right thing to do but wondered if he was just being idealistic. He laughed inwardly and wondered if he really had any idealism left in his heart. The mood in the Oldsmobile was tense, somber, and serious as they ate up the miles.

— ‖ —

Branton Cole was furious as Westcona's chief of security completed his Saturday morning briefing in Dallas. The Alice police department had jailed his two eavesdropping security men the previous evening and refused to release them until their chief of police spoke to the men that morning. The van and all the equipment had been impounded.

"Our men are licensed to carry firearms and there's nothing illegal about the listening equipment," he fumed.

"True, but the Alice cops didn't bother to verify anything until their chief came to work this morning. He cut them loose after talking to them and calling here. They're on the way home now," the chief explained uneasily.

"Did you look at Boyd's and Cade's HR files?"

"Yeah, and there's nothing of value in them. Boyd was hired here in Dallas. He lived in Colleyville with his wife and two kids while he worked in the audit department. He was raised in Oregon and had only worked at a couple of places out there after getting out of the Army. Former Finance Officer who served in Vietnam. Cade came to work right from the Postal Service to our Lindsay, Oklahoma, district. Former Navy enlisted man with almost ten years on active duty. He and Boyd met in Lindsay when Boyd was in that super-trainee program you started in 1981. He was the only one to complete it. Cade grew up in north Texas but never went back home to live after the Navy. He's got a wife and one son who's already grown and moved out."

"So neither is what you'd term a combat vet, right?

"Well, not if you're thinking in terms of actual physical combat on a regular basis. Still, Boyd was an Army officer and his exposure to combat depends on where he was assigned while in Vietnam. If he was part of an infantry division, he lived and worked in a combat zone for sure, and probably couldn't have avoided some fighting. Cade served on aircraft carriers during combat operations. He sure as hell didn't have a desk job. No reason to underestimate what that experience may have provided in terms of mindset and skills."

"Well ladifuckingda. An accounting clerk and a deck-ape. Did you at least check out the McAllen flight plans?"

"Well, we tried but the FAA won't release any information."

"Send a plane with a couple of our more personable pilots, if we have any, to McAllen to see if they can get the information out of the tower staff. Why do I have to think of every goddamn thing around here?" he ranted.

— ‖ —

Global Oil president Mark Streeter was becoming increasingly concerned with Steve Addison's refusal to disclose the Neptune formula. He was furious with Logan and worried about his whereabouts. When he considered the progress Westcona could be making, he cringed. Logan had not been seen in McAllen by Global's security team when they checked all three homes for activity yesterday afternoon. He couldn't be found in Houston, either. Their lack of access to Boyd and Cade made the young Addison their only hope and, while Steve was certainly the trio's weak link, his attitude was hardening due to the forced separation from his wife. Logan needed to be located and controlled or his son might never fall in line. In fact, it was imperative that Global find Boyd and Cade before they did whatever they planned to do with Neptune.

If Logan could be located, Streeter had made the decision to seize and transport him to the lodge but to keep him initially isolated from Steve. Perhaps they could play father and son against each other until they were confident they had all the information each possessed. In addition, Global's board directed Streeter to lead a delegation to Westcona's Dallas headquarters to offer assistance in locating Steve and attempt to bug the security department, boardroom, and Branton Cole's office. Timely information was worth its weight in gold and they just didn't have enough to move forward right now. It would be worth the risk if only one listening device was successfully placed and remained undetected.

— || —

Steve Addison was young, out of his element, and frightened despite his mounting rage. He had never faced any form of real physical hostility in his life. His guards had treated him roughly at first, then almost as a guest. It had him emotionally off balance and disoriented. Now the pressure was being increased as he was again locked in a second-story bedroom. The promised reunion with Shelley was giving way to veiled threats of hurting her if he didn't produce Neptune. With mounting dread, he steadfastly refused to reveal anything until he was safely with Shelley. Plans for what he would do when he next saw his father took shape in his mind…plans that appealed to him more by the hour.

He heard laughter and good-natured yelling from downstairs. His guards were in better spirits, something he hoped was a good omen. While listening for footsteps, he decided to use the time before dinner to examine his room for any indication of where he was or how he might get out. He found advertisements for ski areas in Colorado and Whistler, Canada, along with a flashlight in a dresser drawer. For the first time since being kidnapped, he felt the courage to do more than sit in a chair or lie on the bed. Opening the closet, he found an assortment of fall hunting jackets, outdoor pants, gloves, and caps. He put together a full set and slid them over to one side of the closet. There were also four pairs of lined leather boots. This lodge was obviously set up to entertain people arriving without the clothing they would need in this mountain environment. It was probably used to entertain bankers, lawyers, and outside auditors. Engineers sure didn't get this kind of treatment.

He found a pair of size ten boots and slid them to one side of the closet so he could locate them in the dark. As he pushed the boots into place, he noticed a small service door that was held in place by friction clasps on the closet's side wall. His heart raced when he realized that a utility crawl space or attic area could be his ticket to freedom. He popped the door open and shined the flashlight into the void. A narrow attic—only rafters, insulation, pipes, and heat ducts. He tried to wiggle through the small door for a better view, but the sound of footsteps brought a quick end to his exploration. Hastily dropping the flashlight, he closed the closet door and dove for the bed with his heart pounding like a bass drum in his chest. He would take necessary risks to escape but would need some time without the supervision of his guards to explore this new opportunity. Unfortunately, his guards deliberately kept him off balance by randomly checking on him and otherwise making sure he didn't have time, physically or emotionally, to mount an escape attempt. They were professionals. He would have to give some serious thought to the possibilities this attic space offered.

— || —

After Fletcher's call on Friday night, JT phoned Spencer Wainwright at his Dallas home. He fully explained the situation and asked for Wainwright's help. Wainwright agreed to call JT at the Holiday Inn coffee shop at nine the next morning after expressing shock and some reasonable skepticism in the whole story. JT understood that Wainwright needed some time to sort through the information. He just hoped that Wainwright was worthy of the confidence Boyd apparently had in him. It would take testicular fortitude to get involved in this and JT had never considered many corporate office employees to have much.

JT and Logan stopped at the Alice police department on Saturday morning only to be told the Westcona eavesdroppers were being released and no laws had been violated. The knowledge that Branton Cole distrusted him enough to send eavesdroppers to his home was unsettling. How could anyone question his loyalty after so many years of faithful service? He had trusted and been loyal to the company in ways most employees had never conceived. Now they doubted him? His world was unraveling once again, and he was uncertain as to what his next step should be.

By nine o'clock on this pleasant, brilliantly cloudless morning, JT and Logan were sitting over coffee in a booth at the Holiday Inn when Spencer Wainwright's call was transferred to the lobby house phone just outside the restaurant entrance.

"I've been up all night thinking about what you told me," Wainwright stated, sounding firm and confident. "You're so close to what's happening that it's obscuring your perception. What would you do in Cole's place?"

"I'd do my best to get Neptune," JT admitted without hesitation.

"Right. Now, you can do the most for Fletcher and the company by at least looking like you're joining Cole in his efforts. I'd like to think that Westcona is doing nothing illegal, and that could be true. If it's not, you'll know because you're on the inside. I think you should come to Dallas and mend some fences with Cole."

"I'm not sure he'd even let me in the door. Are you willing to help without anyone knowing about it?"

"Of course I will. I've got a few ideas but we need you on the inside first. Does that make sense?"

"Yeah, it does. But it sounds pretty political for me."

"Politics are a fact of life up here, Jake. Let's play this close to the vest and see what we can do for Fletcher and Westcona."

"Thanks, Wainwright. All right, I'll come up and try to meet with Cole on Monday morning. I'll be at the Greenbrier if you need to find me between now and then. Can we meet Monday night?"

"Call me at the house when you're ready. I'd rather not be seen with you in public," the seasoned auditor said. JT could almost picture him smiling.

Before going back to the house, JT left a message at the front desk for Fletcher, stating that he was going to Dallas and could be reached through Wainwright. He wasn't sure when Fletcher might attempt contact, but wanted him to know that Wainwright was now involved. He then dialed the home telephone number of his FAA friend in Corpus Christi.

"Standridge, this is Jake Taylor. You're a hard man to find when you're away from work."

"Ahhh...hello, JT. That's why they call it days off. What's up?" he asked with some hesitation in his voice.

"I need help with some flight plans that may have been filed in McAllen last week. You might even say it's a life-and-death situation."

"We can't give those out to anyone except the police, and then only with a warrant. I thought you knew that."

"Look, all I need to know is if Global Oil landed any planes in McAllen last week and where they planned to go when they left. I know they had at least one there on Monday and I suspect another on Tuesday. I'm most interested in the Tuesday plane's destination."

"I assume this has something to do with your search patterns all over south Texas the other day looking for cars?"

"That's right. Look, I can't stress enough how critical this is. One person is already dead and others are at risk."

"Then why aren't the police involved?"

"It's too damned complicated to explain and you don't really want to know right now. Trust me on this."

"Shit, JT. Well…okay…destination only. I'll check the flight plans filed in McAllen last week by Global and give you the declared destination only. Son of a bitch. I can lose my pension over this, you know."

"I know and appreciate it, Standridge. I won't tell anyone where I got the information. I'm just trying to keep more people from dying right now. Sooner is much better than later."

"I'll try, JT. I'll try."

Two hours later, the old Falcon blasted down runway 26 in Alice and swept into the south Texas sky where JT stood on the right pedal and pulled her around to a northerly heading. It felt great to be finally doing something, and ripping along at four hundred and thirty knots was just the medicine he needed right now.

— ‖ — Fourteen — ‖ —

AMES APPEARED TO BE A NICE, clean, college town. It was Sunday, and the bright sun reflected off the mostly deserted downtown storefronts.

Yesterday's drive from Kansas City had been easy and quick on the big interstate. While Hollis had been raised on a ranch and later traveled the world, he had never seen or imagined as many hogs or corn fields as he saw passing through Iowa. Fletcher had been concentrating on their Monday morning visit to Ames Laboratory, oblivious to the livestock and scenery. They had settled into a small mom-and-pop motel on 13th Street, just east of the Iowa State University campus. The clerk accommodated their request for rooms on either end of the motel to make it more difficult for anyone to approach one of them without giving the other a chance to help if there was trouble. The little FM handheld radios provided instant communication between the rooms.

Earlier that morning Hollis had knocked on Fletcher's door, pausing only to toss him an Ames Tribune before returning to his room for some solitude and to read the Des Moines Register and Minneapolis Star Tribune he had found in town. It was nice being in a college town where bookstores and news-stands carried out-of-town papers. After lunch, they scouted the Ames Laboratory headquarters building on the sprawling campus. Dealing with a federal agency on a Sunday was just not possible. Their anxiety was taking on a life of its own. They called their wives from a phone booth, telling them where they were and that their mission was almost over. JT didn't answer when Fletcher called his house, so he called the Holiday Inn and received the message JT had left. After dinner, he and Hollis called it an early evening and retreated to their rooms to rest while they had the opportunity…as soldiers always do.

— ‖ —

By seven-thirty on Monday morning, Hollis had polished off six eggs, a half-pound of bacon, and a pot of coffee. After taking a rest to catch his breath and smoke three cigarettes, he was ready to present Neptune to the federal government.

Fletcher was apprehensive and still unsure of how to make his presentation despite having worked through it countless times in the past two days. His previous dealings with bureaucrats had usually resulted in frustration created by a general lack of passion and the unwillingness of government employees to make decisions. He was used to the intense review and quick decisions in the business world, and was not in the mood for red tape, forms, or the stereotypical "that's not my department" government mentality. He did not view Neptune as a social service project and was prepared to demand that the government recognize Neptune for what it was, and take immediate action to purchase it. Would they be willing to pay what it was worth? Could they be trusted during the verification and testing period that would undoubtedly be part of the transaction?

His mind was a swirl of conflicting thoughts as they drove to the campus. The only certainty was that it was going to be a frustrating day.

"What do you think they'll say?" Hollis asked with an ebullience that irritated Fletcher.

"How the hell should I know? They'll probably get all balled up in their underwear and not know what to do. It's the government. What do you expect?"

"Who should we talk to?" he persisted, ignoring the surliness.

"Let's start at the top. No use having to explain this more than once if we have a choice," Fletcher said without conviction.

Fletcher pulled into a visitor parking spot near the front of the lot. Hollis opened the glove box and pushed the release button to pop the trunk.

"What are you doing?" Fletcher asked as he quickly got out and pushed the trunk back down to keep from revealing their weapons cache.

"You want your briefcase, don't you?"

"Hell, no. Nobody sees that formula until we have dollars in a bank account."

"They won't buy it until they know what they're getting."

"They will if we can convince these people that it works," Fletcher said seriously.

Fletcher was surprised by the opulence of the reception area when the elevator doors opened. It reminded him of the executive floors at major corporations. Perhaps that made sense seeing that senior military, government, and business leaders probably came here for meetings.

"They don't do bad for civil servants," Hollis mumbled under his breath.

"May I help you?" asked the young, heavily made-up receptionist as they approached her counter.

"We need to see the man in charge," Hollis responded with as much warmth as he could muster.

"Do you have an appointment, sir?"

"We don't, but we have something he needs to see. It's scientific in nature and extremely important," Fletcher said gruffly.

"Sir, Dr. Edwards is a very busy man. May I ask what this pertains to?"

"It pertains to the most important scientific discovery of the century," Fletcher stated. "Call his office...now, please."

"I'll just check with his secretary," she haughtily responded as she rolled her eyes. "He's probably busy."

Hollis ambled over to a sofa and sat down while Fletcher stood where he was and fought the urge to rip into the snippy little bitch. She appeared oblivious to his anger as she got herself a cup of coffee without so much as offering them any.

More than an hour later a short, fat, balding man in his late forties walked into the reception area. Fletcher was seething.

"Are you the men waiting to see Dr. Edwards?" he curtly asked.

"We are," Fletcher said rising. "Are you Edwards?"

"I'm afraid not. Dr. Edwards is in a meeting that will continue until well after lunch. I'm his administrative assistant. How may I help you?"

"This is more important than any meeting he has. Look, here it is in a nutshell. We work in the oil industry and have a highly inexpensive alternative energy discovery that's more important than any in modern history. Edwards needs to see us immediately. You go interrupt his meeting. Trust me, he'll thank you later."

"That's quite impossible, sir. Dr. Edwards doesn't work with outsiders very often and never without an appointment," the man said with a supercilious smile. "If you have documentation or research papers, I can arrange a meeting with our legal staff in the next day or two."

"We don't have any documents you're going to see today, and we don't want to talk to any lawyers in a day or two. We need to see Edwards right now," Fletcher responded with increased intensity.

"I am sorry, sir but that just isn't going to happen unless you speak to our legal staff first," the exasperating little man insisted. He looked as if he wished he had brought someone from Security with him.

"Yeah, right. Okay, let's go see the lawyers. Once they understand what we have, they'll jerk Edwards out of his meeting so fast his head will spin and then he'll be pissed at you for being an idiot."

"I'll call and see if someone is available," he agreed with the hope of ridding himself of these potential troublemakers as quickly as possible. He dialed from a small desk on the side of the lobby and spoke quietly with someone.

"Why don't you come back after lunch? I'll have a meeting set up for you early this afternoon," he said as he walked away.

Fletcher was nearly out of control and Hollis calmed him as best he could. The only reason they were even at Ames was because Hollis had insisted, and he now was feeling Fletcher's intense vexation at most things *government*. He finally guided Fletcher to an on-campus café and ordered some lunch.

"I see now why you didn't stay in the Army," he chided Fletcher in an effort to lighten the mood.

"The bureaucracy drove me fucking nuts then, too, Hollis. This is like a flashback...but I don't have to put up with it now."

"You know how the system works, Fletcher. Let's just give it a fair shot before we pull the plug on them."

They returned to the DOE building, only to be told to come back the next morning for a meeting with the lawyers. Fletcher was almost apoplectic by this time. Hollis jumped into the driver's seat to keep Fletcher from abandoning Ames before they had the chance to present Neptune. He drove them back to the motel where they changed clothes and became the first patrons of the bar across the street. Hollis accepted the run-around as normal, and reminisced about how he had seen it countless times in the Navy and even more often in the Postal Service. A few J&Bs appeared to smooth Fletcher out a little but Hollis kept the car keys in his pocket just the same.

— || —

JT walked into the anteroom of Branton Cole's office suite on Monday morning just as the Global Oil president, Mark Streeter, was leaving with his security chief. Streeter was easily recognizable from press release photos JT and most oil industry executives had seen in trade publications and newspapers. He had already noticed a small group of hard-looking men in the Westcona security department lobby when he walked into the building from the underground parking lot...and now put it together. Global was visiting. What was Cole doing with Streeter? Had Cole told him that Logan Addison had defected to find his son? JT was smart enough to know that if Global Oil was working with Westcona, he and Addison were in danger. Wainwright had read it correctly; JT needed to mend some fences if it wasn't already too late.

"Mr. Cole, I came up here to set the record straight," JT said.

While he almost always called people by their last names, he thought it prudent to add the formal honorific for Cole on this occasion. "I know you think I've turned on Westcona, but I haven't. I want you to hear this story straight from me."

"Your actions speak for themselves, Mr. Taylor. You're working against us."

"No, I'm not and that's why I came. Westcona means everything to me and I want us to have Neptune. I'll be dead broke if we don't end up with this discovery. While I admit that I've been working on my own, my intentions have always been loyal to the company."

"You're working with Logan Addison *outside normal channels* to use his words. He's not interested in our future."

"Mr. Cole, his son is missing and his daughter-in-law and first grandbaby are dead. I'd hardly say that Neptune, Global, or Westcona are his primary concerns right now."

"What do you want?" Cole bluntly asked.

"I'm here to assure you of my intensions and loyalty, and to offer my full-time services to get Neptune for Westcona. Boyd, Cade, and the Addison kid are important to me, but they won't pay my bills if I'm out of work. I want Neptune for us...and their safety assured. I'm willing to help in any way I can."

Cole looked suspicious yet pleasantly surprised. "You're saying that Addison is only concerned with getting his son back?" he asked with a little more warmth than he had previously exhibited. He hadn't been able to forget the sound of Addison's emotional agony when he'd so clumsily broken the news of the murder.

"Addison strongly suspects that Global killed Shelley and is holding his son. Any loyalty he has to Global is suspended until we get a better handle on Global's involvement, and we'll have a pretty solid confirmation on that shortly. Let me help and we'll get the men back along with Neptune."

"And you suggest what?"

"That we make a more reasonable offer for Neptune after we get the kid away from Global, and bring Boyd and Cade in from the cold."

"Global claims they don't know where the kid is."

"They're lying sons of bitches."

"I know that," Cole said. "Yet it's in both companies' best interest to contain this thing before news of Neptune leaks. Okay, you're off the hook for now, Taylor, but you'd better not be lying to me about this. You keep me informed of everything you do and any contact you have with Boyd."

"I will and I expect to be kept in the loop on what you're doing, too. That information could make the difference in solving this quickly. Oh, and one more thing, Mr. Cole. Please keep your bird dogs away from me from now on. I don't need babysitting. If I find any more people sitting outside my house, I'm not going to call the police or even check out who they are. I'm going to rip off their heads and…well, you know the rest of it. That may not bother you, but this will. Addison and I have reports of both companies' actual and suspected activities surrounding Neptune in safe deposit boxes, and our attorneys have the keys. You and Streeter lose if either of us dies or goes missing."

JT turned on his heels and marched straight out of Cole's office to the elevator. He couldn't get off the tenth floor fast enough.

— ‖ —

Steve Addison was eating a late lunch at the Colorado lodge with three of his guards when Shelley's casket was lowered into the ground on Saturday afternoon in Waco, Texas. His guards made no secret of the fact that they were being relieved in two days, and promised to take Steve to Shelley if he would disclose Neptune. Warning that their replacements were not going to be as pleasant or gentle, they urged Steve to end this foolishness and rejoin his wife before the replacement guards arrived. Steve held firm to his demand to see Shelley before talking about Neptune.

The day had been cool and windy, with a hint of winter in the air. The trees were rapidly losing leaves and snow could arrive with any cold snap. Tall evergreens framed the view from the great-room windows and the setting sun would soon streak the sky with purplish light, casting an eerie glow on the darkening valley. Not wanting to appear eager to return to his room, Steve accepted his guard's offer to play cards near the fireplace. He planned to escape but really wanted some idea of where he was before bolting into the unknown wilderness.

He had skied Colorado and New Mexico, and the scenery reminded him of the west slope of the Rockies. He thought about the steep rock terrain of the Front Range around Denver. There were too many trees here to be on the east side of the mountains. Or maybe Mexico or the Cascades? They had flown long enough to be in the Mexican Sierra Madre but probably not long enough to have made it into the Pacific Northwest. He had flown over those Mexican mountains on vacations with his parents but had never been on the ground there. On further consideration, he thought it was too cold to be that far south. They must still be in the U.S.; someplace in a more northerly state that was so cool this early in the season. Perhaps even the Canadian Rockies. As the card game progressed and the whisky flowed, he began to talk.

"Sure is pretty up here, isn't it?' he said, watching for reaction from his guards.

"Yep, it is. Houston seems like another planet after being here for a few days," one said.

"Yeah, I've lived all over the world but nothing beats these Rockies," Steve added, trying to draw them into a reaction or comment. "I'd like to have a place like this after we sell Neptune."

The guards reacted with enthusiasm at the mention of Neptune, and one poured Steve another drink as they glanced furtively back and forth at one another. He could tell they were anxious for information.

"We know you won't tell us how to make the stuff," one fished, "but how good is it? What does it cost compared to gas?"

"That's why everyone wants it," Steve replied. "It can be used in place of natural gas, diesel, gasoline, kerosene, and stuff like that. Global, or anyone else for that matter, won't drill in this country when crude oil prices are much less than twenty dollars a barrel...and then the oil still needs to be refined. I can make Neptune, which is ready to be put in your gas tank, for about a buck and a half a barrel. That's less than four cents a gallon. I'll bet the cost would be half that if you made it on a large scale."

"You're shittin' me," another guard exclaimed in disbelief. "Why don't ya'll just sell it to Global then?"

"What do you think we've been trying to do? Global *and* Westcona want to steal it from us."

It was obvious that this was the first time the guards had heard the real story and they looked puzzled by it.

"How about some music?" Steve suggested. "Is there a radio around here?"

"Yeah, that would be good," a guard responded as he got up to find a portable radio.

The guard returned with the radio tuned to a country station. The music faded as they played cards, and when the signal finally drifted away completely he reached for the radio to find another station. "This is KJOL radio, 620 on your AM dial, the Christian Voice of Grand Junction, Colorado." The guard stared at the radio in disbelief and embarrassment at his very basic error.

"You know how desolate this area is. Don't try anything stupid; we'll kill you if you force us."

Steve had to mask his excitement as the guards roughly shoved him up the stairs and pushed him into his bedroom. AM radio stations transmit a long way, but religious stations usually operate on lower power than rock or country stations. He suspected he was reasonably close to Grand Junction and now had an idea of which direction to run if he could break out. His mind recalled a map of western Colorado. He must be someplace east of Grand Junction.

Unfortunately, he knew the guards would be watching him more closely now.

— ‖ —

JT circled a few blocks from Spencer Wainwright's suburban Dallas house, checking for any suspicious lights that could mean he was being followed. He then made a series of right-hand turns through the upscale neighborhood just to be sure. The garage door went up as he pulled into the driveway. Wainwright motioned him into the garage, closing the door behind him before he even had the car stopped.

"Fletcher didn't drink scotch until he worked for you," the auditor said with a smile as he poured JT a drink. "I assume that's acceptable?"

"Yeah, thanks. Say, why'd you ever let Boyd get away from you?"

"You know Fletcher; he saw an opportunity and nobody can hold him back when he sets his mind on something he really wants to do even if it's wrong. You're correct, though. I didn't really want to lose him. He was a damn good auditor. A pain in the ass sometimes but a damn good auditor."

"I thought that was a prerequisite," JT said with a smile. "But I don't doubt he was good at it. He seems to be good at most things."

JT explained the details of his meeting with Branton Cole while Wainwright listened intently. The news of Streeter's presence in Cole's office surprised the seasoned auditor, as it had JT. Wainwright continued to listen quietly as he pulled out a notepad and began writing as the details became more complex.

"It sounds like Global isn't making progress with Steve, and they want to find Fletcher and Hollis," he commented after JT finished. "It also looks like Westcona is willing to try to work a deal for Steve. Is that how you see it?"

"To a point. I suspect that Boyd has all the Neptune documentation, but I'm not sure Westcona really cares much about Addison's safety as long as Neptune is in play. In order to defend its claim to the formula, Westcona needs all three men to cooperate, or all three dead. Global only needs the formula. With Boyd and Cade on the loose, Global would have a legal problem when Boyd sues them...and he'd do that in a heartbeat."

"I hadn't thought of it that way," Wainwright admitted. "Wouldn't Global just take Neptune offshore to avoid the U.S. courts?"

"They probably would but they'd still run into legal trouble or serious hostility from other countries and companies if they weren't careful. The U.S. would still be the safest place for them to hold it...I think."

"Do you know where Steve is, Jake?"

"No."

Wainwright rubbed his eyes and forehead with his hands as he thought. "Well, you keep working with his father. In the meantime, I've started a bogus audit of the accounts payable department. One of my people is working with the telephone company and oil companies we have corporate accounts with. We'll know within hours if any of the three uses a Westcona gas or telephone credit card."

"I never would have thought about those credit cards. Good thinking. I'll work with Cole to the extent he'll let me. We need to keep Boyd and Cade out of trouble until we can find Addison."

"Jake, just don't tell Cole where any of the boys are unless we discuss it first. We have to be very careful when we share any information with him. He's a real weasel, you know."

"Yeah, I know he's a sorry bastard. You can call me JT."

— ‖ —

Ellie Cade was happy to have children around the house again. She made cookies with Taryn and Felecia, showed them how to milk a goat, and made ice cream. The girls seemed to enjoy being on a real farm, and Lady was still excited by all the sights, sounds, and smells of a rural environment. Sara and Katie helped as much as Ellie would allow. Ellie decided to allow Lady inside the house at night to comfort Taryn and Felecia, although she thought dogs belonged outdoors. Her dogs always stayed out and would provide ample security should anything or anyone venture too close to the house or barn.

Ellie contacted the Lamar County sheriff to inform him that she had company and was worried about some unusual nighttime activity she had recently spotted in the area. She really hadn't of course, but wanted them watching her farm more closely than they otherwise would. The sheriff was a childhood friend of Hollis's and she had known him since he was a baby.

As she inspected the shotguns Hollis and Fletcher had left behind, she thought they were kind of fancy compared to her old side-by-side double barreled. These were short-barreled combat-style pump shotguns with extended magazine tubes and other things she had only seen in gun magazines when her husband was still alive. Fancy guns that might or might not be good for something, but at least they were twelve gauge. She wondered if Katie could even shoot, what with living in the city like she did. While she knew from experience that Sara could shoot reasonably well, she didn't want any loaded guns in her house that an untrained person might grab and try to use in an emergency. She took one of the fancy shotguns and a box of ammunition out to the edge of her yard and called the younger women.

"Here," she said, handing the shotgun to Katie. "Load up and shoot as fast as you can into that tree stump over yonder."

Katie gave her an amused smile as she scooped up a handful of shells. She turned the shotgun over and loaded rounds into it before smoothly jacking a round into the chamber and loading one more into the magazine. She centered her weight; her knees slightly bent and left foot forward, and fired eight rounds from the hip in what sounded like one continuous, deafening roar. The stump exploded into dust and flying wood chips under the assault. Still smiling, she handed the hot shotgun back to Ellie. "My husband trained me."

Sara took the shotgun from her mother-in-law and reloaded it. She, too, rapidly pumped eight rounds into the remains of the stump just to assure the old lady that she had not lost her touch.

"Good enough," Ellie said, as she walked back to the house. All three shotguns were loaded that night before they went to bed.

—ııı— Fifteen —ııı—

"GOOD MORNING, GENTLEMEN. I'M BARBARA Rowley with the Ames Legal Department. Actually, I am the legal department. Ames has little need for lawyers but when they do, I'm it," she said in a pleasant but matter of fact tone. She walked with cool self-assurance, took a seat at the head of the conference room table, and looked expectantly at them.

She could see that the cowboys who had frightened Dr. Edward's assistant the previous day were pleased to be having a meeting and didn't seem at all put off that it was with a young woman. They also didn't look nearly as tough as had been described to her. Her intent was to listen politely, offer no encouragement, and herd them out the door with a smile on her face. The thought of an actual discovery worthy of Ames Lab resources was far from her mind.

Not wanting this meeting to drag on any longer than necessary, she took the initiative. "I understand you have some sort of a discovery that you're anxious to provide to the Department of Energy. Is that correct?" she asked perfunctorily as she looked at her watch.

"It is. We have an alternative fuel discovery that will change the world," Fletcher said, "though we had a difficult time making anyone here understand that yesterday. We appreciate the value of our discovery and feel compelled, out of patriotism, to offer it to the United States of America...for a fee of course. That's the American way. We're initially thinking its worth somewhere in the vicinity of one billion dollars."

In spite of her usual unflappable demeanor, Rowley found herself blinking several times at the absurdity of Fletcher's response. So much for reality. This was going to be a much shorter meeting than she, and certainly they, had anticipated. Trying to suppress a smirk, she briefly glanced at his partner and caught a glimpse of a self-assured and resolute face staring back.

Her mind worked faster than most, rapid-firing rhetorical questions to herself. She was not highly challenged in her current assignment and knew the administrators and scientists thought themselves too important to deal with things like this, but come on. Annoyance welled within her when she realized these guys had not been adequately screened before being invited to a meeting with her.

Looking Fletcher straight in the eye, she arched an eyebrow and said, "Only a billion? With a B and in American dollars I suppose? You people are out of your minds," she scoffed with a wave of her hand. "I can't believe I'm even sitting here listening to you. What's your background? Are you scientists? Chemists? The best of the best haven't come up with a viable energy alternative but you yahoos waltz in here with this cockamamie story and want the United States government to hand you a billion, with a B, dollars for your trouble? Un-frigging-believable, if you'll pardon my language. Now," she said as she slapped the table and stood, "I've got real business to attend to. Good bye," she abruptly quipped as she started for the door.

Her onslaught caught both men by surprise. Fletcher smiled for lack of knowing what else to do. Hollis realized that this was getting away from them and knew he had to quickly take control.

"You sit right damned down...now," he said with considerable menace in his voice.

Rowley did a slow but deliberate turn to face Hollis, hands on her hips. "I beg your pardon?" she said in an icy timbre as her complexion turned an angry red.

"Sit down or I'll tie your ass to a chair. You're not leaving here until you listen to this," Hollis said in a firm and quiet tone.

Rowley froze in stunned indignation.

"Please, Ms. Rowley. We're being threatened by our employer and really need you to hear us out. We're not nuts and wouldn't be here if this wasn't on the level. We don't know where else to turn...and you need to hear this," Fletcher said as he wondered how far Hollis was prepared to go.

Rowley was obviously not accustomed to being spoken to in quite this manner, and was livid. She reached for the phone but Hollis ripped the cord out of the wall and motioned her to her chair, leaving no further question in Fletcher's mind.

"I'm not going to tell you again," he said as he stood glowering over her until she retreated to her chair at the head of the table.

"We're not chemists or scientists, Ms. Rowley," Fletcher began again as if nothing had happened. He gave Hollis a cautionary glance and continued. "However, we do have a member of our group who is and he's the one who did the chemistry. It's good science that we can duplicate for you today. Dammit, we've got people trying to kill us and you don't seem to think this is worth ten minutes of your time."

Rowley sat in silence for a moment with her eyes closed, probably wondering how she had come to being held hostage in her own conference room. Fletcher could see her hands trembling and felt a tinge of guilty sadness at forcing this on an innocent civilian. Finally, looking carefully at each of them with obvious apprehension, she quietly said, "You'll have to start at the beginning and help me understand what this is all about."

Fletcher calmly began a reasonably detailed history of Neptune, including the assaults, murder, and probable kidnapping. Rowley listened only politely at first, but as the story unfolded she slowly began taking notes. He worked through the convoluted and complicated story right up to their arrival in Ames. She could only stare when he appeared to finish the story, and Hollis walked back to his chair and sat down. Her fear was mostly gone but she still couldn't quite get her emotions under control because none of it made any sense. She wondered why she hadn't heard any of this on the news but realized that only the murder was public information, and deaths in south Texas don't necessarily get much publicity in Iowa unless they involved famous people. Still, this was just plain off-the-wall nutty.

"Let me do a quick recap to see if I've got this right," she said softly as if in physical pain. "You both work for an oilfield service company in south Texas. You accidentally discovered this alternative energy source while drinking beer after a dove hunt in an abandoned orange grove. You've tested this discovery and it will power automobiles, lawnmowers, and some of your heavy equipment. You further believe that your discovery can be used, in its gaseous state, in place of natural gas. The base ingredient for your discovery is seawater, to which you add an assortment of readily available chemicals. The liquefied version of your discovery costs less than four cents a gallon to make. And finally, you want the United States government to pay for this discovery and are thinking that one billion dollars is a reasonable starting point. Is that a fair summation?"

"That's pretty fair," Hollis agreed, finally smiling. "We believe the government should have it but should pay us what we could get on the outside."

"And your chemical engineer who did the work has been kidnapped?"

"We hope so," Fletcher said. "The alternative is that he's already dead."

"After the way you've treated me, how do I know you didn't kill him?"

"That would suggest a money motive, and there'll be more than enough money to make that kind of behavior unreasonable to even the worst type of criminal — which we aren't."

"What about your employer? I suppose they're okay with you just taking off and trying to sell this? Didn't you sign confidentiality and patent agreements when you went to work for them?"

"We did, but we don't feel they apply in this circumstance."

"And your law degree is from? Oh, never mind. And you think the government should just jump right into the middle of this and take your word for it? And why are you at Ames? Nobody up here could tell a pumpjack from a workover rig if their life depended on it."

"Ma'am, you cover a lot of ground without taking a breath. Our employer is trying to get their hands on our discovery, which we named Neptune by the way. Our engineer's father is a vice president with Global Oil and we have reason to believe they're actively looking for Neptune, too. In fact, we think they're the ones who kidnapped our engineer and killed his pregnant wife. For rather obvious reasons, we decided it was best to temporarily remove ourselves from both Westcona's and Global's normal operating area and approach the DOE. We found out about Ames from a library reference book and thought you people would understand Neptune better than most," Fletcher explained.

"And Westcona is your employer?"

"They are."

"I'm familiar with them."

The young attorney took a deep breath, sat back and considered the implications of this preposterous story. While she hadn't mentioned it to the men sitting across from her, she was a native Texan and knew that Westcona didn't hire cretins for the jobs they claimed to hold. Obviously the government would want Neptune if it were real which she still considered highly unlikely. Bringing something this outlandish to Dr. Edwards would certainly impact how she was perceived for the rest of her assignment, and she had no intention of becoming the in-house laughingstock.

Her sharp mind quickly weighed the evidence and impact on her budding career. If Neptune existed as described, or with even ten percent of the potential they described, she'd be criminally negligent in not bringing it to her superiors before these men sold it to commercial interests. After all, the DOE had some of the brightest minds in science working to find things just like this. This could also have national security implications. What had started out to be just another day in Iowa was now something out of a fantasy novel. Still...

She made a decision. She'd give them the opportunity to create and demonstrate their product. In the off chance it appeared to be valid, she'd bring the story and her evidence to Dr. Edwards. Edwards would laugh her out of the office unless she'd vetted it as best she could before bothering him. She was sure she'd just taken complete leave of her senses but her gut told her to move forward. She was now either approaching the high road to a big promotion out of Iowa or the low road out of government service. Or was it the other way around?

"Mr. Boyd, I just can't swallow this yet but you said earlier that you could back it up with science. What are the chances you can provide me a demonstration yet today?"

She watched Fletcher closely for a reaction, and was rewarded with a broad grin.

"Give us the use of a chemistry lab and we'll make you a believer yet this afternoon. We'll need some seawater and the chemicals. Do you have a chemistry lab or agriculture school or veterinary school on campus?"

"Yes to all three. I'm not sure about the seawater though. But we should have any common agriculture and veterinary chemicals."

"Good. We'll create Neptune, although you won't see the actual formula at this point. Fair enough?"

"Fair enough, with one condition. One of our security guards will accompany us while we do this. Is that acceptable?"

"That's fine by us," Fletcher said as she reached for the telephone before remembering what Hollis had done.

"Sorry 'bout your phone," Hollis muttered sheepishly. "And thanks for listening."

She had showered before coming to work and already felt like she could benefit from another.

— || —

Barbara Rowley barged into Dr. Edwards' office and told him what she had just witnessed.

"Have you taken leave of your senses?" he said.

"I know it sounds like it, but I saw them put it together with my own eyes, Doctor. They created a combustible fluid from seawater just as they claimed they could. I'd never consider bringing this to you if I hadn't witnessed it. You need to look at it and form your own conclusion before you dismiss it out of hand."

"Oh, come now, Ms. Rowley. You certainly can't believe these men accidentally stumbled onto what we've been working on for decades."

"Doctor, I saw them do it with my own eyes. Whether or not it can do everything they claim isn't the critical issue. It might be all your people need to make that critical breakthrough. What will happen to your career if we throw these guys out and later find they really have the key?"

They went over her notes, focusing on the implications of Neptune if it existed.

"Are they prepared to repeat this performance under the supervision and observation of qualified chemists?"

"Yes, right now if you want."

"And you seriously think this is possible, Ms. Rowley?"

"Well, Doctor, let's just say they should have a Vegas act if it isn't real."

Doctor Edwards agreed, with obvious reluctance, that it was worth allowing the two men to work for a couple of hours in the lab even though it was probably a waste of time and resources.

"See if any of our people know anyone at Global Oil or wherever they said they work," Edwards instructed. "On second thought, you call the legal or human resource department where they claim to work and see what they have to say. Probably never heard of these fellows."

"They specifically asked that we not contact Global Oil or Westcona until they demonstrated their discovery because they claim to be afraid of what the companies might do."

"Ms. Rowley, please make the call. I'm all ready very uncomfortable with all this and want to know if these men are telling us anything that's true."

Rowley's call to Westcona's legal department set off alarms on the executive floor. The chief administrative officer and in-house counsel confirmed that Boyd and Cade indeed worked for Westcona, but that each was the target of an industrial espionage investigation. He strongly recommended that the DOE have nothing to do with the men. Before Rowley got off the phone, Westcona's head lawyer had their president, Branton Cole, on the line asking to speak with the director of Ames Laboratory. Rowley transferred the call into Dr. Edwards but stayed on the line listening.

"Dr. Edwards, this is Branton Cole, president of Westcona. I understand you have a couple of our wayward sons at your facility."

"We have two men who claim to work for you, and have presented us a most peculiar and startling claim."

"Please, don't listen to their stories or get involved. We're initiating legal action against both men and would hate for the DOE to get tied up in messy litigation. I have a security team coming to your facility tonight to liaise with the local police in arresting them. Your cooperation in keeping them nearby will be greatly appreciated."

"Mr. Cole, we have no interest in your legal issues but I do have a question. Does this Neptune they speak of exist? If so, the implications are immense."

"No, Doctor, we don't think they have what they claim, but they have stolen proprietary information from my company. For the sake of discussion, if Neptune exists, it would be Westcona's property and we'd vigorously defend it in every court in the land. As I said, Dr. Edwards, we'd appreciate your keeping the men around until my people arrive with the police."

Dr. Edwards and Barbara Rowley concurred that Branton Cole was being disingenuous. Denials of Neptune followed by threats of litigation made no sense. Dr. Edwards decided to alert his DOE boss in Washington to these strange events and his concern with the threats made by the Westcona president. But first he informed the Iowa State University president and the university police department of the potential threats and instructed them to keep Westcona security personnel off the campus until he had a reaction and some direction from Washington, DC even if they showed up with the local police in tow. Rowley suggested he expand that order to include security personnel from any outside company, which he did. He was responsible for a federal research facility located on state property, and the City of Ames Police Department would have to understand that reality if they got involved.

"I'm going over to the lab and see how your new friends are progressing," he said to the young attorney. "We need to determine what this is all about before anything gets blown out of proportion…or out of control."

— ‖ —

The listening device planted in Branton Cole's office by Global Oil worked perfectly. They quickly put "DOE" and "Ames" together to correctly identify the Department of Energy's Ames Laboratory as the location of Fletcher Boyd and Hollis Cade.

"Get a security team in the air yesterday," Mark Streeter roared when he heard the news. "I want those people and Neptune under my control by tonight. Make sure they know that Westcona has a team headed up there, too."

— ‖ —

Steve Addison had methodically worked through the problem of the attic space. The opening in his bedroom closet must somehow connect to attic space over the attached garage. At least his engineer's brain told him it should. Now he just needed to summon the courage to do what he knew had to be done. He peered into the recesses of the attic beside his bedroom for the second time. All he could see were rafters, insulation, heat ducts, and Romex cable. It was confusing because he was on the second floor and the attic should have been above him, not on his level.

As he peered into the dim space, it suddenly all clicked into place. The second floor rooms had vaulted ceilings which provided no room for an attic. The second floor had less finished square footage than the main floor because some of it was devoted to interior service areas behind the walls which contained HVAC, water, and electrical service necessities. What about the garage? He plotted out how the downstairs rooms were configured to put the space in context. The garage must be at the far end of the building, but it was hidden from view by the maze of heat ducts. Where else could there be an escape route from the second floor? Most garages had a way into the attic. He realized that once he crawled in, his ability to quickly return to his room would be gone. He would have to take the risk of traversing the attic space while hoping for a way into the garage at the far end of the building. His guards still claimed to be leaving tomorrow when the replacement guards arrived. Tomorrow night would be his best chance while the new guards were not yet accustomed to the building's normal creaks and groans. They could easily mistake them for any noise he might make in the attic. Tomorrow night it was then. He'd been a captive for nearly a week now and it was time to get out of here and find his wife.

— ‖ —

On Tuesday morning, JT was more than ready to leave Dallas and anxious to get back to Alice. His spirits improved when he attained cruising altitude and looked out over the state he so loved. Being alone in the air always improved his attitude.

He hoped his friend in Corpus Christi had the critical flight plan information but didn't dare ask about it on the radio as he approached south Texas airspace. Following normal protocol, he contacted Alice approach and landed the plane.

Logan had a brisket on the barbeque and pinto beans slow-cooking on the stove. The house smelled wonderful. They quickly exchanged information before JT got on the phone.

"Standridge, Jake Taylor. Any luck with those destinations?"

"Hello, JT. I heard you on the radio on your approach into Alice and figured you might call. Westcona had one plane into and out of McAllen last Monday. It came from and returned to Corpus Christi. I think you said you knew about that one. Global had a plane into McAllen from Houston on Monday afternoon and it returned to Houston late that evening. You said you knew about that one, too. Global also had a plane into McAllen on Tuesday afternoon that departed that evening at twenty-two sixteen local time, listing Grand Junction, Colorado, as its destination. Does that help?"

"I think it very well may. Thanks, Standridge. You may just have saved some lives."

JT told Logan about the planes as he mixed them each a drink. Logan blanched when he heard Global's name connected with the destination of the Tuesday night plane.

"I didn't want to believe my company was involved like this, but I guess I half expected they were. We have a lodge near Grand Mesa, just east of Grand Junction, we use for entertaining bankers and politicians. That's where they're keeping Steve hostage," he added coldly.

"Much as I'd like to jump in the Falcon right now, it makes more sense to get organized and fly out there tomorrow. We need to approach the place in daylight so we can see what we're up against. Then again, maybe we should just call the State police and let them go out there. What do you think?"

"I want them for myself," Logan said. "We'd be dead tired if we flew out tonight, rented a car, and then drove to the lodge in the middle of the night. As much as I hate sitting here, let's plan this tonight and leave in the morning. No police."

— || —

A Bunsen burner glowed brightly at Ames Laboratory powered by Neptune in its gaseous state. The chemist observing and assisting Fletcher helped distill the gas to produce a little more than a cup of liquid Neptune before Fletcher asked him to stop the process. Fletcher had shielded his actions, but the man certainly knew what chemicals they had picked up around the campus. What he didn't know was that Fletcher had added four chemicals to their shopping list that were *not* needed or used to produce Neptune. He hoped the subterfuge would buy a little time if the man tried to reproduce their discovery…and that adding the extra ingredients would cause a problem with the mixture if the guy got that far.

"You call Edwards and have him meet us outside where Hollis has one of your lawnmowers," he instructed the chemist.

Twenty minutes later the lawnmower, which had been emptied of all gasoline and run dry in front of Doctor Edwards and Barbara Rowley, roared to life powered by Neptune. Edwards asked the chemist if what he was seeing was good, reproducible chemistry using seawater as a base substance. The dazzled man could only nod in affirmation. Fletcher allowed the engine to run until it died for lack of fuel, then ripped the rubber fuel line off the mower and crushed the plastic fuel filter under his heel. Not a drop of Neptune remained at Ames Laboratory.

"There you are, Doctor. Neptune in action just as advertised," Fletcher said. "Now call your boss and report the good news. We need to know today what the DOE intends to do with this."

"I'm impressed, Mr. Boyd, but you realize the testing is just beginning. It indeed looks promising but we're still a long way from determining its commercial potential or value as an alternative energy source. I'll contact Washington to alert them that we may have a scientific breakthrough on our hands. In fact, let's call right now and report your success.

Dr. Edwards asked Fletcher to wait outside his office while he informed his boss of what he had just witnessed. He was pummeled with questions but held his ground as to what he had seen and the apparent validity of the initial test protocol. Edwards knew that his status within the scientific community carried heavy sway, and was not surprised when the reaction was robust despite having stressed that the discovery was far from properly verified or evaluated from a scientific perspective. He was told to get to work on the verification process, provide security for the men on campus, and send Fletcher and Hollis to Washington the following morning. He opened his door and addressed Fletcher.

"Mr. Boyd, would you and Mr. Cade please be our guests tonight? You've been invited to Washington tomorrow to discuss the legal transfer of your discovery to the United States of America."

"We will, Doctor, as long as they understand they'll need to open their checkbook before we sign any documents or provide details," Fletcher agreed happily.

"Where have you been staying since arriving in Ames?"

"At a little motel on 13th Street. We're fine out there for another night."

"Nonsense. We'll provide you accommodations in our guesthouse and have a nice dinner together."

"It would be our pleasure," Fletcher said.

"Fine, fine then. I'll have someone run over to your motel and get your belongings if that's acceptable. We'll take care of your bill, too."

Doctor Edwards' telephone rang before Fletcher could respond. It was the Iowa State University police chief advising that his men had just stopped a team of Global Oil security personnel and prevented them from entering the campus. No sign of Westcona people yet. Dr. Edwards instructed the chief to put guards on the VIP quarters to assure that these special guests were undisturbed during the night and that they stayed put until he could get them on a plane in the morning.

— ‖ —

The Global security team was furious when they were turned away from the campus by the university cops. They correctly assumed that the men were now being protected on campus, and decided to wait for the Westcona team to arrive. During a call to Houston, the leader was instructed to join forces with the Westcona team so they had a better chance of locating Boyd and Cade without tripping over one another. Mark Streeter authorized *necessary force* to obtain Neptune.

—||| — Sixteen —||| —

FLETCHER AND HOLLIS INSPECTED THEIR rooms with an eye for a fast escape. Regardless of Edwards' hospitality, they couldn't afford to let their guard down. The more time they were away from familiar surroundings the more concern they felt about security. What if Edwards or someone at DOE called Westcona to check up on them?

The rooms were located in the rear of the second floor of what appeared to be a four-story office building converted to small apartments. From the windows, overlooking the rear parking lot, they could see the back of the lab where they had worked with the chemist earlier in the afternoon. Centered between the guesthouse and the lab was a narrow service road that fronted a fifty-yard-deep shrubbery-studded, grassy field that ran up to the back of the lab building. In addition to Fletcher's Oldsmobile, the guesthouse parking lot held only a government olive-drab school bus and two cargo trucks resembling Army two-and-a-half-ton trucks were it not for their blue paint. The windows opened onto a fire escape.

Hollis climbed out to confirm how the fire escape would lower to the ground in case of fire or emergency. Walking around the second floor, they found stairwells on each end of the hallway. Both were unlocked and designated as fire escapes which opened at the bottom floor on the front side of the building. Growing outside the window on the northwest corner, and extending above the roofline was a very large, sturdy oak tree.

Fletcher went out to the car and brought in the handheld radios along with the spare car key he kept hidden behind the license plate. He thought about bringing the Mini-14s into the building but decided against it as they were both carrying handguns. He couldn't conceive of needing more firepower in the current circumstances. Finally, they felt comfortable enough with the new surroundings to settle into their rooms.

Thirty minutes later Hollis knocked on Fletcher's door with a deck of cards he had found in a desk drawer.

"How 'bout some poker?" he asked.

"If you go easy on me. Barbara just called and said she'd be by in an hour to take us to dinner. Sounds like we'll be guests in the faculty dining room. I don't think they want us wandering around the campus tonight," Fletcher said with a smile.

"Oh, its Barbara now, is it? I think Ms. Rowley is from our part of the world even if she has picked up some of that damn Yankee accent. She seemed to know more oilfield terminology than I'd expect from the average Iowan, or whatever they call themselves here. She's not bad-looking, either."

"Seemed to want us to know that she knew something about the oilfields for sure, and the way you behaved impressed her, too," Fletcher chided him.

"Hell, I didn't mean anything by it...just tryin' to get her attention is all. You know she was ready to throw us out so somebody had to do something."

"Well, you did something, that's for sure. I never heard you talk to a woman that way," Fletcher observed.

"She's a damned attorney...so it really don't count," Hollis grinned.

Fletcher gave him the spare car key and radio before they

settled down to a game of nickel-dime-quarter poker. While in the Navy, Hollis had learned just about every game there was to play with a deck of cards and enjoyed beating Fletcher whenever he had the chance. Playing cards had been a tension reducer while aboard ship and it was having the same effect now. Fletcher was not as good a player, but it was just the distraction he welcomed, too.

"I wonder who we're going to see in Washington," Fletcher said absently while Hollis displayed a flush, besting his pair of tens, and pulled the pot of change toward him.

"I've been wondering the same thing. We'll probably have to demonstrate Neptune again for them tomorrow, you know."

"Yeah, well, we'll object if they don't have a chemist there to verify it but I suspect they'll demand it anyway. I'm just concerned that they'll stall long enough for Westcona or Global to get wind of what we're doing. Edwards might even have called to verify our story. We need to be quick about this and make sure the nice government men provide us some security when the brown stuff hits the fan."

The telephone rang just as Hollis relieved Fletcher of his last dime. Barbara Rowley was in the lobby waiting to take them to dinner. They donned their sport coats, turned off the lights, and closed the door behind them.

— || —

The faculty dining room was surprisingly elegant and stocked a full bar. Dr. Edwards recommended a Merlot, which Fletcher and Barbara accepted. Hollis asked for a beer.

Edwards had assembled his senior staff in an apparent attempt to impress the men from Texas and perhaps learn more about Neptune over dinner. The scientists did, in fact, ask many questions while they enjoyed their before-dinner drinks. Naming a potential discovery after a pagan god seemed ridiculous to these august men of science. Those who had taken the time to think through the international ramifications laughingly referred to the discovery as "The Pagan Peril". After all, scientific discoveries of this magnitude had imperiled their creators throughout history when religious orders controlled governments or thought they did. Just ask Galileo, Copernicus, Kepler, Bruno, and many others.

The scientists seemed particularly interested in the men's backgrounds and the story of the discovery. Learned chemists and physicists are naturally skeptical of any major scientific breakthrough, and this group was highly suspect of the story Fletcher related. In fact, the story was hard to believe when you knew the whole truth, and nearly unimaginable without some idea of the chemistry. Dr. Edwards assured them that one of their own, conspicuously missing from this dinner, had verified the creation and that he had personally witnessed the successful combustion of Neptune in the lawnmower that very afternoon. The group enjoyed their dinner while speculating on what this would mean to the world if it really existed. Fletcher got the feeling that they found the whole exercise little more than an excuse to impress each other with their brilliance. Unfortunately, the group didn't come up with anything they hadn't already thought of, and the charade bored him. The hard fact remained; these guys with the prestigious advanced degrees were entangled in useless theory while he and Hollis owned Neptune.

Barbara dropped them off just after nine and promised to pick them up for breakfast at seven-thirty. Fletcher suggested a short walk to relax and unwind after being on the hot seat all evening.

"I wonder where that guy we worked with today was," Hollis mused as they walked around the corner of the building toward the parking lot.

"Apparently he isn't high enough up the food chain to have dinner with the likes of us."

Both men stopped dead in their tracks when they reached the parking lot and looked across the service road to the lab beyond. The place was ablaze with lights and they could see a handful of people through the windows. They walked up into the field for a closer look.

"Sure enough, there's that little bastard we worked with," Fletcher fumed. "They must be trying to figure out Neptune tonight."

They walked back toward their building and into the parking lot where the Oldsmobile was parked. Glancing up, Fletcher noticed that the lights were on in both their rooms.

"I hope it was the guy who picked up our clothes at the motel that left the lights on, Hollis. What do you think about moving the car to a less conspicuous spot for the night, just in case?"

Hollis needed little encouragement. They drove the Oldsmobile down the service road behind their building. A block away, they came upon a maintenance yard containing snowplowing equipment parked outside a small office building, and a huge pile of sand under a large open-sided peaked-top protective roof. Fletcher guided the car around the snowplows and stopped behind the sand pile where the car was hidden from view. They walked back to their rooms feeling a little bit better about their chances of getting out in a hurry should it come to that.

"I'd sure hate to live someplace where the snow gets so high you need earth-moving equipment just to get around," Hollis groused as they entered their building. They found their clothing in their rooms as promised. After calling the ranch and filling their wives in on their terrific progress, they called it a night.

"Keep your radio on," Fletcher urged as he left for his room. He felt vaguely uncomfortable about the scientists working in the lab.

— ‖ —

The Global security team had settled into their vehicle to wait for the Westcona crew. They could see the university police roadblock, and knew the Westcona people would drive right up to it just as they had. Within twenty minutes, a Chevy Suburban following a City of Ames Police Department squad car was turned away after a spirited discussion. It appeared that the city cops weren't going to make a scene over not getting in, but the Westcona leader looked hot.

The Global team followed the Suburban until the squad car disappeared and then pulled Dutch Peltier over with hand signals. The unlikely allies drove to a busy shopping center where they introduced themselves. Both teams used public telephones to call their handlers with the news that they had found each other, and were told to stay near the phone while decisions were made.

— ‖ —

Branton Cole was livid when he realized that he either had a traitor in his midst or his office was bugged. His security chief immediately swept the room and found it. Cole then had a tempestuous ten-minute telephone conversation with Mark Streeter. He hadn't admitted to finding the bug but Streeter had known it when it went dead. He ultimately concurred with

Streeter that they must act together tonight or Neptune would be public knowledge within hours. He wondered what Global was doing to Steve while they played their last card in gaining Neptune exclusively for themselves. It was an ugly thought he didn't want to dwell on.

Infiltrating the campus should be child's play for their accomplished ex-military and former federal agents. They needed to find Boyd and Cade so they could gain control of Neptune before the sun came up. Sharing Neptune with Global Oil would be better than losing it altogether.

— ‖ —

Dr. Edwards answered the telephone at 10:30 as he prepared to go to bed. While he knew it had to involve Neptune, he had hoped against all odds for a quiet and uneventful evening. The university police chief informed him that they had now turned away the Westcona security team along with the City of Ames Police Department.

There would be questions to answer in the morning and he already dreaded the "after the fact analysis" that would undoubtedly take place. The Ames mayor would likely take offense to his actions once he was whined at by the police chief. Still, it was his federal facility and he was sitting on one of the most potentially important scientific breakthroughs of the twentieth century.

"I want you to call out all your people and position as many as needed around the VIP quarters and chemistry lab tonight," he told the chief. "No outsiders get into either building without my personal authorization. Watch the whole campus and please be careful. These people could be persistent if their whole industry is being threatened."

Edwards then called Barbara Rowley and instructed her to be ready to deal with the corporate lawyers and city bureaucrats who would surely be on the phone or their doorstep in the morning. His responsibility was to get Boyd and Cade on an airplane in the morning without incident. In the meantime, he was going to have another glass of wine before trying to get some sleep.

— ‖ —

Steve Addison met the guard replacements on Monday afternoon and was not impressed. These guys were not friendly or at all concerned with his comfort. They grilled him for two hours, trying to pry the details of Neptune loose. They threatened him. They threatened Shelley. They threatened Logan, which surprised him because he thought his father was in cahoots with them. Steve held firm. In the end, they roughly pushed him to his room and left him alone. Shortly after dark, a surly guard arrived with a tray of food. He sat in the corner of Steve's room until he finished his meal and then retrieved the tray, making sure all the utensils were with it before unceremoniously slamming and locking the door behind him.

"You'd better wise up overnight, compadre," the guard warned through the closed door. "You'll be one unhappy sumbitch tomorrow if you don't."

Steve listened carefully as the guard walked down the hall and finally down the stairs. When he was sure the guard was gone, he nervously slipped over to the closet and confirmed that the clothing and boots were where he had left them. He returned to the bed and tried to relax while listening for the guards to retire for the evening. He figured they should be tired after traveling, and sluggish in the high mountain air they were not accustomed to. The sounds of their voices and a radio finally subsided a little after 10:00 p.m. Their body-clocks were probably on Central Time, so they should be getting tired. He made his way to the window and confirmed that the lights were dimmed or out downstairs. The three-quarter moon made it difficult to tell which.

Steve's heart thundered as he crept to the closet and put on the outdoor clothing and boots. He sprung the access-door latches and poked his head into the attic with his ears ringing and sweat already forming on his face. The attic was dark, with no light penetrating from downstairs or the outside. He let his eyes adjust and finally saw faint illumination from the ventilation plates on his end of the building. Switching on his flashlight, he cautiously began a painstakingly slow crawl amid the heat ducts and electric lines, trying to stay on rafters while praying they wouldn't creak under his weight.

Seventy-five feet and twenty minutes into his journey, he reached an obstruction where the heat ducts for the whole upstairs joined. Peering around the ductwork, he could see the end of the building where he calculated the garage to be. His knees hurt from crawling on the rafters and the exposed skin on his face, neck, and wrists was prickling from the loose insulation. The far wall was still another hundred feet away. As he struggled around the ducts and precariously balanced on rafters, the flashlight slipped from his perspiring hand and banged against a rafter before half burying itself in pink insulation. Blood was pounding so loudly in his ears that he couldn't tell if anyone had stirred beneath him or not. Which room was he over?

The sound of a man coughing, followed by footfalls, caused his heart to beat so violently he was sure it could be heard through the ceiling. Sweat ran freely off his forehead and into his burning eyes. After what seemed like an eternity, he heard a toilet flush followed again by the sound of footsteps and finally quiet. His thoughts turned to Shelley and the baby as he fought mounting panic. Was there even a way out of the attic at the far end of the building? Could he get out without being heard? Thoughts swirled in his head. He had to keep going. Twenty-five minutes later, with blood seeping through the knees of his pants, he found the reinforced plywood trapdoor under which he hoped was the garage.

He gently pulled the door up just a crack and listened for a reaction. Nothing. He pulled the door up farther and was rewarded with the smell of vehicles, gas, rubber, and oil. He quietly removed the trapdoor and swung down through the hole, his dangling feet gently probing the air for support. Finally, he felt a soft, cushioned surface and lowered his weight gingerly onto it. It turned out to be the seat of a snowmobile parked directly under the trapdoor. It took him less than a minute to locate an outside door and get through it. He quietly moved along the edge of the building, then toward the woods on what he judged to be a westerly heading. Once into the trees, he moved quickly away from the lodge. Fortunately, Global had created a network of trails on which their guests could comfortably hike, cross-country ski, or snowmobile. And fortunately it had not yet snowed so he wasn't leaving tracks.

He held the flashlight beam low as he trotted as fast as he dared into the night. The ground sloped slightly down to the west, and the silver moon provided just enough illumination to see profiles of the trees over his head. Still, it was much darker in the aromatic forest than it had been around the lodge. Branches slapped at his face and he twisted an ankle and fell twice before slowing his pace to a fast walk. He had seven hours before daylight and wanted to put as much distance behind him as he could. He settled into a rhythm of walking and resting while trying to stay on a westerly heading in the dark. At nearly two in the morning, the trail suddenly ended. Using the moon as his guide, he kept moving through the woods. At least the leaves were off the trees so he could see the outlines of tall pine trees in the moonlight and use them as landmarks while trying to move in a consistent direction. Rest breaks became more frequent as his energy waned in the rugged, undulating terrain.

The glimmer of light in the eastern sky confirmed he was headed west, and his spirits soared despite the mounting fatigue. As the first golden rays of sunlight peeked over the Rockies, he came upon a paved highway that appeared to run north-south. He jogged as fast as his exhausted legs would allow while vowing that they would have to kill him on the spot before they could control him again. He was not going back. He was going to find Shelley.

Steve was still limping along at little more than a slow walk when he heard the sound of a vehicle behind him. His knees and feet were on fire. His face was bleeding where branches had torn skin in the darkness. Blisters were shredded and bleeding on his heels from the new boots. A side-ache was close to crippling him. Tumbling awkwardly into the ditch, he painfully popped his head up and saw a white delivery truck round the corner toward him. After flagging the truck down, the exhausted engineer journeyed in luxurious comfort up Highway 65 toward Mesa, Colorado. The driver asked if he needed emergency medical help and seemed relieved when Steve told him he was only tired after being lost in the woods all night. He handed Steve some towels, a water bottle, his first-aid kit, and the quart bottle of fruit juice he had in the cab. He didn't push for more information as Steve cleaned and tended to his face and hands with water and rubbing alcohol.

— || —

JT's phone rang while he and Logan where preparing to walk out the door for the airport and their trip to Colorado on Tuesday morning. In fact, Logan was outside loading their bags into the car.

"JT, its Steve Addison. Sorry to bother you, but I need help."

"Addison, where the hell are you, boy? Are you all right? Speak to me."

"I'm all right, JT except that Global people are after me. I escaped last night but the sun's up now so I'm sure they're out looking for me. I called my house but Shelley didn't answer.I called Fletcher at the Edinburg yard and they said he was missing and that you were running the district. Do you know where Shelley is...or Fletcher?"

"There's too much to explain right now. Where are you? I'll come and get you wherever you are." JT was nearly yelling into the phone with excitement.

"I'm in a little town called Mesa. It's in Colorado. Global kidnapped me and flew me out here to their lodge. They took my wallet and credit cards but I have some cash in my pocket that they didn't take. I have to get to Shelley."

"What's the nearest airport and how far are you from it?"

"The closest that I know of is Grand Junction. I think I'm about thirty miles away."

"You get your ass over there but stay out of sight and away from the passenger terminal. Don't call the police whatever you do." Thinking quickly about the distance, JT continued, "It'll take me about four hours to get there so use the time to get to the airport. Find the FBO but don't go in. That's the private fixed-base operator not the public terminal building. You'll hear my jet. There shouldn't be many small jets coming or going so we'll be easy to spot. The tail number on my Falcon is N-090ST. Got that? I'll taxi to the FBO. You get to the plane when you see us stop. Don't screw around with anything or anybody. Just get your ass to the plane when we pull up to the building. Got it?"

"Yeah, I think so. What was that number again?" he asked with more confidence than he felt.

"90ST on the tail."

"I'll be watching for you. Please hurry, JT. They're going to kill me if they find me."

"Addison, Steve just called," JT yelled to Logan. "You were right about Colorado. He got away and will be at the Grand Junction airport when we get there. He confirmed it was hostile and needs our help right damned now. Let's grab some weapons and get to the plane.

JT quickly dialed Branton Cole's direct line.

"What is it, Taylor?" Cole barked.

"I just got a call from Steve Addison. He got away from Global and I'm going to pick him up before they find him again. I just wanted you to know that I'll be gone for a couple of days...and why."

"Where is he?" Cole demanded.

"That's not important right now because Addison and I are going to get him and we don't need help. There's nothing you can do except hope we can get to him before the Global people grab him again."

"Bullshit. Tell me where he is and I'll send a team."

"Your team already scared the hell out of the kid and, to be honest, he wouldn't trust any Westcona corporate people now. We'll take care of it," JT said boldly.

"Goddammit, then you pick him up and bring him straight to me. Call as soon as you can. You understand?"

"I'll call when we have him," JT agreed, although he was instantly uneasy with the thought of bringing Steve to Dallas.

The Falcon blasted into the south Texas sky. JT swung her to a three-hundred-thirty-degree heading and began working through their problem with Logan.

"How long will we be in the air?" Logan asked.

"Depends on the headwinds. Let's see…it's just shy of a thousand air miles so we'll be in the air for about two and half hours. Steve should be at the airport by then. If it all works out, we can grab him and get the hell out of there before Global figures it out. Now we just have to decide what we're going to do with him."

— || —

Steve didn't know what to do next. He was hungry, dirty, and unshaven. First things first, he thought. He found a small diner where he ordered food before finding the restroom. He cleaned up as best he could. As he ate, he couldn't help but overhear the banter between the owner and a beer deliveryman who was wrestling keg and bottle beer into the restaurant. Their discussion turned to the man's route, and he perked up when the man said his next delivery was in Grand Junction. He asked the deliveryman if he could hitch a ride, even offering to pay him for his trouble. The man looked him over, noticing the good haircut and clean hands. Though Steve looked pretty ragged and worn-out, he sure didn't look dangerous. The beer truck pulled off I-70 onto the Horizon Drive exit one hour later and roared back up onto I-70 as soon as Steve had dismounted and slammed the door.

With at least an hour to kill, he bought a nearly inedible ham sandwich at a convenience store before walking north to Walker Field, suffering through the sandwich and drinking a Coke as he plodded painfully along. He couldn't seem to get enough food into him, especially meat. He found an unobtrusive bench that provided a good view of the runways but was shielded from vehicle traffic. He could see the FBO just to his right. An hour and twenty minutes later, he heard the sounds of a jet approaching the field. A white Falcon 20 with N-090ST stenciled on her tail floated down out of the sky and taxied to the small building. Steve quickly limped to the waist-high fence and hesitated for two confused seconds before painfully vaulting over it in side-saddle fashion and falling down when his legs collapsed under him on the other side. The hatch was open and his father was waving frantically for him to come to the plane. He staggered up, awkwardly hobbled to the Falcon, and crashed through the already moving hatchway. Logan pulled him in and secured the hatch while the little Falcon rumbled to the runway.

"I thought you were helping Global...and you're not!" Steve said excitedly. He was relieved and thrilled to see Logan.

"No, I'm helping you and that's all that's important," Logan said as he crushed Steve in a bear hug.

"I've got so many questions and so much to tell you. Where's Shelley? I couldn't get her on the phone this morning."

Logan looked at Steve and paused. He tried to speak but his voice failed him. When he began to cry, Steve did too without knowing why.

"They murdered her, Steve. The baby, too," he blurted in anguish.

"No!" Steve shouted. "No, that can't be, Dad. Dad...She's hurt right? In the hospital but they'll be all right...right?" he pleaded.

One more look into his father's tormented eyes drove the horrible news home. Shock so overcame him that he vomited and then nearly passed out from the violent dry-retching and panic. An overwhelming heaviness pressed down on his head and shoulders so powerfully that he doubled over. He choked and fought for breath. Then a primal wail erupted from deep in his soul and drowned out the whine of the twin Garrett TFE731 turbofan engines that thrust them through the sky toward Denver Stapleton Airport. Logan gently pulled Steve up and held his grown son in his arms while they both sobbed inconsolably.

— ‖ — Seventeen — ‖ —

THE JOINT WESTCONA-GLOBAL SECURITY TEAM deftly
made its way on foot through the Iowa State University
campus toward the Ames laboratory buildings. A driver
remained with each vehicle and was in radio contact for possible quick extractions. The vehicles could easily enter the
campus through the athletic field area and go overland rather
than following the paved streets that were guarded by the university police. Darkness was both a blessing and a hindrance as
they watched for signage indicating laboratory or lodging
buildings. They were careful to avoid vehicle and pedestrian
traffic. Students were still actively moving about, and twice the
team ducked behind buildings or shrubbery when university
police cars drove slowly through the area.

At last, student traffic disappeared and they realized they
were into the Ames Laboratory portion of the campus. With little difficulty, they located the brightly lit lab among the mostly
darkened buildings. University police officers were sitting in
vehicles at the front entrance and in the parking lot behind
and across the service road from the building. Dutch Peltier
quietly slipped into the field behind the lab and peered into the
windows hoping to see a familiar face from south Texas, but

recognized no one. He slipped back to the Global team leader and described the activity in the building.

After a brief discussion, they decided this was probably where the scientists were working on Neptune. They scanned the adjacent buildings and parking lots, seeing nothing to indicate where Boyd and Cade might be. However, the security attention being paid to the building across the service road to the rear of the lab troubled them. Were the guards only watching the rear of the lab building from afar? No, it was too dark for effective surveillance from way over there. Something wasn't right. They adjusted their plan, splitting forces to cover the lab and the building behind it.

At exactly 2:00 a.m., posing as DOE security men, the two team leaders approached the security detail guarding the front of the lab building. Dutch calmly asked the men sitting in the car if this was where they were supposed to be to help guard the people working on the new discovery. The driver opened the door and climbed out of his squad car as he acknowledged the question. He was out cold and on the ground before he knew what happened. His partner was no match for the Global team leader and was knocked out and handcuffed before he could defend himself.

— ‖ —

Hollis wasn't sure what awakened him; the gunshot or the handheld radio crackling to life on his bedside table. He answered Fletcher, threw the radio onto the bed, and was quickly dressing when he heard the window onto the fire escape open from Fletcher's room. More shots reverberated off the rear of the building as he poked his head out to see what Fletcher was doing.

One of the university squad cars under their fire escape started toward the lab. The remaining guesthouse guards were already out of their vehicle and turning to challenge some men coming around the back of the building. Shots rang out and Hollis saw both guards go down. He was trying to see how many marauders there were when Fletcher engaged the shooters with his Combat Commander from the fire escape. One bad guy went down but others returned Fletcher's fire. Hollis ducked back into his room as bullets chipped brick off the outside wall between their rooms. He had fantasized about close combat and now was feeling the adrenalin rush and confusion that came with it.

Hollis opened his door just as Fletcher's flew open and they were both into the hallway and running toward the nearest stairway at the northeast corner of the building within seconds of each other. Hollis jerked the door open and was just starting through when the ground-floor door opened and a man clad in black pointed a handgun up the stairway. Hollis fired instinctively and the man went down in a heap. A second man jumped into the stairway and Hollis sent another two-hundred-thirty-grain bullet in response. The second man collapsed on top of the first. No one else appeared as Hollis peeked around the corner into the stairway. He yelled for Fletcher to watch the other stairway but it wasn't necessary.

Fletcher darted past the stairway door, threw open the window at the far end of the hall, and leaped into the big oak tree. He had just caught his balance and shimmied down a few feet when an unfamiliar face appeared in the open window. The man momentarily stared and then started to yell as Fletcher drew and pumped two shots toward him. The man disappeared as Fletcher dropped through the tree limbs as fast as he could without losing his weapon.

He hit the ground hard, stumbling and falling on his backside before looking up to the second-story window. A man re-appeared but ducked out of the way when Fletcher raised his gun to fire. Back on his feet and moving fast, he rounded the front corner of the building just as Hollis burst loudly through the ground floor fire escape door on the other end. Two combatants near the front steps in the center of the building turned at the sound to fire at Hollis. Fletcher double-tapped, knocking one down before his empty weapon locked open.

Suddenly time went into slow motion for Fletcher. He had been keenly aware of all actions taking place around him, but now his vision dramatically narrowed to the antagonist with the gun as his right thumb pressed the magazine release and the empty magazine fell free under its own weight. The man, startled by his partner's collapse, looked over his left shoulder to see Fletcher in the modest light thrown by the street lamps and a building porch light. He began spinning toward Fletcher, still in agonizingly slow motion, bringing his weapon to bear. Fletcher's left hand had already snatched a spare magazine from the carrier on his left hip and was now sliding it up under the gun toward the flared magazine well. He felt the magazine seat in his gun and his left thumb depress the slide release.

The Colts front sight had never left the man during this combat reload and Fletcher smoothly caressed the trigger three times in rapid succession. The gun bucked but he didn't hear the reports. The man crumpled in a heap just a microsecond after he had fired a shot at Fletcher, blowing more brick off the front of the building near his knee. With time, sight, and hearing perception returning to normal, Fletcher forced himself to scan the area for other immediate threats. Seeing none, he turned and ran west down the street away from Hollis and toward the maintenance yard where they had parked the Oldsmobile.

Hollis saw the second man go down under Fletcher's fire just before a squad car and a Chevy Suburban screeched to a stop in front of the building between him and Fletcher's last position. Bullets had ricocheted off the brick building as they whined past, and he assumed they were Fletcher's shots. They were far too close and too personal. More gunfire erupted, matching the intense firefight taking place behind him in the direction of the lab. Hollis ran south down the side of the building toward the lab and into the parking lot under his room. There were five bodies lying on the asphalt.

Suddenly, the deep "whuuuuuump" of a concussive explosion in the lab almost knocked him to his knees, the pressure wave causing pain in his eyes, ears, and chest. Glass rained down as yellow-blue flames shot from the back windows of the lab and men screamed in the inferno.

Shielding his eyes from the falling glass and debris, Hollis jumped into the cab of one of the two-and-a-half-ton trucks parked near the building, hoping it was a former military vehicle that didn't require a key. He flipped the ignition switch on the dash and slammed his foot onto the starter. The old diesel roared to life with a belch of black smoke. He jammed the truck into gear and stood on the accelerator. The old deuce jumped forward as he wrestled it to the left onto the grass along the side of the guesthouse building. Moving fast and without lights, he approached the sidewalk and street fronting the building, wrenching the wheel hard again before crashing down the curb and into the street heading straight toward the squad car and Suburban.

Someone foolishly jumped into his path from behind the Suburban and took a quick shot at him. There was a bright flash, the ping of metal on metal, and then the soft stutter of the big truck's crushing impact on a human body. He roared down the street shifting gears as best he could and veered into the maintenance yard. The truck narrowly missed a big snowplow but caught the edge of the sand pile with its right tires. For a moment he thought the old beast was going to roll but it came to a rapid halt when the engine lugged and died. Hollis dismounted and bolted around the sand pile to find Fletcher starting the Oldsmobile and waving him into the front seat.

"We've got Neptune, right?" was all he could muster as he slammed the door and Fletcher hit the gas in apparent affirmation.

The white Oldsmobile rocketed down 13th Street, onto the I-35 freeway entrance, and accelerated north while Hollis sat in numbed silence. Fighting to light a cigarette, he had to give up when he realized his fine motor skills were not responding. He felt positively giddy, yet sick at the same time...and didn't know why. He looked at Fletcher and saw a sheen of sweat over a look of anger and fear.

— || —

JT, Logan, and Steve made their way to a local hotel after landing and securing the Falcon at Stapleton International Airport. The people at JetCare Flight Support had been kind enough to arrange a rental car and suggest a hotel before servicing the jet. Logan rented a two-bedroom suite so he could keep an eye on Steve and be there for him if he was needed.

They met in the hotel restaurant an hour later. One of Logan's spare shirts was tight on Steve's larger frame but he didn't seem to notice or care. He was clearly numb with grief and in need of his father's company. Logan had mostly recovered his composure but his emotions were raw. While quietly relating the events since his abduction and asking questions about Shelley and the baby, Steve could only pick at his dinner. He was obviously in a state of shock, appearing alert one moment and then confused and muddled the next. Logan's heart was broken at seeing his son in such anguish.

"We have to decide what to do with you until this mess is resolved," Logan told his befuddled son. "Keeping you away from Global will be our first priority, and Westcona's ordered JT to bring you to Dallas. We're not leaning in that direction right now but that's where it stands."

"Do you know where Fletcher is?" Steve asked his father.

"No, but we do know that both companies are after him and your friend Hollis. Last we heard they were trying to figure out where you were."

"He mentioned they were in my old neck of the woods," JT said, "which we took to mean Oklahoma, but we're not sure. We've talked to him since but he wouldn't say where they were because he figured my phone was bugged or just didn't trust us completely."

"They'll be trying to sell Neptune, wherever they are," the young engineer said through an awkward yawn and jerky eye movements as he finished his coffee. He hadn't slept in the past thirty-six hours and now the physical strain, terror, horror, and queasy stomach were causing him more distress than his body could tolerate.

"I need to be alone. You two figure out what to do. I can't think straight...and I don't care."

Under crushing emotional anguish, the young man suddenly stood and reeled out of the restaurant toward the restroom off the hallway.

Logan stood to follow but JT's hand on his arm held him back. "Leave him be, Logan. He has to fight this by himself."

The older men retired to the lounge where JT explained an idea that had been floating around in his head. They agreed that bringing Steve back to Dallas was out of the question. Logan was already effectively out of Global Oil, but JT was still actively part of the Westcona family, at least for now. They worked through a plan that made sense and allowed JT to return to Westcona while Logan stayed with his grieving son. Steve needed his father's companionship while he worked through the trauma of losing his family. There was no time for foolish or emotional actions that could further jeopardize their safety. As cold and harsh as it sounded, nothing was going to bring Shelley and the baby back, but Neptune was still going to change the world. It was simply too important an issue to walk away from despite the Addison's horrible personal tragedy. They discussed going home and leaving the Neptune issue to Fletcher but concluded that Steve would be involuntarily drawn into it no matter what they did. He was in no condition to make that decision but they agreed that continuing in their attempt to locate Fletcher was the least traumatic for him right now. At least they could protect him during the process. They called it a night and returned to their rooms with plans to meet at eight the next morning for breakfast.

As soon as he returned to his room, JT telephoned the nearby Westcona district office located in Brighton. The Denver-Julesburg basin was rich in oil and gas, and all the major domestic exploration, production, and service companies had a presence in the market. The service companies were all located within a mile of each other in Brighton, while most of the exploration and production company offices were located a short thirty minutes away in downtown Denver.

He informed the dispatcher that he was a personal friend of the Westcona district manager, Jeff Neumann, and that he had just arrived in town but had forgotten to bring Jeff's home telephone number. He asked that the dispatcher call Neumann and tell him to call the hotel that evening. His phone rang five minutes later.

"Neumann, you old bastard. Thanks for returning the call," JT said with more warmth than he felt. "I'm in a bind and need the kind of help only a fighter pilot can provide."

"Well, hello to you too, JT," the former naval aviator said. "I'm fine and thanks for asking. It's ten o'clock at night. This can't wait till morning?"

"This isn't exactly Westcona business, Neumann, although in some ways it is. I'm in the middle of a serious shit-storm here, and people have already died in it."

"You're serious?"

"Dead serious but it's more than I can explain over the phone. I need help."

"I'll be there in forty-five minutes, JT."

Jeff Neumann was a talented petroleum engineer and Westcona district manager of eight years. Prior to Westcona he had served in the United States Navy flying carrier-based A-6 Intruders over Vietnam. At six feet two inches, he was just about as tall as the Navy allowed in flight training, even during wartime. A lanky, handsome man with close-cropped red hair and a neatly trimmed mustache, Jeff had a barely controlled action-junkie personality that kept him on the edge of trouble in civilian life. However, his technical education and normally disciplined work environment allowed him to focus and avoid most of the serious trouble many former combat pilots managed to get into after discharge from the military. That did not mean his emotional turbulence was completely or adequately vented.

A post-military marriage had quickly ended in divorce without children. The forty-year-old now lived alone in a quiet Longmont subdivision. Many of his neighbors were IBM employees with technical educations and outdoor adventure lifestyles that fit Jeff just fine. Longmont was close to terrific ski areas, Rocky Mountain National Park, and amazing outdoor recreational opportunities. Still, he frequently craved the jolt of adrenalin he learned to enjoy while flying. His was a healthy, active lifestyle but still lacked the intensity he craved when the dogs of war ran through his haunted dreams.

Jeff had worked in the Mid-Continent Region when JT was the region manager. Neumann had impressed the old warhorse despite being a college boy. This college boy was an engineer and could fly jets in combat. JT admired those skills and liked Neumann's outwardly humble attitude about his military accomplishments even if it was mostly an act. After Neumann's promotion to a district manager position, he had also helped JT with the newly purchased Falcon 20 in Oklahoma City.

Jeff retained current ratings in both piston and jet aircraft, and had enjoyed demonstrating his considerable skills as a jet jock. Once they had the Falcon restored, he'd flown right seat many times showing JT how a jet could be made to do things they didn't teach in civilian flight schools. Neumann had been transferred to Westcona's Rocky Mountain Division as part of the corporate shakeup that sent JT to Alice.

True to his word, Neumann arrived within forty-five minutes. JT laid out the events that had brought him to Denver and explained the Neptune concept. Neumann was nearly struck speechless by the story, but had a heavy dose of obvious skepticism visible on his face.

"This is that super-trainee you tried so hard to run off from Lindsay in '82?"

"The same, but I was wrong about him, Neumann. Boyd's one of us even if he is a little hard to take sometimes. His partner, Hollis Cade, is just as stout. In fact, Cade worked the flight deck on a couple of carriers about the time you were flying. He might have been one of the cat-crew guys who sent you off to work every day. Anyway, they came up with Neptune, along with a scared kid engineer we've got stashed here in a room across the hall. What the hell would you be doing if you were in their place?"

"I'd have to think about it but I guess I'd be doing something big with it. I'm having a real hard time believing this is on the level. I know a little something about chemistry and this just doesn't make any sense."

"No it doesn't, but it sure as hell runs engines. I've seen it. And both Westcona and Global want it so bad they've gone postal before they even know if it really works. That's what's hardest for me to understand."

"Well, at least for now, I want to be part of it but I need to talk some chemistry with the kid. And this Cade guy; wasn't he a service supervisor in Lindsay?"

"That's him. He's a great big bastard. Calm exterior but I wouldn't want him upset with me in a dark alley. We need you to do some flying, Neumann. Maybe even with some combat thrown in if things don't change pretty damn quickly."

— ‖ —

Branton Cole was awakened by the ringing telephone an hour before his usual 5:00 a.m. call from the Westcona security office. He broke into a sweat as he listened to his security chief describe what little was known about the Ames debacle.

"We should expect federal law enforcement to arrive in the next few hours," the chief explained.

It wouldn't take long to identify the dead men as Westcona's, and then the trouble would really begin. They discussed immediate options before Cole hung up and headed for the shower. He called Westcona's corporate counsel and his own private attorney before dressing and heading for the security limousine now idling in his driveway. The Westcona board of directors was being notified of the impending legal nightmare while Cole stared out the tinted windows as the limo made its way through the dark Dallas streets.

— ‖ — Eighteen — ‖ —

FLETCHER HAD THE CRUISE CONTROL set at seventy as they chewed up northbound miles on I-35. The light, middle-of-the-night traffic consisted mostly of big rigs moving toward the Minnesota border. He tucked into a convoy of four fast-moving trucks and adjusted the cruise control to stay hidden among them. It should take the authorities some time to sort through the Ames carnage, and even longer for someone to miss them. He wanted to get into the Minneapolis sprawl before anyone thought seriously about where they might be. Hollis tuned the radio for any breaking news reports but northern Iowa had few all-night stations on the air. So far, their situation had generated only local south Texas news coverage of Shelley's death...and that had not yet been tied to Neptune. Soon the world would start asking questions and possibly put events in perspective. They blew past the Clear Lake exit at 3:30 a.m.

"I've never asked you about Vietnam before, but now seems the right time," Hollis said. "You ever really been in a firefight or kill anyone yourself...before tonight?"

Fletcher was quiet for a few moments as he considered how to respond. He'd never shared much of his military experience with anyone, although it was quite tame when

compared to what many had endured. Mostly it was not
wanting to relive the horror of close combat. The sights,
sounds, smells, and fears weren't what he'd expected, and
finding the words to adequately convey the emotional roller-
coaster of combat was nearly impossible. Then there was what
the experience did to your heart, and how it darkened your
reflection in a mirror, and how you felt when you saw yourself
in a picture with your kids and knew you didn't want them to
know what you'd done. Still, the ribbons Fletcher wore on
his Class A uniform when he came home conveyed ample
evidence of his ruthless competence under fire. He had simply
buried the experience and gotten on with his life, and only his
dreams sometimes betrayed him.

"I have," he answered quietly.

"But I thought you were a Finance Officer."

It was the standard question Fletcher always half expected,
one he knew Hollis deserved an answer to now that his continued safety was at least partially in Fletcher's hands.

"I was. I was assigned to the Finance Company of the 4th
Infantry Division and sent to Vietnam in late '68. The division
deployed in 1966 and I was just another new guy replacing
someone rotating back to the world," Fletcher said.

"So how'd you get into combat?"

"Well, the division was based at Camp Holloway in Pleiku
and operated mostly along the Cambodian border in the
Central Highlands where there was a lot of heavy action.
The Army was naturally worried about morale and always did
its best to recover American bodies, deliver the mail from
home, and make sure people got paid. My unit delivered
payrolls each month and sometimes got caught in bad
situations. Get shot at enough and even Finance people shoot
back. The Viet Cong knew we were making payroll runs, and

the little pricks thought it was great sport disrupting us so our guys didn't get paid on time."

"So you saw some bad stuff and shot back?"

"Affirmative."

Hollis was apparently satisfied with what he heard because he shifted to their current problems.

"Those guys we shot were after us, weren't they?" he asked Fletcher.

"That was my impression. They convinced me when they took out the guards behind our building without warning. When I opened up on them from the window they returned fire pretty damn quick."

"Yeah, I noticed that when some of it got close to me. What if we shot the wrong guys? Could they have been anything other than bad guys?"

"No. They shot those guards without giving them a chance. They obviously wanted us and I'm not sure they cared if we were alive when it was over."

"How'd they think they could get Neptune if we were dead?"

"Either Steve already gave it to them or they thought they could find my briefcase. Maybe both. I'm not sure."

"You think the cops will be after us for murder now?"

"I doubt the local cops will know what to think when they try to reconstruct that mess. Nobody knew we were armed so maybe they'll think we got lucky and ran away in the confusion."

"That part's true anyway. My guts are in a knot," Hollis confided.

"Mine, too. Just try not to think about it."

They rode along in silence.

"We need to get into Minneapolis so we don't stand out on this freeway. Who knows how long it will take for them to start looking for this car. We also need to get rid of the Texas plates or dump the car and steal something else to drive," Fletcher said.

"I've never stolen anything in my life," Hollis said. "How about we just try to find a white Olds like this one and get the plates off it? If we dump this car, some cop will run the plates or vehicle identification number within a day or so."

"You're right. We shouldn't dump the car. JT offered us his cabin in northern Minnesota. Said it was a really rural area. I can't think of a better place to go, can you?"

"I don't know, but we're sure getting a long way off the beaten path. We still need to figure out what to do with Neptune, and there sure as shit isn't anybody up there we could sell it to. It might be best to hide out in a big city where we wouldn't stand out so much. Let's think about that for a bit before we make up our minds."

The miles stacked up behind them as they sorted through all the dangers that might lie ahead.

"How do you think Global or Westcona found us so fast? That seems pretty damn odd to me."

"It is," Fletcher agreed. "Somebody at Ames or in Washington must have dimed us out. That's all I can think of. We'll be getting into the Minneapolis area in an hour and a half, but it'll only be about five-thirty if we keep moving this fast. How about some breakfast at a truck stop once we get up closer to town?"

"I haven't been thinking about food, but I reckon I could stand something. We're going to need to do some shopping, too. I left my toothbrush and extra underwear in Ames and I could use that underwear about now."

— || —

JT turned the television on as he passed it on his way to the shower. It was only five-thirty in Denver but the network and cable news channels were already covering some kind of fire at the Iowa State University campus in Ames. The Des Moines ABC affiliate station, WOI-TV, had a reporter on scene who was describing an overnight explosion and fire that had caused the death of a group of research scientists working at the federal government's Ames Laboratory facility. Details were sketchy but there were also reports of bodies outside the building and across the street from the explosion site. Authorities were not commenting on the cause of the explosion but a news conference was scheduled for 7 a.m. Central time. JT plugged in the coffee maker and continued on to the shower.

— || —

Logan, already showered and dressed, was enjoying his first cup of coffee when he turned on his television a few minutes after 6:00 a.m. A news conference was taking place in Iowa that did not interest him so he switched the channel but found it on that channel, too. Reporters described an Iowa State University campus fire and explosion, and then interviewed federal agents wearing FBI and ATF windbreakers. The agents explained that a group of scientists had been killed in an explosion that had taken place about 2:00 a.m., Central time. Bodies were also found outside, but positive identification of the deceased had not yet been made because some of the victims were not carrying identification. The bodies of the scientists were burned beyond recognition. The FBI representative assured the reporters that fingerprints had already been faxed to FBI headquarters in Washington, and they hoped to identify the victims found outside the buildings shortly.

Logan wondered what government scientists were doing working in the middle of the night. He turned down the volume and retrieved the *Denver Post* lying outside his door. He was scanning through the newspaper and enjoying the early morning quiet when his pager went off. The callback number was vaguely familiar; a Houston number followed by 911. He dialed the number thinking this was the call from his boss to threaten or fire him. They must be guessing he had Steve. The phone in Houston began ringing and he let out a sigh of relief when he recognized his secretary's voice. The number was for her home phone; he had it in his organizer but had never called her there.

"Logan, I just got a call from the office telling me to stay home today. No explanation, no nothing. Just take the day off and come back in next week they said. I had no more than hung up when my friend who works in the security department called. She said there are FBI agents all over the executive floor, and the word is that some of our security people were shot and killed last night up in Iowa! What the hell's going on, Logan?"

It didn't take a second for Logan to tie the breaking news in Ames to his secretary's startling revelation. "I'm not directly involved, Linda, but I think I know something about what's happening. Do what they told you but check in again with your friend if you get a chance. I'm traveling today but I'll call you over the weekend or early next week. From now on, I suggest you not mention to anyone at the office that we've talked. I'll explain when I get back. In the meantime, I'll check in with you at home rather than the office if that's all right with you. I'm going to be out of pager range for most of the next couple of days."

JT knocked on Logan's door a few minutes later.

"I tried your phone but it was busy. Have you seen the news? They just interviewed an Ames policeman who said someone using a Global Oil-issued American Express card rented a Suburban found at the scene. I think we know where Boyd and Cade are."

Logan relayed what his secretary had just told him. "Our boys could be dead," he said, "and that would leave Steve as the only person who can re-create Neptune unless the cops found notes or the formula.

JT stood and stared at him, unable to respond.

"Did you reach your friend last night?" Logan asked.

"Yeah. He'll be here for breakfast. Let's order from room service so we can watch the TV coverage."

Breakfast and Jeff Neumann arrived at eight. Steve came out of his bedroom when Logan finally pounded on his door and told him to get up for something to eat. After making the introductions, the men ate in silence while they watched the unfolding story:

Unconfirmed reports now identify eight of the men found outside the explosion site as employees of Westcona Services Incorporated of Dallas, Texas, and Global Oil of Houston. The men are described as employees of their respective companies' security departments. Five members of the Iowa State University Police Department were also killed, apparently shot to death. Two additional University policemen were found beaten and handcuffed near their vehicle but otherwise unhurt. Ames Laboratory officials are still trying to identify the scientists killed in an explosion and ensuing fire that completely destroyed the building in which they were working. Initial estimates put their number at six. In a bizarre twist to an already outlandish story, Global and Westcona security personnel appear to have been attempting some kind of an industrial espionage mission against Ames Laboratory, the federal energy research

facility here at Iowa State University. That effort went horribly awry. FBI and ATF officials are interviewing senior leaders at both company headquarters this morning in an attempt to uncover a motive for this unbelievable event on this quiet college campus in America's heartland.

"No mention of Fletcher or Hollis," Steve said. Wouldn't they have identified them if they were there?"

"You'd think so, unless they were in the lab with the scientists," Logan said.

They continued watching the coverage.

"If they were found outside, they would have been carrying their wallets…so they should have been identified," JT said. "The FBI may not know about Neptune yet, or at least they're not letting on if they do. They may have Boyd and Cade in custody, or the boys may have gotten away."

Jeff Neumann was beside himself with excitement and wanted to get this Friday morning underway. Now he was convinced that Neptune existed but still took Steve aside and had a quick chemistry discussion. He felt sorry for the kid but continued to grill him with questions.

"We're still going, right, JT?" Neumann said after talking to Steve.

"Yeah, we're sure as hell going. Have you got the Baron reserved?"

"Yep, no problem," Neumann said. "I'll take you all to the cabin and spend the night there. Another club member has the Baron reserved for Sunday, so you and I will be back to Denver tomorrow afternoon and me back to work on Monday morning with no one the wiser."

"Okay, let's get out to the airport," JT said. He caught Logan's eye as Steve walked out the door. "Is he ?"

"Not even close but he seems to be holding it together for the moment. I'll keep close tabs on him. Why aren't we just going to Minnesota in the Falcon, and why do we need Neumann today?"

"Well, for a number of reasons. I don't want anyone to be able to track my plane into Minnesota. Now that the feds are involved, who knows what kind of assets may get thrown into tracking us down if Cole tells them what we're up to. If we don't leave a trail, they won't be able to establish that we made the trip now or when this is all over. Besides, we now have a perfect alibi to prove we only went to Colorado to rescue your son from the evil clutches of Global Oil. That may come in handy when we're in court, which I have no doubt we will be. We also may need Neumann in the future, and I want him to know where the cabin is and how to get out there. Nobody will think to be watching him."

— || —

The Front Range Flying Association's Beechcraft Baron 55B seated six without a lot of extra cabin space. Jeff Neumann belonged to the association and regularly flew a number of their planes. The twin-engine Baron was one of his favorite piston-engine planes, although he didn't often fly it because it was more plane and expense than he needed when he was alone. It was, however, perfect for this mission. With JT in the right seat, Jeff smoothly accelerated down the runway and lifted effortlessly into the thin Colorado air. Seven hundred air miles and three hours and forty-five minutes later, he gently landed the Baron at Thief River Falls Regional Airport in northwest Minnesota.

After renting a car, they checked into the Best Western that was only three miles up the highway from the airport and across from the Arctic Cat snowmobile factory and company head-quarters on the outskirts of town. Arctic Enterprises had stunned the city and snowmobile industry by filing for bankruptcy in 1981 when it closed its facilities and stopped building snowmobiles. The economic impact on the community had been devastating, but the brand name was now making a slow comeback under new ownership and management.

They decided to eat at Lon's, a nearby restaurant recommended by the FBO employee as the nicest in town. The guy was right; it was a nice restaurant with good food. After dinner, they settled in the nearly deserted hotel bar to watch the large TV. A local working girl named Lola was trying to peddle comfort, but no one showed any interest. The TV was tuned to the cable channel carrying the ABC network feed out of Winnipeg in Manitoba, Canada. The Best Western had been hurt the most when Arctic folded, having been built primarily to handle the corporate travelers visiting the plant and headquarters from around the world. Now it was very quiet, and three of the four oilmen attempted to relax on this autumn evening.

Jeff was keyed for action. Steve was silent and disoriented but holding his emotions in check as they watched the news clips from Ames. Nothing about Fletcher, Hollis, or Neptune; just endless speculation as to why two U.S. companies had unleashed their security forces against a federal energy research facility, causing nineteen deaths and destroying a building in the process. The public was incensed and many congressmen were already calling for self-serving investigations. The story quickly spread around the globe when the international press picked it up.

Within a very short time, Jeff moved to the bar to talk to Lola while the others headed for their rooms for some much needed sleep.

— || —

Fletcher and Hollis found a white Oldsmobile Delta 88 like Fletcher's in the Minneapolis Saint Paul International Airport long-term parking lot where Hollis removed the rear plate while Fletcher worked on the front. Fletcher crabbed over to the next car, removed its front plate, slid it under the car to Hollis, and told him to put it on the back of the Olds so the owner wouldn't notice a missing plate when he put his luggage in the trunk. Hollis dropped the plate in his hand as he reached to pick up the plate Fletcher had slid to him when a car rounded a corner and drove toward him. Shielding the two plates with his feet, he stood and pretended to be opening the trunk as the car rolled passed, and then quickly knelt back down and attached a plate to the Oldsmobile. Within minutes they were back on west-bound I-494.

They exited at the Minnetonka ramp where they quickly made the plate change on their car before jumping back on the freeway. Once out of the urban sprawl, Hollis turned on the radio and heard the news about Ames. They were shocked to hear that nineteen people were dead but not surprised that some had been tied to Westcona and Global. They were hugely relieved to learn that no federal agents had been involved and sickened that so many innocents had been murdered by the two companies. It was some consolation that they had not killed anyone that was not willing to kill them first. Their decision to head for JT's cabin was clearly the right one now that they knew the law would be looking for them in short order, if it wasn't already.

When they arrived in St. Cloud, they immediately found a phone booth and called the Cade ranch in Texas. Fletcher talked to Katie and assured her they were safe. Then he listened for a full minute before just handing the phone to Hollis and walking back to the car. Hollis rejoined him a few minutes later.

"Was Katie as upset as Sara?" Hollis asked as he put on his seatbelt.

"More, I expect. She was pretty much out of control and wants us to turn ourselves in right now. She's convinced we're going to get ourselves killed and doesn't give damn about Neptune."

"I got a toned down version of the same suggestion," Hollis said. "They're scared more than mad."

"Well, that makes four us." Fletcher said. "Do you want to go to the police while we're here in town?"

"I've been thinking 'bout that all day. No, I reckon we'd be in so much trouble we'd never get out of it. Let's keep on going."

Fletcher sighed in relief and hoped their decision was the right one. Part of him agreed with the wives and part of him didn't. After lunch and a stop at two stores, they had all the gear they'd need for a short stay in the woods of northern Minnesota.

Four hours later, Thief River Falls appeared on the horizon. It had already been a long day as they pulled into the hotel parking lot. They were exhausted. Each had slept a little in the car but neither had enjoyed a real bed for more than a few of the past thirty-six hours. Hollis wanted Mexican food for dinner and expected the desk clerk to laugh when he asked about it.

"It's yer lucky day if ya don't mind a little drive. Just go out past the airport on Highway 32 about eight miles or so. The St. Hilaire Liquor Store has Mexican food every Friday. And it's pretty darn good, too, ya know."

The men found St. Hilaire and the liquor store where they had a fine northern Minnesota version of Mexican food and a cold beer or two. The liquor store was really a small two-room restaurant/bar. One room housed the actual bar and some booths while the smaller room sported a jukebox, a few tables, and a little more privacy. You could buy a bottle to go if you could catch the bartender's attention. The little restaurant was hopping on an early Friday evening and the men loosened up for the first time in many days. The place had a comfortable feel to it and the natives appeared friendly, although Fletcher and Hollis stuck to themselves. After a hearty dinner, they drove back to the Best Western in Thief River Falls and quickly fell asleep. It had been a long and difficult day.

— || —

News of the Ames shootout spread to the international oil industry throughout Friday night and Saturday morning. The security departments within the international oil community were tight knit, many having known each other for years. Aramco, though now owned completely by the Saudi Arabian government, still employed hundreds of American security experts who had worked for the company since the original Standard Oil, Chevron, Texaco, Global Oil, and Mobil Oil participants controlled it. In fact, many of the senior security officials were former employees of these giant energy companies and, as such, retained a certain camaraderie with the U.S. energy industry and their associates within it. Many counted members of Global Oil's security department as friends.

The news that Global and Westcona security men were killed in Ames was so bizarre that the evening security watches around the Middle East and Africa soon had their telephones, faxes, computers, and high frequency radio nets humming with discussions and theories. Those with shortwave radio or satellite TV coverage at their offices or offshore drilling rigs began feeding breaking information locally via telephone and VHF radio to those who didn't. There might be a nine-hour time difference between Iowa and Saudi Arabia but, with world-wide communications and businesses that operate twenty-four hours a day, they didn't miss a beat with this kind of news. The industry gossip mill was cranking at full speed.

OPEC member-nation intelligence services began to notice the industry chatter and tuned to TV feeds from North America and Europe for more information. Before daybreak in the Middle East, questions were being asked of embassy staffs in Washington, DC, through secure communication links. What had Global and Westcona been after at Ames Laboratory?

— ‖ — Nineteen — ‖ —

BY NOON ON FRIDAY, THE FBI had interviewed Dr. Edwards and Barbara Rowley. Senior DOE officials also met with Justice Department lawyers in Washington that afternoon where they pieced together the Neptune story, along with the evidence they had of Westcona and Global participation in the botched raid.

Westcona's involvement became clear when Dr. Edwards revealed his telephone conversation with Branton Cole. Rowley's collaboration put the icing on the cake. The tie to Global Oil senior management was less compelling and under investigation in Houston. Evidence of Boyd's and Cade's participation in the violence wasn't established, but there was no sign of them or their car in Ames. The scientist with some direct knowledge of Neptune's chemistry was dead, and not a trace of documentation was found in the rooms where Boyd and Cade had briefly bunked. In short, Dr. Edwards and Barbara Rowley, who had only the word of the now deceased scientist and their personal observations as evidence, could merely indirectly confirm Neptune's existence.

The FBI ordered a nationwide manhunt for Boyd and Cade after the Justice Department ordered a news blackout, and their investigators quickly notified Attorney General Ed Meese who had the task of briefing President Reagan. They discussed potential international ramifications and the likelihood of Neptune being real. After a characteristically brief but intensely thoughtful few minutes, Reagan responded with elegant simplicity to the news that was anything but.

"Find them, verify it, and pay them what they ask."

— ‖ —

Justice Department lawyers joined the FBI at Westcona's Dallas headquarters. Branton Cole, while denying any involvement with the Ames raid, was arrested on conspiracy charges on Friday evening. He was released on Saturday morning after posting a substantial bond and surrendering his passport. Westcona's board met in emergency session on Saturday morning and officially relieved Cole of his position. They issued a press release condemning the Ames attack and denying any knowledge of Cole's alleged actions. Federal investigators were promised full cooperation, after which the board quietly formed a crisis management team, headed by Cole, to secretly continue the search for Neptune. Their final action was to approve the hiring of two top criminal defense law firms; one to represent Westcona and the other to represent Branton Cole.

— ‖ —

The FBI and Justice Department lawyers had a more difficult time at Global's Houston headquarters. The mammoth corporation had an organizational structure designed to protect senior executives from regulatory probes and accusation of misdeeds. After hours of interviews with Mark Streeter and other senior leaders, Justice Department lawyers agreed that the highest level at which knowledge could be directly established, at least for now, was at the corporate department head level. For his part, Streeter threw Global's chief of security to the wolves to protect himself. The security chief was arrested on conspiracy charges on Friday evening while the investigation continued. Global's board met in emergency session on Saturday morning where they approved a press release condemning the raid and promising full cooperation and disclosure. A quick show-of-hands vote approved the bond to get their security chief released, and the authorization to hire criminal defense lawyers to protect them from the Justice Department. The security chief would be flown to an offshore drilling rig in the Gulf of Mexico to effectively disappear for the duration. Had his passport not been confiscated, his destination would have been an even less accessible location. His bond was chump-change. Any additional charges against the company over his disappearance wouldn't amount to anything compared to what they were potentially facing. Trillions of dollars were at stake. Nothing would stop them from protecting their company and the future of the energy industry.

— ‖ —

In Dallas, Westcona's corporate director of security was surprised and pleased when he was not arrested, even though Branton Cole had been. The FBI instructed him to stay in town, and to be back at the office on Saturday morning for more interviews. He understood that he was likely in trouble, but the mission to control Neptune was still his first priority. He had been home only long enough to mix a drink and sit down in front of the television when his telephone rang. It was Dutch Peltier calling from Des Moines, Iowa.

"What the hell happened up there?" the security director barked at his team leader.

"The Global guys went into the lab while I took our group across the street to another building that was being guarded. Something happened at the lab that started a firefight. A few minutes later a window opened on the building I was approaching and somebody started shooting at us. We split up and entered the stairways at each end. Shots were fired on the other end as I was approaching my stairway. By the time I got to the top of the stairs, I heard someone outside the window, and when I looked out I saw Boyd climbing down a tree. I tried to yell at him to stop but the bastard shot at me. I ran down the second-floor hallway looking for Cade but he had disappeared, too. There were two bedrooms overlooking the lab with open doors...obviously where they had been staying. Their clothes were still there. I looked around for a minute and heard more shots outside; sounded like from the front of the building. By the time I got downstairs, they were gone and the cops were arriving. The lab had blown up and was on fire. I got the hell out of there."

"How in the hell could two untrained civilians with wives and kids get away from you?" the security chief shouted impatiently.

"There weren't any kids or women. No women's clothes or kids' stuff in the rooms. It was just Boyd and Cade, and they used pretty damned good tactics...almost like they were expecting us. I met up with what was left of the teams at the rendezvous point before we got back to the plane, then had the pilot hop down to Des Moines so we could see what was happening before we were questioned by the local cops, or dared come back to Dallas. We've got rooms here for now."

"Well, the shit really hit the fan down here. The FBI's all over the place. Cole's in jail and I'm probably next. You'll be arrested on murder charges if you turn yourselves in. Call me again tomorrow afternoon here at the house. Hopefully, I'll know more by then. Just keep your head down until you talk to me."

The security chief thought about what Dutch Peltier had said while he nursed his drink and watched television coverage. The media was not letting up on the story. Something else was troubling him but he couldn't put his finger on it. Boyd and Cade must have dropped their wives off somewhere on a line between south Texas and central Iowa. It had to be someplace they thought was safe. He'd had the feeling they were missing something when he looked at the men's HR files earlier in the week. That same feeling niggled at his gut again. What was eluding him?

With a second drink in hand, he got an atlas from his desk and studied the highways between McAllen and Ames. They had surmised that the men had been in Oklahoma, based on the call to Jake Taylor soon after they left south Texas. That meant nothing now, although they had to have been in Oklahoma at some time to have driven to Iowa. They had next shown up in Ames. Had they just gone up I-35 the whole way? Boyd was from Oregon, Cade from Texas. He finished his drink, put the atlas on the bedside table, and shut his eyes.

Something startled him awake in the middle of the night. He remembered looking at their HR records but not their benefit enrollment forms. Those files were in Benefits Administration, not Human Resources. Perhaps a clue as to where the women and kids were hidden was right in front of him after all.

— ‖ —

Hollis was wide awake at six-thirty on Saturday and needed coffee. After plugging in the Best Western coffeemaker, he took a shower while the coffee brewed. Fletcher wanted to meet at seven-thirty for breakfast. Showered, shaved, and now sipping hot coffee, he turned on the television and was shocked to see a news alert that Branton Cole and the Global Oil security chief had been arrested. No mention of Neptune. Hollis poured the remains of the small pot into a paper cup and opened the curtains. Heavy frost was glistening on car windshields as the first rays of sunshine painted pink streaks on the sky. Holstering his Colt and slipping on his new winter jacket, he grabbed his cigarettes and coffee before heading out for a walk around the hotel grounds.

The crisp Minnesota air made him gasp, but he recovered after lighting a smoke and feeling the nicotine-induced super-charge to his cardiovascular system. He walked through the parking lot and around the building, savoring the calm and quiet. An empty cup and cold hands drove him into the hotel lobby for a refill and some warmth.

Two men were sitting in the lobby with their backs to the front desk when Hollis asked the clerk for coffee. They turned their heads at the sound of the pronounced drawl so thoroughly out of place in northern Minnesota. JT's eyes sparkled brightly despite the lack of visible emotion on his face.

"Well damn, Cade. I was hoping you two would have enough sense to get up here."

Logan could only stare in apparent disbelief as JT introduced the two men.

A sense of relief flooded over Hollis. Now they had some help!

— || —

JT, Logan, Steve, Jeff Neumann, and Hollis all grinned as Fletcher walked into the restaurant a little before seven-thirty.

He didn't recognize two of the men but was so elated at seeing Steve again that he grabbed the young engineer's hand and pumped it until his arm hurt while JT was trying to introduce him to Logan and Jeff. The first sense of real calm he had felt since before this all started enveloped him as he took in the smiling faces.

"You boys are pretty famous in some circles these days," Logan told them once introductions had been made and things had quieted down. "Half the country's looking for you, and some of them must want to kill you if you read between the lines in the TV reports."

"They tried, Logan," Fletcher said grimly.

They spent the next half hour over breakfast catching up on what was happening around them without mention of Shelley. Finally, Fletcher gently asked Steve, "How're you doing, buddy?"

"I've...I've been better," the younger man replied with difficulty.

The anguish in Steve's eyes wounded Fletcher but he was relieved he wouldn't have to break the ugly news. Fletcher threw his arm over Steve's shoulder and gave him a consoling squeeze. He had submerged his emotions over Shelley's death but now they came flowing back. No one said a word. Fletcher noticed Hollis's eyes were glistening. He composed himself before trying to speak.

"Why don't you go home with your dad and get some rest," he said. "You don't need to be worrying about any of this for now."

"I've thought about it, but no. Between the companies, cops, and news people, I'd have to go over it again and again for them. I can't do that. I'd rather stay with my dad and ya'll, if that's all right."

"We've got people trying to kill us, Steve."

"So what? You think I care if I live or die? I don't have a life to go back to when this is over."

No one wanted to hear those words but they came as no surprise either. Fletcher thought about it for a moment and realized he would likely be feeling the same way if their roles were reversed.

"Okay — if that's what you want. Let's get to it then so we can put this behind all of us," he said.

JT took them to the rented garage where he kept the Jeep. They loaded empty five-gallon gas cans into the Jeep and Oldsmobile while JT drew them a map to the cabin. He explained how the generator worked and where the tools were kept.

"Boyd, I've been thinking about the ham radio. Whether the FCC would agree or not, I can't see any way around using it. This is a life and death situation and we'll need to communicate."

"That's great except for one minor detail. We don't know anything about operating it."

"It's a little intimidating when you look at the equipment, but you can figure it out. The power and antenna leads will need to be hooked up to the transmitter. I have frequency charts and an instruction manual in a box near the radio. My logbook's in there, too. Find a call sign with a zero in it from the logbook and use it when you call me. A number zero, not the letter O. My call is WD5CL. It's on the cover of the logbook. Look at the frequencies I used when I talked to people with the number five in their call signs and use one of those to try me in the evenings at about the same time noted in the log. If anyone challenges you, just get off the air for an hour or so and change frequencies. Using the ham bands without a license is a federal offense but I just don't see an alternative right now. Speak clearly and slowly. No cussing ever."

"Wouldn't it just be better to use one channel rather than trying to find each other on the air?"

"Ham radio doesn't have channels like you're thinking of them. You're right though, let's just try using 14.155 MHz or right above that if someone else is using it," JT instructed.

"Use the radio as needed and call on the telephone whenever you get into a town that has one."

With that, JT and Jeff left for the airport in the rental car for their return to Denver.

— ‖ —

Hollis gave Steve one of the handheld oilfield radios as he and his father got into the little Jeep CJ. Fletcher and Hollis led the way in the Oldsmobile.

After buying groceries, an assortment of batteries, lantern fuel, kerosene, and gasoline, the two-vehicle convoy traveled east out of Thief River Falls. They followed JT's hand-drawn map and found themselves nearing the Roseau County line an hour later. They missed the small, rutted logging trail on their first pass and had to turn around at the county line and backtrack a little less than two miles until they found the turnoff to the cabin. It was much wilder and more rugged here than Fletcher could have imagined.

The eastbound trail was little more than two muddy tracks through overgrown grass, now brown and dead from the early frosts. Raised less than a foot above the surrounding swampland, it periodically dropped into muddy bogs where they could hear water splashing up under the vehicle as they pushed through to higher ground. Within a matter of weeks, the ground would be frozen and covered with knee-deep snow. The Minnesota Department of Natural Resources groomed the frozen, snow-covered pathway as a snowmobile trail once the snow was deep enough, and wheeled vehicular travel became impossible. A network of narrow trails cut off the main trail would soon create a winter wonderland for hunters, snowmobilers, and the occasional cross-country skier.

They came upon the small cabin, sitting fifty yards off the logging trail, when the odometer showed 2.8 miles from the highway, exactly as JT had told them. After traveling fifty-two miles from Thief River Falls, they were so deeply into the forest it was difficult to conceive of ever being found by anyone. A heavy forest of pine, poplar, and mixed hardwoods surrounded the small clearing where the cabin had been built. The dense summer canopy was now mostly gone, the brilliantly colored leaves having fallen to the ground with the first few hard frosts and stiff winds.

The cabin consisted of a kitchen with a wood-burning cook stove from another century, a living room with a large round table and bunk beds on either side, and a small bedroom with a double bed and some built-in shelves that functioned as a dresser. Off in the corner of the living room was JT's modest ham radio station sitting on a small table. Well water was drawn through a hand pump next to the small kitchen sink. On the counter next to the pump head sat a metal pail of priming water with dead flies floating in it.

Flattened tin cans covered the living room ceiling, protecting it from heat generated by the Coleman lantern that hung on a j-hook to provide light at the big table. Oil lamps were scattered around the rooms for additional lighting. A kerosene heater in the living room backed up to the kitchen wall and shared the single chimney with the cook stove.

The rear of the cabin sat about thirty feet in front of a sheer rock cliff that rose fifty feet straight up behind it, creating shelter from the cold north winds.

Forty feet to the west was a wooden shed with a push rotary lawnmower, miscellaneous gardening tools, axes, saws, a few sacks of powdered lime, and a wood supply. A small generator that vented outdoors sat in the corner on a hand-poured concrete pad surrounded by protective metal walls. The sloped ceiling was also covered with flattened tin cans for protection from the hot generator and the Coleman lantern that hung by another j-hook.

Normally downwind, and just a hundred and fifty feet to the east of the cabin through a bramble of weeds and dead grass, sat a "one-holer" outhouse.

Sweeping up the mouse turds, spider webs, and assorted remnants of other small critters that had taken up residence in the cabin since JT's last visit was the first order of business. They primed the pump and cleared the line of rusty water before filling a pail with enough clean water to wipe down tables and counters.

Hollis and Logan fueled and tested the generator while Fletcher and Steve carried in wood. They fueled the kerosene heater and Coleman lanterns, and put fresh batteries in the flashlights. Hollis cleaned out the coffee pot, frying pan, and a few cooking pots before building a fire in the cook stove and putting a pot of coffee on to brew.

Finally, weapons were broken out to familiarize Logan and Steve with the Mini-14s, .45s, and little .380 ACPs. The .380s weren't much but would certainly make Steve feel a little better having at least some means of protection. Logan still had one of JT's .45 automatics. Steve decided to claim both of the .380s after Fletcher told them he had carried the Walther as a hidden back-up gun while in Viet Nam. Logan was disquieted by the idea of Steve carrying firearms while in his present state of mind, but not enough to try to prevent it when he may very well need them to save his own life. He'd watch his son closely.

Taking a walk outside the cabin, they found the leads for two longwire antennas that JT had strung through the trees.

One antenna was hung horizontally at about forty feet off the ground in an east/west direction; the other was sloped out of a tree atop the rock formation in a southerly direction out over the cabin and anchored into another tree near the logging trail. Fletcher set about making all the proper connections to allow them to switch between antennas from inside the cabin for best directionality...just as JT had instructed him.

While digging around the radio desk, he found a wooden box containing manuals for the transceiver and antenna tuner, a logbook, a notebook of aviation and ham radio frequencies, and a Sony ICF-2010 portable shortwave receiver with its manual. Hollis, a fan of shortwave radio listening since his Navy days, volunteered to be the Sony operator. The radio received both AM and single sideband mode in the shortwave bands, regular broadcast AM and FM, plus the civilian aircraft band. He plugged two AA and three D cells into it when he saw it could operate on battery power.

When they were finally set up for their first night in the wilderness, Hollis took an oilfield handheld radio and found his way to the top of the cliff above the cabin while Fletcher and Logan drove further on the logging trail to see what was on their eastern flank. Using the more powerful mobile radio in the Olds, Fletcher was able to communicate with Hollis until they were just a little over three miles apart...much better range than he had expected. They found nothing but beautiful, empty woods east of the cabin in the five miles they traveled. After carefully studying a map, it appeared unlikely that any antagonists would approach from that direction. There didn't appear to be any highways east of the cabin connecting with the logging trail. In fact, it wasn't readily apparent where the rutted trail even led.

— ‖ —

Logan volunteered to cook that evening, serving ketchup and hot sauce-doctored Dinty Moore beef stew over slices of white bread. While not haute cuisine, they all ate ravenously. They discussed posting an all night guard just to make sure they had a fighting chance in case they had somehow been followed. That seemed highly unlikely, but Fletcher was taking no chances after what had happened in Ames.

He pulled out the bag of military web gear he and Hollis had purchased in St. Cloud on their way north.

"Hollis, come over here and help me put this stuff together."

"We didn't do that in the Navy, you know."

"Doesn't matter; you're in the Army now, hoss."

Fletcher dumped the equipment on the table, separating it into two piles. "We're going to put together two sets and here's yours," he told Hollis as he pushed a pile across the table. "Logan and Steve can wear whichever set comes closest to fitting them."

"No way is all that going on one belt," Hollis said.

"Watch and learn," Fletcher said as he began.

Starting with the pistol belt adjusted to his waist size over his field jacket, he added suspenders, a canteen, two rifle ammo pouches, a daypack, flashlight, poncho, and a fighting knife. Hollis kept up as best he could but needed help in the end. Fletcher then added three thirty-round Mini-14 magazines to each ammo pouch and strapped four hand grenades to the holders sewn to the outside of the ammo pouches.

"I'll be damned," was all Hollis could say when he finally finished.

Fletcher volunteered for first duty and told them to watch how he put everything on so they could do the same when their time came later in the evening. He donned a military shoulder holster centering his .45 Combat Commander on his chest before pulling on his jacket, ski cap, gloves, and finally the web gear. A thermos of coffee, a handheld radio with extra batteries, and his Mini-14 sporting a thirty-round magazine completed the uniform. He turned on the other oilfield handheld radio and handed it to Hollis as he walked out the door and down the trail to the west to take up the first four-hour guard mount.

Logan and Steve shared dish duty while Hollis sat down with the Sony shortwave radio, listening for any news about Global or Westcona. He tuned to regular broadcast AM stations out of Winnipeg, Manitoba, and Grand Forks, North Dakota, international shortwave stations from around the world, and even tuned to 132.15 MHz and heard a Mesaba Airlines flight approach and land at Thief River Falls.

Thankfully and as expected, the only excitement during the night was the changing of the guard every four hours.

— ‖ —

Westcona's security chief arrived back at the Dallas corporate office at nine on Saturday morning as directed. The FBI had obviously spent most of the night rummaging through office files, computers, flight logs, and travel expense reports trying to put the pieces together. After a couple more hours of interviews and methodically repeated questions, the security chief was told he could leave for the weekend. He had given them nothing. He punched the third-floor button on the elevator after leaving his ninth-floor office. Though Benefits Administration was behind locked doors, his master key resolved that issue. Finding the cabinets containing employee benefit enrollment files was hardly a challenge, and he quickly located the two files he needed and stuffed them in his briefcase.

Once home, he made a sandwich and examined the enrollment forms completed by Fletcher Boyd and Hollis Cade.
Boyd's primary beneficiary was his wife Katie. Secondary
beneficiaries were his children Felecia and Taryn. Nothing of
use there. Cade's primary beneficiary was his wife Sara.
Secondary beneficiary was his son, Shane. Nothing to help
there, either. He pushed the files aside and ate. Without really
paying attention, he absent-mindedly thumbed through the
Cade file and noticed an old discolored form under the rest
that Hollis had filled out when he first came to work at
Westcona. That form also named his mother as a secondary
beneficiary and her address was on FM 2820 in Paris, Texas.
Farm country up near the Oklahoma border. Bingo!

Dutch Peltier called from Des Moines at two on Saturday
afternoon. After a brief discussion regarding the events
transpiring in Dallas and Houston, the security chief ordered
Peltier and his remaining men to Mrs. Cade's farm. First they
needed to confirm that she was alive and still lived there.
Then to establish whether or not the wives and kids were with
her. If so, they were to be snatched and flown to Meacham
Field in Fort Worth where they would be met by a Westcona
security delegation.

"It'll be dark when we get down to Paris, you know."

"Just get there and do your job. They have to be there.
I want them in town by tomorrow at the latest. Don't screw this
up again, Dutch. This may be our last hope of getting to Boyd
and Cade."

— || —

The Lamar County sheriff's squad car pulled away from Ellie
Cade's farmhouse at eight-thirty on Saturday evening. Mrs.
Cade had mentioned that her own dogs and her guest's

German Shepherd had been acting unsettled for the past couple of hours though they had not seen anyone around. The deputies dutifully radioed the information to the dispatcher who promptly relayed it to the sheriff via telephone. The sheriff had made it clear that Mrs. Cade was a high-priority lady and that her safety was important to him. His gut told him that something unusual was going on at the farm. He'd known her since he was a kid and she'd never been one to ask for help.

— ‖ —

Dutch Peltier and the other three remaining Ames raiders had been watching the farmhouse through binoculars from a stand of trees near the road where they had enough cover to keep them invisible and enough distance to keep the dogs from alerting. After dark, they quietly made their way toward the house but were kept a couple of hundred of yards out by barking dogs. A sheriff's car came and left without incident. Finally, they caught a break when they saw two girls and a black dog through a picture window. Within minutes, they also visually confirmed the presence of three adult females. No indication of any men in the house.

At midnight, they made their move on the house, an hour after the last light went out.

— ‖ — Twenty — ‖ —

THE RAID UNRAVELED DUE TO THE protective instincts of the Boyd's German Shepherd, Lady. Knowing they couldn't outsmart the farm dogs, the security team had boldly driven right up to the house and knocked politely while gently talking to the agitated dogs. Dutch Peltier stayed in the car. The porch light came on and Ellie Cade answered the door with her double-barreled shotgun protruding out the cracked screen door. She ordered the dogs to be quiet while demanding to know what the men wanted. One of them simply pushed the screen door shut on the barrels while another grasped it and violently jerked the shotgun out of Ellie's hands without a shot being fired. The three quickly entered the house to get out of the dogs' reach, pushing Ellie harshly to the floor in the process.

The dogs came unhinged and set the already alert Lady off like a rocket into the hallway from the girls' bedroom where she had been pacing since the car drove up. She was airborne for ten feet before hitting the lead security agent squarely in the chest as she attacked the man's throat and knocked him to the floor in a flurry of fangs and fur. The other agents kicked and pulled at the dog trying to call off the attack. With the lead agent, the dog, and Ellie Cade still on the floor, multiple shotgun blasts thundered through the little house at chest level. Katie Boyd and Sara Cade had both fired. Sara advanced toward her mother-in-law while Katie backed toward the bedroom sheltering her twin daughters.

Ellie grabbed the telephone from her seated position and hit the speed dial for the Lamar County sheriff. She said her address and then dropped the phone when an H&K P-7 was jammed under her jaw. The shotgun blasts had caused Lady to release the agent for the split second it took him to draw his handgun and push the dog away. He ordered Sara to grab Lady and put her in a bedroom while he used Ellie as a shield from the shotguns. Sara dropped her shotgun and took Lady's collar. Katie saw what was happening and followed suit.

The agent looked unhappily at his two dead compatriots on the floor and yelled out the front door.

"Dutch. Shoot the fuckin' dogs so we can come out!"

Blood pooling on the floor caused the intruder to slip and almost lose his balance as he struggled for footing. He clubbed Ellie and screamed at the younger women to bring the children over to the front door. Gunfire boomed outside and the dogs fell silent.

The girls were quickly stashed in the front seat of the rental car while the agent wiped blood from his neck and motioned Sara to open the rear right passenger door. He snapped a hand-cuff on her left wrist and pushed her roughly into the car. She slumped when he deftly moved his H&K to his left hand and delivered a sharp blow to her neck with his right.

Warning Katie that he would kill her children if she didn't do as he ordered, he walked her around to the left rear door and ordered her in beside Sara while yelling at her to affix the other cuff to her right wrist. He climbed into the driver's seat, pivoted, and hit her on the chin with the heel of his semi-closed fist. She, too, slumped out cold.

Taryn and Felecia were screaming and frightened as the agent ordered Taryn onto the floor and pushed Felecia over to the door. He yelled at them to shut up, then started the car and waited for Dutch to get into the back seat with the unconscious women.

When Dutch didn't immediately get into the car, he looked around in the dim glow of the porch light a moment before a blinding, white-hot spotlight lit up the car.

"Driver! Get out of the car with your weapon high in your left hand."

The agent, dripping blood from his dog bites, slowly got out of the car holding his handgun above his head. Before the deputy could order him to place his weapon on the ground and back away from it, Dutch fired from behind a trailer where he had been hiding. The deputy let out a loud groan and dropped to the ground, firing one shot in the direction of the trailer as he fell. The agent panicked, jumped back in the car and hit the gas sending a rooster tail of dirt into the air as he careened around the squad car and roared down the driveway leaving Dutch standing over the mortally-wounded deputy, and Ellie Cade unconscious in the house.

— ‖ —

Hollis was shivering despite the heavy clothing and army poncho he had wrapped tightly around his torso. He had always thought of army gear as being quiet in the woods but the poncho material was just stiff enough from the cold to crackle when he moved or brushed against branches. Maybe that's why it had been in the surplus store. The sun was beginning to brighten the sodden forest and he was down to his last few cigarettes. It was just before seven o'clock and it had been a long few hours out in the dewy cold.

Not wanting to bang around in the kitchen in the middle of the night and risk waking everyone, he'd decided against bringing a thermos of coffee. It was a poor decision that he regretted and wouldn't make again. He convinced himself that his core body temperature had to be less than 90 degrees. Feeling purely frozen, he stomped his feet, swung his arms, and clapped his hands together to get the blood circulating while his rifle stood unceremoniously propped against a tree. Sailors don't pull guard duty out in the woods with much grace or tactical discipline.

Seldom had Hollis ever been so alone and far from civilization that the silence was this overwhelming. It was so quiet he thought his ears had shut down at one point during the night. Finally, the first hint of dawn arrived and the forest stirred to life with the sounds of birds and small animals. Listening in fascination, he thought he could actually hear the sound of wings brushing the still murky sky. He lit his last cigarette just as Logan's voice crackled through the little oilfield radio and harshly startled him from his reverie.

"You still alive out there, Hollis?"

"Would be if it wasn't for that heart attack you just gave me."

"I've got hot coffee and I'll have bacon and eggs ready by the time you get back. How far out are you?"

"Damned if I know...at least a mile or so, I reckon."

Hollis picked up the rifle with his stone-cold fingers and started walking down the trail. His legs and feet were half-numb as he stiffly and awkwardly gained momentum, loosening up as he walked. He thought he heard a background noise but his breathing was so loud he wasn't sure. Finally he stopped and held his breath, listening carefully. Sure enough, he heard the soft rumbling forest-dampened sound of a vehicle behind him. With surprising agility and speed, he made for a stand of pine trees and sat under them, pulling the green poncho around his exposed legs and feet. He keyed the radio and quietly let Logan know what was happening, warning him to stay off the radio until he reported back. His surging blood-pressure was roaring in his ears as the back of his index finger found and rested against the rifle's trigger-guard-mounted safety, and he began mentally working through his options if these turned out to be the bad guys. As the vehicle slowly rounded a curve and started toward him, he wondered how he'd know. It was a pickup, and appeared to be running without headlights as it idled along at barely walking speed.

Dawn was just breaking and his vision was limited from his hiding place. Finally, he saw an official-looking seal on the door and exhaled sharply when he realized it was a game warden. Of course, there would be game wardens wandering the woods in late October. He let the truck move past before quietly telling Logan who was coming for coffee.

"If he's anything like game wardens in Oklahoma or Texas, he'll be stopping to see you in about ten minutes," Hollis told Logan. "Better not look like hunters because we sure don't have the licenses he'll want to see."

"We'll be fine once I stand these guys down from general quarters," Logan responded in Navy terminology so Hollis would understand that the cabin had been quickly mobilized and prepared for a fight. "You just stay out of sight until he's gone. No sense making him wonder why you're dressed up like GI Joe and running around his woods with a rifle."

Logan continued cooking while Steve and Fletcher tried to look less alarmed and more like they had just gotten out of their sleeping bags, which they had. It was not a pleasant way to be awakened. Logan turned on the shortwave radio to make it even homier when the warden arrived, and the men hid their weapons. Fletcher went outside, lit a cigarette, and headed slowly for the outhouse. The game warden pulled partway up the driveway, gave the place a quick look, and wrote something down. Only then did he get out of his pickup with his eyes on Fletcher.

"Morning," he shouted with a smile. "I'm Joey Andersen, the local warden. You alone or are there others with you then?" he asked, eyeing the cabin and obviously knowing the answer to his own question because there was a car and a Jeep parked out front.

"Howdy," Fletcher said in a friendly voice. "Name's Boyd, and no, I'm not alone. The lazier ones are still inside thinking of having some breakfast. Could you stand a cup of coffee or some eggs?"

"I see where you're headed but I could stand a hot cup yeah, I sure could," he said as Fletcher continued to the outhouse.

Logan, pretending to have just become aware of the warden's arrival, opened the door and greeted the uniformed man.

"The coffee's on and the kitchen's warm. I'm just getting some breakfast together. Come on in and join us."

— ‖ —

Joey alertly entered the cabin and quickly inventoried the people while looking for weapons. He saw none. No need to ask them for hunting licenses at this point. The cook handed him a steaming mug of coffee and motioned him to a seat. They appeared friendly enough and talked with a southern drawl, explaining that they were here for a little R&R and that the guy who owned the cabin had offered it to them for a couple of weeks.

"Whose this place belong to?" he asked innocently.

"Fella by the name of Jake Taylor. We work with him in Texas," Boyd said as he came back into the cabin.

Joey was satisfied when Boyd answered correctly and told him JT had been there but left yesterday. He knew JT from past visits and saw no reason to doubt their story.

"I'll be in the general area most days during the hunting season. There aren't many folks out here during the week but you might see some on the weekends...and they'll be bird hunters with shotguns. Deer season opens in a couple of weeks so you might keep that in mind if you're still here. They'll have high power rifles then."

"Thanks for the warning," Boyd said with a smile.

"We usually keep a pot of coffee on the stove so stop in when you come by again," the cook added.

Joey had noticed four sleeping bags but only three people. He had also seen four plates next to the stove. As he backed his pickup out, he couldn't help but think the car didn't look like a rental, and couldn't imagine why these Texans would be driving a car with Minnesota plates if it wasn't, especially if they had arrived on JT's airplane and had his little Jeep. He turned back to the west and headed for the highway. Maybe he'd call JT tonight just to make sure everything was copasetic. He still had the number someplace. While they seemed like okay guys, he sensed something odd but couldn't quite put his finger on it.

— || —

Hollis had been watching from a hundred yards out and covered the ground to the cabin with the speed of a starving man once the game warden motored past his hiding place. He was cold and hungry. The shortwave radio was still on although no one had been listening to it. He fiddled with the radio while devouring breakfast. Finished, he poured another cup of coffee and lit a cigarette. There was a loud Winnipeg station coming through so he sat back to listen to the Sunday morning news, and it wasn't good. Westcona and Global Oil were involved in more killing, this time outside Paris, Texas. Three people had been killed at a farmhouse, including a deputy sheriff. An elderly woman was injured. Two women and two children were missing. The FBI was on the scene.

— ⅲ— Twenty-One — ⅲ—

IT WAS LATE SUNDAY AFTERNOON in the Middle East and the international energy industry had been following the breaking story all day while North Americans slept through their Saturday night. OPEC member-nation intelligence services were also on the story, pushing their sleepy Washington, DC, embassy personnel for more information. Something of significance was happening and they wanted answers now.

The Aramco President in Dhahran, Saudi Arabia, dialed a private number and smiled when the phone was answered on its second ring.

"Salem, my friend, you are again working long hours," he said with warmth.

"Yes, Ali. I am concerned with many issues that cannot be resolved in a normal work week. To what do I owe the honor of your call, my friend?" Is everything all right at Aramco?" Salem asked.

"Yes, but some in government are becoming distressed with the news coming out of America. They seek information that is not being supplied by Al Makhabarat Al A'amah, and are now asking me what Aramco has been able to discern. I am embarrassed that we have so little to offer. I am hopeful that you have some insight we may have missed, my friend."

"To be sure, Ali, the news is distressing and I, too, am making inquiries within my company. We were initially thinking there was some kind of industrial espionage event transpiring, or perhaps some sort of blood feud between the two firm's security departments. Now those ideas appear unwarranted. Still, I am receiving nothing more than unsubstantiated supposition as to what might actually be happening. Have you made inquiries with our friends at Global Oil in Houston?"

"My information is similar, Salem. I have made inquires of Global but it is a weekend in America, and the people working in Houston seem to be preoccupied with the FBI now in their place of business. That alone causes us distress. Global is too mature a company to be involved in such obvious violence by their security employees. No, there is something more happening. Something is provoking them."

"I also believe that something of significance to your industry is transpiring in America. Some of Global's security people have attacked a government energy research facility and have been involved in other unfortunate events that appear to be related. They have performed poorly, yet they persist. They are assuming considerable risk that makes no sense unless this is a major event. I know little of this company named Westcona, except that it is a domestic oilfield services company that also has a small international offshore drilling subsidiary."

"Salem, the royal family has requested that you contact any trusted friends you may have within Global, on an informal basis of course. It would appear ill-advised to speak to our contacts within their security department, but perhaps your close and valued friendship with Logan Addison could be of help? May I report that you will honor the kingdom with this small favor?"

"Of course, Ali. I am always deeply honored to assist in any way possible. Please give my regards to our benefactors, and expect a call as soon as I can locate Mr. Addison."

Ali Al-Naimi immediately called his contact at Al Makhabarat Al A'amah, the Saudi General Intelligence Directorate, to report Salem's response to their suggestion. They were pleased but still very anxious to get their small special operations team to America. The military team, already airborne, was to find the cause of the stir in America's oil and gas industry. Time was of the essence, and any delay could preclude action ultimately deemed necessary to protect Saudi interests. They would rather be safe than sorry.

Salem winced as his mind replayed Ali's reference to Logan Addison as his close and valued friend. He knew he would always be suspected of sneaking his brother, Mahrous, out of Saudi Arabia when the young man was implicated in a 1979 pro-Iranian insurgency that briefly sized control of the mosque at Mecca. Although Mahrous was ultimately deemed only a rube used by the revolutionary group, his actions had severely strained the family's important relationship with the House of Saud. Salem, as head of his family's business, had turned in desperation to his long-time friend and business associate, Logan Addison, for help. Logan had not asked questions. He had just quietly arranged for Mahrous to be flown by helicopter to one of Global Oil's drilling rigs on the Red Sea, thus giving Salem the time he needed to arrange further transport of his brother to safety in Yemen. Salem's already significant admiration of Logan became an almost brotherly love. He firmly believed he owed Mahrous's very life to Logan, and those of Arab blood do not take such obligations lightly. His hope was that he could someday repay the family debt of honor to his American friend.

This history made Salem uncomfortable asking Logan for another favor, but knew his call would be expected and likely monitored by the Saudi General Intelligence Directorate. He dutifully left messages on Logan's work and home telephone answering machines. He also called Mahrous in Medina, Saudi Arabia, where his brother now managed the family branch operation. Mahrous would make additional inquiries into the events transpiring in America.

— ‖ —

The Westcona plane was waiting at Flying Tigers Airport, a private field southwest of Paris, Texas. The panicked security agent had already lost a lot of blood and was in considerable pain from the dog bites inflicted by Lady. He drove east on FM 2820 to the first junction past the Gambill Goose Refuge sign where he turned south toward the airport. Both women were stirring to life in the backseat but he was not overly concerned with them because they were handcuffed together and should have serious headaches. The blood loss was making him light-headed, and his neck hurt like hell. Thankfully it was only a few more miles to the airport.

Unexpected trouble came as they approached the bridge over Pine Creek and six bright yellow eyes reflected in the headlights. The agent instinctively dropped the H&K into his lap, grabbed at the wheel with both hands, and stood on the brakes to avoid the deer. As he did, an arm hooked around his neck from behind and viciously jerked his head to the right rear. He roared in pain. A second arm snaked around from the other side clawing at his face until a finger found the corner of his right eye socket and another found the side of his nose, and brutally snapped his head around to the left. The car abruptly shuddered to a stop with the right fender against the railing.

The women frantically yelled at the girls to find the hand-cuff key in the man's pocket while they clumsily climbed out. Once free of the cuffs, Katie dropped to her knees and puked while Sara pulled the body out of the car. His right eyeball was lying on his cheek and his left eye had the blank and surprised stare of a dead man. Taryn and Felecia helped Sara roll the body down the incline toward the creek. It was too dark to see how far he rolled and they didn't hear it hit the water.

With Sara behind the wheel, they drove south to Highway 82 where she turned to the west, jumped on the accelerator, and didn't slow down until they reached the Honey Grove exit at Highway 100. She pulled into a secluded church parking lot and shut down the engine. They were confused, scared, and in near panic. Katie was still trying to comfort her daughters and get her own emotions under control. Sara wanted to talk to Hollis.

"We need to talk to the men before we even think about going to the police," she told Katie. "The only reasonable thing is to go back to the ranch. It's the only place they know to find us, and I'm worried about Ellie." Her hands were trembling as she tried to think of what Hollis would do.

Their search of the car interior produced nothing of use. However, the trunk rewarded them with six wallets containing Westcona and Global Oil security credentials and cash. They used the cash to check into a motel and waited for the sun to come up, knowing some time needed to pass before they could go back without running headlong into the police.

— ‖ —

At dawn, a fisherman saw what looked like a body as he guided his twelve-foot aluminum fishing boat under the bridge over Pine Creek. The sun was well above the horizon by the time two FBI agents and a deputy sheriff stood over the chewed-up and broken body on the bank of Pine Creek. The wallet they found on the corpse identified him as a Westcona employee.

"These hotshots sure haven't had very good luck lately, have they?" the junior special agent commented.

— ‖ — Twenty-Two — ‖ —

"WE NEED TO GET TO A PHONE," Hollis said in an uncharacteristically subdued tone. "I'm going to kill them sons of bitches if any of the women or girls are hurt. In fact, I'm going to kill them anyway."

"*We* will," Fletcher said with anger written all over his face.

"I know the Lamar County sheriff and he'll have some answers," Hollis said.

"Look, Hollis. They probably took your mother to the hospital for treatment and observation even if she wasn't badly hurt," Logan reasoned. "They'll have the FBI there, along with your friend the Sheriff, asking her all kinds of questions. Give it a few hours and then call her at the house. You can call the sheriff this afternoon. The guy's probably up to his ass in federal agents right now, and you don't really want them to know you're calling."

Hollis had a Minnesota map unfolded in front of him and was pretty much ignoring Logan.

"There's a place called Skime on Highway 54, or 9 after it goes into Roseau County north of here. That damn highway keeps changing numbers every time it crosses into a new county," he said. "Skime looks pretty small though.

We'd stick out like sore thumbs on a Sunday morning if we hung around for long. We could go farther north up to Roseau. That looks bigger."

Fletcher was looking at the map over Hollis's shoulder.

"I think we should go back to Thief River Falls," he said. "It's big enough that we can hang around for a few hours without being noticed. Remember that little shopping center by the Kmart? Enough people should be around there that we'll just blend right in. Might even be a payphone close by."

Hollis reluctantly agreed. Fletcher suggested they address some security issues around the cabin before they left to find a phone.

"Fletcher, I want you to call my secretary in Houston when you get to town. We need to know what's happening at Global and she's my best source right now," Logan said. "I'll stay here and try to figure out the ham radio equipment while you're gone."

Fletcher forced himself to look critically at the physical layout of the area around the cabin with an eye to defensive improvements. Katie and the girls weighed heavily on him but right now he had to concentrate on the cabin security. He'd be no good to them dead, which he could be if he failed to take all the necessary precautions.

The leaves were off the trees and the field grasses were flattened to the ground, dead from frost. Visibility from a high vantage point would be excellent although it would still be difficult to spot anyone walking or driving down the logging trail from ground level, a lesson Hollis had learned when the game warden approached him.

Hollis suggested they take a look from the rock formation above the cabin. Yesterday he'd discovered that climbing to it entailed walking close to a half-mile along the base of the rock cliff until a game trail traversed up the hill and back toward the cabin. Apparently the game trail was the only reasonable way up—and it would be a difficult and slow climb in the dark. After further discussion with Hollis, Fletcher decided to create an observation post, or OP in military parlance, on the rock. Hollis assured him that they would be able to see for quite a distance around the cabin and would easily detect headlights or flashlights coming down the trail from either direction, especially with binoculars.

Fletcher lead the way as the four men worked their way to the top. They carried an ax, shovel, and an assortment of tools to construct a primitive shelter on the edge of the cliff with heavy boulders and fallen trees. They encircled the makeshift structure with rope at chest height and suspended pine boughs from the rope for camouflage and a token windbreak. Steve had hauled a long piece of heavy rope up with him and was tying knots at ten foot increments.

"I want a quick way down," he said. "That game trail is way too far in an emergency. We can haul stuff up with the rope instead of carrying it all the way around, too."

"We can't leave it visible on the rock face, Steve," Hollis said. "Let's anchor it to that tree and then coil it in the brush. It won't be visible from up here or down below, but we can still throw it over the cliff if we need a fast way down."

"What if somebody managed to get up here without us knowing it? We'd be sitting ducks down around the cabin. You see that hillside straight south across the road from the cabin? How far do you think it is?" Fletcher asked.

"Oh...a good couple hundred yards, I guess," Hollis said.

"If you were down there on the ground, could you hit somebody standing up here?"

"With a rifle, yeah."

"Let's build a fighting position down there before we quit for the day. Then all we'd have to do is get one of us over there from the cabin if anyone did get up here behind us. The trees would partly shield our ground movement from up here."

They made their way back down the game trail and across the road to the hillside directly south of the OP where they dug a four and a half foot deep two-man foxhole to provide cover and concealment. An earthen seat was left in place on the back wall so they could sit and still see over the top. A sump hole was dug into the floor for water to drain into if it rained. Fletcher trotted back to the cabin and returned with four hand grenades that he placed in a hole scooped out of the front side of the foxhole wall at waist level.

"We'll take the M79 grenade launcher up top tonight. It doesn't do us much good down here under these trees but it sure could be useful up there."

"How far will it shoot?" Logan asked.

"About three hundred and fifty meters on flat land. From up there, I'd guess a little farther," Fletcher said. "You just have to remember that our forty-millimeter rounds are high explosive. They'll burst when they hit trees just as if they hit the ground. That's the problem with using them down here in these thick woods. I wish we could practice some but we just don't have enough ammo to play around with. I used to be pretty good with it but that was a long time ago."

He was satisfied that they were now prepared to guard the cabin and return effective fire if someone got up on top behind them. More measures would have to be taken if they stayed much longer or determined their location had been compromised, but this would do for now.

— || —

Steve started lunch while Hollis and Fletcher cleaned up and prepared to go back to Thief River Falls. Steve had listened to the conversation between his father, Hollis, and Fletcher earlier that morning when the men had almost come apart at the seams after hearing about the attack on their wives and Fletcher's daughters. To this point, he had been nearly catatonic, just robotically getting through the day and unable to think clearly beyond complete denial that Shelley and the baby had been murdered by these same bastards. Seeing Fletcher and Hollis so angry triggered a rage in his heart as a potent need for revenge flared alive. His black-hearted intentions would provide the motivation to function for now. Beyond killing those responsible, any future he might have was of no importance to him.

— ‖ —

Sara and Katie had been calling the ranch every half hour since nine o'clock. They were relieved that cops hadn't answered but concerned with Ellie's condition and safety. Finally the older woman answered. A deputy had driven her home a couple of hours earlier, a bit banged up and bruised but holding her own. She'd ignored the ringing phone while the crime scene people were still at the house because she was concerned it might be Hollis, and she had already told the cops she wasn't in contact with her son.

Sara told her they were free of their kidnapper and were coming back.

"The deputies are gone so come on home and park the car in the barn where nobody can see," Ellie said. "I could use some help cleaning this place up."

An hour later, Sara pulled the deceased men's rental car into the Cade barn. Now they just needed to stay out of sight and wait for Hollis and Fletcher to call.

The telephone finally rang in the early afternoon and Katie was relieved to hear Fletcher's voice. After assuring him that they were unhurt and several minutes of tears and sniffles, she was able to explain what had happened. Twice during the conversation she started unloading on Fletcher but Sara motioned her to stop both times.

Sara finally took the phone to talk to Hollis, swearing that they were all unharmed and safe for the moment. She knew Hollis was very likely raging inside, and had no intention of creating more tension for him by playing the weak wife. Not that she wasn't shaken up by the violence...you just don't go around killing people and not have the memory cemented in your head like a bad movie. They could take care of themselves, of that she was certain and told him so. Hollis sounded relieved and a little calmer but she wouldn't give a plug nickel for any Westcona or Global Oil security men if Hollis ever ran into them. He was her staunch protector and wouldn't let this go without a frightful response. She loved and respected him for that.

With the conversation ended on a positive note, the women began helping Ellie with the repulsive cleaning and damage repair made necessary by their shotguns.

A couple of hours later, Ellie heard vehicles approaching and reached for her weapon. The dogs she normally relied upon to sound an alarm were already buried behind the barn. She was thankful to see her son Roy and two young adult grandsons carefully approach the front door. Hollis had asked her to call his brother and get some help for the next few days, just in case the wrong people came back to the ranch. When the Cades circled the wagons, no one was likely to harm them without paying a very high price.

— ‖ —

The Learjet displaying Kingdom of Saudi Arabia markings touched down at New York's LaGuardia Airport late Sunday afternoon. Five men quickly cleared customs on diplomatic passports and flew by helicopter to Manhattan where they made their way to the Saudi diplomatic mission to the United Nations. Arrangements had already been made for five different Saudi nationals to exit the United States using the same passports. This left the five special operations soldiers free to roam unimpeded. The team was thoroughly briefed on the assignment that had been formulated while they traveled. After being fed and returned to LaGuardia, they boarded commercial airliners. Three were Houston bound and the other two boarded a plane for Dallas.

— ‖ —

Fletcher and Hollis took an alternate route to Thief River Falls, this time heading west between Agassiz National Wildlife Refuge and Thief Lake Wildlife Area on Highway 6. They caught Highway 32 and turned south toward town where they found the shopping center on Highway 59 and a payphone outside Kmart. Their call to the ranch relieved their worst fears, although Hollis was still incensed that his mother had been manhandled and his wife struck and kidnapped. Her innocent comment that a man called Dutch had apparently shot the deputy and gotten away in the confusion only added fuel to the ferocity swirling in his head. That was the same bastard who led the fake audit team to Edinburg, and who he had promised a memorable reunion if they ever crossed paths again. It wasn't an *if* any more.

Their second call was to Logan's secretary who was reluctant to talk to Fletcher, fearing he might not really be a friend. Fletcher was able to convince her otherwise, after which she relayed the urgent message from Salem. Fletcher wrote down the curious number, wondering where the call was from.

Fletcher also called JT's home but he was either not yet back from Denver or not answering. He didn't leave a message. Fletcher wanted to check in with JT and assure him of their safety, but even more wanted JT to contact Spencer Wainwright. He had an idea that would require Wainwright's help if the old auditor was willing to go out on a limb for them. It was only two-thirty so they decided to wait an hour or so before trying JT again.

Hollis stopped a man walking out of the store with a World War II commemorative cap on his head, and asked if there was a place in town that might be serving beer on a Sunday. The man directed them back toward downtown where VFW Post 2793 was located on Horace Avenue.

The moment they walked in the door, a lively white-haired man identifying himself as Vern, and wearing an Arctic Cat polo shirt, asked if they were VFW members. He seemed disappointed when they said no. His disposition lightened considerably when they assured him they were both military veterans and were just in town for a short time. He told them he was a past Post Commander and thought it important they join and support their local Post when they got home. They conversed for a few minutes before Vern told them they were welcome as guests, and he rejoined a group on the far side of the room.

Three couples sat at tables near the wall-mounted television watching a replay of World Series game six which had been played the day before, and talking about the upcoming deer season. Life was normal in rural northern Minnesota, at least for the locals.

"I'm going to ask Wainwright to set up a bank account for us to transfer our money into," Fletcher told Hollis as they swigged Budweiser. Coors hadn't made it to Minnesota, so Hollis was grudgingly making do with Fletcher's brand.

Hollis's face was still mottled from the wrath he was holding inside. Fletcher's shoulders were tense and his arm muscles flexed involuntarily as his subconscious reacted to the anger and guilt of leaving his family without his protection. It wasn't easy trying to think tactically without letting the anger impact his planning. Almost impossible, but he was doing his best.

"You think we're really going to get any money for this thing, Fletcher? We're leaving dozens of bodies in our wake, and all kinds of unfriendlies are after us. The cops aren't going to be sociable, either, if they catch up with us. We're in a world of hurt."

"We agreed in McAllen and nothing's changed in Neptune's value. That's why Westcona and Global are willing to kill for it. If they fuck with us again, there're going to be a hell of a lot more bodies. That is an iron-clad-damned guarantee."

Hollis slowly rubbed his red eyes and looked around the room wondering how to respond. He'd never seen Fletcher this pissed off or inflexible.

"Well, where would it be safe to open an account?"

"Offshore someplace. Wainwright's familiar with how Westcona does its international banking so he should be able to help if he dares. I think he worked for one of the auto manufacturers and a big pharmaceutical company before coming to Westcona. He's a pretty bright guy and probably knows more about that kind of thing than most people."

"Offer him a million bucks if we're successful," Hollis suggested.

"Him and a few other people...I expect."

They had another beer before noticing a payphone just inside the VFW's front door. Fletcher tried, again without success, to reach JT in Alice. They decided to go back to the cabin before it was too dark to find the trail.

They traveled in silence, each lost in thought.

— ‖ —

Logan was somewhat familiar with HF radio operations from the time he spent on Global Oil offshore drilling rigs and regional offices throughout the Middle East and Africa. Still, the transceiver's instruction manual might as well have been written in Klingon. Then there was the complicated-looking antenna tuner to complete the confusion. He finally found a cheat sheet that JT had prepared to help him remember how to use the devices. He had no idea what he was doing but followed the diagram and notes as best he could.

Steve went to the shed to start the generator and Logan turned on the power supply and transceiver when he heard the little engine cough to life. He slowly spun the VFO through the frequencies, practicing with the tuner as he moved around the bands and paying particular attention to the protocol practiced by the hams he heard on the air. They were mostly hearing call signs with the numbers seven, one, two, three, and zero in them but no fives like those in JT's call sign. JT had told them to find one in his log that had the number zero in it, and to use it when they tried to call him. Steve picked W0FTU as their borrowed call. Logan tuned up on 14.155 MHz, mustered his courage, and keyed the microphone.

"Is this frequency in use? Is this frequency in use? WD5CL WD5CL, this is W0FTU. WD5CL WD5CL, this is W0FTU calling."

There was no response, just the quiet crackle of static coming from the speaker. Logan waited a minute before trying again.

"WD5CL WD5CL, this is W0FTU calling."

Still nothing except soft static.

"There're two antennas hanging from the trees outside," Steve said. "I noticed that one is oriented east-west and the

other's north-south. I don't know much about radios but I'd
bet there's a logical reason. Let's see if the other antenna works
any better."

They switched to the other antenna, retuned, and tried
again.

"WD5CL WD5CL, this is W0FTU calling."

To their utter amazement, the speaker came alive with
a familiar voice.

"W0FTU, this is WD5CL. How copy?"

"WD5CL, this is W0FTU. Fine copy JT. This is Logan and
we're sure glad to hear your voice."

"Glad to hear you too, Addison. I just walked in the door.
Heard some disturbing news today on my way back from
Denver. Is everything all right up there? Over."

"Not really, JT. We heard the same news, and your boys
went into town to find a telephone. They were pretty upset
when they left, and aren't back yet. I expect them soon.
Everything else is fine. Will you keep the radio on so we can
talk after they get back? Over."

"Affirmative. If this band dies out, try using 3.675. I say
again, 3.675 MHz. Over."

"Copy 3.675 MHz if this band dies. We'll probably shut
down the generator for now but we'll try you again when the
boys get back. Over."

"Fine business, Addison. I'll be here or on 3.675 and listening. W0FTU, this is WD5CL clear on your final. Seventy-
three, Addison."

"Okay, JT. We'll be back to you later. W0FTU clear."

"What does seventy-three mean? You think it's some kind
of a code?" Steve asked his father.

"I have no idea but I've heard others using it when they
sign off. It must mean something like *goodbye* or *have a nice day*

or something like that. These people seem to have a language all their own," Logan said.

Logan was glad to finally have communications with JT. This ham radio was really something. He'd thought it was an outmoded communication service but was now thinking it might just be a fun and useful hobby. While he was confident in the young men's ability to handle themselves, it was comforting to have someone his own age and experience level available. Hopefully, they would be able to check in with each other every evening while they were exiled to the woods. Steve went out to shut down the generator while Logan began lighting the oil lamps and thinking about the evening meal.

— ‖ —

Steve was up on the OP when Fletcher called on the radio from his car. He had hauled the M79 grenade launcher, along with the heavy ammunition, up the game trail and spent the last hour lashing more pine boughs to the framework incorporated onto the rear half of the OP. He hoped that it would provide more protection from the wind-driven rain or snow that would surely strike the minute he came on duty. He had also rolled two boulders into the little outpost and fitted tree limbs and pine boughs between them to create a reasonably soft seat. Small canvas tarps were now stretched across the top of the outpost to further cut the wind and provide a dry place for the *Thumper*, as Fletcher sometimes referred to the M79. The ammunition, binoculars, and a blanket he had dragged up the hill were now out of the elements. His considerable labors should make the nighttime duty less uncomfortable for the others. He didn't really give a rat's ass but they might.

"I'm working on the OP and hauled some equipment up so the first guy on duty tonight won't have to carry so much in the dark. Where are you?"

"We're a couple hundred yards off the highway and headed your way. I'll turn the headlights on so you can watch for us. We had some good news from home today. How's everything here?"

"My dad talked to JT on the radio, and made arrangements to talk to him again tonight. Everything else is okay. I'll stay up here listening and watching for you. I want to see where I first spot your lights and can hear the car."

The men conversed on the VHF oilfield radios while Fletcher and Hollis worked their way toward the cabin. Steve reported briefly seeing lights where Fletcher estimated they were still more than a mile out. They disappeared from view for a moment and then reappeared. Steve didn't report hearing the engine until they were almost in front of the cabin. Sound was muffled in the woods, especially from high up on the OP. They'd have to depend on visual means of alert, or quiet interlopers might surprise them.

Logan had been listening to Steve's side of the conversation on the other handheld radio. Finally, he could hear Fletcher as he closed the last half-mile. Unfortunately, the small handheld radios didn't have much range on flat ground in this heavily wooded area. He was working on their dinner and anxious to hear what they had found out. Steve arrived from the OP about twenty minutes after Fletcher and Hollis rolled in, just as dinner was ready for the four hungry men. They shared the afternoon's events as they ate.

Steve's apparent emotional shift was noticeable and unexpected. He was suddenly participating in the conversation for the first time since arriving. However, his demeanor was more pugnacious and gritty than he had ever displayed in the past. He also seemed a decade older—and with a cold-blooded inhumanity in his eyes that was unsettling.

Logan was shocked to hear that his old friend Salem was looking for him. He figured the Saudis must be getting nervous

with all the bizarre news coming out of North America. Could
they be putting any of this together yet? He hoped not, because
the implications were ominous. Americans, in their self-indul-
gent arrogance, were quick to underestimate the Arab people.
Logan understood the intensity, persistence, and ingenuity they
were capable of when protecting their financial interests.
At least the Saudis weren't openly into all the Islamic fundamentalist jihad bullshit like some of the other countries in that
part of the world.

The men circled around the ham radio as soon as they
cleaned up the kitchen, hauled in some wood, put a pot of
coffee on the stove, and fired up the generator. Logan tuned to
14.155 MHz and could immediately tell the band was quiet.
He retuned to 3.675 MHz and the noise level increased
substantially. After listening for a minute and hearing nothing,
he keyed the microphone and tried to reach south Texas.

"WD5CL WD5CL, this is W0FTU calling."

"W0FTU, this is WD5CL. Good copy, Addison. Did the
boys get back? Over."

"Yes, they did, JT. I'll put Fletcher on and he can update
you."

"Hello JT," Fletcher said. "Bad stuff last night for the wives
and mother. They got lucky today and are now back together.
Hopefully, nobody will think to look there again. Even the dogs
got it from our friends. The women are pretty shook up but
doing okay now. The big guy's brother and nephews are watching over them until we can get back. Say, I need you to call my
auditor friend and see if he might be willing to help us with
some international banking arrangements. I'll call him next
time we get to a phone if he's open to it. Over."

"It's just insane that the cowards went after women, and
they're going to pay a price down the road. Can't say how
I really feel about it on the radio but I'm glad they're safe,

anyway. Yes I'll call your friend and see how he feels about it. Maybe I'll just call him when we get off the air. Over."

"Thanks, JT. I'll pass the microphone back to Logan. Let us know what he says. Over."

"Don't call me at the office. I'll check my answering machine at lunchtime and come right back here after work. That's it from this end. W0FTU, this is WD5CL clear on your final. Seventy-three."

"Okay, JT," Logan said after taking the microphone back from Fletcher. "We'll keep the generator and radio on for another hour or so just in case you have information tonight. If not, we'll try you again on the higher frequency between noon and 1300 hours tomorrow. We'll have the radio back on after 1700 hours. Take care of yourself, JT. WD5CL, this is W0FTU clear."

They agreed on the order of the night's guard mount and then moved into their own personal spheres. Hollis, grumbling about having to hike up the trail, donned his gear while Fletcher filled a thermos with coffee and put extra flashlight and radio batteries into his daypack. Steve briefed him on the OP improvements, and the location of the M79, binoculars, blanket, and extra ammunition before lying down on his bunk and closing his eyes to shut out the world. Logan moved over to the radio, put on a headset, and began twisting knobs and listening to radio chatter. Total darkness enveloped and shrouded them in relative safety once again.

— ⫴ — Twenty-Three — ⫴ —

THE SAUDI SOLDIERS LOCATED MARK STREETER'S home in Houston's River Oaks neighborhood. While only five o'clock on Monday morning, lights were already burning in the estate-home owned by the Global Oil president. Their intent was to observe the security precautions so plans to exploit them could be formulated by the next morning. In the off chance the opportunity presented itself today, they would kidnap the senior executive before he got into the early morning traffic on his way to the office. They assumed the normal electronic monitoring and security cameras were in place on the grounds and were expecting a Global limousine to arrive at any time.

In fact, the electronics were in place and normally a security limo would have arrived at six-thirty. However, this was not a normal morning at Global Oil. Global's standard security procedures were in disarray due to the recent loss of employees in their botched attempts to secure Neptune. Streeter had planned to arrive at the office early to get some work done before dealing with the federal agents, Justice Department attorneys, media, and questions from his own board of directors. Orders to pick him up at five o'clock had apparently not been properly communicated. He called the office and chewed out the security department dispatcher for screwing up his day before it was really underway. Frustrated and impatient, he decided to drive himself to work.

The Saudi team leader was watching the house through binoculars when he saw the garage door go up. He could hardly believe that Streeter was alone in the garage and apparently planning to leave in his private vehicle. The leader motioned the others to drive their van up beside the gate and prepare to block it. Streeter pulled out of the garage and started down the tree-lined, curving, three-hundred-foot driveway, hitting the remote gate-opener button as he approached the street.

Quickly blocking his path, two soldiers pounced on the vehicle before Streeter could react. They jerked open the door, yanked him unceremoniously from his seat, and roughly stuffed him through the van's side door. The leader calmly reversed Streeter's car back through the gate and along the adjacent security wall, shielding it from street view. He punched the remote control and dashed through the already closing gate. They were a block away and moving fast when it clanked shut.

— ‖ —

The Dallas-deployed special ops team staking out Branton Cole's suburban estate was not as lucky. They could see dogs running on the grounds and had no doubt that elaborate electronic security measures were active. A limousine arrived promptly at six-fifteen, dropping an agent at the gate before proceeding to the house.

After picking up Cole, the limo slowed at the gate to retrieve the alert security agent and quickly pulled away before the Saudis could seriously consider a move. They followed at a discreet distance but lost the limo as it accelerated into freeway traffic already headed for downtown Dallas.

— ‖ —

JT called Spencer Wainwright at his Dallas home on Sunday evening as Fletcher had requested. Wainwright was less than thrilled with the idea of opening a bank account, rightfully fearing that his involvement would result in his termination if discovered by Westcona senior management. An internal audit director would have a difficult time finding another job after being fired in what could easily turn out to be a very public corporate scandal. Being fifty-six years old wouldn't help, either.

"Damn, JT. Don't you think this thing is getting a little out of hand? Selling a discovery, or even fighting over its ownership, is one thing. But I think the companies' reactions have been really out of line."

"Yeah…they have. But what the hell choice does Boyd have? He's lost his job, is probably in trouble with the law, and has nothing to look forward to if this doesn't work out. There's no one more dangerous than someone with nothing to lose."

"Nothing to lose? He can still lose his family, more friends, and his own life! You really think we should be part of this? I mean, I'd do most anything for the guy but this is asking a hell of a lot, even for Fletcher Boyd."

"Well, Wainwright, I've had more time to think about it than you have…but yes. I'm going to help him any way I can. Don't you see how this discovery will change almost everything in the world? It isn't going to go away no matter what we do or don't do to help him."

"Have him call me," Wainwright said with obvious mixed feelings.

— ‖ —

JT tried calling Logan on the radio when he got up on Monday morning but couldn't make contact. He'd go home at noon to try again. Logan said they would be monitoring from noon to one o'clock, so it would have to wait until then.

His phone rang just before lunch with the surprise news that a three-man bodyguard unit would be with him by late in the day. He objected and argued that he had no need for protection but the news that Mark Streeter had been kidnapped that very morning changed his mind. Still, it would be damn embarrassing for an old iron-ass like him to have bodyguards. Then there was the issue of privacy when he was making radio contact with the boys. *Who the hell else could be involved in this thing already?* He needed to talk to Logan. He also needed to call Wainwright when he went home at noon and ask him to keep his ear to the ground at the corporate office…and to watch his own ass, too. Somebody must have let Neptune out of the bag, and now anyone privy to the secret had a tit in the wringer.

— ‖ —

Mark Streeter had been pumped so full of drugs that he was incapable of withholding answers to the Saudi's questions. Everything the Global Oil president knew about Neptune, Branton Cole, Fletcher Boyd, Hollis Cade, Steve Addison, Logan Addison, and Jake Taylor was now in their hands. They learned of the botched attempts to seize Neptune and Streeter's own feeling that Jake Taylor knew more than he was telling anyone at Westcona. Logan Addison was also missing, and presumed to be with his son or perhaps even with Boyd and Cade. Their location was unknown.

Being of no further value, Streeter was driven to Memorial Park and dumped like yesterdays garbage. The soldiers returned to their hotel to report their findings to Al Makhabarat Al A'amah in Riyadh for further analysis. They were told to rest in Houston while the intelligence people digested this incredible information.

The Saudi team in Dallas was soon instructed to abandon their mission to kidnap Branton Cole and proceed directly to Alice, Texas, four hundred miles to the south. Jake Taylor was the new target.

— ‖ —

A tightly controlled Cabinet-level committee was already preparing briefing information for President Reagan when news of Streeter's recovery arrived. A medical report followed soon thereafter. This had been a professional operation aimed at gaining important information as quickly as possible.

President Reagan asked for a revised Neptune risk assessment and actionable recommendations. He also ordered an intensified nationwide manhunt for Fletcher Boyd and Hollis Cade. These men were the key to whatever magnanimity or peril this discovery held for the world. The President wanted Neptune contained until its ramifications were better understood. They could sort out the details later.

— ‖ —

Logan took the little Jeep north looking for a payphone. Although he planned to go all the way to Roseau, he was relieved to find one at a country store only three and a half miles up the road in the small town of Skime. He dialed the number Fletcher had given him. What the hell time was it there? Nine hours difference? It was 6 p.m. local time on Monday in Saudi Arabia when Salem answered his telephone.

"Logan, my friend. I am concerned for you. Is everything all right in America?"

"Salem, that's sure a loaded question. Everything and nothing is ever all right in America. You know that," he responded with pseudo jocularity.

"Yes, that is so. I hope you are healthy and prosperous, my trusted friend."

"Salem, I know you didn't call to ask about my health or prosperity. What can I do for you?"

"You are correct, of course. I called because of the persistent rumors of serious problems within Global and a company called Westcona. While my business network is wide, I have no answers for questions being asked of me. Is there something I should know or could tell those with concerns here?"

Logan almost dropped the phone, his face suddenly beaded with perspiration despite the cool temperature. The heavy overcast filtered the sun's warmth but Logan was overheating. He didn't know how to answer his friend and his mind raced as he tried to form a response.

"Salem, I'm very concerned with the recent events involving Global and Westcona. Of course, you're perceptive enough to recognize problems when you hear them. I'm not at liberty to discuss it, although I sincerely wish I could. In fact, I may need your help before it's over," he confided.

"Are you in danger?"

"Yes, as is my only son. His wife and my unborn grandchild were murdered. I can't say more right now. I'm sorry, Salem."

"I am troubled by your words, Logan. As you and your son work in the petroleum industry, I must assume this involves my country's lifeblood. Are you able to confirm my assumption?"

"Salem, I can't say more, and appreciate that your inquiries are not yours alone. The United States government is now involved, and I'm not sure if Saudi Arabia or other OPEC member-nations can be of help. It's an enigma."

"That is an understatement, Logan, but I am also in an awkward position, my friend. I owe you a brother, yet harsh men are asking me difficult questions. I will help you and your son if you are in danger. You must let me help you, as I once allowed you to help my family."

"Thank you, Salem. I will if it comes to that. The best I can do with the other issue is to suggest that the Kingdom, or better yet OPEC, make official inquiries of my government based on news reports and intelligence concerns. I assure you there is a legitimate basis for concern. Please keep my name out of it to the extent possible. There have already been too many deaths over this and I would prefer that my son and I aren't added to the toll."

"You have said much without betrayal, Logan. Please be aware that actions beyond my control may already be under-way. I will honor your request and look forward to the day I am able to repay my debt to you. Please call my brother, Mahrous, in Medina if I am unavailable. He is handling the details of our intelligence-gathering efforts on behalf of the Kingdom. I am sure you are aware that the Saudi intelligence apparatus is act-ing at the behest of King Fahd. I will do my best to shield you from any actions they may be taking. Your friends at Aramco are also concerned for you. Goodbye and be safe, my friend."

— ‖ —

Hollis was listening to the news on the Sony shortwave radio when Logan came in the door.

"I'm afraid the Saudis and maybe OPEC are going to be getting into this soon, Hollis. I just talked to a friend of mine in the Middle East and he had lots of questions about what's happening. He's the guy whose message you brought back yesterday. They know something's up."

"That answers a question or two. Mark Streeter got his ass kidnapped this morning and nobody seems to know who did it. I reckon we're the only ones that already figured it out."

"Yeah, you're probably right. We'll try to raise JT on the radio at noon and see what he has to say."

"Son of a bitch, Logan. I had a talk with Fletcher about giving this thing up when we were in town but he talked me out of it. Now we've got a band of Bedouins after us, too? You think we're doing the right thing?"

"I did at least until I learned about the Saudis…and these guys aren't Bedouins but they'll skin you just as quick. One thing's for sure; we've got to get this taken care of fast or give it up and hope the government can protect us."

"We'd be better off just shooting ourselves than to depend on them."

Fletcher was on the OP watching the logging trail. While they didn't keep a twenty-four hour guard posting, they tried to man the lookout as best they could during the daylight hours and always at night. It was a long walk and a real pain in the ass to get to, but the OP provided the best hope they had of detecting problems while they still had time to react.

They continued to improve the small structure, sometimes for no other reason than to fight the boredom but mostly because nighttime duty was already so miserable that any little thing one could do was appreciated by all. A wooden bench had replaced the makeshift seat Steve had made, and a brown canvas tarp was now stretched and fitted around the rocks to reduce the effects of the cold, biting wind.

— ‖ —

Joey Andersen rolled up to the cabin with a lot on his mind. When he had called JT to confirm that the men were, in fact, his friends and authorized to be in the cabin, JT asked him to watch out for them while inferring they were there for more than just a vacation. Despite JT's assurance that his friends were the good guys if anything bad happened, he was still disquieted. Each time he saw the car, he pondered as to why the Texans had Minnesota plates. He hadn't run them through DMV but still thought it might be a good idea. Of course, JT was a Texan and his little Jeep had Minnesota plates. The difference was that he knew JT parked his Jeep in the rented Thief River Falls garage when he flew his plane back to Texas. These guys appeared to have driven their car all the way from Texas.

Joey also finally met the fourth member of this little gang and was told that Hollis had been out for a morning walk the day he first stopped by. He recalled that the others had just rolled out of the sack and found it hard to believe one of them had gotten up so much earlier and left the cabin. Joey basically trusted JT, yet had a nagging feeling that something wasn't quite right. And the guy named Boyd was missing this time. There always seemed to be one missing. He enjoyed a cup of strong, delicious coffee with the three of them and returned to his duties patrolling the rural area. It seemed he had more questions when he left than when he arrived.

— ‖ —

Fletcher started the generator when he returned to the cabin at noon. Steve had cooking duty and was getting lunch together while Logan fired up the ham radio. It came to life as they began their meal.

"W0FTU W0FTU, this is WD5CL calling."

Logan took his sandwich to the radio and picked up the microphone.

"WD5CL, this is W0FTU. Go ahead, JT."

"Hello, Addison. A few things to report. Let Boyd know the auditor is waiting for his call. I think he'll help but he's not real happy about it. Not sure if you heard the news, but Streeter ran into some trouble this morning. They found him in a park a short while ago, drugged and shaken but unharmed. I have some tough guys coming from the Big D to watch out for my best interests. Sounds like some other organization is getting into the act and my employer wants me safe, although I'm not sure what that will do for my privacy. WD5CL, back to you Addison."

"I'm glad they're sending you some help, JT. We did hear about Streeter and have a pretty good idea of who's involved. I just returned a call to a very concerned friend who's nine time zones east in Sandland. A lot of questions are being asked, and not only in their part of the world. Sounds like Streeter should have received the same treatment you're getting. Everything else is fine here. The boys are working on their big project but haven't settled on their next move yet. Anything else from your end? Over."

"Nothing else here. I'll have the radio on after work. Let's try to touch base then. W0FTU, this is WD5CL clear on your final. Seventy-three, Addison."

"Okay, JT. We'll power back up at five o'clock and keep it on for a couple of hours. Thanks for the help and watch your backside. W0FTU clear."

— ‖ —

Fletcher and Steve drove back to Skime to call Spencer Wainwright in Dallas.

"Spencer, Fletcher."

"Hello, Fletcher. I was hoping you wouldn't call. I'm concerned you've gone completely over the edge. Where are you?"

"Sorry. Can't burden you with that information. We want an offshore account and need your help to do it. Are you willing?"

"To lose my job? Sure, I'm only fifty-six years old with no job prospects on the horizon. Why the hell not? Oh, or did you mean to just get killed? That's an attractive alternative. Why don't you just give this thing up to the feds and let them figure out what to do with it?"

"Yeah, like they ever had a solution to anything. I don't think so. You're wasting my time if you don't have the balls for it. I'll find another way, Spencer. See you..."

"Dammit, Fletcher. I never gave up on anything worthwhile in my life. This is different, though. Are you absolutely sure you want to go through with this?"

"I am."

"I still think you're out of your mind, but I have an idea or two. Do you know where you might be living when this is over? Damn, that assumes a lot, doesn't it?"

"Is our location really going to be important?"

"It will be if you're in some backwater hellhole without telephones or a decent banking system, picking bugs off your ass like a band of monkeys."

"We'll have phones and a real banking system, Spencer. I just want it in a place that's outside the United States and has some seriously strict banking privacy laws."

"I suggest two accounts so you can split things up a bit and limit exposure. Europe has some countries with established banking systems that fit your needs. I think another account, in a different part of the world, would make sense. Someplace in Asia or a South Pacific country."

"Can you do that?"

"Sure, but you'll owe me some money. The brokers here in Dallas charge to set up the accounts, and I'll have to fund them with my own money."

"You won't have to worry about money if we're successful, Spencer. In fact, you can plan on retiring in style if we're successful and you help us. Go ahead with two accounts in very different parts of the world. Anything else you need from us?"

"I'm sure there will be but I don't know what yet. I'll go as far as I can and let you know what else I need. Call me in a couple of days and watch your step out there. You're in way over your head."

— || —

The Saudi special operations soldiers arrived in Alice in time to locate the Westcona yard before Jake Taylor's workday ended. They were surprised when he left the building accompanied by three men who did not look like oilfield workers. One of the men rode with Taylor, while the other two followed in a separate car. The Saudis tailed them the short distance east to Taylor's house near the golf course. Professionals recognize other professionals, and the team was surprised that Westcona had acted so quickly to protect Taylor. They noted his house number and drove down to the corner to see the street name. Confident that they could find the house again, they drove to a restaurant for dinner and to discuss what this meant to their orders.

Kidnapping Jake Taylor was possible, but not without violence that certainly would not go unnoticed in this small town. They checked into the Holiday Inn and changed clothes before driving back over to Taylor's neighborhood to conduct a walking evaluation of the security and get a feel for the general activity level. A car sat in front of the house with one bodyguard in it. They assumed one or both of the others were inside. Returning to their car, one of the soldiers glanced back and noticed a red blinking light high above the house. What was it? They would have to wait until daylight to see what the light was mounted on.

— ‖ —

The off-duty Westcona bodyguard ate dinner in the hotel restaurant and decided to have a nightcap before getting some sleep. His two partners were guarding Taylor overnight and he would resume his daytime duty in the morning. It had been a long day. He stopped at the front desk and asked where the bar was located. The young desk clerk smiled and pointed ten feet to her right at a dark, heavy-looking wooden door.

"We put it right here off the lobby so the sleeping rooms are far away as possible. Quieter for people that way, plus the oilfield people only have to walk in the front door and go straight into the bar. Ain't you one of them Westcona people visiting from Dallas?"

"Now how did you know that?" he asked flirtatiously.

"Oh, we try to know who our real important guests are. Westcona's a pretty big deal down here and we know all your salesmen and managers. You must be here to meet with those *Aay*-rabs that checked in tonight. We don't get many *Aay*-rabs around here."

"Yeah, that's right," the man responded alertly. "I didn't know they were here already. What rooms do they have? I might just call and say howdy."

"Funny, but they only got one room. It's 149 though we ain't supposed to tell people other people's room numbers. Security, you know, but seeing you're here to meet with them, I guess it don't really matter none. Seems kinda strange with both of 'em in one room."

"Yeah, well they live a little differently than we do. There were supposed to be four of them," he said fishing for more information. "Only two arrived tonight?"

"Yep, just the two. They said they were having meetings with somebody this week, so we figured it must be with you...coming all the way from Dallas like you did. Well, like I said, the bar's right there and the house phone's just 'round the corner here if you want to call them."

—⦙⦙— Twenty-Four —⦙⦙—

LOGAN AND JT SPOKE ONLY BRIEFLY on Monday evening, mostly because JT had one of the bodyguards in his house and another sitting outside. They scheduled another call for seven the next morning. His ham radio equipment was set up in the smallest of three bedrooms. However, at fifteen hundred square feet, the house did not provide significant privacy. The bodyguard showed no interest in what JT was doing as long as he stayed in the house. JT knew Fletcher would not have the generator running this late and thus would not be monitoring the radio in Minnesota. The news of possible Arab agents arriving in Alice would have to wait until morning.

"W0FTU W0FTU, this is WD5CL calling on schedule," JT called on Tuesday morning.

"WD5CL, this is W0FTU. Go ahead JT," Logan promptly answered.

"Morning, Addison. My bird dogs are outside so I have a little more privacy right now. We believe some of your friends from Sandland have already made their way to Alice. My guards are thrilled with the idea of some action but I'm not. They talked to Dallas and decided to just play along, at least until they know for sure or the other guys make a move. Anything happen overnight up there? Over."

"Nothing like that, JT. You don't want to mess with my friends. That's a fact. They have a much different outlook on life than what you're accustomed to. Watch yourself. Fletcher talked to his auditor yesterday and they're working on something. We're going to make some decisions this morning. Any chance you might be able to come up this weekend to give us a ride? Over."

"Not with my new shadows, I can't. There's commercial service from the airport nearest you where we landed. Or, I can call Neumann and see if he wants to do some traveling. Over."

"I'll let you know. Are you going to get home at noon, or should we just try again after work? Over."

"Why don't you monitor this frequency from noon to one, and I'll see what I can do. I don't want my new friends to think my radio time is anything other than a hobby so I may have to wait until tonight. Over."

"Understood. We'll have it on at noon and again after five. Watch yourself and I'll talk to you soon. W0FTU clear."

"Seventy-three, Addison. WD5CL clear."

— ‖ —

After breakfast, the soldiers drove straight to Jake Taylor's neighborhood to see what the blinking red light above his house was attached to. To their surprise, it was a tall narrow tower supporting a large horizontally-oriented antenna array and a couple of small vertical antennas. Near the top, just under the horizontal array, was what appeared to be some kind of an electric motor along with the red light they had seen the previous evening. They knew it was some kind of radio station but were unsure of what it was doing in a residential neighborhood. They went back to the hotel and called the Saudi embassy in Washington for technical help.

The embassy communications officer asked them to carefully describe what they had seen. After a few questions, he concluded it was a residential ham radio station with high frequency and very high frequency capabilities. The communications officer explained that high frequency was referred to as HF in knowledgeable radio circles but often called shortwave by those with less technical expertise, or hobbyists who listened to broadcast stations from around the world. It was used for medium and long-range communications. Very high frequency was referred to as VHF and used for short-range communications by businesses, police, fire, aircraft, military, civilian government, and ham radio operators. This information, along with the men's report, was relayed to the team leader in Houston and to the Saudi intelligence service in Riyadh. They were instructed to continue probing Taylor's security coverage and to grab him at the earliest opportunity without creating a police response. New instructions would be forthcoming after the report was analyzed.

— ‖ —

A fresh pot of coffee, a box of stale donuts, and an opened carton of Marlboros sat on the table in front of Fletcher, Hollis, and Steve. Logan had picked up a radio and a Mini-14 before walking to the OP for the morning guard watch. The day was crisp and clear with the temperature registering at thirty-six degrees on the old thermometer mounted outside the dirty and smudged kitchen window. The sun was finally back and a welcome sight with its glinting rays warming their spirits as well as their bodies. The last of the leaves had blown to the ground in the few days they had been at the cabin and it smelled like late autumn.

Fletcher was happy to have some time alone with Hollis and Steve. He knew Hollis was very concerned with how things were working out and was afraid Steve may have been having similar conversations with his father or Hollis. He took the opportunity to frame the news and activity in a positive fashion. Any indication of their former rank within Westcona was long gone. The three had bonded in much the same way combat soldiers have bonded over the centuries. Still, every army needs leadership and Fletcher naturally provided it.

"I have Wainwright opening a couple of offshore bank accounts for us," he told his friends. "He's going to open one in Europe and another somewhere in Asia or the Pacific. Once the money hits the accounts, it'll be outside the reach of U.S. law enforcement and hidden from everyone except the banks and us. We're all going to be very wealthy, very soon."

"How are we going to get the government to send money?" Hollis asked.

"That's what we need to decide," Fletcher continued, thankful that Steve had not questioned the likelihood of their success or indicated he was not going to participate. "We'll have to meet with them eventually. The good news is that we already have them convinced that Neptune is real; at least the scientists at Ames were convinced. Now we also know that Saudi Arabia and maybe other OPEC countries are interested and looking for us. We have to assume that whatever information Global had is now theirs, thanks to Streeter's kidnapping. What we don't know is whether Global and Westcona caved in to government pressure and shared any information about us. I doubt it, but we have to consider that possibility. I'm not sure how long we could last if they all came after us at once. We need to move quickly and get this done before they consolidate their forces."

"You mean that besides Westcona, Global, and the United States government, we should consider selling it to the Arabs?" Hollis asked. "I thought we were pretty much agreed that Neptune should stay in the United States."

"Well, that was the plan…but maybe we should broaden our thinking. Would we be able to live peaceably in the United States after all that's happened? I don't know the answer to that. If we sell it to the government, we might be safe from the Arabs, though. They'd have no reason to worry about us at that point," Fletcher reasoned.

"But if we sold it to the Arabs, our government would have a problem with us enjoying the money. No way would they allow us to just live out our lives in peace. The Arabs would worry that we'd sell it again and ruin their oil industry. They'd have to kill us," Hollis stated without emotion.

"They would," Fletcher agreed. "How comfortable would you two be with moving out of the United States for the rest of your very wealthy lives? We'd have to assume new identities and keep low profiles forever."

"My dad and I talked about that the other day," Steve said. "When you really think about it, that's about the only way it can work. Even if we sold it to our government, the Arabs might still hound us—or prefer we were dead. Our only way out would be if the government gave it or sold it to all the other oil-dependent nations and took the heat off us."

"Selling it to the government and getting some kind of protection, like the Witness Protection Program, might be our best bet," Hollis added. "Still, they wouldn't be happy with us having all that money and then having to protect us on top of it. What kind of life would that be for us? I'm not very good at having strange people around or following rules anymore. I gave that up as best I could when I left the Navy."

"And where could you live without federal protection if you stayed in the States?" Fletcher asked.

"I've always had a hankerin to be the Post Master in Terlingua, Texas, out in the Big Bend. That'd beat the shit out living in the lower Valley around McAllen. "

"Other than chili and beer, there's nothing out there. Are you thinking Sara would go for that?"

"Chili, beer, and hardly any people. Think of it…heaven on earth! And hell yes Sara wants to move. She's already allowed that she'll move out there as soon as she sees balls on a heifer."

"Oh yeah. It sounds likes she's packing boxes already," Fletcher laughed. "So let's get back to our problem. What if our government decides it would be easier to just capture us, take Neptune, and cut us out of the deal?" Fletcher asked. "What options would we have? Take them to court? Threaten to take it to Europe or Japan or OPEC? I can see how they might just like us to disappear, too. Why pay us for something they think they can take by force?"

"I don't like the thought of my own government teaming up with Westcona and Global to catch us, either," Hollis groused.

The men glumly considered what few viable alternatives they really had. At first, they had thought this would be a positive and world-changing discovery but it was turning out to be something completely different. Changes of this magnitude disrupt the international status quo, and history vividly demonstrates that the economic losers usually react poorly to the change. They tend to look for scapegoats and even start wars over things much less earthshaking.

Paranoia was settling on them like a heavy, wet blanket. While they preferred to think the United States would willingly pay for the technology and turn them into world-famous celebrities, common sense told them otherwise. Whoever ultimately owned Neptune would be better off if the men who discovered it ceased to exist. That reality helped them make their decision. Fletcher could see that Steve either didn't care about the transaction or was looking forward to the violence

almost certainly to come. In either case, it appeared that he was
going along with it for his own reasons—and that was fine.

— ‖ —

Al Makhabarat Al A'amah worked feverishly with the information they had cobbled together. The Addison tie between
Global and Westcona was put in place. The father–son issue
was nothing more than a fortunate coincidence, one that could
work in their favor if they could get to Logan Addison. Jake
Taylor's participation and jet airplane were factored into the
equation and his ham radio station was considered to be of
possible importance. Neptune's existence was deemed
absolute. Westcona and Global's failure to contain Neptune was
accepted but not fully understood. How could a company as
large and powerful as Global Oil have difficulty controlling one
of its senior employees? Even more baffling was how Westcona
could fail to control three mid-level employees. In the Arab
world, people willingly complied with official wishes or they
permanently disappeared.

Fletcher Boyd and Hollis Cade were the wildcards. They
knew little of these men but considered them to be at the heart
of the problem. The likelihood that they and the Addison's
were acting together was high. Somehow, Jake Taylor was
actively involved. There could also be others quietly helping
the renegades. Still, the group needed transportation and
communications. If Taylor's aircraft had been used to get them
this far, could Taylor be the only reasonable key to quickly
finding them? Were they using ham radio to communicate?
The Saudis' problem was one of manpower in the United
States. The required resources just weren't available, and they
were reluctant to disclose Neptune to any other nation, even
those they considered friendly.

The director of Al Makhabarat Al A'amah reported his assessment and conferred with King Fahd and his military staff. A decision was made to send a communications expert to Alice to determine whether or not Jake Taylor's ham radio station was part of the equation. After much discussion, a reluctant decision was also made to bring a semi-trusted and economically vulnerable OPEC ally into the mix. The Saudis wanted a last-ditch option as well as an unsophisticated patsy to carry it out on their behalf.

The Iraqi president was more than willing to provide support in North America. After all, Saddam Hussein currently had Iraqi Air Force officers undergoing advanced fighter training at Naval Air Station Meridian in Mississippi as well as at the Canadian Forces Base in Winnipeg, Manitoba. When Iraqi forces had captured more than a dozen F-14 Tomcat fighters in their ongoing war with Iran, they needed specialized tactical and avionics training along with parts and maintenance training. Saddam wasted no time requesting NATO assistance in this opportunity to substantially upgrade his embarrassingly antiquated Air Forces, which then consisted of French and Soviet hand-me-downs. Training was being conducted in the United States and Canada. While the Saudi Arabian Air Force also had pilots training on F-15 Eagles at Luke Air Force Base in the United States, they wanted the blame to fall elsewhere if an attack to contain Neptune was necessary.

The Iraqi leader, whose contempt for the West was anything but secret, was also receiving clandestine intelligence and military assistance from the United States through the CIA. He had enjoyed numerous personal meetings with Vice President George Bush in late 1985 and early 1986. The United States, Canada, and NATO deemed it important to have a strong ally in Iraq, considering the Islamic fundamentalist problem broiling within their neighbor, Iran. Iraq also had everything to lose if Neptune was released to the industrialized world.

— ‖ —

The generator was running and the transceiver tuned to 3.675 MHz at five o'clock. JT had told them to switch to the lower frequency after sundown. Logan didn't understand why the higher frequency they used during the day wasn't useable in the evening but it did seem to work that way.

Fletcher was putting the finishing touches on four ruffed grouse he had cooked in cream of chicken soup. Hollis so enjoyed the plump, succulent game birds that he seldom left the cabin without watching for an opportunity to shoot a few. His only problem was not having the appropriate firearm for the task. They didn't have a .22 or a shotgun to make the task easier and much less messy. He blew the hell out of the birds with the Mini-14 despite his valiant attempts to just shoot the heads off. As long as Joey Andersen didn't show up before the evidence was consumed, everything would be fine with the State of Minnesota, too. He smiled to himself at the absurdity of that thought. They were in survival mode and having the right hunting license wasn't close to being on their radar, although it seemed like it should. That was behavior from another life that already seemed remote. He wondered if they would ever have a normal life again.

"W0FTU, W0FTU, this is WD5CL."

"WD5CL, this is W0FTU. Good to hear you again, JT," Logan said with sincerity. "How are things in your world?"

"Everything's fine here, Addison. Still have my shadows but I guess that's the good news. Did the boys decide anything important today? Over."

"Yes, and I'll be leaving here tomorrow. Is my car still at your house? Over."

"No. I took it over to the Westcona yard where it wouldn't be so obvious. You coming back here? Over."

"Yeah, my flight's scheduled into Corpus Christi at eight-fifteen tomorrow night. Can you pick me up, or send somebody you trust? Over."

"I'll have somebody pick you up in your car. You shouldn't come here. Over."

"Understood. I'll be staying at my son's house down south. I need to tidy up some loose ends for him and then do something for the cause. That should be a real quiet place these days. Over."

"I'll send a second car to the airport so you can head south straight from there. Call me at the house when you get in. I'm anxious to hear what they came up with. Over."

"Will do, JT. It'll be about eleven before I get down there. I'll talk to you then. The boys will monitor here on the same schedule we've been using. W0FTU clear on your final."

"Okay, Addison. Safe travels. WD5CL clear."

— ‖ —

Joey Andersen was still troubled by the Minnesota plates on the Oldsmobile parked at JT's cabin. JT had told him the men were the *good guys*, yet he didn't like it when something nagged at him like this. He bumped into a Roseau County deputy sheriff while having lunch and asked him to run the plate number he had in his notebook. Within minutes, the dispatcher called back saying the plate belonged to an Oldsmobile Delta 88 from Crystal, Minnesota. The registered owner's name didn't ring a bell with Joey but at least the car matched. He hadn't looked at the VIN but it sure was the same type car. Puzzled, he wrote down the owner's name and address before thanking the deputy and driving back into the woods. Rather than solve his problem, it opened up another that didn't make sense.

If these guys had flown in from Texas with JT, why did they have a car owned by someone in a Minneapolis suburb? He'd have to think about that.

— ‖ — Twenty-Five — ‖ —

STEVE, LOGAN, AND FLETCHER WERE awakened by the radio call from Hollis at o'dark-thirty on Wednesday morning. Hollis had drawn the late guard mount, and it was still hours from sun-up and the normal end of his duty. Logan heated water to shave and bathe while Fletcher started breakfast. By four-thirty, the three were ready to leave for Logan's six o'clock departure from Thief River Falls on Mesaba Airlines. Since they would have no further use for JT's Jeep, they planned to return it to the garage while in town.

The wonderful aroma of wood smoke and frying bacon brought Hollis off the OP as they were loading the car with what little Logan was taking back to Texas. Logan handed Steve the big Colt 1911 autoloader he had borrowed from JT as he got into Fletcher's Oldsmobile, and Steve headed for the little Jeep. Fletcher stopped him and told him to drive the Olds so he could spend the trip with his father rather than alone in the Jeep. With Fletcher in the Jeep, the mini-convoy drove west down the dark logging trail as Hollis settled into his breakfast, tuning the Sony shortwave radio for some morning news.

Logan paid cash for his ticket, a nearly full day of travel after layovers in Minneapolis and Dallas. Law enforcement was not looking for him, although both companies dearly wanted to find him. To his knowledge, he was not yet on federal radar, assuming neither company had told the whole story. Even if the local police became aware of his presence in McAllen, it would appear quite reasonable for the missing engineer's father to be there taking care of the house. Still, the clock was ticking on the feds making the connection between Shelley's murder, Steve's disappearance, and Neptune. He wouldn't be able to stay at Steve's house for very long, but he didn't need much time to clean up and secure the house, make his calls, and disappear again.

— ‖ —

The Saudi communications specialist flew to Corpus Christi on Wednesday morning and rented a car for the forty-mile drive to Alice. By lunchtime, he walked up to the Holiday Inn front desk to check for messages from his compatriots. Earlier that morning, the two Saudi special ops soldiers had watched Jake Taylor and two bodyguards leave Taylor's house and go directly to the Holiday Inn where they conferred with a third bodyguard before leaving with Taylor for the Westcona yard. Taylor had only one guard during the day? Perhaps this was a weakness they could exploit. Obviously the Westcona body-guards had rooms at the Holiday Inn.

Realizing they must keep an even lower profile around the hotel for fear of being made by the Westcona security detail, the soldiers decided to move to a motel located south of Highway 44 in the more industrialized area of Alice. Fewer comforts and amenities, but certainly more covert for their purposes. The two soldiers were checked out and waiting in the lobby when the communications specialist arrived.

The trio made the short drive to Taylor's house, in the northeast quadrant of the small city, to show the specialist the antenna and tower. He studied the tower, estimating it at sixty feet in height, and quickly identified the primary antenna as a multi-band beam antenna. To most people, it looked like an oversized outdoor television antenna laid on its side so the elements were horizontal to the ground. Knowledgeable radio people knew it was a directional antenna used for long-range communications in what the general public thought of as the shortwave bands. A single-wire antenna, which he recognized as a quarter-wave dipole used on the eighty meter band, was attached high on the tower and draped toward a tree on the back of the property.

Taylor's setup included a rotator which allowed him to point the beam antenna to any compass bearing from inside the house. The longest antenna elements extended about forty feet across the yard, just about to the six-foot cedar fence separating Taylor's house from the neighbor's. The fact that the yard was fenced did not please the specialist but the fact that the antenna elements extended nearly to the property line did.

He had hoped to be able to approach the tower base while Taylor was transmitting but could see that would be difficult. However, he had a piece of equipment that would work nearly as well if he could get to the fence on the neighbor's side and nearly under the antenna elements. After reviewing Taylor's normal schedule with the soldiers, he asked to be driven back to his car so he could check into the motel and sort through the suitcase of equipment he had brought from Washington. He would be back when the sun went down and Taylor came home from work.

If Taylor used his HF radio, the specialist would attempt to determine the frequency being used and then tune his portable receiver to hear what was being said or at least Taylor's side of it, depending on the distance to and quality of the other station's transmitting system. It might take a few days but he should be able to confirm or reject the use of the radio for the purpose suspected by his superiors.

When the specialist got to his motel room, he called the Saudi embassy in Washington and directed a technician to purchase a Radio Amateur Callbook at a local ham radio shop to find the call sign of Jake Taylor, licensed in Alice, Texas. Although not critical, he wanted every advantage in his quest to identify Taylor's transmissions. Taylor wasn't the only ham in Alice so having his unique call sign would help. Now it was going to be a waiting game requiring some luck on his part.

— ‖ —

After dropping Logan at the airport, Fletcher made good on his promise to call the Cade ranch and assure the women of their safety. Hollis had insisted although Fletcher may have otherwise foregone the call. He was tiring of Katie's negative attitude.

"Are you and the kids doing okay?" Fletcher asked.

"Yes, no one has tried to kill us or kidnap us again," she said sarcastically.

"Don't think for a minute that hasn't been worrying me. I know how hard it must have been for you, but they shouldn't be looking for you in the same place again."

"Fletcher, they found us once and they can find us again. I can't do this much longer. In fact, I'm at my wits end right now. It's unfair of you to be leaving us here in danger, especially when it's for nothing more than money. Dammit, I've had to shoot one person and help break another's neck. I'm beyond sick about all this and I want it to end."

"I'm sorry about that, Katie, and I wish I could undo everything that's happened to you — but I can't. If it helps any, try to think about it as them doing it to themselves. They forced it...you didn't do anything but defend yourself."

"Bullshit. Your little mind games don't change anything or make it right. You need to get back here and take care of us. That's where your priority should be. You need to give your discovery to the government and have them protect us."

"But they won't protect us. That's the whole problem," Fletcher said. "If they'd pay us what it's worth and be able to protect us, I'd do it in a heartbeat. But they wouldn't and couldn't. That's why we have to finish this ourselves."

"I might not be here when you return...if you return," she said. "You're out of control and putting money above our safety. You're sick, Fletcher."

"Katie, don't talk like that. I love you and the girls, but try to see this from my perspective. The government isn't going to help us. We're on our own. I just need a little more time to get this settled. I promise."

Fletcher reluctantly hung up but stood in the phone booth for a moment collecting his thoughts. He knew he was right about the government, just as he knew Katie and the girls were safe. *Why can't she see this for what it is?* Of course she was afraid for the girls, and he understood that. Up close violence and being forced to defend yourself is horrible. While they had always talked about the subject and agreed they should be able to protect themselves, perhaps talking about it and actually doing it were far too different to reconcile for Katie. After all, she had no serious training or experience to fall back on like he did.

He knew he and Katie were drifting apart and probably had been for years, but he didn't like what he was hearing from her. His emotions were vacillating between pride in her performance, sadness over the state of their relationship, and disappointment in her attitude. Husbands and wives should change and grow together but his gut told him that wasn't happening in their case. He had to push the thoughts out of his head for now and gas up the Jeep before meeting Steve at the garage.

They needed to buy groceries and make another phone call but it was still too early. A comfortable looking coffee shop in downtown Thief River Falls caught Fletcher's eye. As good a place as any to pass the time and get out of the cold. Before heading back to the cabin, they would gas up the Oldsmobile, buy another ten gallons of kerosene, and find some lantern fuel. Too bad they didn't have seawater and the chemicals they needed to make Neptune. It would have been much easier than chasing around looking for all the different fuels they needed today.

The coffee shop was surprisingly full which made them overly-cautious until they studied faces and decided everyone looked like a local. Mostly retired men enjoying the early-morning company of old friends, much the same as in any rural community.

After two cups of coffee and their second breakfast of the day, they made their way to the Kmart for lantern fuel and new t-shirts, socks, and underwear. It was much easier buying new than trying to find a place to wash the old and they were in great need of washing. It was after ten-thirty when they came out of the Kmart.

Fletcher returned to the Oldsmobile to pick up a roll of quarters and a small notebook before going back to the payphone in front of the store to begin the next phase of Neptune. He dialed the number on the business card resting on the notebook.

"Doctor Edwards speaking," the director of Ames Laboratory said.

"Fletcher Boyd here, Doctor. I won't stay on the line long, so I want you to answer my questions quickly. Is the government still interested in purchasing Neptune?"

"Mr. Boyd, where are you? There are people looking for you all over the country."

"Quickly, Doctor. Do you want Neptune or not?"

"Oh my. Yes. You need to turn yourselves in and talk to the authorities. We want Neptune very badly…I can't stress that enough."

"Give me a name and number to call. I'm sure somebody told you what to say if I called, right?"

"Indeed. They assumed you wouldn't turn yourself in but I have to ask. They promise to protect you and Mr. Cade if you could see fit to trust them."

"Would you trust them after what happened in Ames?"

"That was your employer and Global Oil, Mr. Boyd. The Justice Department knows you were attacked and were only defending yourselves if you were even involved in the violence. I'm sure they wouldn't worry about that issue if you turn yourselves in."

"Yeah, right. Nineteen people killed and they wouldn't even ask us about it. Time's up, Doc. Who do I call?"

"You will be calling the White House, Mr. Boyd. They set up a special number so they won't miss your call. You will be speaking with a Mr. Smith who is a special assistant to the President."

Steve looked at his watch as Fletcher hung up the phone.

"You were on for a minute and twelve seconds. How long does it take to trace a call?"

"I'm not sure. Longer than that, I think. Let's get gas, find a grocery store, and think about this before we make the next call," Fletcher suggested before he relayed what Edwards had said.

The men discussed their options while picking out food that would be easy to heat at the cabin. Turning themselves in was not a viable option. Calling the White House made them both nervous, especially considering the array of technology they feared could be used to pinpoint their location during the call.

They found a phone booth near the grocery store and, after a deep breath to focus his mind, Fletcher began feeding quarters into the telephone.

"Mr. Smith, this is Fletcher Boyd. I'm hanging up in thirty seconds so listen up. Neptune will cost you one billion dollars, with a B as in *Bravo*. You will wire the money to an offshore account of our choosing. There will be no criminal charges against my friends or me. You will provide us with new identities. Repeat what I just said."

"One billion dollars wired offshore. No criminal charges. New identities," the man smoothly responded. "I'll need to get approval. How can we reach you?"

"I'll call you," Fletcher said. He hung up the phone and looked at Steve.

"Twenty-five seconds."

"Good. Let's head for the cabin."

— ‖ —

Sara Cade invited Katie on a walk with the twins and the dog. Felecia and Taryn seemed to have recovered from what they had witnessed over the past few days — at least on the surface. Thirteen-year-olds are amazingly resilient yet Sara wondered how the little girls were suppressing the horrors. They acted carefree and happy as they ran into the field with their dog, chasing each other around while Lady jumped and barked. Sara knew the girls missed their father and were confused by what was going on. Still, they certainly trusted Katie and Fletcher to watch out for them.

"You were a little emotional with Fletcher this morning," Sara said quietly as they watched the girls play. She had heard Katie's side of the conversation with Fletcher.

"He has no right putting us in this situation," Katie shot back. Her eyes welled with tears and she quickly wiped them with her sleeve before continuing. "We've killed people and you seem to think that's all right."

"We defended ourselves from people who were trying to kidnap us. There's one hell of a difference," the older woman said. "Why are you upset with Fletcher? You've been married to him for a long time, and this is the same Fletcher I met five years ago when he came to Lindsay. What's changed? Am I missing something?"

"No, but my daughters are in jeopardy. Fletcher has no right to do that to them...to us," Katie said vehemently, her tears now gone. "I know this is all about their discovery and what it could mean to the world but that doesn't give me any sense of security for the girls. I just can't sit here day after day hoping the girls don't have to witness more brutality. I just can't do it anymore."

"Look, Katie. Fletcher certainly didn't mean for all this to happen. Our guys have obviously been double-crossed by both companies and probably the federal government. They've defended themselves and kept us out of danger as best they could. From the sounds of things, they're doing a pretty darn good job of it for guys just flying by the seat of their pants. They aren't doing anything to you and the girls to deliberately cause you any harm."

"Nothing to me and the girls? What are you talking about? Think what this has already done to them. I know Fletcher is out there someplace trying to make a deal, but I'm the one left here with the girls trying to keep some semblance of normalcy in their lives. What kind of life will we have once this is over? Things will never be the same. What happens if he's killed?"

Sara knew better than to push Katie on that subject because she was also afraid of what might happen to Hollis. She was terrified of life without him and missed him terribly already. Still, she had endured separation before and trusted him to do what he felt he needed to do. They walked in silence while Sara considered another approach to help Katie deal with her fears. Though she felt a lot of annoyance when she thought about what Katie had said to Fletcher earlier that morning, she knew she had to curb her remarks.

"Do you have any concept of how hard Fletcher has worked to give you and the girls the lifestyle you have? Do you have any idea what he's gone through? Is going through? "

"I just want a nice quiet life for the kids. We don't need all the things he buys us. I want him home at night and focused on us, not his job and where it might take him over the next ten years. I'm tired of his always reaching for more, and I want him to slow down."

"You married him but seem to have conveniently over-looked the fact that he's a striver and always has been. You must have found it attractive at one time. Guys like him don't change, they keep looking for opportunities. Now he's got his hands on something that will make us rich beyond all reason and you just keep poking at him with a sharp stick. If you think he's going to change now, you're in a dream world. He may not be perfect or everything you want in a husband but he deserves better than you're giving him right now. That's my take on it, anyway. I support Hollis and I'm sure not going to give him any reason to doubt my devotion or feelings about what he's doing. You shouldn't either."

With that, Sara walked back to the house leaving Katie to ponder her words. She could see that Katie no longer loved

Fletcher and it made her heart heavy. Sometimes love just isn't strong enough to endure all the pressures of life and time. Katie would have to work through her feelings on her own but Sara had no doubt about the conclusion she would reach.

—ǁ— Twenty-Six —ǁ—

HOLLIS WAS ENJOYING THE SOLITUDE while Fletcher and Steve were in town, although he was tired from his late guard duty. He hated to waste the time sleeping so he busied himself with a few chores. After splitting some firewood and hauling it into the cabin, he found an old canvas tarp in the shed and staked it over the foxhole. Sitting on cold, wet dirt wouldn't be very comfortable if they ever needed to man it. Of course, it would probably be an emergency situation if that happened, so it hardly mattered. By then he was getting hungry and a little sleepy.

With the Sony shortwave radio tuned to an AM broadcast station in Winnipeg, Hollis fixed a summer sausage sandwich and hoped Fletcher remembered to stop at the grocery store before coming back because his sandwich finished off the sausage and nearly the bread supply. Some mustard wouldn't be bad either.

It was cold in the cabin and the sky was darkly overcast. *What happened to the sunshine?* Not quite cold enough for snow but damned close. Hollis lit a fire in the cook stove and put another pot of coffee on to brew. He also warmed a pot of water that he used to clean up a bit, noting how low his clothes supply was getting as he donned the last of his clean under-wear and socks. Hearing nothing of interest on the radio, he turned it off and sat gazing out the window, savoring the rich aroma of the freshly poured Navy-strong coffee that sat cooling in front of him. Deep in thought or perhaps momentarily nodding off, he suddenly became aware of engine noise. Startled, he quickly checked the handheld VHF radio to make sure it was on. Fletcher would have called when they were within a half-mile just to let him know they were coming in. The radio was on but he hadn't heard a thing.

Just in case it wasn't Fletcher and Steve, he picked up his Mini-14 and dodged away from the window. When a car door slammed he peeked out and relaxed when he saw the white Olds. Embarrassed at letting a vehicle drive right up to the cabin without detecting it, Hollis realized he must be more tired than he'd thought. This wasn't something he was likely to own up to as they came through the door.

"Didn't have the radio on, huh?" Steve asked.

"I did but the volume must have been turned down," he said.

Steve threw him a large Kmart bag full of underwear, t-shirts, and socks. He sorted through them as Fletcher briefed him on the telephone calls to the ranch, Ames, and the White House. He was happy to hear that his brother and nephews were watching over the women and shocked that Fletcher had actually called the White House.

"Did you call Wainwright about the bank accounts?" he asked.

"No, because he only just started his project on Monday," Fletcher said. "Two days isn't enough time to get much accom-plished. I'll call him before I call the White House again. I'd like to make sure Logan's working his side of the plan before going any further with the government. Anything happen around here while we were gone?"

"Not really. I covered the foxhole with a tarp, chopped some wood, and had lunch. That's about it. You really called the White House?"

Fletcher just grinned.

Locking eyes with Fletcher, he shook his head in disbelief, smiled, and walked out the door to help Steve unload the car. He really didn't want to talk about his day. *The White House?* He picked up the kerosene cans and went to the shed with Steve trailing right behind with the lantern fuel. Now that the others were back, he was going to crawl into his sleeping bag for some much needed rest. *The White House!*

— ‖ —

Joey Andersen had just left the Grygla Community CO-OP store and was waiting to turn east onto State Street when he saw the white Oldsmobile approaching from his right. He glanced at the front plate to make sure it was the same car and was surprised that the number was not the same as he thought he remembered. Still, the windows were dark-tinted and it was headed in the direction of the cabin. He had long ago learned to distrust coincidence and this would have been a big one. Maybe he was confusing the number he thought he'd written down. With no cars behind him, he checked his notebook for the plate number he'd jotted down out at the cabin. They were different. More than a little perplexed, he pulled into the Grain Bin Café for lunch and to consider his next move. Was there another white Oldsmobile Delta 88 with dark-tinted windows out here in the north woods? He was sure there wasn't.

Thinking back to his first contact with the men, he remembered that the car had been parked nose in to the cabin and that he had jotted down the rear plate number. He should probably just stop by this afternoon and resolve the issue once and for all. JT had said his friends were in some kind of situation and that they were the good guys. Good guys? What the hell did that mean? While he'd never had any reason to doubt JT, this still made him uncomfortable. He'd give them the benefit of the doubt but he needed to find out what was going on so he could get his mind back to being a game warden.

— ⅲ — Twenty-Seven — ⅲ —

EACH FBI AGENT TASKED WITH ANSWERING the special line installed to receive Neptune calls was instructed to answer to the name of Mr. Johnson. The line was trunked through the White House switchboard but actually rang in a small office located at the agency's J. Edgar Hoover Building.

Federal authorities were methodically piecing together the story surrounding Neptune, yet didn't have scientific confirmation that Neptune really existed as it had been described. The Ames Laboratory scientist with first-hand knowledge was dead and his notes were burned. In fact, the United States government knew little more than what Dr. Edwards described from Ames. That and the irrefutable and mounting evidence that Westcona and Global Oil had made at least two deadly raids in their quest for the discovery.

The Justice Department was getting very little useful information from either company. They were trying to put together details of the Mark Streeter kidnapping and were wondering if yet another, more sophisticated, group was behind that event. It was obviously too well executed to have been the work of Westcona, if their participation in the Ames and Cade ranch raids were any indication of their tactical expertise. The bureaucratic finger pointing had already begun with a Justice

Department memo stating the Department of Energy was negligent in not providing Boyd and Cade immediate military-level protection and transportation to Washington after Dr. Edwards had first called with the startling news. While bright minds dominated the Justice Department ranks, they were significantly behind the information curve on this story and they knew it. Boyd and Cade were the only players the government had any knowledge of…and they were missing.

The FBI was unsure of how many people were involved with Neptune or how tightly knit the group was. Their review of Boyd's and Cade's Westcona HR records had been followed by a review of each man's military record. While both had honorably served in combat zones, there was nothing in their military training that specifically provided the kind of expertise the men were demonstrating. Boyd had been awarded a purple heart, and one of his Officer Efficiency Reports had noted his participation in a handful of combat operations that had developed around him while he was discharging his duties as a finance officer. Still, he had not officially been an assigned combatant in any of these episodes. Neither did the men's educational credentials indicate the requisite chemistry skills to work with Neptune. FBI analysts concluded there must be other people involved on some level. They also knew that group dynamics often change significantly when this level of violence or money is involved. Behavioral specialists were adjusting their knowledge base in an attempt to predict how non-criminals like Boyd and Cade could be expected to respond to these unusual circumstances. The electronic recording and tracing equipment had been active when Boyd called, but he had not stayed on the line long enough for his location to be established. These guys were either very good or very lucky.

Boyd's telephone demands had been relayed up the chain of command to FBI Director William Webster, who had been instructed to immediately forward news of any contact to the

White House Chief of Staff, and United States Attorney General Ed Meese. Webster hand-carried the information to the White House. Within minutes, he was in the Oval Office with key presidential advisors and the attorney general. Webster played the recording for President Reagan, who listened intently and then asked to hear it again.

The President stared out the window at the beautiful autumn day while appearing to replay the recording yet again in his mind. His brow wrinkled in concern and thought. "Mr. Boyd is a man of few words. He also doesn't seem to trust us. Didn't Dr. Edwards assure him of his safety if he brought Neptune to us?"

"Yes, he did, Mr. President," Webster said. "But Mr. Boyd and his friend have been through a lot in a short time. He's being very cautious. I think that's understandable in the circumstances. If only half of their story is true, they're doing well just staying alive."

"Based on their performance in Ames, you should hire them," the President said with little indication he was kidding. "Are we absolutely sure this Neptune is what they claim it to be?"

The attorney general spoke up. "We're taking the word of Dr. Edwards at Ames. Two energy industry companies are apparently willing to commit multiple murders to get their hands on whatever it is they perceive it to be. We're investigating and while we know they're lying to us, we can't prove it. It appears more than reasonable to assume Neptune is genuine. We can't afford to think anything else, sir."

"Is there any question that Neptune is worth the billion dollars they're demanding?" the President asked.

"Mr. President," the secretary of defense answered, "we have folks working on the potential impact this could have on our country and the world. It sounds good on the surface;

nearly free energy for our citizens and industrial base. But under the surface are many more complex considerations we have yet to work through. The instability this could inject into the balance of world power is mind-boggling. Many of the oil-producing countries are almost completely dependent on oil revenue for their very economic and political existence. Take that away, and they could sink into civil war and extreme poverty. Refugees would overrun international borders into the stable, industrialized nations. Disintegrating governments would have nothing to lose by attacking their neighbors just to survive. On the other hand, you now have the Soviet Union on the ropes. Neptune could solve their economic problems and create a whole new military crisis if they recovered quickly enough and became emboldened by their newfound wealth. No sir, the possibilities are frightening and overwhelming right now and I'm sure I've barely scratched the surface of possible ramifications. We must control this discovery until we better understand its impact on the United States. It very well may be worth a billion dollars just to keep it off the market and preserve the international status quo."

The President gazed at the assembled group. He had hand-picked these advisors and trusted their judgment. Still, he alone was responsible to the American public. He obviously concurred that bringing Fletcher Boyd and Hollis Cade under government control was vital for everyone's safety and well-being.

"Ed, are we prepared to provide them with new identities, and not prosecute them for any crime we may discover they committed?" the President asked the attorney general.

"You realize that they may have committed serious crimes including murder?"

"Does self-defense constitute murder, Mr. Attorney General?"

"That depends on the circumstances and how we want to handle it, Mr. President."

"Then I ask you again, based on what we know right now are we prepared to not prosecute them in exchange for their discovery?"

"Yes sir, if that's what you want."

"Then let's get on with it without overcomplicating our response. This is developing quickly and we certainly aren't in any position to negotiate." The President reached for the jar of jellybeans on his desk. "It might well be that Neptune would do more harm than good. If Mr. Boyd wants to speak directly to me, tell him I'll be happy to do so. This will take common sense and more than a little finesse.

— ‖ —

Spencer Wainwright received word from Zachrich International Trust, the private offshore service provider he had hired, that the bank accounts were open and that he needed to fund each with one thousand U.S. dollars. He was amazed at how quickly this had happened with so little identification or cash. A passport and drivers license satisfied all requirements. Fortunately, he still had a photocopy of Fletcher's documents from when he was an auditor. Besides the Cook Islands and the Swiss account, he elected to add accounts in the Cayman Islands, Macao, Panama, Bermuda, Hong Kong, Singapore, Monaco, and Belize. While that increased the cost and complexity of the plan he had developed, it was still more than reasonable and necessary.

Wainwright told his assistant that he had an errand to run and would be back in an hour. He drove to his bank, obtained a twenty-thousand-dollar bank draft to fund the accounts and pay the fees, and made his way to the Zachrich International offices. He was back at work within an hour.

The accounts were jointly titled in his and Fletcher's name. The plan assured that tracking the cash would be next to impossible...if money ever showed up at all. Now, he just needed to let Fletcher know that money could be moved. A ripple of excitement made the hair on his arms and neck stand up when he thought about what was going to happen.

— ‖ —

Branton Cole met with Westcona's crisis management team at the Greenbrier Hotel to avoid the prying eyes of Justice Department lawyers still working in his office. News of potential Arab agents nosing around Alice brought Cole's blood to a boil.

"Why wasn't I notified of this when you found out?' he thundered at the assembled executives.

"We just got the report and couldn't find you. We handled it," the Westcona security chief said in a steady tone.

"I don't suppose you thought to send more men to Alice."

"Ya think? Yeah, three left this morning," the chief responded insolently.

Cole ignored the comment and thought furiously about how any Arab nation could have detected the link between Neptune and Jake Taylor. Logan Addison? Boyd, Cade, Steve Addison? No, they wouldn't be following Jake Taylor around Alice if they'd been in contact with any of those people. Suddenly it hit him like a lightning bolt. Streeter! They had the information Mark Streeter had. They had siphoned what they needed out of his conniving head and dumped his stinky ass on a park bench when he was of no further use. No muss, no fuss, and no cops. Why was he the only one around this company who could think?

"Find out who the fuck these ragheads are and what they're doing," he barked. "You people need to get off your asses and start thinking. That or you'll be kicking rocks down the street," he roared as he stormed out the door.

— ‖ —

Joey Andersen turned onto the logging trail and stopped. He was authorized to be armed but seldom wore his duty belt because it was heavy, uncomfortable, and just plain unnecessary most of the time. Nothing much ever happened in the woods of northwest Minnesota. When it did, he had plenty of warning. Still, something told him to put it on before driving to the cabin. He had long ago pared it down to only his Smith & Wesson Model 10 revolver, a leather pouch containing two HKS speed loaders, a compass, and a pair of handcuffs. He'd also been issued a handheld radio but it was nearly worthless out in the woods. Instead he relied on the more powerful mobile radio installed in his pickup.

Like many game wardens, he kept a box of assorted winter survival gear and a heavy sleeping bag stored behind the seat of his crew cab 4x4 pickup. A State of Minnesota issued Remington Model 870 twelve gauge shotgun and a Model 700 bolt-action rifle chambered for .308 Winchester were stored away in a rack behind the seat. Also thrown in with the survival gear was a personally owned .22 revolver he sometimes used to dispatch animals struck by vehicles or too sick to be saved. That was one of the few things he disliked about his job. Quickly and humanely harvesting a game animal for food was one thing. Putting down sick or injured animals he knew were suffering was something else.

It was just after three on Wednesday afternoon when he pulled the truck off the soggy trail and stopped at the bottom of the driveway instead of pulling up to the Oldsmobile parked in front of the cabin. He was almost fifty yards from the car, and couldn't clearly see the rear plate because it was parked at an angle and the plate was muddy. The Jeep was gone and he wondered who was in the cabin. He focused his binoculars on the plate. It was not the same as the front plate he'd seen in Grygla.

He got out and started up the driveway on foot. A quick walk around the car told the story. The front and rear plates were different. Keeping a close eye on the cabin, he pulled his notebook and pen from the shirt pocket under his jacket, walked around to the driver-side's windshield, and wrote down the VIN located on the front dash.

The muddy ground ten feet to his right belched as three quick shots rang out from high and behind him the moment he turned away from the car. He froze for two long seconds before reaching for his revolver. The grass just a yard from his right boot erupted as three more bullets tore into the damp ground with hollow thudding sounds. Someone yelled for him to put his hands in the air, and he carefully did as he was told.

— ⫴ — Twenty-Eight — ⫴ —

THE SIX SHOTS BROUGHT HOLLIS out of his sleeping bag so quickly and violently that he tore the zipper from the fabric in the process. He had his Mini-14 in his hands as he opened the door wearing nothing but his skivvies, surprised to see Joey standing beside the Oldsmobile with his hands in the air. Steve stumbled up behind Hollis a moment later, rubbing sleep from his eyes. Fletcher was yelling at them to disarm Joey while he came down the rope. Hollis uncomfortably kept his rifle pointed in Joey's general direction while Steve, now half dressed, approached the ashen-faced game warden. Hollis returned to the cabin for his clothes when Fletcher came around the cabin.

Fletcher pushed Joey through the door wearing his own handcuffs before Hollis had his boots tied. Steve followed, carrying Joey's duty belt over his shoulder and a miserable look on his face.

"Joey, Joey…you dumb son-of-a bitch," Fletcher said.

— ⫴ —

Late October sunsets are fast and early in south Texas. The Saudi communications specialist was sitting just off North

Texas Boulevard watching Lincoln Street for Jake Taylor and his bodyguards to drive past on their way home. The specialist had already walked past the house, checking for the safest adjacent yard from which to attempt his frequency gathering activity. He had noted a reasonably well-hidden area in a next-door neighbor's yard where he could get right up against the fence and nearly under the beam antenna's longest elements. The dipole draping off the tower and secured to a tree on the back of the property could be a problem if Taylor was using eighty meters. He wasn't sure if his frequency counter would read that far. There was no indication of a dog, and he hoped he could slip in under a gnarly mesquite tree growing close to the fence. In the worst case, he could get onto the golf course behind the houses and try working his magic from the back of the yard. It wasn't dark enough just yet but it would be very soon.

The soldiers waited down the street from the Westcona yard to pick up Taylor and his guard as they left work. The Westcona district manager had been going directly home these past few days, but tonight they noted with some dismay that his white Oldsmobile turned west toward Highway 281 instead of the customary easterly route to Lincoln Street and his house. They followed him south on 281, watching with anticipation when they saw his right turn signal blinking as he approached the Holiday Inn. Perhaps there would be a lapse in security that would allow them to quietly escort their target away right under the noses of his guards.

Assuming Taylor was in the bar, one soldier opened the heavy door and peered into the dimly lit room. He could see a wooden bar along the right wall, and a jukebox to his immediate right just inside the door. It was busy with the local oilfield crowd, almost all of whom wore cowboy hats or baseball caps. Picking individuals out of the crowd was difficult due to the headgear, similar clothing, and smoke-filled dim light. They all looked alike.

He sat down on a barstool and ordered a beer. Using the mirror over the bar to scan the room, he finally identified his target and was surprised that Taylor was sitting at a large round table with his three guards and another three who also looked the part. Only Taylor and the soon-to-be off-duty guard were having a drink. The other five were drinking coffee, another sign that distressed the Saudi. He noticed one of the men glancing in his direction with more interest than seemed appropriate; or was it just his imagination? He was self-conscious in a bar, and certainly uneasy with a beer in front of him.

Leaving the beer untouched, he left to inform his partner that Westcona might have sent reinforcements. The soldiers positioned themselves down a short hallway close to the men's room and restaurant entrance where a side door opened to the outdoor pool area. If Taylor walked down there by himself, they'd push him out the side door and quickly to their car. If not, they had done their best tonight.

The communications specialist grew fidgety when Jake Taylor did not drive past shortly after five o'clock, as the soldiers had said was his custom. Could he have driven another route home? The specialist started his car and drove down Lincoln to make sure. The house was dark and the yard so black he couldn't see the shrubs he knew were planted along the front of the structure. He drove back to Texas Boulevard and took up his position. It was shortly after six-thirty when Taylor finally approached the stop sign. There was the customary security car and a van following him tonight. All three vehicles seemed to be traveling together. The specialist needed to get into a position where he could detect the frequency Taylor used if he attempted to contact anyone on his radio. Would he even use the radio when he had all those people with him at the house?

The specialist had a variety of radio frequency measuring devices in his bag; a grid dip meter, an absorption wave meter, and the one he felt most likely to help him tonight, a military-grade digital frequency counter. Considering the level of security that had arrived at the house, he'd never get into the backyard and up to the tower base where he'd need to be to use either of the first two meters.

He put the frequency counter in his bag, added a small red-lensed flashlight and calmly walked down Lincoln Street toward the house. It was very dark, and he was wearing dark clothing as he slipped into the next-door neighbor's yard from the side farthest away from Taylor's house. A few moments later he was around the back of the neighbor's house and snuggled up to the fence under the mesquite tree, and nearly under the antenna elements.

Taylor's house was ablaze with lights, but the neighbor's house was nearly dark. He turned the frequency counter on and shined the flashlight on the display panel, shielding the dim light with his body as best he could. A door opened on Taylor's side of the fence and he listened nervously while someone walked around the backyard smoking a cigarette, apparently making sure any gates were shut and locked. Carefully shielding the dim red light shining on the meter with his cap, he hoped no telltale glow was visible between the fence boards.

The display jumped to 14.155 MHz and the specialist burned the number into his memory, although was somewhat confused by what he saw. He had expected to see a lower frequency considering the time of day. The display went back to zero, then back to 14.155 while he watched. He was pulling a pen from his pocket when the meter again went to zero. He knew Taylor must be retuning to a lower band, and was hoping he was still using the big beam antenna mounted on the tower. Nothing for over a minute. The specialist took a chance when he stood and held the meter up over the top of the fence to get it just a couple of feet closer to the eighty-meter dipole strung off the tower. With his flashlight in his mouth, he saw the meter display 3.675 MHz. That was more like it. He patiently watched while the meter dropped to zero and moved back to 3.675 after another long thirty seconds had passed. That's it! Taylor was using that frequency. He needed to write the number down before he forgot it. He fumbled for his pen while crouching behind the fence with the little flashlight still between his teeth. Detecting movement in his peripheral vision, he instinctively looked toward the house shining his red beam at the window in the process. A powerful white beam from the neighbor's window lit him up like he was in full daylight. Within seconds the interior house light came on and he saw an old woman with a telephone to her ear. He bolted for the rear of the yard repeating the frequency over and over as he ran.

By the time the bodyguards cleared the fence into Mrs. Walter's yard, the specialist was over the rear fence, onto the golf course behind the houses, and running west to his car. He narrowly missed being seen by the police as their cruiser rounded the corner onto Lincoln just as he burst out of the bushes a hundred feet north of them onto Texas Boulevard. He sped south a few blocks to Schallert Elementary School, pulled into the parking lot, and quickly tuned his portable receiver. Nothing! Leaving the radio on, he drove back to his motel where he continued to monitor after calling his control in Washington. He hoped the old lady had not seen the equipment he was holding when her light was on him. The bodyguards could gain valuable information if they realized someone was interested in Taylor's ham radio activities.

— ‖ —

At 1900 hours, Fletcher had the transceiver tuned to 3.675 MHz. Joey was handcuffed and seated in the kitchen.

"WOFTU WOFTU, this is WD5CL calling."

"WD5CL, this is WOFTU. Hello JT," Fletcher said in a formal voice. "How do you copy?"

"Fine copy, Boyd. Everything okay up there? Over."

"Well, we put Logan on a plane this morning but we have a little problem and could use your help."

"What kind of a problem? Over."

"Your friend the game warden is now our guest. Seems his curiosity got the best of him, and we've had to ask him to stay with us."

"He's with you now?"

"That is correct. He's in the kitchen as we speak, and I'm sure he's listening."

"If he can hear me, then he needs to hear this. Andersen, I already told you these guys are model citizens that you should watch over. You listen to their story "

Suddenly, JT stopped transmitting.

"WD5CL. Are you there JT?" Fletcher said.

Nothing but silence for another fifteen seconds. Finally JT responded.

"Sorry for the delay, Boyd," he said. "It seems we have some commotion going on outside. Andersen, you listen to their story and believe it. They're not exaggerating or making anything up. I'll be back on the radio in the morning at seven to answer any questions. I gotta go. WD5CL clear."

Joey didn't like sound of what might be happening at JT's house in Texas. He wanted to be relieved by what JT said but was now even more confused over why he was a prisoner if these were such exemplary citizens.

The men brought him into the big room and sat him at the table. After placing a bottle of Scotch on the table, Fletcher sat down and pushed a glass over to him.

"The cuffs stay on for now," he said. "We have a story that will surprise you. It will sound far-fetched, but I assure you it's absolutely one hundred percent the truth. Now listen up."

Joey stared in wide-eyed disbelief as Fletcher explained Neptune. He took particular notice when Steve and Hollis nodded in agreement as Fletcher moved through the discovery and then explained that the two big companies had been after them for nearly two weeks. Arabs were already involved and in the United States. His blood pressure spiked when it dawned on him that these were the guys from Ames! He silently thanked his lucky stars that he had not followed through in reaching for his revolver earlier in the day. He tried an anxious smile but his face wasn't working. Perspiration formed over his lip as he pushed his empty glass toward Fletcher.

The good news was they hadn't killed him. Calls to the White House? Maybe they really were trying to do the right thing. Even so, it put him in a shitty position as a sworn law enforcement officer. What was his responsibility to his badge? He decided that not getting killed was responsibility number one. Of course, he now understood why they couldn't let him go.

"You're in a bit of a fix then, eh?" Joey said, trying to sound nonchalant.

"That's one way of looking at it." Fletcher agreed. "And so are you."

—‖— Twenty-Nine —‖—

IT WAS WELL AFTER MIDNIGHT BEFORE the communications specialist received a return call from the Al Makhabarat Al A'amah in Riyadh. They had been working with an agent at their Washington embassy to confirm Jake Taylor's ham radio call sign while analyzing the information reported earlier that evening. There was still no real proof that Taylor was communicating with the men they were seeking, but neither was there reason to believe he was not.

They instructed the specialist to monitor the frequencies Taylor had transmitted on, and reminded him of how HF propagation works during different times of the day. He acknowledged but was annoyed. Why did those sitting behind a desk on the other side of the world find it necessary to treat him like a novice rather than the expert he was? He certainly knew which frequencies would be used for long-range communications at different times of the day without their *help*.

At the same time, the Saudi intelligence directorate ordered their Washington, DC, and Ottawa, Canada, embassies to monitor the two frequencies, listening for the call sign WD5CL between the hours of 1130 to 1300, 1630 to 1830, and 2200 to 0500 hours Zulu, covering the most logical times Taylor would be home. If they were able to confirm that Taylor was speaking with Fletcher Boyd and his friends, their mission was to obtain a beam heading to the station Boyd was using so they could ultimately triangulate the men's location using a technique known as radio direction finding.

The specialist had already noted that Jake Taylor's beam was pointed in a northerly direction, but he would have to go back during the day with a compass to get an accurate bearing while hoping that Taylor had not swung the beam after trying to contact Boyd on twenty meters. After all, Taylor had used the wire dipole antenna to communicate on 3.675 MHz, so the beam heading could be meaningless. It would certainly also help to have other monitoring locations more geographically separated to make triangulation more effective. But then the world is seldom a perfect place. First, they needed to find out if the men were even in radio communication. Otherwise, this could be nothing more than a waste of time and resources.

— ‖ —

Logan saw the hellish, revolting mess there was to clean up at Steve's house in McAllen and immediately headed for a hotel. There was no way he could consider staying at the house where there had been so much hope and happiness but was now reduced to a morbid and painful reminder of better times. The medical examiner and police had done little more than remove Shelley's body and scrape up some of her brain matter. He called seven cleaning companies before finding one willing to do the job.

The cleaning crew was working as he sat in his hotel room and prepared for a call to his friend in Jeddah, Saudi Arabia. Salem would be winding down his Thursday workday at his construction company headquarters in the next couple of hours. Logan's mind kept returning to the murder and what he was going to do when he found those responsible.

He forced himself back to the present and realized that Salem had been asked to call him only because of their friendship and would not likely be the man he would deal with going forward. That troubled him. With so much at stake, he knew he could not trust many people from Saudi Arabia. Still, there was no other way. He dialed the phone.

"Salem. It's Logan."

"Logan. It is wonderful to hear your voice. I trust you are well?"

"For now. Look, I know you got pulled into this because of our friendship. Circumstances are changing quickly and I need a contact name and number that will take you out of the discussion. No offense intended, but I need to deal with a decision maker and I don't want you in the middle. Can you help me?"

"Of course, I will do what I can for you, Logan."

"Are you aware of the issues we're dealing with?"

"Only as of today and I am not sure I have all the details. Even so, this is a difficult problem that will require great wisdom and courage to resolve without bloodshed."

"That and a whole lot of money. I don't want you involved. You had nothing to do with it, and nothing good can come of it for you or your family. Who should I be talking to? I have a message from the Neptune participants to your Kingdom, or OPEC if Saudi Arabia has already brought in the other member-nations."

"I am authorized to deliver any message you have from your son and his friends. Someone else will take over once I have relayed your message," Salem said quietly. Logan could hear the tension in his friend's voice and understood the pressure he was under.

"Please tell them that Neptune may be purchased for two billion U.S. dollars, wired to accounts of my son's choosing. I will personally deliver Neptune to a mutually acceptable location because I am not aware of the science. Assuming you play by the rules, my son and his friends will move abroad, establish new lives, and have nothing more to do with the United States or Neptune. They will have to trust you to leave them alone, and you will have to trust them to forget Neptune."

"Why would they turn their backs on their country?"

"They feel betrayed by their employer and the United States government. The incident in Ames had a significant impact."

"As a businessman, I understand. My family is wealthy, yet I have learned that wealth does not buy happiness or shield you from the rest of the world. Look at the trouble endured by my family as each successive generation gained financial independence. Always more trouble that I must deal with. Working within the family business is all that seems to keep us out of trouble. Have you not told your son these truths?"

"I have, Salem, but he and his friends are young and under stress. My daughter-in-law was killed while carrying my first grandchild. The boys were attacked and forced to kill to stay alive. Their families have also been attacked. No, my friend, I'm afraid social graces and gentlemanly behavior are not part of their deportment right now. In Texas, people like them are sometimes referred to as *seriously pissed-off cowboys*, if you follow my meaning."

"I do indeed, my friend. How may we contact you?"

"I'll call you tomorrow at this same time. Thank you, Salem."

— ‖ —

Joey heard the late-night changing of the guard and sleepily realized he was witnessing an operation run with military precision and solemnity. He flushed with embarrassment at the thought of how he had initially approached the men, assuming they were nothing more than casual bird hunters or vacationers even though his instincts and training warned him there was more going on. He had driven in and out of their camp, completely oblivious to the intensity level. These men were fighting for their lives, and he had acted like a real country bumpkin. But perhaps that's what had saved him when he forced them into action.

Obviously, there had always been someone on duty with a rifle watching his actions as he approached and left the camp. Just as obviously, the men had always been very close to weapons when he was at the cabin. He wondered how well equipped and experienced they were. Fletcher could handle a gun pretty damn well, that was for sure. Former military?

Joey didn't go back to sleep after Steve took the last watch at three o'clock. Instead, he used the time to think about what these men were involved with and how it applied to him. He wished he had heeded JT's request to watch over the men rather than sticking his nose into their business. After much consideration, he concluded that the men were sincere with their outlandish story. Still, federal authorities wanted them and he was a sworn law enforcement officer. He heard Fletcher get up, call Steve on a handheld radio, and put coffee on the stove at six-thirty. He clumsily struggled into his pants and boots, and walked to the kitchen still in the uncomfortable handcuffs. He just pointed outside and they made their way toward the outhouse while Steve came off the OP and Hollis slept.

— ‖ —

A half-hour later, Fletcher sat down at the radio when he heard JT's voice.

"W0FTU W0FTU, this is WD5CL."

"Morning, JT. This is W0FTU. Things calm down yet?" Fletcher said.

"Just a little trouble last night, Boyd. Seems we had a prowler next door who could be related to your business. Can't be sure right now. I talked to Addison late last night and he's safely at his destination. Said to tell you he's making his phone call this morning. How are things with Andersen?"

"Nothing's changed. We'll see how his pulse is beating over breakfast. Say, we'll be needing some wings soon. This thing's going to ratchet up pretty fast when it happens. Will you or Jeff be able to help us on short notice?"

"I'll let him know what's happening and see how his schedule looks. One way or the other, you'll have transportation when you need it. Oh, I forgot to tell you the auditor called yesterday. Says his mission is complete. He'd like a phone call."

"Excellent. It'll be good to get out of here. If it gets much colder, we'll be marooned in this wilderness until spring. Okay, we'll have the radio on at 1200 and again after 1700 hours. Anything else, JT?"

"Not from this end. We'll talk later, probably after work. Be careful. WD5CL clear on your final. Seventy-three."

"Okay, JT. You watch yourself, too. W0FTU clear."

They sat down to the breakfast Fletcher had started and Hollis had finished.

"You had time to think over what we told you last night?" Fletcher asked Joey.

"Yeah, that's about all I've been thinking about. I take it there's a lot of money involved with Neptune."

"More zeros than we can keep track of," Fletcher said.

"Maybe you could use some help only a law enforcement officer can provide."

"We've been doing fine on our own—but what are you getting at?"

"Well, I like my job and worked hard to get it. Still, I know now that I'll never make a whole lot of money doing it. The state pension plan is pretty good but—

"You want a cut of the money to fund your retirement in better style."

"Just a thought," Joey said. "I could help if you could see your way into trusting me. I won't hurt any civilians but I can help with information. And nothing builds loyalty better than being part of the deal."

Fletcher looked hard at the game warden.

"Hollis suggested we just shoot you because we could die if you blow the whistle on us," Fletcher bluffed.

"I'm surprised Hollis said that, but it sounds like you could die either way. I can help if people start poking around looking for you, and that might just make the difference," Joey countered. "I drive around this area all day, every day, and have access to all the law enforcement communication systems. I know the people in four sheriffs' offices and all the state troopers that work this part of Minnesota. And, I can also spot outsiders a mile off. You need my help."

Fletcher looked at Hollis and saw concern in his trusted friend's eyes. The money wouldn't matter if they really cashed in, but could they trust Joey?

Joey looked uneasily at Hollis and then back down at the table.

— ‖ —

In Washington and Ottawa, the Saudi and Iraqi radio rooms were manned. They heard the radio traffic between Taylor and a station identifying as W0FTU on their military-grade radios and antenna arrays. All four radio operators got fixes on W0FTU, noting the names JT, Boyd, Addison, Jeff, and

Anderson. The military attaché at the Saudi embassy in Washington looked up W0FTU in their recently purchased Radio Amateur Callbook and saw the call sign belonged to a ham in Duluth, Minnesota.

He plotted each embassy on his map and extended lines from them in the direction each claimed to have received the strongest signal from W0FTU. The key would be the direction of Taylor's antenna bearing coming from Texas. He called the specialist at the motel in Alice and told him to get over to the house with a compass, and the specialist called back within thirty minutes. The attaché drew a line from Alice at seven degrees east of due north. It intersected the other four lines coming from Ottawa and Washington. They didn't cross at one spot as he had hoped but rather suggested an area located in northwest Minnesota, northeast North Dakota, or southern Manitoba. This confused him because Duluth, where W0FTU was licensed, was over on the western tip of Lake Superior on the far eastern side of the state. However, it was now clear that Taylor was in radio communication with their targets, and their location was approximately identified.

— ‖ —

The Westcona security director caught on to what his agent in Alice was implying. The man outside Taylor's house had something to do with radio communication based on the eyewitness report of Mrs. Walters. Jake Taylor was a ham radio operator and used his station regularly. Arab agents were in Alice. Therefore, this was an Arab agent trying to discover who Taylor was talking to on his radio. Hot Damn! This could be the break they needed. He went to the Westcona communications center and had a long conversation with the senior technician. Yes, they could listen in but would need to know the frequency being used. The security man was frustrated and angry that the Arabs had thought of this first and probably already had the frequency information they needed. Sensing the strong emotion, the technician offered a possible solution.

"Look, just have your people in Alice look at Taylor's log book by the radio. Hams log their contacts as they make them, and include the time, frequency, and call sign of whoever they communicate with. Have one of your guys take a look at the book and call back with the frequencies and call signs of whoever he's been working in the past couple of weeks. Taylor may not have logged them all if he's worried about security, but old habits die hard and he might have written down the frequency at least once. Also have them see which direction his antenna is pointed. They can read the beam heading right off his rotator control in the shack. It's worth a try."

An hour later, the Westcona communications center was monitoring 14.155 and 3.675 MHz with confidence they were again on the right track.

The Westcona radio people didn't need to be told to shoot an azimuth to the transmitter Taylor was talking to when he came up on the air at seven o'clock that morning. They couldn't triangulate, but got a solid indication of the direction Boyd's radio signal was coming from. They had a Radio Amateur Callbook in the communications center and quickly established that the call sign was issued to someone in Duluth, Minnesota. But Duluth wasn't on the line they drew on a map from Dallas. Something wasn't right.

— ‖ —

Before JT left for work, he called Jeff Neumann's home number in Longmont, Colorado. The phone rang unanswered. He called the Westcona yard in Brighton but Jeff had not yet arrived. Where would he be at 6:15 a.m. if not at home? *Probably with some skirt,* he thought with amusement and a little grudging admiration. He left a message with the dispatcher for Jeff to call him at home that evening to discuss some airplane problems he was having.

— ‖ —

Hollis rode with Joey in the pickup as they drove north on Highway 54 toward the payphone in Skime. Fletcher was leading in the Oldsmobile. They had decided to avail themselves of Joey's offer but were concerned with his apparent willingness to help them for money. Then again, who could really blame him? They were all turning their backs on their past lives for money…a lot of money…life changing money. Still, cops normally value their badges pretty highly and they were watching Joey carefully. Joey mentioned that he had to check in with his dispatcher or someone would come looking for him, and they agreed to allow it on this trip.

With Hollis listening intently, Joey keyed his microphone and called the Department of Natural Resources dispatcher. She asked where he was and what his plans were for the day. He gave her a false location and said he'd be patrolling the woods in western Lake of the Woods County near the Red Lake Wildlife Management Area. He also told her he might be out of radio range during the day, but not to worry about him. He'd call again that evening or first thing in the morning. She seemed satisfied.

— ‖ —

When Fletcher stopped at the payphone, Hollis directed Joey in next to the Oldsmobile. Fletcher pulled a small notebook from his pocket, fed quarters into the payphone, and started dialing.

"Hello, Spencer," he greeted his former boss in his Dallas office.

"Hello, Fletcher. Glad you called. I have an account set up for you, and it's ready to use right now."

"An account? We talked about at least two."

"I'm trying to keep this simple, Fletcher. I gave this a lot of thought and decided you only need to worry about one account right now. We can deal with other accounts later," he said. "I'll read you the information if you have something to write with. I'll also give you the bank's phone number."

Fletcher didn't like surprises in the best of times, and he sure as hell didn't like it now. Still, he thought he could trust Wainwright and didn't want to stay on the phone. This kind of money could turn anyone's head. Wainwright read the information for the Swiss numbered account while Fletcher carefully recorded it in his notebook and fought niggling feelings that his mentor might be pulling something.

"Okay, Spencer, but this better work the way we discussed. Watch for some substantial activity in it soon…like ten figures' worth."

Fletcher then called the hotel where Logan was staying in McAllen, hoping he would answer the phone…and he did. Without fanfare, Fletcher gave Logan the account number needed to complete his assignment.

Lastly, Fletcher reached deeper into his stash of quarters and started pumping them into the telephone. He motioned to Hollis when Mr. Johnson answered on the first ring.

"What's the answer, Mr. Johnson?" he asked the FBI agent.

"Is this Mr. Boyd?"

"Cut the crap, Johnson. What's the answer?"

"The answer is yes. We'll pay what you ask, and agree to the rest of your demands. We'll need to meet and take possession of the product before we transfer the money. When and where can we do that?"

"In your dreams, pal. You'll transfer the money first or there's no deal."

"The President has offered to personally talk to you and resolve any concerns you have."

"Not a chance in hell, ace," Fletcher responded flatly.

The FBI agent began objecting but Fletcher hung up the phone without listening. He looked at Hollis. He'd have to think about how to meet with the feds. Turning over one billion dollars without having Neptune was a problem the feds were going to have to deal with.

"Fifty-two seconds," Hollis said out the truck window.

"Longer than I wanted," Fletcher said as he turned to the sound of gravel crunching under tires.

A sheriff's car pulled up next to the driver side of the game warden's pickup and a young deputy began talking to Joey. They chatted for a few minutes as Joey told him he was waiting to use the phone to call his girlfriend. The deputy laughed and drove off. Fletcher expelled the breath he wasn't aware he had been holding.

Fletcher and Hollis discussed the short conversation with Mr. Johnson and agreed it would require another call. They drove up to Wannaska and found another payphone. Pumping in quarters, Fletcher motioned to Hollis when Johnson answered.

"I understand your concern but you have no choice. Bring us new identities and a letter signed by the Attorney General and the President stating we will not be charged with any crimes related to this transaction or any of our activities leading up to it. You fill in the proper language. We'll be back to you with a location when the money shows up. "

"What's the account number," Johnson asked.

"Thirty-nine seconds," Hollis said when Fletcher hung up after reading off the number.

— ‖ — Thirty — ‖ —

By Thursday afternoon, the Westcona security director had called a number of police and private detective friends he and his senior managers' maintained contact with from their active law enforcement days. Those working as private detectives were somewhat understanding of his plight. Those still on public payrolls were less so. All he was asking was for someone to check property records for land owned by Jake Taylor within the State of Minnesota. At least he reasoned that it had to be in Minnesota. While these were public records, the only other way to do it was to travel to or call each county and request ownership or tax information. That could take weeks or longer. With almost eighty thousand square miles broken into eighty-seven counties, Minnesota was clearly too large for his resources. He needed the computer checks that cut through red tape and county bureaucracies that only law enforcement or well-connected private detectives could muster with the immediacy he required. Two contacts promised to look into it for him but he wasn't going to hold his breath.

As he sat back and stared at the map of North America on his wall, he wondered how Boyd and Cade had made it so far so fast. His eyes drew a line from Dallas to Winnipeg. Something wasn't right. Taking two pushpins and a long piece of string over to the map, he placed a pin in each city, wrapped the string around the pins, pulled it taut, and stood back. The string didn't go over Minnesota at all. It passed directly west of Minnesota through the Dakotas.

"You said the transmitter Jake Taylor was in communication with was on a line between Dallas and Winnipeg. That doesn't make sense based on some other information we have."

"I said Winnipeg because it's the closest big city to the heading in the far north. Our heading was really slightly to the east of Winnipeg. Does that help?"

"Maybe. Bring a protractor and the exact heading up to my office!" he said as he slammed the phone down.

They quickly determined that the true heading line transected only the westernmost Minnesota counties and perhaps one or two more counties to the east once the line moved farther north into the state. The area under and close to the line covered twenty-four counties if the heading was accurate. That was a far cry from all eighty-seven Minnesota counties.

He immediately tasked five employees with the job of calling the courthouses in each of the twenty-four target counties, starting from the south and working north to the Canadian border. Once the work was underway, he called Branton Cole.

"Mr. Cole, I think we may have a break in locating Boyd." He explained his reasoning and what they were doing about it.

"Look," Cole responded testily, "you're assuming a lot to think they're actually in Minnesota, and I don't put much stock in this radio direction-finding voodoo. Too many things can make it inaccurate and useless. Go ahead and keep trying but don't bother me again unless you're successful."

"Yes, sir. But please hear me out on this. Minnesota is the only place that makes any sense. We know the transmitter is almost straight north of us. We know Taylor is a hunter and fisherman who owns his own airplane. Minnesota has some of the best hunting and fishing up there, unless you keep going into Canada. He probably wouldn't do that because it'd be a hassle with his firearms and plane. The other states, between here and there, are farm states. Minnesota is where he'd have his cabin. It just has to be."

"Maybe, but you've got nothing but magic radio-waves and some feeling that you'd buy land there if you were Taylor. You're not, and I'm not buying your bullshit. Now get off the phone and find me those men."

The security director listened to the dial tone for a moment, and then hung up in frustration.

— ‖ —

Al Makhabarat Al A'amah looked at the location of OPEC member-nation embassies and missions in North America. Most had embassies in Washington, DC, along with delegations to the United Nations in New York City. All had embassies in Ottawa, Ontario, the Canadian seat of national government. Only Venezuela had sovereign facilities anywhere else, and those were in Chicago and Miami. What they needed were transmitter fixes from places other than the northeast United States or southeast Canada to more precisely triangulate their target's location. A directional fix from Miami or even Chicago could considerably narrow the search area.

Venezuelan intelligence officers assigned to their Miami and Chicago embassies were pleased to be part of an OPEC operation, accepting the request without feeling compelled to report the activity to the Venezuelan ambassador. This was OPEC business, not a matter of state. Their daily lives were largely uneventful, so this opportunity to exercise some of their skills was a welcome distraction. They soon had receivers tuned to 14.155 and 3.675 MHz with directional antennas pointed toward Minnesota.

— ‖ —

Logan Addison's secretary brought him up to date on the gossip permeating Global Oil's Houston headquarters. She told him that most of the federal agents and lawyers had mysteriously disappeared late that morning, and that Mark Streeter had come back to the building at noon, accompanied by a doctor and phalanx of bodyguards. He was meeting with his senior staff, according to the secretary gossip line. She also reported that Streeter had received a call from Branton Cole soon after arriving but had not taken it, instead asking for a number where he could reach Cole later in the afternoon. Finally, she said that Global's Houston-based security staff had been paged and ordered back to the office.

Logan pondered the information, wondering if the feds were really pulling out or if Streeter's ego was just acting up again. The feds would only have left if ordered to do so by the Justice Department or a higher authority. That could mean only one thing. Fletcher had worked a deal for Neptune and someone in a high position didn't want anything to short-circuit the agreement. Then again, maybe Global had succeeded in bamboozling the federal agents and lawyers. He dismissed that idea as unlikely, which left only one reasonable assumption. If the government had agreed to a Neptune deal, he'd better accelerate his portion of the plan. He looked at his watch as he picked up the telephone and dialed across the world, hoping his friend hadn't gone to bed early.

"Salem, its Logan. I want you to let your handlers know that I will deal only with you, and that I need an indication very soon of where this thing is going. Sorry to put you in this position, old friend, but things are heating up on my end and I don't have the time I thought I had."

"I understand, Logan, but I am not sure I am authorized to be your sole contact. I am just a simple construction contractor with fortunate ties to the Royal Family. I am not in a position to make decisions for them or demand that they move at a speed other than what they are comfortable with."

"I'm sure this conversation is being recorded, Salem. Let them listen to it and decide what to do. They risk losing Neptune if they don't follow my instructions. I know they think this could be a hoax, but they must have had your economic people calculate the potential impact on your economy. The United States government believes Neptune is viable based on tests done at Ames Laboratory, and they've already agreed to pay a substantial fee for it. Both Westcona and Global Oil are still trying to buy or steal it. If Saudi Arabia or OPEC wants it, they need to kick it up a notch. It's up to you folks to make the next move, and it needs to happen now. I trust you, Salem, and I know the King has faith in you. Hopefully, he's fully aware of what's happening. I'll call back in twenty-four hours for an answer. Take care, my friend."

With that, Logan hung up the phone. He had never been so abrupt with Salem, and hoped his friend understood the pressure he was under. Decades of experience had taught Logan that the Arab people respond poorly to boorish manners, or to any form of demand unless they are allowed to negotiate. He sincerely hoped Salem would forgive the disrespectful treatment.

— || —

Salem immediately called his Al Makhabarat Al A'amah contact to report the second call from Logan. They pretended it was news to them, but no doubt already had a tape of the conversation moving within their chain of command. After being instructed to sit tight, he promptly ignored the orders and traveled a few miles to the home of a trusted friend from which he called his brother, Mahrous, at home in Medina and explained what was happening. Mahrous had asked Salem to keep him abreast of Logan's travails, understanding his brother was likely under tight surveillance.

Mahrous had never forgotten the kindness shown him by Logan Addison when he was in trouble with Saudi authorities and the Royal Family many years ago. While Salem, as senior member of their family, was responsible for repayment of family debts of honor, Mahrous felt personally obligated and would do anything he could to help Logan. His younger brothers and cousins didn't necessarily share his feeling of indebtedness to the older American, but knew their father and uncle, Sheikh Mohammed, would never have permitted such a debt to go unpaid. And still, with few exceptions, the family members would treat it as their own out of respect for the family name, and despite their personal feelings.

For the first time, Mahrous asked Salem for details of what was happening to Logan. To that point, he had accepted his brother's offered information without asking for what might not be his to know. Now he felt that he needed to do something to help.

"Brother, I will fly to the United States to help our friend in his time of need. Do we know where he is?"

"We do not, but I agree with your noble gesture. Go to Houston and stay in contact with me. I will locate Logan and direct you to him. Thank you, brother. You bring honor to our family," Salem said.

A company jet bearing only Mahrous and two pilots lifted into the dark Arabian sky bound for Houston, Texas. It was a long flight, and he would be busy once he arrived. Reclining in the seat and covering himself with a blanket, he tried to sleep...but couldn't. His mind and heart were troubled by another sibling's behavior and attitude. Born to wealth and high station, the younger brother was well-educated and traveled. He was bright, brighter than Mahrous himself. Yet, at twenty-nine years of age, he was still not contributing to the business or the family as he should. The youngster was far too interested in Islamic fundamentalism, and that zealotry was not compatible with their business. Because Mahrous was on a family mission, he had not asked any non-family to accompany him, even to the exclusion of security personnel. He had requested that his youngest brother come along, but the young man had laughed, stating he would not help any American. Any obligation Mahrous and Salem felt to this American was theirs alone according to the youngster. After all, he had been a mere child when Logan helped save Mahrous from certain imprisonment or worse, and he felt no obligation to get involved now. Mahrous was disappointed and even a little afraid to let Salem know what their brother had said. Salem had responsibility for the international business and should not be bothered with minor family problems. Mahrous had also been a problem to his family as a young man, but had straightened himself out with Salem's help. Now it was his turn to help by getting his younger brother under control and into a position to contribute.

He would revisit family issues when he returned to Saudi Arabia. The younger generation was always difficult to understand, focus, and motivate. As he drifted off to sleep, he wondered if other families had as much difficulty with their youngsters.

— ‖ —

Fletcher, Hollis, and Joey returned to the cabin in time for a late lunch. The frosty ground had turned wet from a slightly warmer drizzle that had fallen during their short absence. Snow was only a few degrees away. Steve, tired from his early morning guard duty, had taken a nap after they left to make phone calls but was now up and busy working on his gourmet luncheon specialty, wieners and beans.

"I had the radio on from noon to one-thirty listening for JT, but he didn't call," Steve told the group.

"That's 1200 to 1330 hours," Hollis growled. "You need to get with the program around here, son."

"He didn't call then either," the young engineer said without humor.

The men ate and questioned Joey about how he thought he could help. Fletcher was impressed with Joey and the way he'd handled himself while they were out making calls. He was also thinking about how helpful it would be to have someone tied into law enforcement watching for problems away from the cabin.

They had attracted very little attention since arriving in northern Minnesota the prior week but realized their luck couldn't hold forever. The critical issue was whether Joey really believed their story and was honestly willing to help for a cut of the money. Nobody in his right mind would turn them in knowing they could be killed by the action unless that person was power hungry and wanted to put a big star on his resume. Joey didn't seem like that kind of guy, but neither did he strike Fletcher as someone willing to sell his badge for money. Well, he had said he wouldn't hurt anyone while helping, so perhaps that was how Joey was rationalizing his offer— and it was a dazzling amount of money.

Fletcher decided that Joey would better appreciate what they had if he had a deeper understanding of Neptune, and asked Steve to expand on the chemistry theory. Steve looked surprised but went ahead. Joey appeared transfixed at the science as it unfolded before him.

"I basically understand the theoretical science because of my biology undergraduate degree," Joey said. "Still, this is tough to buy without seeing it work or knowing the chemicals you use."

"We've made it and used it many times in both gasoline and diesel engines," Fletcher assured him.

"And your employer tried to kill you for this," Joey flatly stated. "That doesn't surprise me at all. Think of what they'll lose if this gets out, eh?"

"The whole oil industry will nearly vanish," Steve said. "They might still make lubricants, but the fuels would disappear. Global already killed my wife before kidnapping me. I escaped and JT rescued me in his jet. These guys have been chased and shot at all the way from Texas. Their wives killed some Global or Westcona guys who tried to kidnap them, too."

"Now we know that Saudi Arabia is sniffing around and taking steps to figure it out. They might even have some of the other OPEC countries helping them," Fletcher added.

"I don't think the United States government is working against you," Joey said. "I heard all kinds of things about Ames and the people who died down there. They're blaming Westcona and Global for that, not you. In fact, the bulletin I read doesn't even mention you were involved in any violence, or that you should be considered armed and dangerous. You're to be detained and protected at all costs according to the FBI. So somebody's sure trying to help you with this thing."

"But we sure as hell are armed and dangerous," Hollis grunted. "Fletcher, did the White House guy say anything about charges against us?"

"He said they agree to all our demands. That includes no charges against any of us, and new identities. That doesn't mean they're not out looking for us though."

"No, they're still pushing every police agency in the country to find you. For some reason, our little group of game wardens didn't take it too seriously. Why would people like you be in our woods?" Joey said. "That, plus I don't think the government has a very good idea of what's really been going on with you guys. If they did, they'd be pulling out all the stops."

Hollis pushed back his plate, picked up a rifle and coat, and headed out the door.

"I'm going up on the rock," he grumbled.

— ‖ —

"W0FTU W0FTU, this is WD5CL calling."

Their seven o'clock evening contact was seldom much off the scheduled time. The men had already cleaned the kitchen, and Hollis was settling into some relaxing time listening to news on the Sony shortwave receiver after standing guard during the afternoon hours.

"WD5CL, this is W0FTU. Go ahead, JT."

"Hello, Boyd. I just got off the landline with Neumann. He's willing and able to fly out there whenever you need him. Just let me know and I'll contact him. Sounds like he can get the Baron without much notice. I also talked to Addison and he said he expects a response from his friends by tomorrow afternoon. Over."

"Thanks, JT. If you talk to him again tonight, let him know things are progressing on our end, too. We've got an agreement worked out but need to settle the timing and a few details. We should be good to go for next week. Over."

"Fine business, I'll let him know. How's Andersen doing? Over."

"Better than I expected. He thinks he needs to be getting back to work and wonders if that's all right with us if he helps us out. We're leaning that way. Over."

"You're in the best position to make that call, Boyd. If you feel inclined to agree with him, my experience says that's a pretty good choice. I'm sure you've explained the consequences to him. Over."

"He understands. You have any other news? Over."

"Nothing more from this end. We're still trying to sort out who's running around here at night, but no other problems. You know, the sooner this thing's resolved the better I'll sleep. Over."

"You and me both. Okay, JT, we'll let you go and will be listening for you tomorrow. W0FTU clear."

"Okay, Boyd. Stay safe and let me know when you're ready to travel. W0FTU, this is WD5CL clear. Seventy-three."

— || —

The Venezuelans in Miami and Chicago recorded and got a solid fix on the station identifying as W0FTU. Once all the stations had presented the beam headings they thought were correct from their locations, the Saudi military attaché plotted them on another map. He added the beam heading from JT's house to get a plot from the south. This time the lines crossed more closely. It appeared the transmission was originating in an area of northwest Minnesota close to the Red Lake Indian Reservation. The isolated area appeared to be slightly south of the Canadian border and well north of Highway 2. Still a large area, but small enough to send people into with the hope of identifying the precise location.

A call to Riyadh resulted in an order for the Saudi teams in Texas to fly to Minnesota at their earliest opportunity. That the Neptune men were discussing leaving by air was of great concern. They needed to find these men before their secret could disappear again.

— || —

The Westcona communication center was focused on monitoring Taylor's evening contact with Boyd, and luck was with them. The supervisor immediately notified his boss with the beam heading and a transcript of the conversation. Within an hour, Branton Cole convened a meeting of the crisis management team in his Dallas office.

"Why the hell wasn't this recorded so I could hear exactly what was said?" he exploded. "This doesn't even make sense. Who's Noonon? What's a baron? Which Addison is working with which friends? What progress is Boyd making? Who's Anderson? I need to hear them say it to understand the context, goddammit. You people are idiots!"

Few could ever keep up with the rapid-fire thinking and questions for which Cole was famous. News that Boyd had a solid deal in the works terrified them almost as much as hearing they were going to fly out of their hiding place. Two more significant errors had been precipitated by Neptune's pagan influence to further bedevil Cole's decision making process. The communication center supervisor mistakenly transcribed Jeff Neumann's last name as "Noonon", and not one of the senior corporate leaders associated the name with their own district manager in Brighton, Colorado.

In their muddle, the group blindly supported Cole's snap decision. They needed resources now. Cole dialed Mark Streeter's home number in Houston. Global Oil's strength and considerable resources must be brought into the fray again, or all was lost. The security director strongly objected and reiterated his conviction that his people would have the property located by Friday evening. Why bring Global back into it? Cole again rejected the argument out of hand.

Global's liaison team, headed by Streeter himself, was in Dallas by 10:00 p.m. With the corporate behemoth's substantial influence, they had the location of Jake Taylor's Minnesota property as the Friday morning sun weakly lit the Dallas skyline. It would be a bright, sunny day with temperatures forecast in the low eighties in north Texas. Things were looking more promising for the oil industry.

— ‖ —

The Saudi corporate jet landed at Houston Hobby Airport in the Friday predawn hours. Mahrous was exhausted despite his uneasy sleep over the Atlantic but took time to call the home and office numbers he had for Logan Addison, leaving messages with a call-back number for the hotel. Finally, he called Salem to inform him he was safely at his destination. After a light room-service meal, Mahrous fell into the soft bed. He knew he had to sleep fast because Houston would be awakening shortly.

— ⫶ — Thirty-One — ⫶ —

JEFF NEUMANN SLEPT FITFULLY ON THURSDAY evening in his Longmont, Colorado, home. The three-bedroom house was purchased more for investment purposes than actual need. Since his divorce in Oklahoma, Jeff discovered that he needed far fewer creature comforts than his former wife had found reasonable. Still, renting was a waste of money when real estate investments usually increased over time. Unfortunately, this premise was not holding true in the 1986 metro-Denver market. The area was experiencing record-high foreclosure and mortgage default rates due to the simultaneous slump in the energy and high-tech industries.

IBM was transferring and laying off employees at their facility located on the Highway 119 diagonal between Longmont and Boulder. Many of Jeff's neighbors were among them. Peripheral companies, depending on IBM for their existence, were quickly relocating or going out of business. Denver's attempt at becoming the Silicon Valley of the Rockies was falling flat, as was the new airport project. The oilfield was slumping horrendously in the Denver-Julesburg Basin, and the inevitable consequence was a moribund housing market. Homes were remaining on the market for longer and longer periods, now rapidly approaching eighteen months before sellers caved in to low offers to escape the mortgage after moving out of state. Jeff wasn't sure he could even sell his house for the mortgage balance. While he enjoyed living in Colorado, he knew he couldn't eat scenery once he lost his job. Unlike many residents, he would not be staying around just because the mountains were beautiful or because he thought it stylish to live in Colorado. Jeff was a flexible world-traveler and becoming weary of the impending doom permeating his industry. Change was good and he was ready.

The former naval aviator was infused with energy and eager to take to the sky on Friday afternoon. Westcona's headquarters was one time zone east, giving Jeff an hour's time advantage. His Dallas-based boss was prone to afternoon meetings away from the office, especially on Fridays, giving Jeff additional cover when he had things to do and didn't want to have to think about a call from Dallas. He felt no need or desire to debate his abrupt vacation request, the reason for it, or anything else for that matter. He was tired of Westcona and the whole damned industry.

After his Thursday evening telephone conversation with JT, Jeff's picture of Neptune and where the action was headed became much more clearly defined. He needed to get to the cabin where Fletcher would brief him on his specific role and what he might expect as a partner in their plan. JT claimed to have no knowledge of Fletcher's plan and Jeff believed him. He understood operational security from his military years and just hoped the action would be in keeping with the magnitude of the discovery. JT's only instruction had been to take his own individual weapons, cash, passport, and a parachute. His blood was running hot…and it felt appallingly good. The Baron was reserved for nine days starting at noon, and he planned to be in the air shortly thereafter. Returning to Colorado wasn't necessarily on his itinerary.

— || —

Fletcher started the generator on his way back to the cabin from his graveyard-shift guard duty at 0630 hours. The eastern sky was just beginning to lighten when seen from the OP, but it was still dark down at the cabin. He was cold, damp, tired, and hungry. Light mist and fog shrouded the woods even though the forecast called for clearing skies and cooler temperatures. Hollis would likely be tuning the ham transceiver before he got inside for some of the hot breakfast he smelled wafting from the cabin. Today was a day of decisions, and for the last four hours he'd been thinking about what they needed to do and what loose ends might still need to be dealt with.

Breakfast was unusually quiet. Everyone seemed lost in his own thoughts about what direction this might take in the coming days. Fletcher had decided to turn Joey loose knowing it was in their best interest to have another set of eyes on the ground in case they received unwanted attention. He was now convinced the Saudis were actively hunting them just as hard as Westcona and Global. The feds were a conundrum but he had to assume they were also in on the chase despite the fact they had a deal in the works. Just a little heads-up help from the game warden might make the difference between success and failure.

"W0FTU W0FTU, this is WD5CL calling," JT called at 0659 hours.

"WD5CL, this is W0FTU. Go ahead, JT," Hollis responded.

"Morning, Cade. Just a couple of things. Your ride will be there late this afternoon. He'll buzz your location and talk to you on 123.45 MHz. Come out and wave a red jacket or blanket or something so he'll know everything's okay and that you'll be on your way to pick him up.

Monitor that frequency on the Sony. Remember to move the mode switch to AM if the radio doesn't switch itself when you tune to the air-band. I don't remember if it does or not. Copy?"

"We copy, JT. Yeah, I know how to run the Sony. What else? Over."

"Your pilot's taking next week as vacation and can do whatever you need. Addison should have word on his efforts by about now, I expect. He was going to call his contact first thing this morning. Things changed yesterday at his place of employment. It seems their unwanted company unexpectedly packed up and left. Same thing happened in Dallas. You might be able to make something of that. Over."

"Fletcher's nodding his head so I guess it means something to him. We'll give Logan a call in a little while. Thanks for getting us transportation. I don't expect we'll need him for that long but it's good to know we have the option. Anything else? Over."

"Not this morning. Just watch for your ride and take care of yourselves. I'll have the radio on this evening. W0FTU, this is WD5CL clear on your final. Seventy-three."

"Okay, JT. We'll talk then, and thanks. W0FTU clear."

Fletcher threw a handcuff key on the table in front of Joey. He had been in the cuffs except when driving to Skime with them to make phone calls.

"You're free to go, partner. I'd threaten you, but if you dime us out we'll be dead long before we could get to you.

"I understand," Joey said as he removed the cuffs, rubbed his wrists, and slid the cuffs into his pocket. "I need to get cleaned up and back to work before the State of Minnesota gets curious. You can keep my handheld radio although you won't pick up anything from down here in the woods. If you take it up on that rock where you shot at me from, you should be able to hear the state repeater that our radio system operates on. Not sure you'd have enough power to get into the system from way out here though. I'll be watching for strangers and anyone from law enforcement who's showing any interest in you. You're making the right choice."

"Joey, you'd have hit the ground dead if I had shot at you," Fletcher corrected with a crooked grin. "You have no idea how close you came to meeting your maker."

"I didn't then, but I do now."

Joey looked excited and animated. It took him less than ten minutes to gather his few belongings and reassure the men that he would do his part as a real partner. He explained again that if he keyed his microphone in the truck to talk to them, the repeater would pick up his signal and relay it to his dispatcher and other game wardens to hear over a wide area.

"Next time someone's up on the rock, try getting into the state system by keying up without saying anything and see if you hear the repeater respond. You'll know if it does. Just don't talk on it if it's reaching the repeater except in a real emergency. I'd hear your message but so would everyone else on the net."

With that, Joey drove away from the cabin.

"Let's give Logan a try before we dial for White House dollars," Fletcher said as Steve prepared for a few hours on the OP and Hollis cleaned up the dishes. Steve had decided he would rather be on the OP than in the cabin if trouble arrived while the others were gone.

Twenty minutes later, Fletcher and Hollis were following Joey's path on their way to the pay phone in Skime. Fletcher still had concerns about Joey, but knew they had bigger ones that were more likely to bite them in the ass if they didn't get some work done quickly. The sun hid behind the clouds making the drizzle and fog even more chilling. So much for weather forecasts.

"I hope to hell it doesn't snow," Hollis said.

By the time they turned off the rutted trail onto Highway 54, wet flakes were falling like little anvils straight down out of the sodden sky. Nothing was sticking to the ground...yet.

— ‖ —

Logan dialed Salem's number in Jeddah. He had not slept well. The stress was mounting as he considered the danger they faced from every quarter. The feds would try to take them alive and without violence. State, county, and city cops would be more afraid of the men if they read between the lines and realized what might have really happened in Ames. All too often, armed men with government-sanctioned authority tend to react with force more quickly as their level of training, experience, and organizational discipline decreases. Westcona and Global security people would kill them without hesitation to protect their employers, avenge their lost comrades, and salve their bruised egos. Neither would the Saudis, and whomever else they had involved, hesitate to use extreme violence to protect their hold on the industrial world provided by their vast oceans of oil. Yes, it seems the boys have painted themselves into a corner.

Salem answered on the second ring.

"Logan, I have good news. The funds have been wired to your account. At least the instructions have been given to make this happen. The bank is in western Europe so the transaction may not be able to be confirmed until Monday morning when the bank opens. You may still have time to confirm the transfer if you do so quickly."

"That's good news, Salem. I'll call when we finish up here. Is there an official message to go with this news?"

"Yes, there is, Logan. My benefactors expect to meet with you as soon as the wire is confirmed. They have appropriate resources already in the United States and require a call to set up a Monday meeting at the latest. Tonight or tomorrow is preferred. Considering the critical importance of this transaction, any hint of deception or procrastination will precipitate unrestrained reactions that will be dangerous to the world."

"We don't respond well to threats, but I understand and will talk to the boys as soon as possible, Salem. I'm not in constant or immediate communication with my son or his friends. They've been forced to flee, as I'm sure you can appreciate. However, I see no problem with a Monday meeting to deliver the product. Certainly sooner if the funds transfer is verified and travel arrangements can be made. There will be no deliberate deception or procrastination. Anything else?"

"Only this, my friend. My people are very anxious. I am trying to help you in every way possible. Not everyone on this side of the world feels the way I do. Please understand that, Logan."

Logan profoundly sensed the threat in Salem's words, yet was thrilled with the prospect of a clean transaction. He checked his watch and did a mental time calculation. It was just after 3 p.m. on Friday in Switzerland. He dialed the bank only to find the funds transfer desk had just closed. It would reopen at 9 a.m. on Monday, which meant 2 a.m. Texas time. The money might be in the account but there would be no confirmation until then. He considered calling Salem back but didn't when he realized the Saudis already knew. They not only knew but had deliberately timed it to give themselves the weekend to find Steve and his friends. Scimitars, khanjars, and jambiyas were being honed and that seldom bode well for enemies of Allah. Logan involuntarily chilled at the thought of cold Arab steel.

He dialed his secretary who relayed the message from
Mahrous. She also told him that Mark Streeter was already out
of the office for the weekend. Even his secretary didn't know
where he was; only that he had taken a company plane and
a handful of executives with him the previous evening.
She would call a friend in the Aviation Department to see if
anyone knew their destination.

Why would Mahrous be in Houston? Was this the help
Salem had obliquely mentioned? He dialed the hotel. It took
Mahrous a few moments to convey his message, but soon the
two men were speaking candidly about what was happening.
Mahrous made no secret of the fact that Neptune was being
aggressively hunted, as was Logan. The Saudis would use any
leverage they could to extricate Neptune from the young men
who possessed it. Mahrous sounded surprised when Logan
told him of his earlier conversation with Salem. His reaction
was one of wariness and exasperation.

"I'll land in McAllen in about two hours to help you,"
Mahrous said.

— ‖ —

Fletcher dialed Logan but got a busy signal. Too impatient to
wait, he quickly dialed the White House from the pay phone in
Skime. The falling snow was now mixed with sleet and beginning to accumulate in a gray slush on the gravel and grass. Mr.
Johnson answered on the first ring.

"The President has authorized your payment. When and
where do we meet?" the FBI agent asked.

"We don't until I confirm the money is in our bank
account. Has it been moved?"

"No, but it will be yet today. You have our word on it."

"Gee, that sure makes me feel better. This is how it will work. Unless I get a confirmation from the bank today, we wait until next week to hand it over. Do you think the Swiss bankers are working this weekend?"

"Where do we meet next week?"

"I'll call you." Fletcher slapped the phone onto its cradle and turned to look at Hollis.

"Twenty-five seconds," Hollis called out after looking at his watch. Fletcher again dialed Logan.

"Logan. Fletcher. Looks like success on this end. How about you?"

"They claim to have already wired the money. I tried to confirm it but the wire transfer desk is closed for the weekend. I told them you'd have Neptune for them on Monday after we confirm the transfer."

Fletcher was dazed by the news and had to pause for a moment to think. They had anticipated a tough sale but suddenly both parties were willing to wire money today? On a Friday afternoon when they knew it was too late to confirm? Not likely! This was just too easy and too good to be true. Had they figured out where the men were hiding? Why else would both parties be timing their transaction this way if they weren't attempting a setup of some kind? No, this was turning into a real turd sandwich. He and Hollis needed to get back to the cabin right damn now and prepare for the worst.

"Logan, I was just told by the feds that they'll wire the money today, too. I told them I'd turn Neptune over next week. This is the news we hoped to get, but it smells bad and the weekend timing vexes me. What're you thinking?"

"Well, neither group is exactly trustworthy now are they? You're exactly right; it doesn't pass the sniff test. There's another surprise that might help, though. I have a highly placed Saudi friend arriving in McAllen in the next couple of hours to help us. He thinks he owes me a debt of family honor and is trying to make good on it. This isn't over by a long shot, according to him. I think we'd better keep our heads down over the weekend and see what shows up in the bank on Monday morning or on our doorsteps between now and then."

Fletcher wasn't sure what to say. Was Logan under duress? Was this friend of his really a friend? "Logan, are you safe? Just clear your throat if you're in danger."

"No, you've got it all wrong. I couldn't be more safe or happy to see my friend Mahrous. His brother is my contact in Saudi Arabia, although he isn't very happy with the arrangement. They own a little construction company over there. They want to help Steve and me, and you get helped by default. We'll be talking to his brother in Jeddah and hope to have better information about what's really going on. Now, where do I tell them I'll have Neptune on Monday?"

"Jeff Neumann's flying here this afternoon or evening. We'll be able to be anywhere by Monday. Let's keep it someplace far enough out of the way that everyone will have to scramble a little to get there, and not have time to set up many surprises. How does Green Bay, Wisconsin, sound to you?"

"Green Bay, Wisconsin? Where the hell did that come from? It's as good a place as any, I guess. Never been there and didn't have plans to before now. I'll call JT and see if he can fly us up there. Or, Mahrous has a plane and he may still be around to do it. JT can let you know what the plan is on the radio tonight."

Fletcher hung up and redialed the White House.

"I'll call you on Sunday night with the location. You have our new identities and papers signed by the President ready by then. I'll show up as soon as the bank confirms the transfer of funds," he said to Mr. Johnson before hanging up again.

— ‖ —

Saudi government officials, military leaders, and special guest, Iraqi President Saddam Hussein, were meeting in Riyadh when news of Salem's successful contact with Logan Addison arrived. Now the Americans might become careless since they knew the money had been wired. Saddam Hussein assured the group that his trusted Air Force officers training in Winnipeg, Manitoba, were prepared to scramble a plane and attack the Americans if so ordered. He would only require a specific target location to destroy Neptune.

The group was satisfied that their special operations team would be landing in Thief River Falls late that afternoon with portable radio direction-finding equipment and the weapons necessary to resolve the issue once the targets were located. The Iraqi fighter aircraft represented an option they would not hesitate to use if the Americans tried to flee with Neptune—or double-crossed them.

—ııı— Thirty-Two —ııı—

JT CALLED LOGAN IN MCALLEN WHEN he came home for lunch, inviting him to stay in Alice once his business in the Valley was complete. All the Westcona bodyguards had departed that morning after the Arab team unexpectedly checked out of their motel and left town.

When Logan arrived with Mahrous in tow, JT was initially alarmed but calmed quickly when Logan introduced his friend from Saudi Arabia. They retreated to his home for a strategy session and information exchange. Logan found a bottle of Scotch and poured two glasses, looked questioningly at Mahrous, and then poured the third. The men sat down at the kitchen table to lay out what they collectively knew.

—ıı—

By Thursday afternoon, Jeff Neumann had packed all he figured he would need. He called his bank and told them he would be by at lunchtime on Friday to pick up the thirty-five thousand dollars from his savings account. Remembering how little parachute training he'd been subjected to in the Navy, he reluctantly made arrangements to pick up a chute as Fletcher had instructed. He really didn't know much about manually jumping out of airplanes and hoped the damned thing wasn't for him. He stuffed a shoulder holster for his old Browning Hi-Power into his bag along with three spare magazines, five boxes of nine-millimeter ammunition, and a couple of military-style fighting knives he had in his basement. The thought of bringing a rifle or shotgun passed through his mind but he decided against it.

Before getting in the car on Friday morning, Jeff changed his mind and grabbed a Remington 870 pump-action shotgun and four boxes of twelve-gauge goose loads. Not an ideal defensive load but they'd do the job if he did his. Hurrying, he banged the gun on the door frame while putting it in his car. Irritated, he yanked the shotgun from the case, carried it to his workbench and wrapped a crumpled-up jacket around the gun's receiver to protect the finish. He slipped it into a vise and made short work of the last nine inches of barrel with a hacksaw. The ventilated rib looked like hell. Smiling ruefully at his handiwork, he smoothed the burrs with a file and then duct-taped the flopping rib to the barrel. He now had a much handier, but purely ugly, nineteen-inch-barreled shotgun with no choke. That cranked his mood up several notches as he headed for the Westcona yard in Brighton.

His morning was spent tying up loose ends, straightening up his office, and killing time. He filled out a vacation request form and asked his secretary to fax it to Dallas late in the day. By noon he was out the door thinking he might never return to the job he had once so enjoyed. After a quick stop at the bank, he soon had the Beechcraft Baron on a forty-degree heading at eight thousand feet.

Four hours later and out of daylight, Jeff tuned his radio to 123.450 MHz and keyed the microphone, trusting Fletcher had the radio on at the cabin.

"I'm close and heading your way. Should be over you in about five minutes. Shine a light when you hear me."

He had planned to arrive before sunset but was behind schedule. As he watched the dark forest for lights, he hoped they had the generator on to provide him a reference point. Three minutes later he spotted lights and banked to starboard. Someone was swinging a red lantern outside the brightly lit cabin. Satisfied, he keyed his microphone again.

"I'll be waiting at the airport."

— ‖ —

When Jeff walked into the Thief River Falls airport FBO, he was surprised to see a subdued group of six middle-eastern-looking men at the counter. He almost had himself convinced that it was his imagination when an animated discussion broke out between the group spokesman and counterman over fuel availability. Apparently the fuel truck operator had left for the day and was not expected to return. Jeff caught bits and piece of the Arabic/English translation taking place among the group. A dump of adrenalin coursed through his veins as he walked back out to the Baron. He'd go back in when the Arabs left, hand the guy his credit card, and ask that they refuel the plane whenever the fuel man came back.

Just as he was completing the tie-down procedure, a Beech King-Air landed and taxied over near the Baron. The hatch opened and nine cramped men clawed their way out, stretching and bitching as they scuttled down the short steps after a long flight. The pilot exited last and ambled over to Jeff.

"They have fuel available?" he asked with a soft drawl. Because Jeff had been around the oilfields since getting out of the Navy, he could place regional dialects without difficulty and this one was pure east Texas. The slight drawl Jeff had acquired while working in Texas and Oklahoma had morphed into a more "mid-west unidentifiable" after living in Colorado for the past few years. The hair on the back of his neck stood up in warning.

"Can't say for sure. There're some people arguing about it right now. The fuel truck guy went to dinner and may not come back tonight. I decided to wait until morning. Where'd you come in from?" he asked with feigned innocence.

"We flew out of Love Field in Dallas today. Up from Houston last night. Business trip for those boys. A wasted weekend for me," he drawled. "See you around."

"You bet," Jeff said as he walked close enough to the King-Air to confirm the small Global Oil emblem painted on the fuselage beside the open hatch.

Steve Addison was sitting out front in Fletcher's Oldsmobile, drinking a can of Budweiser, when Jeff walked around the side of the building and up to the waist-high chain link fence.

"How was your flight?" he asked as he got out of the car.

"Good," Jeff said, brimming with excitement as he passed two duffle bags and cased shotgun across before vaulting the fence. He felt younger than he had in years. "We've got a real shit-storm brewing," he said as he popped the top on a cold beer he found in the front seat. He dug through his bag looking for the Browning Hi-Power as he filled Steve in on the Arabs and Global people while they made their way out of town.

— || —

Joey Andersen went home to shower, shave, and change uniforms before making an obligatory stop at his Thief River Falls office to show them he was still hard at work. The other game wardens were smoking and joking over coffee when he came through the doorway into the large bullpen area.

"Hey, look what the cat dragged in," someone yelled when he saw Joey. "Been pretty busy out there, have ya?"

Joey sat down and shot the breeze with the group while trying to enjoy a cup of atrocious State of Minnesota coffee. He had never figured out why the office coffee was so bad, yet everyone gathered after shift if they were in town to drink the foul stuff. He thought of the strong, rich coffee Hollis brewed and smiled to himself. The wardens were sifting through reams of paperwork that had accumulated over the past few days when one of the men held up a flyer for everyone to see.

"Look at this shit. The feds are still looking for those bad boys from that lab down Iowa way. They even want us to be watching for them. Now what in the hell would guys like that be doing out here?" he asked as everyone laughed. "They probably hit the Idaho border within two days of shooting up Ames."

A shift supervisor nodded and mentioned he would stop by the Pennington County sheriff's office to see if there was anything more on the manhunt. Joey rubbed the handcuff-chaffed skin on his wrists and wondered why they would think Fletcher and Hollis had shot up anything in Ames?

"I didn't know they shot up Ames," he said. "That's not on the flyer."

"Hell, yeah. The feds haven't openly said so, but the scuttlebutt is that they found .45 shell casings and an empty Colt magazine with Boyd's prints all over them at the scene. I heard they found a match in the military database. They must be former Rangers or Green Berets or some damn thing like that to have kicked ass like they did."

Joey quietly pondered his decision to help...and got up and left without saying goodbye.

—|||— Thirty-Three —|||—

JEFF'S FRIDAY NIGHT ARRIVAL AND news of the Arab and Global Oil security teams in Thief River Falls galvanized Fletcher. His instinct to get back to the cabin and prepare for the worst had been dead on.

With Logan off in Texas, Jeff settled into his vacated bunk.

"This is a hell of a way to start a weekend," Jeff said. "My timing couldn't have been better to catch those assholes at the airport."

"It was—and we're sure as hell glad you're here," Hollis said. "I can't figure how they found us so soon. You think the feds are on to us, too?"

"Odds are that the feds aren't far behind, Fletcher said. "It'll be a bitch if they all come at us at once. If the feds do show up, we'll only have that one chance to turn ourselves in and that's if we're lucky. Those other guys will try to kill us without any conversation."

No one had a comment.

Fletcher had talked to JT on the radio at seven that evening, just an hour before Jeff arrived with the news. There was no mention of any problems from Alice, or reason for them to be more concerned with their security than they had been.

Spencer Wainwright knew a little about their plan, but didn't know their location. Who had given them up? Joey?

Fletcher unsuccessfully tried JT on the radio. Jeff's assurance that neither group appeared frantic to get out of the airport put them somewhat at ease. Perhaps both were operating from the same intelligence and weren't exactly sure where the cabin was.

When Jeff arrived, he was already wearing his shoulder-holstered Browning Hi-Power. Now he was sitting on his bunk methodically loading his shotgun and stuffing extra ammunition in his jacket pockets. In just a week at the cabin, they had already become a little lax with wearing their web gear and carrying extra ammunition. Not any longer. For Jeff's benefit, they reviewed the location of the grenade launcher and hand grenades before settling in for the night.

— ‖ —

Saturday morning's radio conversation with JT revealed that the Saudis were still not sure where the cabin was located and that they were depending on radio direction-finding equipment to zero in on the transmitter. JT was very careful to not disclose the source of his information over the radio. The appearance of the Global Oil team was an issue no one had an answer for, but JT warned that Westcona almost surely had people on the Global plane. The companies were working together. Fletcher cut short their conversation to make it more difficult for the Saudis. He had the information he needed to finalize his plan.

The noose was tightening and Fletcher knew it. They were cut off for all practical purposes. They couldn't use the ham radio for fear of leading the Arabs right to them, or leave the cabin to use the telephone without the risk of being spotted.

Either action could result in the loss of Neptune—and probably a quick death. Fletcher was working on a plan—one that might just get them out alive. Would the others go along?

When Joey Andersen came by the cabin early on Saturday morning, it was quickly apparent that he was completely loyal to Neptune...or at least to the dollars he stood to gain. He also seemed to hold them in higher regard than he had before they let him loose. News of hostile teams in the area clearly shocked him. Apparently his offer to help hadn't adequately factored in the likelihood of real life bad-asses actually showing up in his normally quiet and tranquil woods. This was now the real deal...not an esoteric intellectual exercise. His predictable initial response was to get law enforcement help, but they quickly quashed that notion.

They poured him a cup of coffee before Fletcher ordered him back out to the highway to watch for anyone snooping about or preparing a raid. Joey seemed comfortable with that assignment and was plainly happy to be trusted. Before he left, Fletcher asked him again about the likelihood of anyone finding a way to the cabin from any direction other than the trail they had been using, and was again assured there were no readily available maps that would show the logging and snowmobile trails that ran to the east of the cabin. There was no way in from the north or south, at least none any attackers could find and use. It was just too rough and unknown to all but the most ardent local woodsmen. That was consistent with what Fletcher had seen when he and Logan had driven east from the cabin when they first arrived.

Joey loaded his shotgun and rifle, and placed them where they could be quickly reached before driving west to Highway 54. He caught a glint of reflection in the early morning sun from the OP and knew Hollis was watching him through a riflescope or binoculars. Hollis would have a good view of anything happening on this trail, but that would be small consolation if a dozen or more armed professionals made a run on the cabin.

Fletcher's new plan had come together quite well in a short time. He presented it without fanfare before anyone decided to muddy the water by bringing up other ideas.

"Any suggestions or comments?" he asked. His plan was elegant in its simplicity yet bold enough to scare anyone in his right mind.

"The only other option is to make a run for it and hope to get free of all these people until Monday when the banks open, right?" Steve said.

"That's right," Fletcher said. "The Arabs don't know exactly where we are, and therefore are less of an immediate threat than the company security team. But, the Arabs have an airplane in Thief River Falls and could cut us off if we made it there and tried to escape in the Baron. On the other hand, the company team might know where the cabin is on a map, but finding it is another matter. That would almost certainly have to be done on the ground and in daylight. Even starlight scopes or night vision goggles would be difficult to use in these dark woods without some moonlight, and I doubt that either company outfitted their security department with them. The security team also has Global's airplane and enough people to split into two groups if they wanted. One to attack us and one to block us from getting out if we did defeat their attack team. The Global plane could even be in the air during the attack as a spotting platform."

A fight looked inevitable; quite possibly with the security team and then the Arabs in quick succession. They were cornered. The only thing working for them was the Baron, and the hope that neither group knew for sure that Jeff had already arrived.

"I didn't join up with you guys to turn tail and run," Jeff said. "Seems like you've been doing too much of that already.

It's easy to talk about fighting. Now let's see if you've got the balls you think you have."

Fletcher didn't appreciate Jeff's statement, but understood it and knew he was right. Running only postponed or repositioned the inevitable fight. They needed to stay alive to confirm whether or not money was in the bank on Monday morning, and evade or defeat the security team and Arabs. But Monday seemed like a long way off right now.

"Hollis, "Fletcher said. "You wanna run for it or try my plan?"

"If I thought we could get clean away and hide until Monday morning, I'd be all for it. But I don't reckon we can. I'd rather fight them right here than let them ambush us somewhere."

Fetcher smiled in agreement. He looked at Steve and could tell from the look on Steve's face that he wanted a crack at the people who murdered his wife. No need to even ask.

He could see Jeff was satisfied with the decision, but obviously had something else to say.

"If we pull this off, I'm going to be out one airplane that I don't own, and my job. We've never talked about a cut for me."

"*We* have," Fletcher answered calmly. "You'll never have to think about working again when this is over. Good enough for now?"

"Good enough."

They would have to stay off the ham radio to keep the Arabs in the dark as to their specific whereabouts and deal with them at the airport or on the road, as necessary. The initial contact would be with the security team, and it was only reasonable that they do it in a place that gave them tactical advantage and the element of surprise. If the security team was not aware that their presence had been detected, the men could

lie in ambush and take on the numerically superior force
before escaping through the trails to the east. Now, they just
had to be on their toes, prepare the ambush, and keep the
security team from the knowledge that they were expected.

Fletcher wasted no time in making assignments. Hollis
would occupy the established foxhole position across the road
from the cabin. Steve and Jeff would set up fighting positions
from slightly higher ground to the south of Hollis. That would
create a picket line in the woods to meet the attackers
with withering fire to the west. Fletcher would man the OP to
provide fire-support with the M79 grenade launcher, and
suppressing rifle-fire as needed. When the security team was
neutralized, they would assemble on the Oldsmobile, prepositioned east on the logging trail. Then it would be off to the
airport on an untried route Joey assured them would be
passable.

They'd brief Joey and give him his assignment when he
stopped by at lunchtime.

—‖— Thirty-Four —‖—

WHEN BOYD RADIOED JAKE TAYLOR on Saturday morning, the Saudi soldiers were already in the field with portable shortwave radios and directional antennas. They had scattered out from Thief River Falls to gain the physical separation needed to make triangulation more effective. A little luck was needed and they got it in short order. Three were able to get a reasonable compass fix on the signal, and by noon had plotted the likely location of the cabin as north and east of Thief River Falls, somewhere south of the Canadian border. They called their report in to Riyadh and were ordered to move further into the field and attempt to locate Neptune. The information would be studied to identify the most likely airports for the Neptune men to have their plane arriving or already waiting.

Two soldiers bought food at the CO-OP in Grygla and ate as they drove toward their new target area. They were astounded at how wild this part of the country was. No rolling open desert. No flat steppe-like terrain. Just a claustrophobic pine, poplar, and hardwood forest that appeared to go on forever.

In Riyadh, Al Makhabarat Al A'amah studied all the northwestern Minnesota airports and landing strips from the information they had. They could see a number of airfields that would be convenient for the men they hunted. Until today, those men had no reason to suspect their location was compromised, so convenience rather than security should have been the major factor in selecting an airfield. That would mean Thief River Falls, Bemidji, Roseau, or even Grand Forks, North Dakota. With the new updated information from the special operations team, they eliminated all except Thief River Falls and Roseau.

Winnipeg was also not far way. Another meeting in Riyadh resulted in updated instructions to the Iraqi Air Force officer at the Forces Canada base:

Be prepared to leave on short notice to identify and destroy a small or medium-sized civilian aircraft taking off from Roseau or Thief River Falls, Minnesota. The plane will likely be a multi-engine piston plane, but could be a corporate jet. More instructions to follow.

The young captain couldn't believe what he was reading. This had to be some sort of training protocol to ready him for future combat missions when he returned home. Surely it wasn't an actual tactical alert. Then again, it certainly could be part of a surprise training drill meant to create stress. Orders were not his to question, no matter how odd they might seem. He was there to train, so train he would. His first step was to check civilian air-band radio frequencies used in northwest Minnesota and preset the radios in the fighter, and secondly to get live ammunition aboard his aircraft. He was surprised at how easy that task was, which furthered his conclusion that this was a training exercise and he was being allowed to arm his jet as part of the exercise. They certainly would have stopped him if it wasn't.

— || —

The Westcona communication center delivered a recording of the Saturday morning radio communication between Boyd and Taylor to the tenth-floor executive conference room being used as the command center for the combined crisis management team. Their joint field team had stayed at the Thief River Falls Best Western on Friday evening and was eating breakfast when Mark Streeter and Branton Cole made a call to the hotel. The two presidents had agreed that telling the field team that their quarry already knew of their presence would be counterproductive. The team-members were professionals, and professionals always approach each mission with every conceivable contingency in mind. No sense in heightening the stress by confirming their attack was anticipated. Boyd, Cade, Addison, and whoever this pilot was certainly couldn't be a match for them.

Streeter and Cole instructed Dutch Peltier to leave one man with the pilot at the airport just in case Boyd got lucky again and made it that far. Peltier had been appointed team leader only after Cole informed Streeter that Peltier was a former Navy SEAL, despite his knowledge that it was untrue. A few nasty jabs at the Global Oil president for letting the young Addison escape in Colorado sealed the deal. Streeter didn't like Global Oil people reporting to a Westcona employee but it seemed reasonable in the circumstances.

They also firmly reminded Peltier that they were operating in a very rural area where people like them could not go for long without raising eyebrows. They were encouraged to keep a low profile and execute their mission no later than at Sunday's first light. Both senior leaders were concerned that Peltier would abort the mission and return to Texas if he knew Boyd was expecting the attack. That was not an option. The security men were expendable. The mission was not.

"What about the Arabs?" Peltier asked.

"Kill them," Cole and Streeter said in near unison.

"I can't just shoot people on the street."

"Then make sure you don't bump into them, but kill them if they get in the way," Cole said again.

Peltier assigned one man to stay with the Global pilot, and told the others they constituted the attack team. They reviewed weather forecasts and maps, and the final raid details were set in place. It was much colder than expected, requiring the purchase of a few last-minute winter clothing items before four of them moved out to recon the area. According to their maps, there was only one way into the property Jake Taylor owned. No escape route if things went south on them. They needed better information and the recon team was tasked with obtaining it.

— ‖ —

Mahrous called Salem from Jake Taylor's house, asking when there might be a better time to call—a prearranged code telling Salem to go to a friend's house where Mahrous would call within thirty minutes, hopefully without being monitored by Al Makhabarat Al A'amah.

"I understand the men have been approximately located and a team is already on the ground trying to find their precise location," Salem said before Mahrous could begin.

"And their orders?" Mahrous asked.

"I think you already know that, brother. I have other disturbing news."

"What could be more disturbing?" Mahrous asked.

"I just spoke with our brother in Medina, Salem said. "He tells me that our government has teamed with the Iraqis and now has a fighter aircraft poised in Winnipeg to destroy Neptune by the end of the weekend."

"Do you believe this report to be accurate? Why would we or the Iraqis have a fighter plane in Canada?" Mahrous asked.

"Yes, I believe it is accurate. The Iraqis have pilots training in Canada just as we have pilots training in the United States. I do not know if they could get one armed and into an attack without being stopped by Canadian and US forces, but I have no doubt they would try."

Logan was enraged when Mahrous explained what Salem had reported. He tried calling Fletcher on the radio but got no answer. JT was already a step ahead and packing a bag. Picking up the Alice telephone directory from JT's counter, Mahrous found a number for the nearest FBI office and dialed the number.

"An Iraqi fighter is poised to enter United States airspace from Canada yet this weekend and attack U.S. citizens. This is related to Neptune, a crisis of which you may not yet be aware. Many lives are at risk. You must immediately call your superiors in Washington with this information."

With that, he hung up. What else could he do or say without being detained?

"Let's get the Falcon headed north. It'll be dark when we get up there and we may be too late even then," JT told an agitated Logan. Mahrous already had his bag near the front door.

An hour later, they were cruising at forty thousand feet.

"We've got severe weather ahead, Addison. I can try to get around it but it looks like the whole center of the country is one hell of a mess. We can go over it, but I'll need to put down once for fuel between here and Thief River Falls. I'd rather not get low on fuel with that much weather below us."

"Don't even think about putting this thing down before Thief River Falls," Logan said.

"May Allah be with us," Mahrous prayed quietly.

— ‖ —

The newly minted twenty-four year old FBI special agent assigned to the San Antonio field office had heard about the weekend calls from local crazies. He had also heard of the pranks played by more senior agents. It was Saturday morning and he was stuck manning the office while everyone else was out enjoying their weekend. An Iraqi fighter? Coming out of Canada to attack U.S. citizens? Neptune? None of this babble made any sense. His first instinct was to share in the laugh and give the guy credit for a lively imagination. Upon reflection, he wondered if he shouldn't call the SAC just in case there was something here he didn't understand…but hesitated and put the phone back down without dialing. Finally, he decided not to take the bait but to cover his own ass by filing a report for review and action when the rest of the office returned on Monday morning. Let the boss see what he had to put up with as a new agent and just how good his judgment was.

— ‖ —

Steve manned the OP with the oilfield and game warden radios while the others drove toward the highway with a chain saw, a pruning saw, and a couple of axes. They turned around at the highway, pulled back onto the trail, and stopped as Joey squealed to a halt. He had been watching the turnoff from a distance.

"What are you doing?" the game warden asked.

"We're going to make it tough for anyone to drive down the trail," Fletcher said as he opened the passenger door and got into Joey's truck.

"Word's out that you and Hollis shot people in Ames," Joey said.

"We'll be shooting some more if they make another run on us," Fletcher responded without explaining what had happened in Ames. He quickly briefed Joey and sent him back down the highway to watch for bad guys.

They pulled down the trail thirty feet, stopped, and dropped a large maple tree across the trailhead with the chainsaw. Moving back east toward the cabin, they cut trees at bends in the trail and let them fall in a haphazard fashion to block vehicle traffic. They did the same whenever they arrived at an awkward curve or approached a particularly swampy spot, and stacked brush and branches on the downed trees to make it appear that the road ended or was permanently blocked.

Any decent four-by-four pickup or SUV with some ground clearance and a talented driver could get over, around, or through most of them. A car couldn't. People with little experience in the woods wouldn't know what to make of the obstructions. By the time they got back to the cabin, they had created six tactical barriers behind the maple tree blocking the trailhead at Highway 54. Anyone coming in would be walking or making a lot of racket. In the darkness, it would be almost impossible to quietly traverse, though it wouldn't even slow down military troops. All in all, not bad for a hasty defense under the circumstances.

— ‖ —

Fletcher checked everyone's gear, making sure each man had his fair share of ammunition. He checked flashlights, fighting knives, and hand grenades. He reviewed how to arm and throw a hand grenade with all three men, none of who had ever done it in anything except their dreams. Finally, he went over the operation of the M79 grenade launcher that would be used from the OP when the time came. If something happened to him, any one of them might need to know how to employ it. Because it operates like a single-shot, break-open shotgun, it was easy to describe without having it in his hands.

Once comfortable that each man was as prepared as he was going to be, Fletcher took them down the drive to the foxhole and reviewed fields of fire while reminding them that forty-millimeter grenades would be raining down from the OP once the ambush was sprung. They went over the location of the prepositioned hand grenades in the foxhole and where to throw them without hitting overhanging branches in darkness.

Finally, Fletcher helped Jeff and Steve dig rudimentary fighting positions on the slightly higher ground just south of the foxhole Hollis would occupy. They placed the first about forty yards from the foxhole, and the second another fifty yards farther south and slightly west. This provided a concave line from which the men could direct devastating fire on anyone approaching from the west. Fields of fire were cleared and their fighting holes were concealed with brush and tree limbs. All this preparation activity was new and intriguing to two ex-Navy guys and a career civilian.

Jeff carried all of his shotgun shells to the center position, claiming it as his own. Steve would occupy the outpost farthest to the south and away from the cabin. Both men continued to dig in the cold earth to make their holes just a little deeper as they contemplated what it would be like to have bullets thumping into the dirt around them.

Fletcher went back to the cabin, made a sandwich, and headed to the OP for his tour of guard duty. From his high vantage point, he carefully noted the location of the new fighting holes so he wouldn't inadvertently fire on them or drop a forty-millimeter grenade too close.

Hollis and Jeff ate a quick lunch and decided to follow Fletcher's suggestion of walking slowly west toward the highway, flanking the logging trail and watching for any signs of intrusion while Steve got some rest after his early guard duty. Fletcher had told them to be watching the easternmost barrier and down the trail beyond. Any infiltration by the security team would be a reconnaissance probe, not an attack. Hollis looked back toward the OP but couldn't see Fletcher, although he could see the outline of the little structure they had built to stay out of the weather. Nobody else would notice.

— ‖ —

Joey was sitting on the side of the road in his State of Minnesota pickup truck near the junction of Highways 54 and 6 when a van pulled over behind him. He'd seen it coming in the mirror and was instantly suspicious. There were a lot of SUVs and pickups out here on Saturday afternoons, but he seldom saw a van. Mothers with too many kids drove vans around town. Businesses delivered their products in vans. It just didn't fit out here in the woods. He unsnapped the safety strap but left the revolver in his holster as a man got out from behind the wheel and approached. Joey could see someone in the front passenger seat and a couple more in the back.

"Hello, officer," Dutch Peltier said with a southern drawl. "My friends and I are driving around looking for a good place to hunt deer when the season opens. Pretty country. We're trying to find a way to get over closer to the Red Lake Wildlife Area and can't seem to get farther east than this highway. Do ya'll know of a way to get back over there?" he asked in what seemed a friendly, down-home fashion.

He immediately assumed these guys were the security team, and knew exactly what they were after. They wanted to know how to get to the cabin from the east side where they'd have a real advantage over Fletcher and the men. Fletcher had been very serious when telling him these men were well trained and dangerous.

"Nope, you can't get over there from here. You can get as far east as Fourtown if you go down to the north side of the Red Lake Reservation, but there's no way into the wildlife area from there. We call it a wildlife area for a reason. It's wild as all get out, eh?" Joey said with what he hoped was a friendly smile. "You can get a little closer by going up to Lake of the Woods County and then south toward the wildlife area from Roosevelt, but even then you don't get too far except on foot or horseback."

"No kidding. I would have thought there must be trails back through there for the state or county people to use," the man persisted.

"Nope. We usually ride horse or snowmobiles to get in. Sometimes we get a chopper ride. Shoot, there's more than two hundred thousand acres that belong to the wildlife management area alone. Then add the state forest and its more land than you can cover in years if you're on foot. The hunting's good most places, but you need to come in the north side for the best of it. The state puts some biologists in every summer for a bit, but there's no road to follow," Joey lied.

"Well, thank you sir. We figured you'd know if anybody did. Thanks again."

Joey watched as they drove north on Highway 54 toward the cabin cutoff. He let them disappear over a rise before pulling out onto the highway and slowly following behind. When he got to the cutoff, he saw they were stopped on the west side of the road and pointed in a southerly direction. They must have missed it and turned around when they hit the county line. He smiled when he noticed the big maple tree blocking the trail, waving as he drove past the van.

Did they know this was the right trail, or had they just gotten lucky and stopped when they came to a road in the general area where they suspected the cabin to be?

Joey keyed his microphone. "OP, you have Texans on the highway but it looks like a scouting party only. Four of them and they'll be on foot. Good job with that tree."

"Thanks," Fletcher replied.

— || —

Hollis was the first to detect the approaching men from his hiding place among the trees behind a deadfall thirty yards off the trail. He motioned to Jeff, who was fifty yards across from him on the other side of the rutted trail. The recon team was moving slowly, single file and well dispersed. None appeared to be carrying a long gun, but Hollis assumed they were carrying handguns. The team had followed the trail for nearly two and a half miles, probably figuring they were getting close to the cabin. As the point-man approached the last obstacle, he stopped and dropped to one knee with his right hand up signaling the others to a halt.

Hollis watched as the man peered down the trail trying to see around the trees and branches that were blocking his view. Finally, the man turned and motioned to his nose. It suddenly hit Hollis. The man had detected wood smoke from their stove and halted the group's forward progress. The leader motioned the others down while he crept around the obstacle and continued alone toward the cabin. Back within fifteen minutes, he motioned the three others back toward the highway. Hollis watched them retreat west and, when the men were well out of sight, keyed his radio and spoke quietly.

"Fletcher, four of them got close to the cabin before they smelled smoke. One came in alone to check it out and now they're all headed back toward the highway. They had no idea we were watching. You want us to follow and make sure they don't leave? "

"No, stay put. Let's give them a chance to get back to their car and see if Joey reports that they're leaving. I don't want these guys to know we saw them."

Within forty minutes, Joey reported the men were south-bound on Highway 54. Hollis and Jeff made their way back to the cabin while Fletcher descended from the OP.

Fletcher told them to get a few hours sleep. It was going to be a long night — and a real bitch of a day tomorrow.

—‖— Thirty-Five —‖—

JT, LOGAN, AND MAHROUS WERE UP well before dawn on Sunday morning. Kansas City was as far as they had been able to go before the massive storm sweeping across America's heartland drove them to ground and quickly closed around them before they could fuel and get back in the air. Even Logan agreed it was time to put down when he saw the size and color of the storm on the plane's radar.

The northern edge was somewhere over southern Minnesota following a path to the east-northeast. They were near the southern edge that had stalled overnight, dumping a mix of rain and snow across a six-state area. Ground and air traffic was at a standstill. Winds were being reported in the fifty-five to eighty mile-per-hour range throughout the central plains. JT's watch displayed the date, November 2. Snowstorms and blizzards had been known to occur this early in Minnesota, but an early storm of such severity was unusual even there.

Logan made two calls to Salem from the hotel. Being very careful of his word choice, Salem could only tell them each time that nothing new was happening as far as he could determine. JT thought of calling Branton Cole but knew it would be a waste of time. Cole was set on obtaining or destroying Neptune and nothing was going to change that. Even if he could convince Cole to call off the hunt, he knew Global would continue. Instead, he dialed Joey Andersen's home number hoping to catch the game warden before he left for his Sunday morning patrol. The call went unanswered. There was nothing they could do but wait out the storm.

— || —

Joey had spent Saturday night sitting in his truck, tucked into his warm winter sleeping bag. He had pulled off Highway 54 a quarter-mile south of the cabin cutoff, backed carefully through the shallow ditch and up into the woods, and painstakingly camouflaged his truck in a position where he could still see the highway. His job was to warn Fletcher if the attack team arrived. Just in case he needed law enforcement help, he had called his dispatcher on the radio to confirm they could copy his signal from his hiding place. Someone on the OP had been monitoring the call on the handheld radio he had left them and immediately keyed the microphone twice in rapid succession to let him know the transmission had been heard and they knew he was watching the road.

The sound of two passing vehicles awakened Joey from a light sleep at five-thirty on Sunday. Startled, he nearly panicked when he realized he had dozed off. Quietly, he opened the door and crept toward the highway where he could look north toward the cutoff, thankful that he had disabled the interior dome light in his truck. The moonless sky was still very dark as he felt his way down through the ditch, spotting the tail lights of two vehicles pulled off the road. He figured they were planning to attack during civil twilight between six-thirty and seven.

Carefully, he scanned the men with binoculars, establishing that eight of them were putting on heavier clothing and preparing weapons. It was too dark to see what they were carrying but he could tell they had long guns. When they backed the vehicles down the cutoff and up to the fallen maple tree, he caught the outline of an M-16 in the headlights. While the rifles were probably civilian-legal, semi-automatic-only AR-15s, Fletcher would have some serious firepower to deal with. The team walked down the trail at a quarter to six. They could be at the cabin in as little as forty-five minutes if they hurried.

Joey hightailed it back to his truck and tried not to sound winded or alarmed when he announced, "OP, you have eight, repeat eight, Texans coming your way on foot with ARs."

"Copy eight with ARs. Thanks and *do not* follow them in," Fletcher warned.

Joey waited ten minutes before picking up his rifle and walking to the parked vehicles. He felt hopelessly under-armed with his bolt-action rifle and .38 Special revolver after seeing what the assault team was carrying. Using his Buck Woodsman knife, he punctured the front tires on the van and car before walking forty yards back toward his truck and into the brush to find concealment under the low overhang of a heavy pine tree. The frosted, snowy branches chilled him when they brushed against his face and neck, and the moisture from the snow-melt ran down his throat onto his chest. He shivered.

Heart pounding, he waited for the sounds of battle. No matter the outcome, none of the assault team was going to drive away today. He could have sheriff's deputies on scene with a radio call to his dispatcher if anyone came out alive and he couldn't handle it.

— ‖ —

Fletcher had been on the OP since ten on Saturday night. He was comfortably bundled into his sleeping bag despite the penetrating cold that was preceding the storm still a few hundred miles to the south. After today, they would have no need for the sleeping bags. Body bags might come in handier for whoever discovered the Armageddon he was going to set in motion.

Hollis had radioed at one in the morning and said the thermometer showed fifteen degrees as a light, grainy snow began falling from the gloomy clouds. The wind repeatedly gusted and died in some weird Siberian pattern while his eyes watered and nose ran. From the radio broadcasts they had followed earlier on the Sony, it sounded as if an early-season snowstorm of unusual proportions was really blasting a large portion of Minnesota. Duluth was on the leading edge of the storm, already experiencing wind gusts to eighty miles an hour as the huge weather mass moved toward it. He hoped Neumann was half as good as everyone thought he was.

When Joey radioed at 0547 hours, Fletcher quickly called the cabin on the oilfield radio with the warning. He suspected they were gulping the last of the coffee if Hollis had been up long enough to brew it. Hollis would be smoking between slurps. He hoped they were up to what was ahead. Hell, he hoped he was up to it. The thought of ambushing people was repugnant even under these circumstances, but he didn't know how else to save their skins. He knew Hollis and Jeff would be calm on the outside but wondered if Steve was really mentally prepared for the actually fighting. There was sometimes a vast difference between thinking about revenge and actually doing something about it, especially for someone who had never been openly violent in his life—and Fletcher was quite sure Steve had never been. Fletcher had seen trained soldiers freeze in their first taste of combat, and was concerned that Steve would either freeze or over-react and get himself hurt.

Fletcher nervously checked the M79, and arranged the ammunition so he could reload quickly. Then he trained his binoculars on the woods and began watching in earnest. The dusting of snow made for better contrast against the dark rocks and deciduous trees, but looking down through pine trees was difficult as they danced with the wind. He thought he saw movement when Hollis, Jeff, and Steve left the cabin but wasn't sure what he was seeing. It was still too dark for an attack or an ambush. He dropped down below the OP wall and lit a cigarette.

He was trembling slightly but told himself it was the cold.

— ‖ —

Joey had learned to enjoy the absolute quiet of the pre-dawn woods. When most people are first exposed to the nearly complete silence, they feel disoriented. Sometimes they quietly hum to assure themselves that they have not gone deaf. They can hear their own heartbeat and the nearly nonexistent sounds made by small animals as they begin their day. It unnerves many but Joey was accustomed to it. It was one of the many benefits of his chosen profession, and he never tired of quietly waiting for the sun to peak over the horizon as the birds and animals awaken. However, on this particular morning, his heart was beating loud enough to block the sounds of nature he usually treasured. He had heartburn and felt slightly disoriented and uneasy. Nearly uncontrollable urges to call for reinforcements ran through his mind. As the minutes ticked past in agonizingly-slow motion, he felt helpless.

A faint hum grew more audible as he moved out from under the tree to listen. It was a vehicle coming from the south. Not all that unusual on an early Sunday morning during bird season. Still, most grouse hunters tend to wait until the sun is well into the sky before venturing into the woods. Many an experienced local hunter claimed that no self-respecting grouse ever moved around much before nine. While not exactly accurate, it made for a good story. Maybe it was duck hunters headed for Lake of the Woods? No, it was too late in the morning for them to be this far south.

The car stopped on the road, its occupants apparently looking at the van and car parked at the cutoff. Joey was only forty yards away but well concealed. Most hunters move on when they come upon a spot where others have already entered the woods. As Joey focused his attention on the car, the passenger door opened and a man stepped out shining a flashlight into the other vehicles and then on the ground near the flat tires. His voice carried; he laughed and spoke in what sounded like Arabic to Joey. Although he had never heard Arabic, or any other Middle Eastern language, he had heard French and Spanish. It wasn't anything like those languages or the German he had heard in World War II movies. The men sounded excited, or at least it seemed so by the tone of their conversation.

He was surprised when he saw a light come on. Someone had popped the trunk and was removing what appeared to be a radio receiver. They put the radio on the hood before pulling out something that looked like an outdoor television antenna on a short mast. They connected a wire from the antenna to the radio. One of the men was looking at a map with his flashlight while the other was doing something with the radio. Joey's heart sank. He ducked back under the tree wishing he was at the truck where he could let Fletcher know the Arabs were close. He felt for the safety on his rifle.

— ‖ —

It was now almost light enough to see in the woods and Fletcher had been observing the dark forms of the attack team for several minutes. He counted six ghostly figures floating among the trees in the early morning dawn. They were fanned out on a north/south-oriented line that stretched about two hundred yards out from the rock cliff under the OP, with some on each side of the trail. He assumed the other two were under him and close to the face of the cliff. The man farthest out was slightly south of where Jeff was set up with his shotgun. *Show time!* He could see Hollis and knew exactly where Jeff and Steve were although he couldn't quite pick them out in the gloom.

Fletcher keyed his radio twice without saying anything. Hollis understood the signal and quickly motioned to Jeff. He saw Jeff's movement when he motioned to Steve. It was just light enough for them to see one another but Steve was still invisible to Fletcher.

It was seven o'clock and daybreak when Fletcher fired the first high-explosive forty-millimeter grenade into a small clearing between and well in front of Jeff and Steve. One attacker screamed in agony and went down before he had a chance to join in the fight. Fletcher reloaded and rained fire on the attackers as fast as his hands would move, rapidly laying it on or slightly behind the attack team to push them forward into the hidden killing zone. Some of his rounds hit in the pine trees where they exploded and rained heavy branches and steel fragments to the ground. He picked up his Mini-14 when the attackers moved so close to the fighting positions that he dared not continue M79 fire for fear of hitting his own men.

Fletcher heard Jeff let loose with a war-call like an Indian in an old B-grade western movie before he popped up from his hole and quickly pumped two twelve-gauge goose loads toward the man approaching from his immediate right. The man crumpled in a pink mist as the heavy lead pellets tore into his face and throat. Still yelling, Jeff shifted fire to his left where another man had apparently engaged Steve. The sound was deafening, terrifying, and exhilarating at the same time.

Gunfire was erupting all along the line of contact and reverberating off the cliff. Jeff was suddenly up and moving toward Steve's position, firing on the run. Another opponent's head exploded like a ripe melon as the shot ruptured his temple area. Jeff stopped his charge, dropped to one knee, and appeared to be loading his Remington before crabbing toward his fighting hole and ammunition stash, seeking additional targets as he fluidly moved.

Fletcher had not seen Steve and momentarily wondered if Jeff's aggressive action had been to protect him. Had Steve frozen when the shooting started? Had he been shot? The action was fearsome and frighteningly loud after the quiet of the dawning day. Fletcher saw two men approaching the area near Steve. He wanted to yell a warning but knew it wouldn't be heard over the gunfire. Suddenly, Steve engaged the man he apparently could see the most clearly, the farther of the two approaching him. He unleashed a rapid string of shots at the running form before abruptly shifting fire to the closer man who rose up off the forest floor with his rifle pointed directly at him. The marauder fired and dropped back to the ground. Fletcher saw Steve reach for his ear and then crouch back down. A moment later, a hand grenade lofted from Steve's fighting hole and its deafening blast blew body parts into the air. Steve jumped up and pumped three quick shots into the area of the explosion before bounding into the woods toward the men he had just engaged, screaming at the top of his lungs. He appeared fearless and out of control. The crackle of gunfire moved closer to the cabin and Fletcher shifted his attention.

Just 150 yards from the OP, Hollis was burning through ammunition at a prodigious rate. He was firing at fast-moving forms and they were returning fire as they ran. People were running, dropping to the ground, popping back up, and shooting again. Fletcher wasn't sure who was hit and who wasn't. Confusion reigned. Suddenly, one attacker came running straight up the driveway toward the cabin, plainly framed in the driveway and silhouetted against the cabin for Hollis to clearly see. He took quick advantage of the tactical blunder when he leaned into the Mini-14 and caressed the trigger. The man crashed to the ground as though he had been pole-axed. Hollis then fired at attackers out of Fletcher's view under the OP and near the cabin.

Out of nowhere, an attacker Fletcher had not yet noticed engaged Hollis from behind a tree and small rock outcropping between the trail and foxhole. Hollis directed rapid fire on the man's position, changing magazines again. The man stayed carefully hidden, just popping his rifle out and firing blindly in Hollis's direction. Fletcher could see the man and quickly fired on him. Hollis couldn't tell Fletcher had shot the man and was apparently taking no chances. He grabbed a hand grenade, pulled the pin, and let it fly. The spoon flew off with a ping as the grenade arched nearly thirty yards before hitting the ground and bouncing among the rocks and nearly into the man's lap. The explosion rocked the earth, shattering the cold air with fury. The tree tipped, almost blown off at the base with lengths of intestines draped over its branches and body parts scattered for yards.

Fletcher saw Jeff and Steve running north toward Hollis. They approached from the rear; Steve sliding into the foxhole with Hollis while Jeff sprawled out on the ground behind it. Fletcher could see them talking and pointing at the cabin, and wondered how many attackers were left.

"Fletcher, the last of them's under you and close to the cabin. Drop grenades on him!" Hollis shouted on his radio.

Fletcher quickly began throwing hand grenades over the cliff, letting them drop near the cabin. He couldn't see where they were landing but knew he had hit the cabin with at least one when a shower of debris jumped into his view. Then he heard the crackling of fire and smelled smoke. *The cabin must be on fire!* He had tried to throw them so they would land in a straight line along the base of the cliff where he suspected someone would run. The explosions echoed deafeningly. And then there was silence. He saw Hollis, Steve, and Jeff craning their necks from cover as they looked for survivors without exposing themselves. The smoke from the burning cabin made it difficult for Fletcher to see.

"You've got one running west along the cliff below you," Jeff radioed.

Fletcher lobbed two more grenades over the edge.

Hollis and Steve were firing toward the cabin with their Mini-14s.

Without warning, Hollis lumbered out of the foxhole, motioning Jeff in and tossing him the Mini-14 as he ran toward the trail. Jeff and Steve waited until Hollis turned west on the trail before opening up again with their rifles. Hollis ran close to fifty yards before cutting into the woods towards the cliff and out of Fletcher's vision.

— ‖ —

When Hollis reached the cliff he bent over, hands on his knees, trying to catch his breath and listen for movement. His breathing was ragged and labored. The cigarettes were working against him as he coughed, gagged, and spit. Thirty seconds later a figure came crashing along the cliff base, almost colliding with him. It was Dutch Peltier, the Westcona team leader from Edinburg and the ranch, and he had been running hard.

"Well, lookey what we got here," Hollis wheezed to the momentarily startled man as he ripped Peltier's rifle from his hands.

"Hey man, it's over," Peltier said as he backed away.

This time Hollis didn't let down his guard or underestimate the man's willingness to fight. Hollis threw the rifle to the ground and smiled. Peltier charged directly at him doing a hesitation step just before getting into reach, leaping into the air and rotating his body while swinging a foot around at Hollis's head. Hollis ducked back to avoid the blow. Peltier landed gracefully and struck a martial arts pose as if he truly expected Hollis to fight him with his fists. Then he smirked with confidence and again began closing the distance between them. His arrogance only served to inflame Hollis's last nerve. Hollis reached to his belt.

Steel flashed as they collided in an explosion of fury and rage. Hands and feet violently pumped with numbing speed as they brawled, crushing bone and ripping skin. Hollis recoiled under Peltier's assault as impacts buffeted his head and pummeled his gut. He twisted away, slashed Peltier across the upper arm, and then lunged with his knife...burying it to the hilt. Peltier staggered back and stopped with his eyes wide in disbelief. Blood sluiced from his arm wound and he became visibly faint. Hollis stepped back and wiped his bloody hands on his pants before pulling the Combat Commander from his holster.

"You fucking killed me," Peltier gasped as his hands closed around the handle protruding from his belly.

"I told you in Edinburg you'd better steer clear of me, and then you went after our women. You're a coward, *Dutch*, and I'll see you in hell."

Hollis raised the big Colt and shot Peltier in the forehead, blowing brain matter out the back of his skull.

"*Now* I fucking killed you, you worthless piece of shit."

His blood was pumping so hard he thought his head was going to explode. He desperately wanted more fight from Peltier and stepped toward the crumpled body with savagery in his eyes…and paused. After staring at Peltier's erupted head and struggling to pull himself back from the brink of darkness, he slowly walked away from the body. Only combat veterans can fully comprehend the primitive blood-lust he had just so thoroughly and briefly enjoyed. It damn near called for a cigarette to complete the moment. Back under emotional control and embarrassed at the feelings, he would never reveal the primal, barbaric yearnings that had flashed through him.

— ‖ —

Fletcher radioed Jeff and Steve to count bodies as he readied himself to provide what suppressing fire he could from the OP. They had confirmed six bodies when they heard the shot from the cliff base. No one could see the area Hollis had ventured into. A few tense moments later, Hollis walked out onto the road and motioned to Fletcher that he was okay. Fletcher radioed that they now had seven bodies and to watch for the last man.

"You blew one to hell next to the cabin with a grenade," Jeff radioed back. "That makes eight."

From first shot to last, it had taken less than nine minutes to fight the battle, but it seemed an eternity. An intoxicating exhilaration overwhelmed the rage and terror Fletcher felt during the battle. His knees and hands began to rattle, knowing his well-conceived and executed ambush had been a deciding factor in their victory. Intelligent preparation, sound tactics, and a few pieces of very basic military weaponry in the hands of modestly trained but highly motivated men had triumphed over those with technically superior skills and training. On paper, Dutch Peltier and his squad should have easily taken them. But Fletcher had learned long ago that life doesn't happen on paper.

— ⫶ — Thirty-Six — ⫶ —

THE SAUDI RADIO DIRECTION-FINDERS scattered around northwest Minnesota had been prepared to monitor the normal 0700 hours transmission by the Neptune people. They felt confident they could zero in on the location with one more opportunity. In the end, the team sitting out on Highway 54 didn't really need their directional antenna to find the action on this crisp Sunday morning. The outbreak of gunfire rapidly grew to the crescendo of a full-blown firefight. While muffled by nearly three miles of heavy forest, the intense small-arms fire punctuated by the grenade explosions, left little doubt as to the location of Neptune. They were too late! Whoever these cars belonged to had solved the riddle. There must be others involved as well because someone had slashed the front tires to prevent a getaway. There was no quick way to sound the alarm so they hurriedly turned south and drove to Grygla where they had seen a payphone in the early morning hours.

When the news was relayed to Riyadh, immediate decisions were made. The soldiers were told to return to Thief River Falls and report to their team leader. The Saudi's instructed Saddam Hussein to scramble his jet and attack anyone at or leaving a building in the woods at the location identified by the soldiers, and to destroy any suspicious planes leaving the Roseau or Thief River Falls' airports starting in one hour. The planes must be destroyed by any means and at any cost. Neptune must not disappear or fall into the wrong hands, if it hadn't already.

— ‖ —

Joey heard the gunfire and thanked the good Lord he was well away from what sounded like a war. It was an amazing thing to hear, even from a distance. He wondered what the men had that was exploding or if it was the attackers with some kind of heavy weapon. He'd put his money on Fletcher having some military hardware or dynamite-based improvised devices.

Within three minutes of the attack, the Arabs had spun their car back out onto the highway and started south. Joey considered going after them but decided to stay put. He had to see who came out of the woods, or hear something from Fletcher before doing anything in response. He went back to his truck to wait for Fletcher's voice on the radio, sweating so heavily that he didn't need to start the engine for warmth. His discomfort was escalating to near terror when he thought about what would happen to him if this whole episode came to a bad conclusion. Ten minutes after it started, he heard Fletcher's voice.

"OP here. Everything went as planned. Copy?"

Joey keyed his microphone twice in affirmation without saying anything in response. In spite of his frayed nerves, he finally got the windows defrosted and was able to pull out onto the highway. The Arabs were at a payphone in Grygla when he passed through on his way to Highway 1 where he planned to meet up with Fletcher. Still breathing hard and trying to bring his emotions under control, the road looked as if it was pulsating and everything seemed to be moving in slow motion.

— ‖ —

Fletcher slung his Mini-14 and awkwardly rappelled down the rock, bruising and burning his hands as they skidded and slid through the knots Steve had tied in the rope. Smoke was billowing into the sky and the intense, churning heat from the fire was making the pine trees sway as if in heavy winds. He hit the ground running.

They rallied at the Oldsmobile where Hollis already had a first-aid kit open on the hood and was working on Steve's ear.

"What happened to you? Fletcher asked Hollis whose left eye was swelling shut. His lip was split and blood was crusted under his nose and along his chin. Fletcher could also see blood on Hollis's pants and hands, one of which was swelling at the knuckles.

"Nothing. Peltier and I had a little discussion about his behavior, and I changed his outlook on life," he said before returning to Steve's wounds.

Steve's hair and one shoulder were bloody but he seemed to be standing without difficulty. Fletcher rinsed his hands with water from a canteen and found some salve for his rope burns. They looked worse than they were. Jeff rummaged in the trunk and emerged from behind the car with a shirt and a pair of pants.

Steve's ear undoubtedly hurt but Hollis told him it was going to be fine. A bullet had torn a ragged hole through it before grazing the side of his head. Flesh wounds. Bloody but hardly life threatening. Fletcher was puzzled as to why Jeff had the clothing until Steve turned around. His jacket and pants were plastered with muddy blood. He appeared to have been in a slaughter house before rolling in dirt. His face was devoid of emotion but his eyes appeared alert and cognizant. Hollis had a sad, knowing look on his face as he patted Steve on the shoulder and guided him to the fresh clothing without words.

Fletcher grasped what Steve had done but didn't realize Hollis did, too. After all, how could Hollis understand that dark divide over which Steve had traveled when he ran into the woods? Not all combat trauma is visible, nor could theirs be dealt with right now when more violence was on the horizon.

After stepping into the fresh clothing, Steve and the group jumped in the Olds and accelerated east with Jeff behind the wheel to spare Fletcher the discomfort of having to use his burned hands and Hollis the difficulty of trying to drive with one eye swollen shut. Branches slapped and low-hanging limbs pounded the car as it careened along the overgrown trail to nowhere. Other souvenirs from the fight included bullet holes punched through the front doors and a bullet-creased rear bumper. Aside from that, the car was still in pretty good shape. Steve popped two aspirin and took a swig of beer before passing it to Hollis. Hollis raised it in silent salute and drained it as best he could as the car bucked and bounced. They were scuffed and bloodied, but alive.

— ‖ —

The Canadian Forces Base switchboard operator patched the international call through to the Iraqi Air Force pilot's BOQ. Without preamble or explanation, he was ordered to scramble his F-14 Tomcat and cross the international border into Minnesota to destroy a building in the woods and kill any people around it. The caller provided the building's GPS coordinates and also instructed him to track suspicious small aircraft departing airports in Roseau and Thief River Falls, and to destroy them if he felt they might be fleeing the area. He was assured that this was not a drill and that the safety of his family, still in Basra, was at risk if he failed. The American targets had information that could destroy his country and they must not be allowed to do so.

His mind reeled with a dozen questions as the caller abruptly disconnected. What was he being ordered to do? Why? He had assumed his earlier alert message had been part of his official training but it was now crystal clear that was not the case. Beads of perspiration broke out on his forehead as he thought through the magnitude of his orders. The Canadians or Americans would surely shoot him down before he could complete this mission. How could he tell if a plane was fleeing or just flying away? A building in the woods? The coordinates they gave him wouldn't help if he was streaking over the border fifty meters above the trees. Madness! What about his family? He couldn't let them down by not following orders. What options did he have? None if he wanted them to live…and there wasn't time to think about it. He steeled himself to his new and utterly horrible reality.

While tracking multiple aircraft was an easy task for the Tomcat's AN/AWG-9 radar, staying off Canadian and American radars long enough to complete this mission was going to be more difficult. He had been training with Forces Canada on fast, low-altitude attacks, and would now see how well the Tomcat's Mach Sweep Programmer, or MSP, really functioned as it automatically adjusted the wing angle for optimal flight performance at low altitude.

His original thought had been to take the fighter up on his own but, with the added requirement of tracking multiple aircraft, he would need the help of his radar intercept officer who normally flew in the aircraft's other seat.

By 0815 hours both men were walking to their supersonic, twin-engine, variable-sweep-wing warbird, hoping the Canadian response to their take-off would be slowed by the lackadaisical attitude he had noted in the tower personnel, especially on weekends. His RIO was frightened of what he understood their mission to involve, but even more frightened of the consequences of disobeying the order.

They were challenged and turned away by maintenance personnel and a roving air policeman at the hangar. It was 0915 hours before they were able to sneak back to the Tomcat when the maintenance crew left for a coffee break and the air police were elsewhere. Soon thereafter, the two Pratt & Whitney TF-30P-414A turbofan engines hurtled them into the sky with nearly forty-two thousand pounds of thrust. They flew north and deliberately established radar contact before dropping low, swinging around to the south, and heading for northern Minnesota.

— ‖ —

The drive east from the cabin was made difficult by the rutted path, but could have been worse. Jeff was fighting the Oldsmobile's steering and road suspension system as they repeatedly bottomed out and slid dangerously close to trees on the half-frozen mud and dead grass. He instinctively ducked when a large branch overhanging the trail caught the top of the windshield causing a spider-web of cracks to radiate across the glass. They came to a slightly more established north/south trail after ten miles and were on pavement thirty minutes later when they got to Fourtown. Following Highway 89 south, they came to the Highway 1 junction after traveling another twelve miles. Joey Andersen's State of Minnesota pickup truck was parked seventeen miles west at the County Road 28 junction.

"You sure made a lot of noise back there," Joey said quickly, his emotions now mostly under control. Fletcher could smell cigarette smoke coming from the pickup and knew Joey didn't smoke. *Combat nerves,* he thought. Combat can turn anyone into a smoker.

"Yeah, and a fire. We owe JT a new cabin," Fletcher said with a tight smile.

"Two Arabs had just arrived with some radio stuff when the shooting started. They took off right away but I let them go. They're up the road about twelve miles on the phone right now."

"They'll be waiting for us in Thief River Falls then" Fletcher said. "Anything else?"

"No, I left as soon as you radioed," Joey said. "Was anyone walking out to the road?"

"Not hardly," Hollis deadpanned in a half-hearted John Wayne imitation.

"What happened to you?" he asked Hollis after seeing his face.

"Nothing."

Jeff grabbed his small duffle and shotgun and got into the truck with Joey for the ride to the airport. Fletcher handed him one of the oilfield radios through the window and got back into the Oldsmobile, this time with Steve behind the wheel. They were an easy thirty miles from the Thief River Falls airport and the freedom it represented.

"Now we only have Arabs and federal agents to watch for," Jeff said with a nefarious smirk as they pulled onto Highway 1 with Steve following behind. Joey gave him his best grimace.

— ‖ —

Fletcher noticed a car occupied by four people sitting near the airport entrance. He fully expected the Saudi team to have at least one lookout nearby and these could be the guys.

Who else would be sitting around the entrance on a Sunday morning, and where were the rest of them?

Joey lit up his lightbar as he drove through the gate onto the concrete apron, behind the passenger terminal building, and down to the general aviation aircraft area with Steve following closely behind. The Global Oil King-Air was still sitting on the apron beside the Learjet 55CLR the Arab group had arrived in on Friday evening. The Lear had its hatch open and he could see someone in the cockpit.

Jeff jumped out of the pickup and checked the fuel on the Baron. It had not been refueled as he had requested on Friday, but that was okay. He set about calculating the Baron's remaining range based on his fuel usage from Denver to Thief River Falls. He had not taken off with a full fuel load, but it had been reasonably close. The Denver to Thief River Falls leg was about seven hundred miles, and Duluth was another two hundred miles to the southeast. Lake Superior, which started at Duluth, was three hundred fifty miles long. The range of a fully fueled Baron is about eleven hundred miles, perhaps a little less with today's weather. All things considered, the Baron would crash into Lake Superior if he tried to fly the length of the lake without taking on more fuel. Perfect. He filed an IFR flight plan for Green Bay, Wisconsin, identifying himself as the pilot along with three passengers departing within the hour. Duluth was listed as an alternative airport in case the weather turned bad.

Fletcher ran into the terminal in search of a payphone.

"Mr. Johnson," he said to the generic FBI agent, "We're under a little more pressure than we'd anticipated so you get your instructions earlier than promised. Bring what we asked for and meet us at the Executive Air building at Austin Straubel Airport in Green Bay, Wisconsin, tomorrow at 0900 local time. We'll have confirmed your wire transfer by then and will be prepared to hand over Neptune. One of our group, the one carrying Neptune, will not be with us in case you've decided to play games. Once we're in possession of our letter signed by the President and have our new identities, the last member of our little band will come in. Don't screw with us. Westcona and Global tried that again this morning and came up short. You'll better understand when you find the bodies."

Fletcher rejoined Hollis and Steve who were watching for the men they had seen sitting at the airport entrance. They finally spotted the car just outside the gate they had passed through to get onto the apron, but they didn't see anyone other than what looked like a couple of middle-aged locals working around the private planes. Suddenly, five Arab-looking men were standing near the waist-high chain link fence that separated the private planes from the public area outside the terminal parking lot. Fletcher walked to the Oldsmobile with its trunk up and made a scene of removing an old briefcase they'd found at the cabin, carefully passing it to Jeff. Jeff carried it to the plane, making sure the Arab's could clearly see it. A few moments later the right prop began to rotate.

The Saudi soldiers made their move. Running across the two hundred feet of concrete apron toward the Baron with unholstered handguns, they appeared determined to grab the briefcase Jeff had carried aboard—just as Fletcher had hoped.

Fletcher, Hollis, and Steve had purposely kept the Oldsmobile between themselves and the Saudis. They jerked open the doors to pull out the Mini-14s. A loud boom resonated over the sound of the Baron's right engine before they came up to engage.

Joey had lowered his passenger-side window while watching the Arabs prepare their attack. Jeff's short-barreled Remington was still in the truck and the young game warden drew his first blood with it when he protected his partners from deadly threats.

Fletcher didn't waste a lot of time wondering what had made Joey do it but was glad he had because another shot immediately rang out from the direction of the Global Oil King-Air, punching through the rear window of the battle-scarred Oldsmobile and tearing a hole in the dash. Fletcher swung to his right and fired twice into the open hatch. A body fell partially out as he pivoted back to the charging Arabs. Hollis and Steve were already firing and made quick work of the remaining attackers.

The immediate threat had passed but another was just beginning. You can't have a gunfight at an airport without drawing some attention—even at the tiny Thief River Falls airport on a quiet Sunday morning. They had to act fast.

The left engine roared to life and Jeff taxied the Baron toward the runway. Joey, with emergency lights still blazing, led the Oldsmobile off the apron and back out to Highway 32. He motioned them south as he pulled over and stopped on the side of the road. Steve roared around him and was in St. Hilaire within minutes. He slowed to the speed limit, drove past the place Hollis and Fletcher had eaten their Mexican dinner just a scant nine days before, and followed Highway 32 to U.S. 2 where he turned east. Fletcher was crouched over in the front seat beside Steve, and Hollis was lying across the back seat with his eye now completely swollen shut.

— ‖ —

Joey watched the Oldsmobile disappear before looking back at the airport. Jeff had taken off in the Baron and was already swinging around to the southeast toward Duluth. He wondered how many calls the police had already received, and how he would explain his presence at the scene. Keying his microphone, he called the dispatcher to report a shooting at the Thief River Falls airport and that multiple ambulances were needed. Before he could clarify the information, the roar of a small jet drowned out the dispatcher's questions and the solution popped into his head.

"Dispatch, the people doing the shooting just left on a small jet. I can still see it. I'm at the airport and don't think any of the perps are still here, except the ones who got shot."

With that, he drove back into the airport and up to the bodies lying on the concrete. The Global Oil King-Air, piloted by the sole remaining member of the ill-fated company contingent, lifted off as Joey studied the man he had shot. He realized he'd better get Jeff's shotgun out of view, and tucked the Remington behind the seat and covered it with some winter clothes. Soon he was joined by state, county, and city police officers. A couple of fire trucks roared to the scene followed by a rescue squad and two ambulances. The confusion appeared to have peaked and no one had even found the bodies at the cabin yet.

Joey explained his fabrication to a group of cops and then sat drinking coffee while they argued over jurisdiction and who should be notified to catch up with the Learjet. Fat chance of that happening.

He drove back to his headquarters hoping nobody had connected the white Oldsmobile or his pickup to the shooting. Why didn't he feel any remorse over killing a man and lying to the police? Something had changed in him, and he wasn't sure it was for the better. He felt very alone in Thief River Falls by himself. Could he trust Fletcher? He'd better be able to because his law enforcement career was toast.

–⫴– Thirty-Seven –⫴–

NEWS OF THE ERRANT F-14 TOMCAT gone missing from Canadian Forces Base Winnipeg was quickly relayed to the 119th Fighter Wing, part of the North Dakota Air National Guard based at Fargo's Hector Field. Also known as the Happy Hooligans, the 119th was responsible for interceptor alert coverage over the north-central United States.

Within moments of hearing that an unarmed Iraqi Tomcat had departed without clearance and disappeared from the Canadian base, a Happy Hooligan F4-D Phantom began searching for the plane over eastern North Dakota and western Minnesota. Another Phantom was immediately launched as a precautionary measure.

The Phantom's radar painted the sky, revealing six civilian aircraft in the immediate vicinity. One small jet appeared to have just taken off from the Thief River Falls area, but the crew saw no indication of a military aircraft. Nothing appeared to be out of the ordinary. The pilot made contact with CFB Winnipeg, asking for an update on the missing plane.

— ‖ —

The Saudi Learjet pilot was searching for the Baron that had just taken off with the briefcase. His radar showed multiple planes in the area but couldn't isolate the Baron. He had seen a King-Air preparing to take off behind him and that would only add to the cluttered skies in a few moments. The Saudi tuned his radio to 123.400 MHz, the frequency commonly used for air-to-air contact, and keyed his microphone asking the Baron pilot to respond. Nothing. He re-tuned to the other commonly used air-to-air frequency, 123.450 MHz, and tried again. Still no response.

His efforts did not go unnoticed, however. Just as he was preparing to re-tune his radio to 121.500 MHz, the air emergency frequency, he detected a fast-moving military jet approaching from his four o'clock. It blasted past his cockpit and began an immediate tight turn back toward him. Another military jet flashed past on his left side, so close that the Lear bucked violently in the turbulent air. The Saudi fought for control and, in mounting panic, made a course correction away from the military jets and back toward the perceived safety of the Thief River Falls airport.

— ‖ —

The Iraqi Tomcat pilot was caught off-guard by the almost immediate American response. While he had attempted to complete his initial mission soon after departing Canadian airspace, his high speed and low altitude limited any chance for success over the heavily forested area. He had seen smoke and a fire on the ground but had not identified it as the building he was supposed to destroy.

He made a quick decision to go after aircraft, the mission the F-14 was best equipped to perform. There were planes all around but he couldn't identify his target. Was it the Learjet? Was it the King-Air? What about the other planes in the area? One thing was certain; he couldn't follow Saddam's orders with this American Phantom climbing up his ass.

The element of surprise was on his side when he engaged. The American Phantom was obviously trying to intimidate him into turning back to Canada, but he courageously pulled his Tomcat into a tight turn and surprised the American by coming around behind him. The moment he had weapons lock, he unleashed an AIM-9 Sidewinder missile at the unsuspecting Phantom. The missile, traveling at two-and-a-half times the speed of sound, blew the American Phantom out of the sky in a sudden, violent, blinding flash of yellow and orange.

That resolved the immediate military threat and now he could concentrate on the other planes. There was no time to consider options. He had his orders and his family was in mortal danger if he failed. The RIO was tracking the Learjet and quickly directed him to it. The Lear pilot was taking evasive maneuvers but was no match for the Tomcat. Just as he attacked with his M61 Vulcan twenty-millimeter cannon on the first pass, the corporate jet unexpectedly dove for safety, narrowly avoiding the cannon fire. He pulled the Tomcat around and opened up for the second time with the Vulcan. This time smoke billowed from the Learjet as it turned over and began a death dive, exploding in a spectacular crimson and black fireball when it hit the partially frozen ground.

The RIO quickly directed him to the King-Air that had just taken off. The King-Air pilot gave no indication that he was aware of the military action, and was bringing his craft around on a southerly heading toward Minneapolis when he was hosed with twenty-millimeter cannon fire. The heavy projectiles raked the cockpit and the plane plummeted to the ground, striking the earth in a ferocious smear of metal, fuel, and flesh. It had been like shooting fish in a barrel. Now it was time to disengage and think about his next move. Surrender was out of the question, and failure would result in the death of his family back in Iraq. His only motivation was to be successful enough that the Iraqi President would honor him as a dead hero and leave his family alone. He turned the Tomcat to a 200 degree heading and flew on the deck.

— || —

Jeff was pushing the Baron as fast as she would fly toward Duluth and Lake Superior. Bits and pieces of radio traffic he was hearing indicated something very wrong was happening behind him. Another half hour would put him close to Duluth, assuming he could still slip away unnoticed. He was uncomfortably strapped into the parachute and had his small duffle attached to a coil of rope and lying behind him on the floor. His current course would put the Baron over the eastern end of Lake Superior, north of Munising, Michigan, before it ran out of fuel and dropped into the cold, deep water. At least that was the plan and it didn't include him getting wet.

The weather was deteriorating as he flew directly toward the storm now moving past Duluth and out over the big lake. Fletcher's plan hadn't factored in this storm or what sounded like some kind of a military response behind him. What had sounded so achievable at the cabin was now looking less so as he mentally prepared for the parachute jump that would hopefully land him somewhere in the vicinity of Duluth International Airport. At least he'd be able to see the ground once he fell through the clouds, bobbing under his silk canopy.

— ‖ —

JT, Logan, and Mahrous lifted off from Kansas City as soon as the storm cleared on Sunday morning. They desperately hoped they weren't too late to save the men, but couldn't turn around and go back to Texas without trying. JT called Minneapolis Center while still over Iowa and confirmed his intent to over-fly the Twin Cities and continue north. The response was unexpected. They were ordered to either land in Minneapolis or turn around and return south. The FAA had declared a large portion of Minnesota, North Dakota, South Dakota, Wisconsin, and the Michigan Upper Peninsula closed airspace. Only military aircraft were allowed into the area and no further explanation was offered. They landed in Minneapolis with crushing frustration and angst over the young men's fate.

— ‖ — Thirty-Eight — ‖ —

NEEDING SOME SEPARATION FROM THE action and a moment to think, the young Iraqi captain flew the Tomcat on the deck, relying on the MSP to keep his wing-angle properly adjusted. The farmland flashing past the cockpit was flat as he tried to evade the search radars so frantically scouring the sky. His mind raced and he momentarily toyed with the idea that he may have already completed his mission — that he could keep going and just land at the first airport he found without being shot down. Perhaps his target had been the Learjet or King-Air. Slowly but with great clarity, the sad realization hit him. It didn't really matter because he couldn't be sure. He was fully committed and could only protect his family by shooting down any planes around Thief River Falls. Ultimately, one of them would be the correct target. The lives of these strangers would have to be sacrificed to save his family. There was no escaping his destiny.

A plan formed in his mind as he bled off time and speed. He still carried a full load of AIM-54 missiles that were capable of simultaneously engaging up to six targets at ranges out to one hundred and twenty miles. His radar system could track as many as twenty-four targets at a time. Pulling the Tomcat around to meet his fate, it was time to re-engage before the fleeting opportunity vanished like a wisp of smoke.

— ‖ —

Jeff Neumann was rapidly approaching Duluth and the storm raging out over Lake Superior, but the city was still mostly shrouded in clouds that were blowing east with the storm. He was flying in bright, magnificent sunshine that shone like a golden floodlight on the dark, swirling clouds below. It was cold, windy, and setting up to be one hell of a day. He readjusted his heading, preparing to let the autopilot guide the plane down the length of the lake to eventually crash. At least that was the plan. Who knew where she would end up once she got into the high winds out over the water. He gently backed off the throttles, engaged the autopilot, and took a few minutes to reflect on how wonderfully beautiful the world was even on a stormy day. Lighting a cigarette and savoring the rich, full flavor, he stared peacefully into the eye of the storm. Running on adrenalin with his heart thumping wildly in his chest, he opened his soul to the wonders before him. It was time.

Struggling carefully in his seat, he took the rope attached to his small duffle-bag and tied the end to his ankle. Wanting the bag to ride on his thigh, he pulled the slack loop up under his belt and then tied the bag in place with the loose rope. Once under silk, he would let it dangle beneath him so he didn't have to contend with it when he landed and tried to roll, as he had seen so many times in the movies. He struggled to push open the hatch, grimaced, and roared with excitement as he launched himself into the wild, shrieking wind.

— ‖ —

Steve pulled off Highway 2 in Bemidji. Hollis requisitioned a quarter from the Oldsmobile's cup holder and plunked it into a payphone to call the local airport. He was told that Mesaba Airlines had seats available on a Minneapolis-bound plane departing at 2:00 p.m., assuming the airspace was reopened. Using civilian time felt good after being immersed in twenty-four-hour military time over the past few weeks. He reserved three seats with a promise to pay when they got to the airport. Puzzled by the news of the airspace closure, he could only speculate on what might have happened after they left Thief River Falls. Would the Feds have done that to single out the Baron if they thought Neptune was aboard? *How in the hell did the Feds get involved so quickly?*

To the best of his knowledge, they weren't being followed and no one seemed to be giving them a second glance. Fletcher felt relatively safe checking into a motel before heading to the airport. Showers, shaves, and clean clothing were overdue. Fortunately, they had tossed what they needed into the car the previous evening. A stop at a drugstore scored a black eye patch for Hollis whose eye looked like hell.

Now feeling human once again, Fletcher pondered what to do with the car. Leaving it at the airport for the cops to find and ultimately trace to them was not an option if their plan was to work. The feds had to believe they were all dead and Neptune destroyed.

Pulling up to a seedy-looking bar, they waited for anyone to leave or arrive. Within fifteen minutes, a young Native-American arrived as if ordered from heaven. They offered him the car if he would drive them to the airport. Hollis admitted that the car was hot and could use a new home. The man's eyes lit up after looking over the once-beautiful white Oldsmobile, even if it did have a few bullet holes, scratched paint, a cracked windshield, and a shattered rear window. Less than two hours later, the car was in a Red Lake Indian Reservation chop-shop being dismantled, and the young man was happily selling the weapons and gear he found in the trunk.

The boys were already on a Minneapolis-bound Mesaba Airlines Convair 580 propjet. They caught a connecting flight to Dallas at 6 p.m.

— || —

The Iraqi F-14 Tomcat pilot solemnly set his final plan in motion when he climbed to an altitude that allowed his radars to work their magic. He was on a forty degree heading north of Brainerd, Minnesota, and moving at Mach 2 when the RIO painted the sky. The Hughes AN/AWG-9 long-range radar identified seventeen aircraft within one hundred twenty miles of the fighter, the farthest just passing Duluth. Six aircraft were selected by the RIO, all still within the one-hundred-twenty-mile range of their missiles. Each was also within two hundred miles of Thief River Falls and thus a possible target. Six AIM-54 Phoenix missiles dropped from the F-14's pylons and accelerated to three thousand miles per hour while homing in on the individual planes assigned them by the weapons system.

The young captain had only time to momentarily savor his success before an AIM-9 Sidewinder missile followed by an AIM-7 Sparrow impacted the fast-moving Tomcat within a heartbeat of each other. The second 119th Fighter Wing's F-4D Phantom had done its job, but not before five explosions rocked the normally tranquil Minnesota sky. Miraculously, one targeted Cessna passing east of Grand Rapids escaped sudden death when a malfunctioning Phoenix scudded harmlessly past, unnoticed.

— ‖ —

As Jeff hurtled out of the Baron, the loop of rope tucked under his belt snagged on the seat frame. Entangled, knocked senseless, and pinned to the outside of the plane by the crushing airflow, Jeff traveled with the Baron over the western shore of Lake Superior. The last Iraqi missile flashing across Minnesota obliterated the eastbound Baron in a bright orange fireball, sealing his fate.

— ‖ —

The United States military was quick to put most of the story together once information streamed to the Pentagon from Hector Field in Fargo and CFB Winnipeg. Secretary of Defense Caspar Weinberger was summoned to the White House family quarters to brief President Reagan.

The President soon convened a meeting in the Situation Room with trusted advisors and Vice President Bush where he ordered the airspace re-opened with no public explanation as to why it had been closed. The FBI, FAA, and National Transportation Safety Board ordered additional people to Minnesota to open investigations. The President wanted to know who was on the downed civilian planes, and suggestions on how to best explain why two military fighters and seven civilian airplanes had been shot down on a blustery November Sunday morning over the United States. He personally called Canadian Prime Minister Mulroney to request cooperation with a "proper presentation of events" to citizens on both sides of the border. And most importantly, he demanded in an uncharacteristic manner, "Where the hell is Neptune?" Every potent adjective in the English language understated his black mood.

— ‖ —

JT pushed the Falcon toward Thief River Falls once the airspace was re-opened. He, Logan, and Mahrous had been forced to watch the story unfold in front of a television in Minneapolis as they were regaled with what little was known of events taking place in northern Minnesota. In fact, the news media knew very little about what had happened. Grim and silent, JT knew in his heart that whatever they'd find when they landed could only be bad.

Surprisingly, the airport was business as usual when they arrived. There was little indication that men had been killed in a short but intense firefight on the concrete apron earlier in the day. Mahrous had no winter clothing so they stopped to pick up some gear at Kmart before driving to the cabin in JT's uncomfortably small Jeep CJ.

It was already dark when they arrived at the turn-off. Flares were burning on the highway and it appeared that some-one had put a chainsaw to a large maple tree that had fallen across the trail before being skidded out of the way. A car and a van with flat front tires had also been pushed aside, and the deep, muddy ruts indicated some heavy equipment had been driven in during the warmer afternoon hours.

JT knew there would be a cop convention at the cabin, but was surprised to see a fire truck pulled up near where the cabin used to sit. The whole scene was lit up like downtown on Saturday night with the aid of portable generators and racks of bright lights. In addition to the firefighters, there were also representatives from the Marshal and Beltrami County sheriff's offices, the Minnesota State Patrol, and the FBI. A row of boots were sticking out from under a tarp laid over what remained of eight bodies. The cabin had burned to the ground and explosives of some kind had blown trees down.

"Son of a bitch," JT uttered under his breath.

One of the deputies waved them up the driveway before motioning them to a stop. Keeping his hands in plain view, JT identified himself as the owner of the cabin. When Logan produced identification showing him to be a Global Oil employee of some significance, questions began in earnest. The FBI assumed control when Mahrous bin Laden identified himself, and suggested they contact Vice President George Bush on his behalf. Even JT did a double-take when Mahrous revealed his last name. He had no idea who Mahrous really was until that moment, and it caught him by surprise.

They viewed the mangled and shot-up remains before perfunctorily announcing they could not identify any of the bodies. The FBI agents thought it odd they should be so indifferent and unaffected by the casualties, and correctly surmised the bodies were not those of the Neptune men. Soon thereafter they were frisked, disarmed, and informed they were now in protective custody.

— ‖ —

"I'm way past wore out. You want me to call my brother and have him come get us or can we just find a hotel and crash for the night?" Hollis said to no one in particular as they were getting off the plane at DFW Airport.

"Bad choice of words, Hollis, but I'm for the hotel," Steve agreed. "I could use another hot shower and a drink of Scotch. My ear hurts and I'm so damned tired I can hardly stand up."

"We'll get you a purple heart as soon as the store opens in the morning," Hollis growled.

"Yeah, and we need to make a call to Switzerland as soon as they open their doors. That should be about 0200 hours our time," Fletcher said. "We'll either be very wealthy or SOL."

"Hell, we're all dead anyway," Hollis said, "or so everyone better sure as hell think when they piece together the clues we left." He stifled a yawn and ran a hand through his hair.

Fletcher picked up the courtesy phone to arrange a ride to the hotel. His hands hurt but they would heal. Having slept on the flight from Minneapolis, he felt better than he had in days. He wondered if Jeff was already at the hotel so he could get an idea of how that end of the plan had worked. Their families and JT didn't know of their little ruse and must be shattered by what they thought had happened if the Baron's crash had already been reported. *It might be too soon for that.* They'd call the ranch and let the women know they were safe as soon as they got to the hotel.

— ‖ —

The White House had the story close to correct even before they had all the details. Information provided by JT, Logan, and Mahrous bin Laden confirmed what they already suspected. It appeared the Iraqi Tomcat had shot down the U.S. Phantom because it was interfering with his mission to destroy Neptune. He then shot down the Saudi Learjet and Global Oil's King-Air thinking one of them might be his target. After breaking contact to escape the second Phantom, the Iraqi lost track of his quarry and had been forced to rely on intuition and his radar weapons system to help identify other potential targets. He fired missiles at five aircraft a moment before being blown out of the sky by the other U.S. Phantom. The Iraqi missiles hit the civilian airplanes, including the Baron piloted by Jeff Neumann who was flying Boyd, Cade, and Addison to Green Bay to hand over Neptune. The other civilian planes were just in the wrong place at the wrong time. A Minnesota game warden was somehow involved in this mess, apparently helping Boyd escape. A small group of Arabs had attacked the Neptune people as they prepared to depart Thief River Falls on the Baron. It was fairly certain that Saudi Arabia had a hand in the mission but Mahrous bin Laden denied any Saudi or OPEC involvement – at least to the best of his knowledge. He continued to maintain that he had only been trying to help a friend. The initial government conclusion was that Neptune was lost along with the men who created it.

— || —

JT, Logan, and Mahrous bin Laden were escorted back to Thief River Falls and provided lodging at the Best Western on the federal taxpayer's nickel. It was quickly confirmed that bin Laden was a highly placed Saudi national and senior executive of the forty-thousand-employee, international construction company, bin Laden Brothers for Contracting and Industry. His oldest brother, Salem bin Laden, had run the company since the passing of their father and company founder Sheikh Mohammed bin Laden in 1967. The company enjoyed close ties with the House of Saud, the royalty of most Middle Eastern countries, numerous European governments, and the Bush family in the United States. An Air Force fighter escort was ordered by the White House for the bin Laden corporate jet as it was flown from Texas to Thief River Falls to pick up Mahrous and take him home after a telephone conversation with Vice President Bush.

While the trio waited for the bin Laden jet to arrive, the FBI continued questioning the men, trying to glean more information about what had really been happening behind the scenes in the hunt for Neptune. The mesmerizing story unfolded: from the despicable Global Oil and Westcona involvement to the bin Laden family's sincere effort to help their friend

Logan Addison save his son from harm. Jake Taylor and Addison were obviously sick with grief over the loss of friends and a son.

Joey Andersen was arrested and lodged at the Pennington County jail. Eye-witnesses placed his pickup on the Thief River Falls airport tarmac during the shooting, and DNR dispatchers provided statements that Joey had been making unusual and suspicious radio transmissions in the twenty-four hours preceding the events. He maintained his innocence but investigators were having difficulty with his story.

Mahrous bin Laden's flight home was long and emotional. He felt like a total failure because he had not been able to repay his debt of honor to the Addison family. He and older brother Salem were incensed with their younger brother, Osama, for withholding critical information when it could have been used to help the Addison's. Osama bin Laden would not be happy when his older brothers finished with him. Of course, family business would be conducted in private.

— ‖ — Thirty-Nine — ‖ —

THE DFW AIRPORT HYATT REGENCY seemed palatial as Fletcher, Hollis, and Steve settled into their rooms. The same fictitious names they created to purchase airline tickets in Bemidji had come in handy again at the front desk when they checked in. For the first time in many days they felt their lives were well out of danger's grasp. How could they be in danger? They were already dead! In the privacy and comfort of individual rooms, they watched the television coverage from Minnesota and Washington, DC. News that seven civilian planes had crashed that morning sent chills down their spines. They knew better than to believe such nonsense. Just more government spin aimed at controlling the population with illusion and lies. The planes had been shot down. The only question that remained was of Jeff's fate. Had he jumped before the Baron was hit? Just prior to 10:00 p.m., and in time for the national news, a special report was issued to the press. A local Dallas network affiliate picked it up and added a local connection.

Today was a rough day for aviation in northern Minnesota. Two National Guard jets collided in mid-air while conducting weekend exercises. Members of the North

Dakota Air National Guard's 119th Fighter Wing, based at Fargo's Hector Field, were apparently slightly off course when they collided over northwestern Minnesota. There were no survivors. The military is investigating.

In another surprising but unrelated aviation catastrophe, seven civilian planes crashed today after departing the airport at Thief River Falls, Minnesota, marking this as one of the worst days in American general aviation history. Federal investigators are already on scene, and sources close to the investigation have revealed that contaminated aviation fuel may be to blame. All seven planes are believed to have landed and refueled at the Thief River Falls Regional Airport this morning before departing and crashing around the state. While not all the victims' names have been released, we do know of a local Dallas connection. Authorities have identified a group of friends, employed by Dallas-based Westcona Services Inc, as among the dead. The plane in which the men were traveling crashed into Lake Superior just east of Duluth, Minnesota, after departing Thief River Falls an hour before the crash. The pilot has been identified as Jeffrey Neumann of Longmont, Colorado. Passengers included Fletcher Boyd, Hollis Cade, and Steven Addison all of McAllen, Texas. A Westcona corporate spokeswoman told us that Neumann had also worked at their Edinburg facility near McAllen before transferring to suburban Denver. The men were on a hunting trip. Some of you may recall that Westcona has been in the news recently with reports of the deaths of multiple security department employees, some involved in the mysterious violence at the federal energy research facility on the campus of Iowa State University in Ames. Certainly tough times for this local company.

After watching the newscast, Fletcher was thankful they had already called the ranch and assured the women of their safety. Sara would be driving Katie and the twins to Dallas in the morning. He wished he could have contacted JT and Logan but just couldn't risk word getting out at this point, nor did he know where they were.

He was exhausted and the others appeared equally so. Fletcher knew that Hollis was a tough bastard and coped well with just about anything, but what worried him was the devastating emotional turmoil Steve had to be enduring. Adding today's experience to losing his family could take anyone right over the top. The young engineer seemed to have moved from shocked denial directly to nearly insane anger…and that wasn't healthy. He needed to grieve like any normal human. Hell, they all did.

Try as he might, Fletcher couldn't calm his mind long enough for real sleep. An hour later his phone rang, and soon thereafter Hollis was knocking on the door.

"One hell of a day, Fletcher. I can't believe we got out of there alive."

"Yeah…I'd say. Not sure my knees are done knocking yet."

"Shit, Fletcher. We killed a dozen men today, and I'm not sure I even feel bad about it. I should, but I just feel kind of numb."

"A wartime mindset does that, Hollis. That's what we had to create in our heads when this all started. We'd all be over-the-cliff wacko if we hadn't shut down our emotions and compartmentalize the fear. You had to have done that during Vietnam. I sure as hell did."

"Yeah, but I never saw it up close like this. And I never actually pulled a trigger with a man in my sights before. The difference is…well…it's just way different."

"Different? How? You didn't know what those planes you helped launch off aircraft carriers were doing while they were gone? You were in combat operations…just as much as the people who pulled the triggers."

"Maybe. I just never thought of it that way until now. I don't much like it."

"Join the club. Why do you think so many people never quite recover from being in a war? Hell, the distilleries and divorce lawyers would be out of business if it weren't for veterans trying to cope with civilian life."

"What I can't figure out is why our military was willing to shoot us down," Hollis said. "I guess that's why I just can't get all worked up over killing those guys. Everyone we met seemed to be trying to kill us."

"Well, if it makes you feel any better, I'm not going to lose much sleep over those guys either. The innocent people on the private planes are the ones I'll never be able to forget. And Jeff's starting to concern me, too. He should be here by now, unless they still had the Duluth airport closed this afternoon and he couldn't get a flight out."

"Yeah, I'm getting a bad feeling about him ever getting here. He may have gotten hurt on his jump or something…but you're right, something happened."

"Or, maybe he forgot which hotel we agreed to meet up at, or the fake names we're using—but I doubt it."

Whether or not they were really rich, they played their usual nickel-dime-quarter poker while waiting for the bank to open in Switzerland. Still no telephone call or knock on the door from Jeff, and that served to heighten the tension.

At 2:15 a.m., Fletcher dialed out and the call was routed to the Customer Service Desk at the Swiss bank. He carefully read the account number and waited patiently for the clerk to look up the account.

"Sir, that account has a zero balance."

Fletcher turned to cold granite. Finally, when he could breathe again, he asked to speak with a manager who calmly explained that this was the third call he'd received on this account in the past quarter-hour. Yes, two wire transfers had come in on Friday afternoon. However, the bank had followed its written instructions to immediately wire the money to other accounts, none of which were in Switzerland.

"Who wired money into the account?"

"The governments of the United States and Saudi Arabia and both parties have already called this morning claiming the wires were in error."

"Who instructed you to move the money?" Fletcher demanded.

"When Mr. Wainwright opened the account, he instructed us to immediately transfer the funds as they arrived," the manager said.

Fletcher lit a Marlboro, poured another drink, and dialed a local number. His hands were trembling with rage.

"Where the money, Spencer?" Fletcher barked at his former boss and mentor when he sleepily answered the phone.

— ⫶— Forty —⫶—

JAKE TAYLOR'S VOICE CRACKED AS HE TRIED to finish his prepared remarks at the memorial service in Dallas. His eyes fell on Taryn and Felecia Boyd, Fletcher's beautiful twin daughters, and the words stopped, replaced by searing remorse and mounting nausea. Unable to continue and with tears forming, the once feared and still revered Westcona manager pivoted to his left, saluted the large portraits of his dead friends, and returned unsteadily to his assigned seat between Spencer Wainwright and Logan Addison. Logan's emotions were running high and his anti-stress medication was working its magic. JT regretted not having taken one himself.

As Branton Cole smoothly continued the accolades and praise for the four Westcona employees lost in the tragic plane crash into Lake Superior, JT was aware of Cole carefully studying him. As Cole's calm, melodic speech to more than fifteen hundred employees, family, and friends continued, JT drifted into his own confused, emotion-wrenched thoughts. What would two little girls and two widows do now? Who would fill the ugly hole ripped in their aging parents' lives? Who would end up paying the price for this mindless violence; the survivors? Was someone going to be held responsible? They shouldn't be dead. They were good men with the bold, fearless outlook on life that men his age often lost when they finally came to terms with their limitations. Soft music filled the auditorium as the drone of Cole's voice ended. JT jolted back to reality with all the rage and fire for which he was known. Before the security men seated near him could react, he was on his feet and charging toward Cole.

"You killed them, you rotten son of a bitch! You could have had it all, but you killed them and now your goddamned company has nothing. Nothing!"

Spencer Wainwright got to JT first, but couldn't stop his forward momentum. Two FBI agents who had been standing in the wings adjacent to the lectern intercepted and forcibly escorted JT away from Cole and out of sight. Katie Boyd joined them and did her best to calm him. Assuring the agents that she would get him to his car, she nodded to Wainwright to open the door into the service hallway as she guided JT out with the agents following close behind, ready for another outburst. Only when Katie finally coaxed JT through the outside door and into the parking lot did the agents relax and return to the ballroom. Logan was drowsy from the Valium, confused by the activity, and doing his best to keep up.

"Listen to me, JT," she demanded, firmly grabbing his arm as if talking to a child. "You have to calm down. Stop this!"

She paused, nervously looking in all directions to be sure they weren't being watched.

Speaking in a hushed tone she explained, "There's something you don't know and couldn't know until now." With a slight hesitation, she made direct eye contact and carefully continued. "The boys are alive, JT. Everything's okay. Do you understand me?"

His head snapped up with his eyes open wide, looking at her as if she were completely out of her mind.

"Alive?" he shouted. "What the hell do you mean they're alive?"

He had her by the shoulders, almost shaking her as his face distorted in disbelief.

"Quiet!" she hissed as she shook free of his grasp and tried to appear calm. "They're alive. Well, not Jeff Neumann," she said quietly, looking around to make sure no one was watching. "He really did go down with the Baron. Please, please calm down and listen. Fletcher, Hollis, and Steve weren't on the Baron. It was all a diversion. Those planes they said crashed last week were really shot down by an Iraqi fighter before our Air Force shot him down. The Iraqis were trying to stop Neptune, but Fletcher outsmarted them. Jeff was supposed to parachute out but something went terribly wrong. He either bailed out over Lake Superior and drowned, or was shot down before he could get out. We'll never know what happened to him."

Logan had been standing idly by, watching and listening to Katie and JT until her words finally got through his cloudy mind.

"Steve's alive?" he stammered.

"Yes, he's alive and we're going to him now," she said as Sara and the twins pulled up in the van Westcona had provided them while in Dallas.

Katie motioned Felecia and Taryn to the back row of seats while pushing JT and Logan into the center row. She jumped in the passenger seat and they were off for the hotel.

— ‖ —

The anger JT felt at being at being kept in the dark was short-lived, eclipsed by the elation of knowing the men were alive.

He realized they had used his emotions to sell their deaths, and marveled at the cruelty. He felt Logan shudder and realized the overwhelming torment Logan had endured while believing he had lost Steve had been too much. Now the profound emotions exploded in a cacophony of passion, and Logan broke down. The girls began crying, and soon Sara pulled over so they could all allow the tempest to consume itself and she could drive again.

— ‖ —

Fletcher was watching the hotel driveway from the fourth story window and Steve had already made his way to the lobby. Leaving JT and Logan in the dark as to their fate had been a difficult but necessary decision.

He watched the van approach and Steve dash into view. The door opened and Logan burst out and into his son's arms. Fletcher could feel the jubilation from where he stood. JT got out and put his arm around Steve, nearly fighting Logan for position. Katie, Taryn, and Felecia spilled out, and Sara drove the van to the parking lot while the group disappeared into the lobby. Fletcher asked Hollis to open the door and they waited for the elevator chime.

JT burst into the room with a broad smile that vanished once he had vigorously pumped their hands and pounded them on the shoulders.

"That was a damned shitty thing you did to us, Boyd," he said once the door was closed.

"I know it was, JT, and we didn't do it without a lot of thought. You and Logan needed to be displaying real emotion, and we were depending on it to convince anyone with any doubts as to our deaths. I hope you did it well."

"Oh, he did that very well," Katie said. "I thought the FBI was going to have him in jail for a moment there. He scared the bejeebers out of Cole when he went after him."

"Damn, JT. I didn't know you cared," Hollis kidded him.

"Yeah, well it was still a shitty thing you did to us."

"Now you can all go home appearing to have properly mourned us. Logan, will you be able to hide Steve in Houston until he decides where he wants to go? We still have a few things to work out but he'll be ready to travel in a few days." Fletcher asked.

"I sure as hell can and will. You'll all have to get out of the country, right?"

"Right. We have big decisions to make and you guys need to spend some time together working out your future," Fletcher said.

"You got the money?" Logan asked.

"Oh yeah. We sure as hell got the money and there's plenty for all of us...and I do mean all of us. That won't ever be a problem again. Steve can fill you in and you can work out what's best for you," Fletcher said.

— ‖ — Forty-One — ‖ —

BRANTON COLE WAS UNEASY ABOUT EVERYTHING related
to Neptune. While few things scared him, the FBI's demands
and threats convinced him to change his attitude. They released
him only after extensive debriefing and with the understanding
that any mention of Neptune would land him in a federal insti-
tution for much longer than he cared to consider. They made it
emphatically clear that Neptune did not and had never existed.
It was never to be mentioned, discussed, or acted upon again.
There would be no exceptions, and he was expected to drive
that point home within Westcona. He worried that JT's
emotions could make that responsibility difficult, but he would
make every effort to comply with the government instructions.
He knew how extremely fortunate he was, and that only the
overwhelming desire of the federal government to keep
Neptune a secret was saving him from a surefire conviction.

Mark Streeter had grudgingly endured the same treatment
from the Justice Department and was operating under the same
set of limitations and potential penalties. But, he couldn't let it
go. His immense ego continued to override any semblance of
common sense. When Logan returned to Houston and his job
at Global Oil, Streeter immediately forced him into retirement.

Streeter wanted Logan out of the organization while a gaggle of chemists worked at an offshore Global Oil facility to re-create Neptune. He was also preparing to move his headquarters to Scotland to avoid continued scrutiny by U.S. officials.

Katie Boyd and Sara Cade had been fully debriefed early on and provided blanket immunity from prosecution, including for the deaths at the Cade ranch, in exchange for all the Neptune details they had, and their perpetual silence. Thereafter, they quickly received their husbands' life insurance proceeds along with checks for a million dollars each from Westcona as a good-will gesture, though only after the federal government lawyers strongly suggested that keeping the women quiet was in Westcona's best interest. Westcona had immediately tapped Global Oil for half the payment. Playing the roles of grieving wives, Katie and Sara gladly accepted the money and returned to their McAllen homes to begin living a more normal life, albeit without their husbands. Sara was lonesome, but Katie was not. The price had been too high. She was grateful that Fletcher had survived, but had no intention of continuing their marriage. Not after what Fletcher had put her and the girls through. Not after what Fletcher had done for money.

— ‖ —

Sitting on Spencer Wainwright's very secluded suburban Dallas patio, Fletcher and Hollis were dazzled at their riches and very thankful that Wainwright had taken the precaution of moving the money out of the Swiss account as soon as it arrived. The seasoned auditor's training and experience hadn't allowed him to trust any bank or government. His involvement had not been detected, and he fervently hoped it would stay that way. The instructions he had so carefully crafted directed the Swiss bank to immediately split the money eight ways and re-wire it to accounts all over the world. The money was subsequently reconstituted in two accounts, one in Luxembourg and the other in the Cook Islands. This subterfuge worked beautifully to make tracking the money nearly impossible. The United States and Saudi Arabia were jumping through hoops trying to find it, but failing miserably. Banking secrecy laws, manual bookkeeping systems, and anti-American and anti-Arab sentiment in many parts of the world foiled their efforts at every turn.

If Wainwright had been offended by his protégés' initial reaction of distrust and embitterment at the news of the zero-balance Swiss account, he never let on. He understood the pressure Fletcher had been under and was happy to help him through the banking details once he calmed down. Wainwright was now back at work while the newly wealthy trio temporarily enjoyed themselves at his home after their families and JT had gone home to perpetuate the illusion.

"We owe some people for helping us," Fletcher said. "Any suggestions as to who and how much?"

"With three billion dollars, we can kinda do whatever we want," Hollis said as he drained a frosty can of Coors. "We sure couldn't have done it without JT or Logan."

"Or Spencer, or Joey," Steve added quietly. "My dad only helped because he was trying to help me. Maybe it would be better if I just gave him something out of my share. Or all of mine because I really don't much care."

"No," Hollis and Fletcher said in unison.

"Your dad risked his life, and we all owe him," Fletcher continued. "Any one of them could have gotten us, or themselves, killed. Some worked a little harder, but we wouldn't be sitting here right now if it weren't for each of them. Let's decide right now?"

"Well, my dad's already pretty well off," Steve said. "I'd still like to know he's a millionaire a couple of times over, though. Is that too much?"

"Steve, think about it. We have three thousand million dollars, and I want a clear conscience when I look back on this," Fletcher said.

Hollis ran back into the house and returned with another beer and a calculator he tossed to Steve.

"If we gave each guy a hundred million bucks, what would each of us have left?" he asked the young engineer.

"I don't need a calculator. If we gave away four hundred million, we'd still have two-point-six billion...or a little more than eight hundred and sixty-six million each. Would that still be enough for you?"

"I don't even know how much that is, but I reckon it would do," Hollis laughed.

Fletcher pulled out a box of cigars and passed them around. They sat on the patio smoking and considering how the four new mega-millionaires would react to the news.

Steve was crestfallen and depressed, but still trying to be part of the group he now viewed as brothers. He also needed comfort and guidance from his father. In fact, he was glad they had succeeded but didn't want to think about his lonely future that held no joy. He had nothing to go home to...no reason to live. They had their dreams and he wouldn't be part of them...or of anything for that matter. Emotionally and physically drained, he was trying to be happy for them but couldn't quite summon the energy.

"I wish there was something we could do for Jeff, but I can't think of what it could be. He died like he would have chosen but it seems to me like there should be more," Fletcher said to no one in particular.

"I don't know what we could do either but he can't spend it now. Let's just decide where we want to live, divide up the money, and get on with it," Hollis said as he drained another Coors.

"That's a little harsh," Fletcher said.

"Nobody chased Jeff around the country shooting at his ass or threatening his family. Look, I liked the guy but he wanted a fight and some action...and he got it. I'd be all for giving a full share to his wife and kids except he ain't got any. There's really nothing else to decide.

"Well, there is. What you want to do with Neptune," Steve said.

"I've been giving that some thought," Hollis said quietly, drawing lazily on his cigar.

"It seems to me that Neptune's been nothing but trouble for anyone who's known about it. I hate to say it, but our government wasn't even smart enough to take it when we offered it to them. They just plain failed. Are these the people we want to trust with it? I'm not sure the world is ready for something so big," he concluded.

"You know Westcona, Global, and the government are probably already trying to figure it out," Fletcher said.

"Well, then let them figure it out and decide. I think we should put our Neptune in a safe place and just sit on it for now," Hollis urged.

"Somehow that seems wrong, but I can't come up with a rational argument to the contrary, especially when it would put so many people out of work if it wasn't handled right. I don't want that on my head, too. Steve, what do you think?"

Steve shook his head in apparent disinterest.

"I'll make hard copies and floppies of the files for each of you. I'll put mine in a safe deposit box in Houston. You do with yours what you think is right. I'm going to talk to my dad and then figure out where to go."

"Sounds like a plan to me," Fletcher agreed as Hollis nodded his head.

— ‖ —

Salem and Mahrous bin Laden spoke with other family members and made their decision. Osama was a problem the family could no longer tolerate. The bin Laden family would not tolerate his boorish, self-centered behavior that was so inconsistent with their values. His bizarre distortion of Islam into a hateful, destructive tool of death revealed mental-health issues for which he refused treatment or counseling. Something was very wrong, and he would not be allowed to continue working for or be part of the family if he refused help. At age twenty-nine, Osama bin Laden was provided the assets his brothers deemed rightfully his, and shown the door.

— ‖ —

"Are we absolutely positive the men were on that plane? President Reagan asked his advisors. "Is there any chance we missed something?"

"Yes, they were on the plane, and no, I don't think we missed anything, Mr. President," responded Secretary of Defense Caspar Weinberger. "There is no credible evidence they shared Neptune with anyone or left documentation. We've been through both company's computer systems, and inter- viewed their families, friends, and acquaintances. Unfortunately, we couldn't locate the airplane wreckage in Lake Superior. No bodies, either. No sir, the damn Iraqis got lucky on this one and we need to punish them for it," he concluded.

"Ahem," FBI Director William Webster cleared his throat and interrupted as politely as he could. "I have confirmation that Mahrous bin Laden called our San Antonio office and warned us of the imminent Iraqi attack; even that it was being launched from Canada. We blew it."

"What do you mean, we blew it?" the President exploded.

"The junior agent answering the phone that Saturday thought it was a prank either by the other agents or by some local nut. He put it in Monday's business for the Special Agent-in-Charge. Mahrous bin Laden did warn us as soon as he knew something specific."

"Well, it seems we messed this thing up from start to finish, and now you tell me we could have avoided it by acting on a warning that was actually received by the FBI? George, did bin Laden or King Fahd give you any good information?" he continued with the Vice President. "They must have known something was going on."

"Yes sir, I'm sure they did, but the King won't confirm they knew anything. He doesn't have much good to say about Saddam Hussein, but he has to support him because the Iraqis are the buffer between his country and the Ayatollah Khomeini in Iran. You'll recall that we're training some Iraqi pilots right here, too. The bin Laden's are respectable people and operate one of the largest construction companies in the world. I suspect their intel was better than the Saudi government's, and that's how they caught on to it. Obviously, Salem and Mahrous bin Laden have an especially close friendship with Logan Addison so they tried to help him when they determined Logan's son was involved. I'd say we owe them a debt of gratitude, even if we did fail to act on their warning," the Vice President said.

President Reagan blanched when reminded that Iraqi pilots were being trained in the United States. The Joint Chiefs had objected to the Iraqi leader's requested training on their newly captured F-14 Tomcats, but he had overruled them as a political expedient. The United States had to support Saddam Hussein to provide some stability in the Middle East, but it was not a situation he had liked then and sure as hell didn't like now.

"Yes, you're right, the bin Laden's tried," admitted the President. "Make sure we throw them some work if we build anything in their part of the world," he suggested. "Let them know how much we appreciate their help. Sounds like the young brother made the real connection and blew the whistle on Saddam. What's his name? Osimi? He must have a good network."

"Osama, Mr. President. Osama bin Laden. I'm sure we'll be hearing a lot about him in the future," agreed Vice President Bush.

"Now, what I want to know is how we're going to prevent something like this from happening again. Here's how I see it. Three fine American's made the discovery of the century. They took it to their employer, who tried to steal it from them. They brought it to us, but we failed to accept or secure it. These men then had their employer and another American company try to kill them, and we didn't even bother to protect them; they had to do that themselves, too. Half the Arab world heard about it and found them before we did in our own country. We then allowed an armed Iraqi fighter to violate our airspace and shoot these American's down while they were trying to bring it to us again. The Iraqi shot down a total of eight airplanes, including one of our interceptors. We discovered we'd been specifically warned that this was about to happen, but thought it was a joke. As a result, Neptune was destroyed and these fine young Americans are dead along with dozens of others. Finally, to top it off, we lost one billion dollars in the process. Does that about sum it up?" The President made sure his sarcastic tone wasn't lost on anyone.

No one answered as he locked eyes with each in succession.

"I'm not convinced those men are really dead," President Reagan continued in anger.

"Why did the Swiss sandbag us when we asked about the account ownership? Why wouldn't they just return the money once we explained this was part of an intelligence operation gone badly? No, this doesn't feel right. You'd better start tracking that money and find out where it went. Watch those men's wives and see what they're up to. Find out who set up that Swiss account. It has to be someone other than those men, and that someone is probably sitting right under our noses— maybe with our billion dollars. Then I want you to round up the Iraqi pilots we're training and quietly send them home. If the Joint Chiefs want to keep their airplanes, I'll support them. I should have listened to them in the first place. And lastly, if the Neptune men were able to pull this thing off without military or government assistance, then we sure as hell need to find them and *hire* them. They're much more skilled and aware of what's going on around them than anyone we have working for us!

The assembled men still had no answers or comments as they waited for more from the President.

"Considering the critical nature of relationships within the Middle East, it's best for the world that we let this whole thing die a quiet death. Neptune's gone, at least for now, and the Middle East should calm down. The press would never let go of this story, or think it through before blowing it all out of proportion if they ever got wind of it. No, they can't find out what happened or there won't be another Republican president for fifty years, and that's a sobering thought. Mr. Vice President, that should really scare you if you have any designs on my job. I'm going upstairs for a nap. That will be all for now, gentlemen."

— ‖ — Forty-Two — ‖ —

WITH NEARLY UNLIMITED CASH, FLETCHER and Hollis had no difficulty establishing new identities. Money talks.

Hollis and Sara had purchased two hundred acres of forested land where they built a log home with all the upgrades they had always dreamed of. The sparsely populated eastern slope of the Southern Alps was remote enough for Hollis, yet close enough to both coasts and the city amenities Sara enjoyed in Christchurch. Stunningly beautiful mountains surrounded them, with the Tasman Sea to the west and the South Pacific to the east. Nothing in New Zealand was really very far away, the whole country being no larger than the state of Colorado. The fishing and hunting were unrivaled. Hollis had plenty of wood for the fireplace, and excellent shortwave listening for world news. They had found a low-stress, calm, idyllic place to live.

"Hey, look what's in last Sunday's Dallas Morning News...and Houston Chronicle," Hollis pointed out to Sara and Fletcher.

Both newspapers described the brutal killings of Westcona president Branton Cole and Global Oil president Mark Streeter. Cole had been found shot to death at the bottom of a freeway exit near his home. Police attributed the shooting, which also resulted in the death of Cole's bodyguard, as random. Just bad luck. Streeter had been eviscerated as he left a posh Houston restaurant after his bodyguard was distracted in an altercation with an unidentified man. There were no suspects in either murder.

"Well, I guess there's justice in the world after all," Sara said with some concern in her voice. "Pretty strange, though."

"That's an understatement," Fletcher said. "You'd sure think the local cops would be pulling out all the stops to solve both, wouldn't you?"

"I would have at one time," Hollis said. "Now I see the mysterious hand of the Justice Department waving off the local cops for fear of bringing up Neptune again…but I tend to be paranoid anymore."

"Yeah, you do. Still, they didn't just happen to die during the same week." Fletcher said.

"You thinking what I'm thinking?" Hollis asked.

"I'll try to raise JT on the radio when I get home," Fletcher offered. "He's been hard to find lately, but its dove season in Texas right now. Then there's the time difference."

"Well, thanks for the supper and drinks, Mrs. Cade or whoever you are these days. I need sleep," Fletcher said to Sara as he drained his glass and stood to go home.

"Thatcher. We're the Thatcher's now. Remember? You can stay here if you don't feel like driving, Mr. Beckwith," she offered.

"I still prefer Boyd, but thanks. I think I'll just mosey on home. Do they "mosey" around here?"

"Not that I've heard. Thanks for coming over, Fletcher," Sara said with a smile.

"Thanks for having me. You know I can't resist your okra."

— ‖ —

Fletcher's rented farmstead was just outside Springfield, on the South Pacific side of the island. He'd considered buying property, but was still unsettled by Katie's refusal to let him back into her life. She was adamant and wouldn't leave the States. She would not be married to him. He knew he'd not been the best husband in the world; perhaps they had just grown apart. That thought helped him cope but he knew deep down that it was just a rationalization. He'd repeatedly put his career before his marriage and family. That had started the growing apart he preferred to think of as natural when it wasn't. Seldom is one person completely to blame for a relationship coming apart, but he knew he was likely more to blame than Katie. Then he had endangered their lives for money—and that had been a complete disconnect for her. Still, he missed Felecia and Taryn terribly, and couldn't help but feel he should be playing a larger role in their lives. Then again, he wouldn't be in this situation if he'd done that when he had the chance.

News that Katie had returned home to Oregon with Taryn, Felecia, and Lady followed and confirmed what Fletcher had nearly already accepted. Their marriage was indeed over. Fletcher set up Cook Island accounts for his daughters and funded them with one hundred million dollars each. He also set up an account for Katie and sent the information to her at her parents' address in Portland. She had not responded or touched the money.

A tower supporting a television antenna sat on the old homestead when Fletcher rented it. It was the kind of television antenna tower most farmers and many city dwellers had as standard equipment before satellite dishes and cable TV. It wasn't as tall or sturdy as the tower JT had in Texas, but it got his directional beam antenna high enough to work the world with his new ham radio station. Fletcher had worked hard to pass his New Zealand ham radio license exams, something Hollis and Sara were studying for now. From his brief exposure to it at the cabin, he had come to admire how ham radio worked and helped save their lives while in the Minnesota wilderness.

Up and out of the shower by 8:00 a.m., he glanced at the clock he kept set to Central Time in the United States. It was early afternoon yesterday in Hargill, Texas, as he poured a cup of coffee. Maybe JT was home and had his radio on.

Once the Neptune dust settled, JT had retired and returned home to Hargill in south Texas. Logan Addison had purchased a beautiful new home just sixty miles away in Boca Chica, on the southern tip of Padre Island. The men spent considerable time together due to their similar backgrounds, wealth, and mutual enjoyment of hunting and fishing. Although both were still tolerating some attention from the IRS and FBI over suspected financial windfalls and their part in the Neptune saga, neither had anything to say about the subject. The feds surely could not prove any misconduct on either man's part. Both kept their money in offshore accounts, much to the consternation of the U.S. Treasury Department which couldn't establish how much either man really had. Logan had helped Steve relocate to Luxembourg and, with the help of Salem bin Laden, found the care Steve needed if he were to ever be normal again. Steve was still living at an ultra-exclusive mental health facility that dealt only with the very rich on a highly confidential basis. Spencer Wainwright had stayed on the job in Dallas. He truly loved being an auditor and had no intention of retiring despite his considerable wealth.

"WD5CL WD5CL, this is ZL2CDR calling."

"ZL2CDR, this is WD5CL. Hello, Beckwith. Up kind of early, aren't you?"

"Hello, JT. Yeah, just after 0800 local time. I've been listening but haven't heard you on the air for a while. Just thought I'd check in and see what's going on in the northern hemisphere. Over."

"Oh, not much. Addison and I shot at some doves this morning and I just got back home. We had a good time; lots of white-wing around this season. Didn't hit many though."

"Any or many?"

"You haven't changed, have you Beckwith? Addison got a few but they were a little fast for me...again."

"You been up to anything else lately?" Fletcher asked.

"Oh, Addison and I took a little vacation in his new Winnebago a couple of weeks ago just touring around Texas. This retirement thing is pretty easy to get used to. How are you doing, Beckwith? Over."

Fletcher's mind went to the newspaper accounts they had read the previous evening in the week-old Dallas and Houston newspapers.

"Doing just fine, JT. We've been doing some fishing and just enjoying life in general. Spring's a pretty time down here. Are you and Logan getting settled into your new homes? Over."

"Yeah, we're both settled in. He's got a pretty nice setup over on the coast. We get in some fishing when I go over there, and we hunt dove or pigs when he comes over here. He's planning a trip to Europe for Christmas this year. Sounds like the engineer is doing a little better and might even move into his own place pretty soon. He sends his regards, by the way. Over."

"I'm glad to hear it, JT. He's a good kid and I hope he can get well. What are you doing for Christmas? Over."

"Well, if my daughters spend the holidays with their mother, I don't know what I'm going to do. Addison invited me to go along with him, but I haven't committed until I see what the kids are doing. You know how that is, they can't ever tell you what's up until the last minute. WD5CL, Over."

"WD5CL, ZL2CDR returning. Yeah, I know how that goes. If your kids are busy and you don't want to see Europe this winter, you're sure welcome to come here. Will the Falcon fly that far? Over."

"Aw, that's too far to mess with flying on my own. Thanks, Beckwith. I'd enjoy Christmas in the summertime. I'll push the girls for an answer and let you know soon. I'll make the trip one of these days anyway, just to see you folks and drink a little J&B."

"Hey, I meant to tell you about a couple of good scotches I found down here. One is Ballantines and the other is Sheep Dip."

"Sheep Dip?"

"Yeah, it's a single-malt that's really good."

"Can't you buy J&B there?"

"Sure."

"Then I'll stick to J&B and you can have your Sheep Dip. I'll be down anyway."

"Good, we'll all enjoy seeing you. Say, we heard the news about our old corporate friends. Kind of a surprise, wasn't it? Over."

"Yeah, we heard about it on our trip. This old world can be a tough place, can't it? That old Texas saying about what happens to you if you mess with a bull isn't all that wrong, I guess."

Fletcher didn't respond to JT's comment but changed the subject instead.

"Ah…have you heard anything from the warden? Over."

"Yeah, I have. He moved to Alaska a few weeks ago. I sold him my old cabin site for a dollar, and he'd planned to rebuild it. But he was getting so much static at work that he just up and quit his job. His quiet little patch of woods just wasn't the same as it had been. I helped him organize his finances like we did ours, and off he went. I'll get his address for you once he lets me know where he settled. Over."

"Thanks, JT. Well, it's a beautiful spring day here and I've got lots to do. I'll let the Thatcher's know that you might be down for Christmas. They have a really nice log home in the mountains about an hour from here. Let me know when you make a decision. Over."

"Will do, Beckwith. No chance you'll be going to see the kids over the holidays?"

"I don't think that's in the cards, JT. I wish it was, but it's not. Take care of yourself, old man. I'll talk to you again soon. WD5CL, this is ZL2CDR clear on your final. Seventy-three, JT."

A ripple of emotion reminded JT of how much he missed his pain-in-the-ass, college-boy, young friend. He put down his microphone when he knew he couldn't trust his voice to remain steady, reached for the Vibroplex paddle sitting on the desk, and pounded out his final in high-speed Morse code:

Good Morning and Godspeed son   ES73   SK ZL2CDR DE WD5CL

— ‖ — Acknowledgements — ‖ —

WRITING A FIRST NOVEL IS A MORE ambitious project than I ever dreamed. While the writing part can be a very solitary activity, the work required to turn the manuscript into a presentable story is anything but. That credit goes to a handful of extremely talented and motivated friends who pushed, pulled, cajoled, and inspired the project to completion.

Norma Parker challenged me to write a book, and encouraged me when it was nothing more than a hand-written outline, a dozen rough chapters, and a stack of blank paper. Unfortunately, life "happened" and the unfinished manuscript languished in a desk drawer for far too long.

My wife, Diana, dusted off the manuscript and urged me to complete it. Her effort as a critical story consultant and eagle-eyed pursuer of details was hugely important to the process. She kept me focused, on point, and working when it seemed there was no end in sight. She deserves a dusting of stardust for her tireless efforts in helping me bring it all together.

Arlene Prunkle, my professional editor, taught me what I should have known before I started and was instrumental in turning a rough product into what it is today. Working with a professional editor for the first time is a humbling experience for any new writer, but Arlene's gentle encouragement and patience made the process educational and amazingly positive. Her technical expertise and story-line suggestions made a huge impact on the readability and overall quality of my writing. Any parts that still need polishing are my fault alone, and very likely contrary to what Arlene suggested.

I sincerely appreciate the impact each of these fine ladies had on my work.

Jim McCulloch

CPSIA information can be obtained at www.ICGtesting.com
Printed in the USA
BVOW081928181012

303339BV00002B/3/P